THE
PARIS
CHILDREN

 A NOVEL *of* WWII

GLORIA GOLDREICH

sourcebooks
landmark

Published by Sourcebooks Landmark, an imprint of Sourcebooks
P.O. Box 4410, Naperville, Illinois 60567-4410
(630) 961-3900
sourcebooks.com

Library of Congress Cataloging-in-Publication
Data is on file with the publisher.

Printed and bound in Canada.
MBP 10 9 8 7 6 5 4 3 2 1

*This book is dedicated to the memory of the million and a half
Jewish children who perished during the dark days of World War II.*

הבצנת

A NOTE FROM THE AUTHOR

The Paris Children is a work of biofiction based on the life of Madeleine Levy, the granddaughter of Alfred Dreyfus and a heroine of the French Resistance movement. While I have adhered as closely as possible to the chronology of her too-brief and tragic life, which was dedicated to the rescue of endangered Jewish children, I have exercised the novelist's prerogative and created scenes and relationships based on my own imaginings. I have relied on many primary sources, but I want to especially acknowledge *Dreyfus: A Family Affair* by Michael Burns (Harper Collins, 1991) and *Suzanne's Children: A Daring Rescue in Nazi Paris* by Anne Nelson (Simon & Schuster, 2017).

PROLOGUE

RED, WHITE, AND BLUE FIREWORKS DANCED THROUGH THE cobalt evening sky. The excited shrieks of children and the vigorous patriotic music played by the wandering street musicians mingled with sudden bursts of song. As always during the week before Bastille Day, Parisians flocked to the streets to celebrate. The sounds of holiday exuberance drifted through the open windows of the Levy salon, but the assembled family sat in a silence born of sorrow, indifferent to the gaiety below.

Their hands clasped, their heads lowered, they dared not look at each other, fearful that an exchange of glances might unleash a torrent of grief. They struggled to assimilate the warning words murmured in a measured, muted tone, heavy with regret by Dr. Pierre Paul Levy, who swayed uneasily as he spoke. Alfred Dreyfus's son-in-law had, during his long medical career, advised many families of the imminence of a loved one's death, but on this summer night, he was issuing such an edict to his own family.

"I have asked you here to tell you that you must prepare yourselves for the inevitable. He will die. Soon. Very soon," he said, aware that his voice was barely audible.

His wife, Jeanne Dreyfus Levy, turned to him, her fine-featured face blanched of color, and spoke very softly.

"You are certain, Pierre Paul?" she asked, although she knew the question to be unnecessary. Pierre Paul was renowned for his diagnostic expertise and the accuracy of his predictions. He was all too familiar with the ominous progress of the disease that was slowly and deliberately ending Alfred Dreyfus's life.

"There is no doubt," he repeated firmly. "His kidneys are failing. Death is rapidly approaching."

Jeanne nodded and went to the window, closing it firmly and drawing the crimson velvet drapery, blocking out both the sight and the sound of the revelry that intruded on their nascent sorrow. It was ironic, she thought, that her father, who had survived a wrongful conviction of espionage, five long years of exile and imprisonment on Devil's Island, and then heroism on the bloody killing fields of the Great War, would now die of a simple abdominal ailment. She sighed and returned to sit beside her mother on the sofa, encasing Lucie's cold hand in her own and gently massaging each of the elderly woman's fingers.

"But Grand-père will not die before Bastille Day?" Etienne, the youngest of the Levy children, asked and then blushed with shame at the irrelevance of the question.

"Yes. Almost certainly before Bastille Day," his father replied sadly.

Pierre Paul Levy would not, could not lie to his family. As a doctor, death, whether sudden or lingering, had long been his constant companion. His own sorrow at this new impending loss was contained, but he grieved for Jeanne; for her brother, Pierre; Lucie, her mother; and the children of the family, his own sons and daughters, his nieces and nephews, whose innocence would be shattered by the death of their grandfather.

Braced for their grief, he rested his hand on Jeanne's shoulder, but his gaze was fixed on Madeleine, his younger daughter.

She sat opposite him beside her sister, Simone. Her eyes were closed; long, dark lashes damp with unshed tears swept her high cheekbones, and her dark hair fell to her shoulders in a cascade of curls. She was seventeen, a very young seventeen—too young, he thought, to suffer a loss so profound. He had long recognized the special bond between Madeleine and her grandfather, the mysterious tenderness that had comforted and sustained them both from the earliest days of her childhood. Their love was palpable.

"They need each other; they understand each other," Simone had once told him, speaking with the precocious maturity that always surprised him. "Madeleine reads his lips, and Grand-père reads her heart."

Pierre Paul had recognized the truth of her words. When Madeleine, a child of eight, fell ill with scarlet fever, Alfred Dreyfus had remained at her bedside day after day, night after night. The very first word she had uttered when she emerged into consciousness after that life-threatening sleep was *Grand-père*. And that grandfather, a man who seldom displayed emotion, had wept as he bent to kiss her cheek. But Alfred Dreyfus had been dry-eyed days later when he told the newly recovered child that her illness had damaged her hearing.

He and Jeanne, her own parents, had been cowardly, Pierre Paul acknowledged, in delegating that difficult task to Alfred. But they had listened as he told their daughter the truth.

"You must treat your difficulty in hearing as a gift. You will learn to concentrate and read the lips of those who speak to you. Such concentration will give you great understanding of both the speaker and the words being spoken," he had said, and Madeleine, ever courageously accepting, had nodded.

She had not understood his words then but they had remained in memory, to be retrieved when needed. She was perhaps retrieving them now, Pierre Paul thought.

There was, he realized, an odd reversal of roles. Just as her grandfather had sat beside her bedside when she was a child, Madeleine had remained beside his bed during his illness. Throughout the spring of her last year as a lycée student, she had spent long afternoons and evenings at his side, hours scavenged from her studies and her commitment to the children in her troop of Jewish Scouts. The children filled her with joy. Her grandfather's deteriorating condition filled her with despair.

She had watched him grow thinner and thinner; she had seen how his skin, as brittle as parchment, had yellowed with the onset of jaundice. She, a doctor's daughter, had known that he was dying.

Pierre Paul, staring at his daughter's lovely face, marveled that he had thought only of Madeleine's fragility, never recognizing her remarkable strength. He recognized it now, and taking her hand, he led her into the dining room where the family gathered around the table to sip tea gone cold and discuss all that had to be accomplished given that finality was upon them. Funeral arrangements. Announcements to the press and the military. Alfred Dreyfus was a historic figure, a Chevalier of the Legion of Honor. Lists were drawn up, responsibilities divided.

That done, inevitably the conversation drifted to the

ominous news from Germany that haunted their every waking hour. The cruelty of the Nazi regime, the reality of the evil so close to their own threatened border, could not be ignored.

War, Pierre Dreyfus thought, was as imminent as his father's death.

"The reports from Berlin are frightening," Pierre said gravely. "Anti-Semitic legislation is being passed, and Jews are suffering terribly. Professions are closed to them. Children are forced from their schools, terrorized by the bullies of the Hitler Youth. Terrible things are happening, and the worst is still to come."

"Those laws will be struck down. Hitler will not survive in the land of Schiller, Goethe, Beethoven, and Bach," Pierre Paul countered. "You are too pessimistic, Pierre."

"No," Pierre replied firmly. "I am not pessimistic enough. Perhaps you forget that my father was persecuted in the land of Voltaire and Racine."

"And exonerated. France is not Germany," Pierre Paul retorted.

"But Adolf Hitler is now Germany. Only today he said that he supports the Italian invasion of Ethiopia. After all, if Italy is allowed to invade Ethiopia, then why should Germany not invade France? Hasn't he already said that Germany has a legitimate claim to Alsace?"

They shivered at the mention of Alsace. Alfred Dreyfus had been born in the hamlet of Mulhouse, and their extended family still lived there. Alsace endangered meant the Dreyfus family itself was endangered. Hitler's threats pierced their hearts.

Pierre's voice faded, and his shoulders sagged. His own question was rhetorical. The futility of the argument wearied him. Close as they were, he and his sister's husband had long held opposing political views.

"Even in the unlikely event of a German invasion, Frenchmen will act with courage and honor," Pierre Paul insisted.

Madeleine shivered. The mention of the cruelty the Jewish children of Germany were enduring filled her with fear. If Germany invaded France, the children she mentored might suffer the same danger. She thought of their bright faces, their high, sweet voices, and was overcome with fear.

She stared across the table at Simone and her brothers. Simone, sensing her distress, pressed Madeleine's hand reassuringly and the boys smiled. As members of the Éclaireurs Israélites, the Jewish Scouts, the Levy siblings shared their uncle's perceptions, acknowledged the reality of Madeleine's apprehensions, but this was not a night to disagree with their father, nor was it a night for the Dreyfus family to be at odds with each other.

It was Lucie who raised her hand and spoke very softly. "Let us not argue," she said. "Instead, let us all pray for that which is important for all of us. Peace of our country and our people. Peace for Alfred."

Her words soothed them into silence. Madeleine helped Lucie adjust her cape.

"I will see you tomorrow, Grand-mère," she said.

"Yes. Tomorrow. *À demain*," the old woman said and kissed her cheek.

Madeleine awakened very early the next morning and cycled swiftly from her parents' home to the small student café on the Left Bank where her close friend, Claude Lehmann, waited for her. He frowned as he turned the pages of *Le Monde*.

"Bad news again?" she asked, sliding into the seat opposite him and gratefully dipping her croissant into the bowl of café au lait which he had so thoughtfully ordered.

"When has there been good news?" Claude asked and sighed. "These are dangerous times. The *éclaireurs* must be prepared to confront the difficulties that are yet to come."

She nodded. His inferences were veiled, but she understood his intent.

"I cannot say more," he continued, "but you understand. The Jewish Scouts need you, Madeleine. There is work to be done."

"I know that," she said, her voice firm, her face flushed.

"Of course." He lowered his eyes. "Your grandfather is no better?" he asked gently.

"He will not get better, Claude," she said tonelessly, and he reached across the table and touched her hand.

"Be strong, Madeleine," he said, rising and gathering up his books. "I'm sorry that I must leave. I have an early seminar."

He struggled to find words of comfort to offer her, but it was she who found the words that eased their parting.

"Do not worry about me, Claude," she said. "Study well. We will talk very soon. For now, au revoir."

"Au revoir," he repeated and hurried off.

Looking back as he turned the corner, he saw that she sat motionless at the table, staring down at her empty cup. He should not have told her to be strong. Madeleine was strong enough. He should have, instead, kissed her on both her cheeks and placed his hand tenderly upon her head. Regret slowed his steps as he mentally cursed his shyness.

Alone, Madeleine sat in luxurious silence, lost in a whirl of memories.

"Flowers, mademoiselle, flowers for Bastille Day? Special today. Red, white, and blue."

A small boy, panniers of flowers draped across his narrow shoulders, interrupted her reverie and smiled hopefully at her.

"Yes. Of course," she said, and reaching for her purse, she counted out two franc notes.

He handed her a large bouquet tied with a tricolored ribbon.

"And I also want to buy those beautiful lilacs," she added and smiled as he handed her the fragrant purple blossoms.

Lilacs, Madeleine knew, were her grandmother's favorite flower, and she herself favored them. She threaded a single sprig through her long, dark hair, and newly energized, she drained the last of the now-tepid coffee, mounted her bicycle, and sped to her grandparents' apartment on the rue des Renaudes.

Lucie Dreyfus opened the heavy oaken door, her smile, as always, calm and gentle. Even at this moment of crisis, her quiet dignity had not deserted her. Her thick white hair was neatly gathered into a chignon, and she had affixed a white lace collar of her own tatting to her black dress. Madeleine noted that although Lucie's fine-featured face was pale with fatigue, her high cheekbones were lightly rouged. She took the lilacs that Madeleine held out to her and inhaled the sweet aroma gratefully.

"They are beautiful, Madeleine," she said. "I am glad you are here. Only a few minutes ago, your grand-père asked for you."

"He is awake then?" Madeleine asked.

"A kind of waking sleep. His eyes open. They close. He speaks, then falls silent. But do not be frightened, Madeleine. He does not seem to be in pain."

"I am not frightened," Madeleine assured her.

Claude's words drifted back to her. *Dangerous times*, he had said. Life, she thought sadly, was more frightening than death.

She took the vase of red, white, and blue flowers into the dimly lit sickroom where her uncle Pierre sat beside his father's bed.

"Is he asleep?" she whispered, setting the vase down on a small table.

"Not awake. Not asleep. A fugue state, I think your father calls it."

She nodded and sat beside him. They did not speak again although now and again their eyes met, and now and again they leaned close to the sick man as he whispered words that neither of them could discern. They looked up when Lucie entered and watched as she passed a damp cloth across her husband's forehead, moistened his dry lips with slivers of ice, and then bent to lightly kiss his cheek.

Alfred Dreyfus opened his eyes and turned to Madeleine.

"*Ma petite. Ma Madeleine.*" Her name, spoken in his rasping voice, was laced with love.

"*Chantez.* Sing." He closed his eyes and drifted back into the odd half-sleep that she knew would very soon end in death.

She hummed quietly and then lifted her voice in the lullaby her grandfather had so often sung to her. Ever aware of her hearing difficulty, he had enunciated each word clearly and she had committed the lyrics to memory. Like many with hearing deficits, music and melody presented no difficulty for her.

"*Entends-tu le coucou, Malirette?* Do you hear the cuckoo, Malirette?" she sang.

Pierre added his strong tenor to her sweet alto. In tender duet they lovingly caroled Alfred Dreyfus into his final sleep. Their voices grew ever softer as his breath rose and fell until, at last, it ceased. Lucie entered, glided across the room, placed her hand on his heart, pressed her cheek to his mouth and her lips to his pale eyelids in a farewell kiss.

"He is gone," she said, her voice breaking. "He has left us."

Pierre enveloped her in his strong arms, and she rested her head on his shoulder. They stood together in silence, united in their shared sorrow, in the enormity of their loss. Madeleine, in turn, placed three blossoms, one red, one white, one blue on her grandfather's heart, its beat forever stilled.

Through the open window, she heard the tolling of church bells and counted them. *Une. Deux. Trois. Quatre. Cinq.* She would remember always that at five o'clock in the afternoon, on the twelfth day of July, with the sun still high in the sky, death had come to her grandfather Alfred Dreyfus.

It was at Lucie Dreyfus's insistence that the funeral was held on Bastille Day.

"Our people honor the dead by burying them as soon as

possible," she said firmly and her family nodded obediently. Her quiet serenity vested her with an authority that her children and grandchildren recognized and accepted.

"I am glad that your grandfather will be buried on Bastille Day," Pierre murmured to Madeleine. "You know how dearly he loved his France."

"I do," Madeleine replied as she carefully placed the flag of France across the plain pine coffin.

The funeral cortege left the rue des Renaudes at daybreak and proceeded slowly from the Champs-Élysées to the Montparnasse Cemetery across the Seine. Even at that early hour the streets were thronged with holiday crowds waving tricolored flags. Red, white, and blue balloons soared through the air. Children rolled their hoops; young couples danced to the music of wandering musicians, but they paused respectfully as the hearse rolled slowly by.

At the Place de la Concorde, cavalry troops halted their exercises and turned their horses to face the vehicle that carried the hero of Monmorency to his final resting place.

At the cemetery, Madeleine and Simone, wearing black linen dresses, with black straw hats perched precariously on their carefully swept-up hair, stood beside Simone's fiancé, Anatol, and listened as Rabbi Julien Weill intoned the traditional Hebrew prayers. It was Madeleine who moved forward to support her grandmother as Lucie swayed slightly, her lips moving in silent repletion of the liturgy.

Pierre Dreyfus intoned the mourner's Kaddish, and Madeleine was deeply moved by the cadence of the prayer and the lilting strength of her uncle's voice.

"Amen," the small group of mourners intoned as Pierre concluded, his head lowered, tears streaking his cheeks.

"Amen," Madeleine repeated and very softly added the words so meaningful to Alfred Dreyfus: "*Liberté, égalité, fraternité.*" Liberty, equality, fraternity. His credo, her heritage.

One by one, family members stepped forward to lift the shovel, heavy with the dark earth that would blanket the pale wood of the coffin. It was a Jewish tradition, the final act of love and respect a family accorded a departed loved one.

"Your turn, Madeleine," her brother Jean Louis said and handed her the shovel.

She shook her head and chose instead to kneel beside the open grave. Lifting a clump of moist soil and dropping it onto the coffin, she murmured, "Au revoir, Grand-père. Shalom, Grand-père." She sat beside Simone on the journey back to the rue des Renaudes where Lucie Dreyfus would now live alone.

"Are you all right, Madeleine?" Simone asked.

The Levy sisters, from childhood on, had sensed each other's moods. Dearest of friends, devoted sisters, they were mutually protective of each other. Their interests and inclinations, their desire to work for those less fortunate, were shared. Simone was already completing a course of study in social work and Madeleine, newly graduated from the Lycée Molière, would continue her studies there.

"No. Not yet. But I will be," she replied.

"Yes. You will be," Simone agreed.

The sisters busied themselves in their grandmother's kitchen, arranging platters of hard-boiled eggs and circular pastries, the traditional post-funeral foods that symbolized the continuity of life even in the face of death.

Madeleine carried a tray into the dining room and then went into the study and closed the door behind her. The windows of the dimly lit, book-lined room, where she had spent so many happy hours with her grandfather, were tightly shut; the summer heat hung heavily in the air. She opened them and a fragrant breeze, sultry with the scent of primroses, brushed her cheeks. She looked down at the street, teeming with celebrants waving their flags and singing with sweet spontaneity. A group of dancing children in the portico of the building parted to admit visitors arriving to pay their respects to the mourners. She thought it both strange and wondrous that the joy of the dancing children and the sorrow of the newly bereaved could meld with such ease. It was an awareness that had come to her that very morning as she and her grandmother had set the table for the meal of consolation that would follow the funeral.

Lucie had cautioned her to handle the gold-rimmed Sevres serving platters with care.

"My very first wedding gift," she had explained. "I was afraid to touch them. I was such a silly girl. A bride at nineteen. So happy, so in love. The same age as Simone is now. And Alfred was perhaps a year older than Simone's Anatol. We could not stop smiling, Alfred and I."

Madeleine had nodded, marveling that on this sad day, her grandmother remembered herself and Alfred aglow with joy. "Simone has made a wise choice," Lucie had added. "Don't you think so, Madeleine?"

"I do."

Her answer had been honest. She thought it wonderful that Simone had found love and contentment with Anatol, a brilliant young law student, but she herself yearned for the adventure of an independent life, a career vested with meaning that might, in some small way, make the world a better place. She wanted to be challenged, to be tested by life.

She picked up the framed drawing of the Dreyfus family home in Mulhouse, shaded by a pear tree. It was the work of an unknown itinerant artist, but Alfred Dreyfus had treasured it. Madeleine studied it, lifting it toward the light just as the door opened and Claude Lehmann entered. Wordlessly, she held the picture out to him and he smiled. By odd coincidence, he was a son of Mulhouse, and his family and the Dreyfuses had been neighbors.

"Ah, the pear tree. I climbed it often enough. In the summer I would pluck a fruit and suck it dry as I sat in its branches," he said.

"And I too climbed it during our summer visits. Perhaps you were hiding in the leaves then and I did not see you," she countered.

"Perhaps."

He smiled, the endearing smile she had noticed at their very first meeting when she had been new to the Éclaireurs Israélites, and he had spoken with that rare combination of passionate seriousness and wistful humor.

"Scouting is a great tradition," he had said. "It teaches us to be self-sufficient and to confront nature in all its beauty and all its challenges. And we, as Jewish scouts, will soon face situations that will require all our courage and all our skills. What is happening to Jewish scouts in Germany, the Blau-Weiss, may soon happen here in France, and as scouts, we must be prepared for such danger."

Even as he spoke, there was a murmur of dissent.

"France is not Germany. What is happening there could never happen here," a tall boy shouted defiantly.

Claude smiled that wonderful, tolerant smile.

"Let us hope not," he said. "But there is no harm in preparing for that which may or may not happen."

He then led the assembled scouts in the spirited singing of "La Marseillaise" followed by "Hatikvah," the anthem of the Jewish people.

Claude had come up to her and held out his hand.

"I hope my words did not frighten you," he said.

"No. I hope that we will not face such dangers, but I agree that we must be prepared. Fear must have no home in our hearts," she replied gravely.

"I do not think that you frighten easily."

"Nor do you, I would guess."

That first exchange had been the foundation of their caring friendship. Their eyes had locked in mutual recognition and understanding.

Simone, ever sensitive to her sister, had taken note of their closeness.

"Are you and Claude perhaps more than just friends?" she had asked Madeleine teasingly, looking away from the pad on which she was sketching designs for her wedding invitations.

Madeleine leaned over and admired her sister's skillful calligraphy even as she shook her head.

"Claude and I are good friends, no more than that," she asserted truthfully.

His friendship was important to her, but he was not the center of her universe. Her life stretched before her, an unexplored sunlit road leading to an unknown and unknowable future.

Still, on this sad day of her grandfather's funeral, she was grateful that Claude was with her, offering his quiet support and his tacit understanding of her grief.

He took the drawing from her and studied it intently.

"Perhaps, one day, we will climb that pear tree together, Madeleine," he said. "We will reach its crown, look down on the valley, and gather enough pears to make a sweet Alsace compote. It will be a happy day."

"Will we ever be happy, Claude?"

The question came unbidden and filled her with shame, but it did not surprise him. He smiled that wonderful whimsical smile, and taking her hand, he stroked it gently, slowly, calming her with the tenderness of his touch. He understood her. He recognized the source of that sudden sadness; he shared both her fears and her hopes for the future. On this day of loss, he offered her his strength and his condolence.

They went to the window and watched as the sun began its slow descent. Bastille Day had come to an end. All of Paris was enveloped in the melancholy azure of *l'heure bleue*, the enchanted hour between twilight and the advent of darkness. They turned to each other, silently acknowledging that the day of sadness had ended and a new beginning awaited them.

ONE

THIRTY DAYS PASSED, EACH DAY EMPHASIZING THE DREYFUS family's new reality. Alfred was gone. On that thirtieth day, known in Hebrew as *shloshim*, the family gathered again to observe the ancient Jewish tradition of the second phase of mourning.

Dutifully, if reluctantly, the family assembled in the rue des Renaudes apartment where Lucie greeted them with her usual serenity. The scent of her famous lamb cassoulet drifted in from the kitchen. Madeleine, delayed by her interview at the Institute of Social Work, entered the crowded room and felt the swell of affection as the family welcomed her. Despite the assault of death, the Dreyfuses were united, alive, and enduring.

The room hummed with the murmured melody of memories. Her cousins spoke with lilting sweetness of the happy Sundays they had shared in the salon. Aline Dreyfus, Pierre's younger daughter, recalled Alfred teaching them the spirited *tanzette a la schellette*. Seizing Etienne's hands, she and he sprinted merrily across the room in the rapid Alsatian dance.

"Grand-père smiled when he taught us that dance," Jean Louis said. "I remember that because he did not smile often, did he, Madeleine?"

"No, he didn't," his sister agreed. "He was often very sad."

"He had every reason to be sad. France, his beloved France, had disappointed him. Because he was a Jew, vulnerable and unprotected," Pierre muttered.

The bitterness of her uncle's tone surprised Madeleine. Pierre Dreyfus, himself a hero of Verdun, inducted into the Legion of Honor, had always been a vocal patriot of La République.

Times had changed. "France now values and protects its Jews. Our children will never know fear and hatred," her father asserted.

Pierre shrugged.

"Would that I could believe you, Pierre Paul," he said bitterly. "But I believe that the curse of anti-Semitism remains very much alive in the hearts and minds of many of our fellow citizens. Soon, all too soon, the hatred that infects Germany will spill across our border and those who persecuted my father will persecute all Jews. You are a doctor, and you know that cancer is not easily contained or ever cured. Anti-Semitism is a cancer, and we have already seen its symptoms. Only last week there were anti-Jewish demonstrations on the Grand Boulevard. Such demonstrations will spread. A mitosis of irrational hatred. One rally this week. Two rallies next week. A contagion of evil."

He poured himself a large glass of brandy and drank it with his eyes closed.

Madeleine glanced at Simone, who shook her heard warningly. They said nothing, unwilling to contradict their father although they recognized the truth of their uncle's words. Only days earlier they had attended a performance of a new play entitled *The Dreyfus Affair*. The drama critic of *Le*

Monde had called it a sympathetic portrayal of Alfred Dreyfus's innocence and his unwarranted ordeal. They had clutched each other's hands as the actress who played Lucie had moaned, "Our children should be pitied."

Those "children" had been Jeanne, their mother, and Pierre, their uncle. Simone and Madeleine had wept but were jerked from their sorrow by the vitriolic reaction of the audience. A cacophony of fury exploded in the theater.

"No pity for those Dreyfus children. Did the Jewish traitor pity France?"

"Down with the Jews!"

Simone and Madeleine had rushed from the theater, fleeing that chorus of ignorance and hate. Seated now in their grandmother's salon, the fear they had felt that night was reignited.

Pierre strode to the window and stared moodily down at the street. Their father sat in grim silence.

Jeanne Levy spoke at last, turning to her brother, her voice melding plea and assertion.

"Pierre, surely you realize things will get better. There is a great deal of economic uncertainty in our country now so people look for someone to blame. But as soon as commerce picks up and the franc is strong again, everything will be all right," she said.

Her skin was mottled. She clasped and unclasped her hands nervously, as though trying to convince herself of the truth of her own words. Pierre sighed. It was difficult, Madeleine knew, for siblings to deceive each other. When he spoke to his sister, his eyes were soft but his words were harsh.

"Face the truth, Jeanne. France is a box of dry kindling. A

few sparks of hatred from the German border, and the fires of anti-Semitism will blaze again. The Jews of France, the Jews of Europe, are an endangered species. Things will not get better. No. They will get worse. Much worse."

"Pierre, enough. This is not a time to quarrel. Not a time to discuss our plans."

Marie Dreyfus placed a calming hand on her husband's shoulder. He nodded mutely but turned to his mother as her quivering voice shattered the uneasy silence.

"Pierre, you cannot mean that you are thinking of leaving France. How can you think of emigrating? You and your family are safe here. You are a hero of the Republic, a decorated veteran. Would you abandon me? Look around the room. Would you leave Jeanne and her family, your cousins, everyone who is dear to you?"

Pierre strode to his mother's side and embraced her.

"I'm sorry, Maman, but yes, we probably will leave France. Not immediately, but if the Germans invade, we will not hesitate. I have already visited the United States Embassy and obtained visa applications for my own family and for you and Jeanne and her family. For now, such visas are an insurance policy, but we will use them if we must," he said.

Madeleine, ever the peacemaker, was determined to break the tension in the room, the tense silence. Smiling, inviting their approval, she shared her news.

"I want you all to know that I have been officially accepted by the Institute of Social Work. Just as Simone finishes her certification, I will begin my own training," she said.

Her eyes were bright, her face flushed with pride.

"Mazel tov!"

Lucie Dreyfus embraced her granddaughter.

"That is wonderful. You and Simone have chosen such important work. Your grandfather would have been so proud of you."

Peace was restored. They relaxed and gathered at the elegantly set dinner table where they spooned Lucie's fragrant casserole onto their plates and exchanged family memories.

Pierre turned to his sister.

"Do you remember, Jeanne, how we used to hide in the doorway of this very room and eavesdrop when Maman and Papa held meetings of Le Comite de Bienfaisance, the Committee for Jewish Charity?" he asked.

"I remember how I choked on the smoke from Monsieur Rothschild's cigar," Jeanne said, smiling. "You had to leave the window open all night after he left, to get rid of the odor, Maman."

Lucie laughed.

"I forgave Baron Rothschild and tolerated his smoking because he wrote us very large checks to support the refugees from those terrible pogroms in Eastern Europe. Your grandfather was a great believer in what he called 'charitable action.' He wrote as much in his journals."

She motioned toward the small pile of moleskin notebooks that she had placed next to her own table setting and opened one, the place marked with a red ribbon.

She handed it to Madeleine, who read the single marked paragraph aloud.

"'Charity is not sufficient. What is needed above all is openness of heart, material deeds.'"

Her voice broke and tears streaked her cheeks. Her grandfather's mandate was her legacy.

"And that is exactly why Madeleine and I will be social workers," Simone said, turning to Lucie. "We believe, as he did, in material deeds. When we were small girls, we went with you and Maman to the Pletzl, that old Jewish quarter of the Marais, and distributed food and clothing to the poor Jewish refugees from Eastern Europe. Charitable action. Material deeds."

Lucie smiled sadly.

"And now we go to the Marais and Belleville to help Jewish families who are fleeing Germany. These are new and even more dangerous times, and our help is desperately needed," she said.

Madeleine turned to her uncle.

"You see, Uncle Pierre, there is so much we have to do for our people here in France. They need our assistance, our protection."

Simone nodded vigorously.

Pierre Dreyfus looked at his young nieces, moved by their beauty and their courage. He was proud of them, and he feared for them. He chose his words carefully, unwilling to reignite his sister's resentment or his mother's sorrow, but he would not disavow his intent.

"We must each follow the dictates of our own hearts, our own consciences, Madeleine. My family and I must choose our destinies, and you must choose your own. Let us wish each other bonne chance, good luck, good fortune. We will all need a great deal of luck in the dark times that will soon be upon us."

A frozen silence followed his ominous words. It was his wife who turned their mood from solemnity to gaiety.

"But we have much to look forward to. Simone, how do your wedding plans progress? And where is your handsome Anatol?"

"He is at an important meeting of scout leaders, but I hope he will be here in time for dessert," Simone replied, blushing as she always did when she spoke of Anatol.

"I certainly hope so. I made my *apfel* strudel because I know it is his favorite," Lucie said. She touched Pierre's cheek lightly. Her son was chasing shadows that might never fall. Germany would not dare to threaten France.

There was a knock at the door, and Simone hurried to open it. Anatol and Claude entered, their faces ruddied by the evening breeze, the blue-and-white scarves of the Jewish Scouts loosely knotted around their necks. Anatol carried a white rose, which he handed to Simone.

Her family clapped as she smiled and tucked it behind her ear. Etienne slipped out of the chair beside Madeleine and nodded to Claude, who grinned and took his place.

Dr. Pierre Paul Levy pressed his wife's hand to his lips.

"Our girls are very beautiful," he whispered.

Jeanne nodded. "So beautiful and so young."

He discerned the sadness and fear in her voice. "Everything will be all right," he said softly. "We are in Paris, the city of love, the City of Light."

"Darkness has been known to fall on light," she replied, but she lifted her glass as Pierre Dreyfus proposed a toast to his father, whose memory they had assembled to honor, and to the République they all loved so well.

"*À la France. À la famille Dreyfus.*" Their voices were strong, their eyes dangerously bright, fear and hope comingling.

Later that night, Claude and Madeleine walked through the silent streets. Claude spoke of an important meeting of the Jewish Scouts. "There are many leaders who think we should join the *tzofim*, the scouts in Palestine," he said.

"And what do you think?" Madeleine asked.

He did not answer but remained silent even as a group of students singing "La Marseillaise" passed. Madeleine added her voice to theirs.

"And my uncle Pierre wants us to emigrate to America," Madeleine countered, her voice soft. "Ah, Claude," she said, "how can we abandon our France?"

"We must pray that France will not abandon us," he replied, and with those words, she remembered the raucous voices in the theater and how she and Simone had fled that unexpected chorus of hatred. She shivered.

"You are cold," Claude said, and tenderly, he draped his blue-and-white scarf over her shoulders.

WINTER

TWO

M ADAME DANIER, THE DEAN OF THE INSTITUTE OF SOCIAL
Work, glanced down at the folder on her desk and smiled
at the dark-haired young woman who stood before her.

"Good morning, Mademoiselle Levy. Please sit down."

"Thank you," Madeleine said, grateful that the dean spoke
loudly and clearly. She sat at the very edge of the indicated
chair and leaned forward, her eyes fixed on Madame Danier's
face. Her hearing was only peripherally impaired but she was
training herself to read lips, a prudent measure, she told herself,
which hopefully would never be necessary.

"I have the records of your coursework and examinations
here, and I congratulate you on your excellent performance."
Madame Danier beamed with pride at her outstanding
student.

Madeleine blushed.

"I worked and studied very hard, madame," she replied
modestly.

"I also note that today is your birthday."

"Yes. My twentieth."

Madeleine relaxed and fingered the crimson woolen neckerchief that had rested beside her breakfast setting that morning.
It was, of course, her grandmother's handiwork. Madeleine had

been pleased but not surprised. Lucie Dreyfus never forgot a birthday.

"It is coincidental that you should receive this today. Consider it a well earned, very special birthday surprise," Madame Danier said.

She held out a thick white envelope, which Madeleine grasped, her hands trembling as she opened it very carefully and withdrew an embossed document. Her eyes filled as she read it.

"My certification!" she exclaimed. "I did not expect to receive it so soon."

"Indeed, you passed all your examinations and completed your coursework in record time. You now have the title of *assistante sociale*, a qualified social worker."

Madame Danier reached across her desk and took Madeleine's hand in her own.

"I am not surprised. I knew you would succeed from the moment you began your studies. You and your sister, Simone, are among our most diligent and accomplished students."

The dean spoke with quiet restraint. She was not a woman who lavished compliments easily, but she had observed the Levy sisters with great admiration. Madeleine was always willing, and Simone had managed demanding assignments despite her husband's dangerous illness and the needs of her small daughter.

"It has been our privilege to study here, especially during times such as these," Madeleine replied quietly.

"Yes. Your training will be important if events continue on this sad trajectory."

They sat for a few moments in silence. There was no need for additional words. Grim news had haunted them week after week, month after month, as Adolf Hitler's vicious actions accelerated, filling the world with fear and trembling. France had felt the impact of the Nazi regime as scores of terrified German Jews fled across the border, seeking refuge from the torrent of abuse and hatred in their native land. Conventional resources were overwhelmed, but social programs were swiftly organized by the Institute of Social Work and the French Jewish community.

Madeleine's father and her brother Jean Louis, himself a medical student, ran a free clinic in the Marais where they treated malnutrition, rickets, the scars of vicious beatings, and limbs distorted by badly treated fractures.

"We do not ask what caused the scars, the fractures," Dr. Levy had said wearily. He no longer spoke of Germany as the home of Beethoven and Schiller.

Madeleine and Simone had scavenged hours to assist their mother and grandmother in the distribution of food and clothing.

"How is Simone managing?" the dean asked hesitantly. "We have heard of her husband's illness."

"Yes, Anatol has meningitis, but my sister is very strong," Madeleine replied. "She is a wonderful mother and we do our best to help her. My mother, my grandmother, myself."

Madame Danier nodded.

"Of course. It is known that the women of the Dreyfus family are strong. Strong and brave."

"Thank you for those words," Madeleine said.

She committed them to memory. She would repeat them to Simone and perhaps to her mother and grandmother. Such encouragement was reassuring during this sad time of watching and waiting as Anatol hovered between life and death. She sighed and wished fervently that she could believe in her own strength, her own courage.

Madame Danier leaned toward her, speaking with an odd hesitancy.

"Mademoiselle Levy, I have a special assignment for you. An emergency has arisen that requires an immediate home visit. A teacher in the Pletzl has reported that a newly arrived Jewish family from Germany is in urgent need. There are three children so severely malnourished that she fears for their very survival. We want to offer them assistance from the special fund established by the Jewish community, but we cannot do so unless an accredited social worker gives an assessment of this situation. No one but yourself is available. Could you do that today?"

"Of course," Madeleine replied immediately. "After all, I am now an *assistante sociale*. This will be my first case." She smiled proudly.

"Then I must wish you bonne chance," the dean said as she handed Madeleine the flimsy folder that contained the family's details and an evaluation form.

"And happy birthday," she added, but Madeleine, hurrying out, her head averted, did not turn to thank her for her good wishes.

Too late, Madame Danier remembered that her newly qualified student had a slight hearing deficit. She shrugged.

No matter. Such an impairment would not hamper Madeleine Levy, vested as she was with determination and compassion.

Madeleine traveled to the Pletzl on a crowded Metro car, the scent of newly baked baguettes reminding her that she was hungry, very hungry. She clutched her briefcase, regretting that she had not thought to tuck a croissant among her papers and vouchers. She had not had time for lunch and doubted that she would be home for dinner, given that an important meeting of the scouts was scheduled at that hour. Emerging from the Metro, she was relieved to see that a buxom elderly woman, wearing a grease-stained white apron over her heavy, dark winter coat, stood beside a brazier on the rue des Rosiers, shouting out the virtue of the crepes she offered for sale.

"*Crêpes, délicieuses. Fraises du bois. Pommes. Fromage! Crepes, delicious.* Strawberry. Apple. Cheese!" she shouted as she warmed her large hands over the glowing coals.

Madeleine hurried over, pointed to a strawberry crepe, and handed the vendor a franc note.

The plump woman smiled and scooped the crepe into a cone fashioned from a creased sheet of newspaper, adding a generous sprinkling of powdered sugar.

A small girl, her fair hair matted, her painfully thin arms sticking out of the sleeves of her much-mended plaid coat, wearing boys' boots and thick, mud-spattered stockings, sidled up to the cart and stared wistfully at the array of crepes. Her lips were dry, and hunger was in her eyes.

"Would you sell me half a crepe for three centimes?" she asked shyly.

The vendor averted her eyes, but Madeleine pulled another franc note from her purse.

"Do you want strawberry or blueberry?" she asked the child.

"Blueberry." The answer came in a whisper, but the small girl smiled as she bit into the sweet delicacy.

"*Danke, Fraulein*," she murmured and then quickly corrected herself. "*Merci, mademoiselle*," she said in a stronger voice.

"Bon appétit," Madeleine said. "But perhaps you can now assist me. I am looking for rue Lascin."

"But that is my own street," the child replied. "I live on the rue Lascin. I will take you there."

Madeleine walked beside her, both of them munching the last of their crepes. They made their way through a maze of hovels into a narrow alley cluttered with overflowing dustbins. Ragged children darted in and out of the debris in urgent play, shouting in French and German, Yiddish and Polish.

"This is rue Lascin," the child announced importantly. "You must tell me the number you want."

Madeleine glanced at the information sheet.

"*Dix*. Number ten."

"But that is where I live. Number ten," the child said.

"Do you know the Hofberg family?"

The small girl thrust her small shoulders back, and for the first time, she smiled.

"I am Anna Hofberg," she said proudly and led Madeleine into the dark, fetid vestibule of the tenement.

Slowly, they climbed the narrow stairwell. Large-eyed

children clustered on each landing. The mingled odors of carbolic acid and overcooked cabbage drifted from open doorways. The banisters were draped with damp underclothing, singlets and shirts worn to a thinness, trousers and faded dresses patched and darned.

"We live at the very top," Anna said apologetically. "My mother says that is good because we do not hear other families walking overhead. We are not used to that. In Berlin we had our own house. A big house. I had my own room. And so did my brothers. The quilt on my bed was pink, and the curtains on my window were the same color. My mother had a sewing room and my father had a study. I miss my quilt, my curtains. It was a beautiful house."

Her voice quavered, and Madeleine feared that she might cry. Impulsively, she took the child's hand.

"I'm sure it was, Anna. But your parents were wise to leave it. A house is just a house. Your safety is more important than any house. And Germany is not safe for our people. Not now. Perhaps not ever."

"But how do we know that we will be safe here in Paris? How do we know that we will be safe anywhere ever?" Anna asked plaintively.

Madeleine was silent. It was the same question Pierre Dreyfus had asked the previous evening when he had revealed his determination to take his family to America.

"How do we know that we will be safe in Paris? Or anywhere in Europe? I am certain that war will come, and I must seek safety for my children." His voice had been weighted with misery, and his words of warning were etched into Madeleine's memory.

She understood, standing in the stairwell of the decrepit tenement, that this waif shared her uncle's premonition, his desperate fear. How could little Anna be assured of her safety in Paris or, indeed, anywhere in a Europe threatened by Nazi power? She touched Anna's shoulder lightly and forced herself to smile as she struggled to find words of reassurance.

"France is not Germany. The French are good people. We believe in love, not hatred. You will be safe here, Anna. We will keep you safe," she said. "I promise."

A foolish promise, she knew, but one she would try to keep.

They reached the top floor. A thin, fair-haired woman stood in an open doorway, tapping her foot impatiently, her lips clenched, fear in her eyes.

"Anna, where have you been? I was so worried."

She spoke in German, harshness and concern blended in her tone, but seeing Madeleine, she addressed her in the stilted and rudimentary French of a new arrival.

"You must forgive me, mademoiselle. I was concerned about my daughter," she said apologetically.

"I understand. Anna was kind enough to accompany me when I told her that I had been sent to visit the family Hofberg," Madeleine said, careful to speak softly, calmly.

"You are certain that it is the family Hofberg you are seeking?" Anna's mother asked.

Her question was hesitant, laced with fear. Madeleine understood that visitors were alien to her in this new land. Alien and threatening.

"Yes. I am certain. May I come in so that I can explain why I am here?"

"She is a nice lady. So kind," Anna whispered.

Her mother hesitated, then nodded, and Madeleine followed her into the apartment. The bare floor was scrubbed clean, and bare mattresses were thrust against the peeling wall. The curtainless windows sparkled. A table had been improvised from a plank of wood and cinder blocks, but a graceful crystal vase, containing a single yellow rose, stood on its splintered surface. Small Anna perched on a battered sofa, cotton stuffing pouring out of its faded floral-patterned cushions.

"Frau Hofberg, allow me to introduce myself," Madeleine began. "My name is Madeleine Levy and I am a social worker, an *assistante sociale*."

She spoke her new title with subdued pride and paused before continuing.

"A teacher in your son's school contacted the Institute of Social Work. Your son told her that he was hungry and felt weak because he had not eaten, that there was no food in his home. The teacher feared for his health and turned to us. We want to offer you assistance from a fund made available to us by the Jewish community of Paris. The *kehillah*."

Frau Hofberg nodded in recognition of the Hebrew word for *community*, but her voice trembled when she replied, speaking with an odd comingling of pride and embarrassment.

"I thank you but we do not need charity. A kind neighbor has lent us money for bread and milk. We will, of course, repay her when my husband finds employment. He knows business. Upholstery. There is no illness in our home. I keep everything clean, very clean."

The words poured out in a jumble of German and French.

Frau Hofberg's eyes were very bright, her color high. Anna gripped her mother's hand, and two boys ran in and stood protectively beside her. Their pallor and the wariness in their eyes saddened Madeleine.

"These are my brothers," Anna said. "Samuel and David."

Madeleine held her hand out to them, and as they each touched it, she felt the fragility of their fingers, the bones shining through the thin covering of skin. *Malnourished*, the teacher had reported. *Starving*, Madeleine would amend when she wrote her report.

She turned to their mother.

"Frau Hofberg. It is not charity we offer but assistance. The Jewish community is one family, and families always help each other. And so the French Jewish *kehillah* wishes to help you as you would surely help us if our situations were reversed," she said, impulsively drawing Anna close and patting her head.

The gesture was not lost on Anna's mother. Her expression softened. She sat on the sofa and motioned Madeleine to a seat beside her.

"Of course. In Germany, before the bad times came, our family always did what we could for those in the community who needed help," she said.

"I am certain of that," Madeleine assured her. "Then you surely understand why I am here. May I ask you how and why you came to Paris?"

She knew the answer, but the details would have to be included in her report. She took no notes but listened as the weary woman sighed and spoke very softly, her every word awash in sadness. "The Hofberg name is not unknown in Berlin.

My husband's family lived there for generations. We owned a prosperous upholstery business with many employees, both Jewish and non-Jewish. My husband is a veteran of the German army and was awarded the Iron Cross for his valor in the Great War. Our life was pleasant until Hitler came into power.

"Everything changed in that time of darkness. All pleasure and ease vanished from our lives. Gentile friends and neighbors shunned us. Samuel and David, like all Jewish children, were expelled from school and were terrorized by gangs of Hitlerjugend. Swastikas were painted on the windows of our emporium. We washed them away. We were determined to be patient and wait for the season of hatred to pass. We were sure that we were safe, that things would soon get better. We placed my husband's Iron Cross in the front window of our home on Goethestrasse. Could cruelty and danger come to a street named for Goethe?"

She laughed bitterly and continued.

"Then came 'the night of breaking glass,' Kristallnacht. The plate-glass windows of our store were shattered, the merchandise looted. We hid in the basement of our home and saw the shards of glass from the front window fall in a gleaming shower onto the pavement of Goethestrasse. The Iron Cross was plucked from its red velvet casing, the case itself tossed onto the street. My son David rushed out and picked it up, muddied as it was, and a man with a swastika armband chased him, shouting, 'Tomorrow will be worse. Tomorrow every Jew will be dead and our Germany will be *judenrein*, free of Jews.' We did not wait for that tomorrow. We left for Paris that very night.

"We dared not go to the bank to withdraw our money. We took only what we could fit into our rucksacks and valises. I sewed my jewelry into the hems of our coats. What money we had in the house, we used for train tickets, and here in Paris, we sold the jewelry to pay the rent, to buy food. But I did snatch up a small crystal vase that had belonged to my mother and thrust it into my bag. I buy a flower every morning and place it in the vase. A foolish luxury, I suppose, but a rose costs only a centime and it reminds me of the life that was lost to us. It reminds me that there is beauty in the world. We have only a few pieces of jewelry left so I buy very little food. You are right. Our children are hungry. And too soon, yes, they will be ill. I am a mother who must watch her children go to bed hungry. I am a mother who fears for their lives."

"Your children will no longer be hungry, Frau Hofberg. And they will not fall ill," Madeleine responded. "I do not think you are foolish. I think you and your husband were very brave to save your children's lives."

She opened her briefcase and withdrew a wad of vouchers from the Federation of Jewish Societies.

"You can buy food with these in the large market on the rue des Rosiers. The kosher butcher and the greengrocer on the corner will also accept them, and I will give you others when you need them. My grandmother and my mother will visit you and bring you whatever clothing you may need for the children. The Jewish Federation will help find employment for your husband. This is what we Jews do for our families, for those in need. You would do as much for us, would you not?"

Tears of gratitude silvered Frau Hofberg's cheeks.

"This is the first kindness we have known since Kristallnacht," she murmured.

Madeleine nodded.

She knew about the night of breaking glass.

She had attended a rally at which her uncle Pierre had delivered a speech condemning the Nazi regime for its destruction of Jewish property, its assault on Jewish life. His passionate denunciation had been interrupted by outbursts of anti-Semitic rhetoric from a band of hoodlums, but Pierre had persisted. His reward had been a brave editorial in the widely read newspaper *Ordre* with the headline that read: "The Son of Captain Alfred Dreyfus Strongly Condemns Nazi Persecution."

Who in France would speak out against German cruelty when her uncle left for America? Madeleine wondered.

Heavyhearted, she glanced at her watch. She did not want to be late for that evening's meeting of the Jewish Scouts.

"May I offer you a glass of water, mademoiselle?" asked David, the elder of the two Hofberg brothers.

Even as Madeleine nodded her assent, an idea came to her.

"Frau Hofberg, perhaps your sons may accompany me when I leave here. I am going to a meeting of Les Éclaireurs Israélites, the Jewish Scouts. Perhaps you have heard of them."

It was David who replied.

"Of course we know about them. Samuel and I were members of the Blau-Weiss, the Jewish Scouts of Germany," he said proudly.

Frau Hofberg hesitated.

"I do not know if it will be safe for them to go. My sons have no documents. I do not want them to get into trouble if they are stopped by gendarmes. In Berlin the Jewish Scouts met in secret, but even so, many of them were arrested and sent to concentration camps."

"There are no concentration camps in France," Madeleine assured her. "There will be no difficulty. Gendarmes in Paris do not challenge young boys. I myself am a Jewish Scout and so are my younger brothers. Here in Paris, we have no need to meet in secret. We are simply young people who want to learn more about our Jewish heritage and the wonderful world of nature. We go on hikes and outings. We sing, we dance. There are groups of Jewish scouts throughout France—in Lyon, in Marseille, in Toulouse. There were even troops of scouts in Alsace. But, of course, that was before."

Before. She uttered the word in a regretful whisper. It did not have to be explained. Frau Hofberg understood that their world was divided into *before* and *after*. *Before* the rise of Hitler. *After* his reign of terror began.

Madeleine herself would always remember the happy days of *before* when she and Claude had visited Mulhouse on a trip with a group of scout leaders. It had been exciting to be in the village that had once been home to both their families. They had stolen away from their group and climbed the pear tree that had so often sheltered each of them in their separate childhoods. Seated on the thick-leafed branches, looking down on the sylvan scene so distant from a Paris newly haunted by the fear of war, she had turned to Claude. Hesitantly, she asked a question so simple that it caused her to blush at her own ignorance.

"Is this happiness, Claude? You and I sitting in a tree with sunlight on our faces?"

How tremulous her voice, how gentle his response.

"Yes. I think it must be," he had replied and twirled a tendril of her dark hair about his finger.

Neither of them had spoken of the dark foreboding, their unacknowledged fear that these few hours might be all the happiness they would ever know.

Madeleine sighed and turned her attention back to the young Hofbergs.

"Please, Mama. We should like to go."

They spoke in unison, and Anna flung herself onto her mother's lap.

"Me too. I want to be a scout. I want to sing and dance," she pleaded.

They all smiled, a sunburst of pleasure.

"Anna, tonight's meeting is for older scouts, but I will take you to a meeting of children your own age next week if your mother allows it," Madeleine assured her.

Frau Hofberg nodded, patting Anna's head.

"This meeting—where will it take place?" she asked.

"At the small synagogue on the corner of rue des Rosiers. We will be giving out apples and cheese. Your boys will be able to bring some home. And tonight we have a speaker from Germany, Leon Cohn."

"But Leon Cohn was our Blau-Weiss leader. Remember the tricks with knots he taught us, Samuel?" David asked excitedly, and his brother nodded. A small piece of their abandoned boyhood had been restored to them.

"Do not come home too late. Your father will be concerned," Frau Hofberg said. She hugged her daughter.

"Do not worry, Anna. Mademoiselle Levy will not forget you," she whispered.

"Of course I will remember you. I promised, didn't I?"

Madeleine smiled and watched as Anna removed her unlaced boots and passed them to Samuel. She noticed, for the first time, that he was barefoot. She studied his feet, estimated his shoe size. She would have to tell her mother to scavenge a pair of boots in his size.

She stood and knotted her new crimson scarf about her neck, her grandmother's lovingly crafted gift reminding her that it was, after all, her birthday. She smiled to think of all that had transpired on this first day of her twentieth year— her certification, her intervention in the lives of the Hofberg family, and small Anna's trusting smile gifting her with the assurance that the profession she had chosen was important and meaningful, that she, Madeleine Levy, had the power to lighten the lives of others. And the day had not yet ended. She wondered if Claude had thought to buy her a gift and chastised herself for the selfishness of the thought.

"We must hurry," she told the boys.

She did not want to be late. She did not want Claude to worry about her. She thrilled at the idea that, of course, he would worry. She smiled and checked her briefcase to make sure that the embossed document of her certification as an *assistante sociale* was safe within its folder.

THREE

THE BASEMENT MEETING ROOM OF THE SMALL SYNAGOGUE was crowded, but Claude stood in the doorway and led Madeleine and the Hofberg brothers to the seats in the front row that he had saved. He knew that she preferred to sit close to the speakers so that she could be assured of hearing every word.

Madeleine introduced the boys and directed them to the long trestle table spread with platters of apples and cheese. She proudly whispered her news to Claude.

"I was awarded my certification document today."

He grinned.

"Wonderful. You earned it in record time."

"Only because I took courses and did fieldwork during the summers. Just as you have done. It is as though we are racing against history."

"Let us hope that it is a race we will win," Claude replied.

She nodded and reflected that it would be wonderful if they could simply allow their lives to proceed at an easy pace. What would it be like to have the luxury of leisure and the carefree pleasures of sunlit days and star-spangled nights? She sighed. Perhaps they would know such luxury, such pleasure, when Hitler was vanquished and the fear they lived in was gone from their lives. Perhaps next month, perhaps next year. *Perhaps never.* The unbidden thought thudded against Madeleine's heart.

As though aware of the darkness of her imagining, Claude took her hand in his. He understood her all too well. He knew that if war engulfed Paris, now more a probability than a possibility, the Sorbonne would close and the university degree that he had struggled toward for so long would be forfeit. He shuddered as the daily news bulletins grew increasingly ominous. Hitler had appointed himself war minister, bellowing new threats even as Germany occupied the Sudetenland. Of course France was in his sights. That certainty invigorated Claude and intensified his determination. There was so much to do, so much that needed his energy, his commitment.

He smiled at Madeleine.

"I have not forgotten that it is your birthday. Let us celebrate in our own small way after this meeting."

"Celebrate?" she asked, startled.

The very word, uttered in this room, at this time, had an alien ring. Celebrations belonged to a world at peace.

"Yes. Celebrate," Claude repeated. "Carpe diem. Seize the day."

She smiled. It was an expression Simone and Anatol had used when they had insisted on marrying despite their youth and the uncertainty of a future that portended more threat than promise.

"Now is the time when we must have the courage to seize the day," Simone had declared, and she and Anatol had indeed seized the day. They had been breathless with joy at their wedding, exuberant at the birth of their daughter. But Anatol's devastating illness now punctured that defiant optimism. Poor Simone. Poor Anatol. It was with a heavy heart that Madeleine motioned the Hofberg brothers to the seat beside her and noticed that they shared only one apple and one slice of cheese. She understood that they were saving the other one for their sister. That small act of kindness caused her eyes to burn with unshed tears.

Her brothers, Jean Louis and Etienne, joined her, and she introduced them to Samuel and David.

"Jean Louis is studying medicine," she told them. "He will be a doctor like our father."

"I was preparing for the medical school examination in Berlin," David said. "Until the Nazis expelled all Jewish students from the Gymnasia."

"Then you might think of studying here," Jean Louis suggested. "I will help you."

"Perhaps."

David's reply was hesitant, and Madeleine understood that he would not allow himself the luxury of hope. Jean Louis had persisted in his studies despite the fact that as the threat from Germany mobilization grew stronger, the French government was calling up its own reservists. Her brother might soon have to exchange the white coat of healing for the gray army uniform of death. Her heart sank and she drew closer to Claude. Would he too be called up, Claude, her friend, her heart's companion?

New arrivals continued to pour into the room.

"I've never seen a meeting so crowded," she whispered.

"That is because Robert Gamzon, the founder of the Éclaireurs Israélites, as well as Leo Cohn, the leader of our

German comrades, will be speaking. Tonight may well decide the future of the Jewish Scout program throughout Europe. Our movement will have to prepare for new challenges," Claude said, all lightness gone from his voice.

He stared straight ahead. Madeleine shivered, frightened by the unusual somber mood that had so suddenly fallen upon him. What knowledge did he have that she was denied? she wondered. Why this new pessimism in his tone? He had often told her that their generation would confront extraordinary challenges, but they would meet them with courage because they had youth and idealism on their side.

She had been less sanguine, more fearful. Did Claude now share her own premonitions of a hovering disaster? She thought not. She was conditioning herself to show courage but he had been born to bravery. Still, she noted the sadness that shadowed his angular face as the conversation subsided into silence.

A tall, thin man strode up to the podium, Robert Gamzon, the founder of the French Jewish Scout movement, *les éclaireurs*. History had already claimed him. He was a communications officer in the French army, and while he wore that uniform, his neckerchief was the blue-and-white bandanna of the Jewish Scouts. He greeted his young audience with a casual wave of his hand and an engaging smile.

"Shalom," he said. "Shalom, *chaverim, amis*. Welcome friends. Welcome comrades."

They responded with enthusiastic applause and vigorous cheering.

"Shalom, Robert Gamzon," they shouted. "Shalom, *chaver.* Shalom, *ami! Vive la* France. *Vive les* Éclaireurs Israélites!"

Madeleine, who had never before seen the legendary leader, studied his handsome, smiling face. She was suffused with admiration at the patience and control he emanated. He waved his hand rhythmically until silence was restored, and when he spoke, his voice resonated with conviction. She listened carefully, each word saturated with vitality and commitment. He was, she realized as he spoke, the ideological architect of her own future, a future dedicated to the saving of lives, the saving of children.

"Dear friends," he said. "We meet at a perilous time. The storm troopers of Nazi Germany are massed at our borders. We pray that they will not invade our beloved France, but we recognize that we, the Jewish youth of our brave République, must be prepared should the worst happen. We must have a plan to protect our children. We must fight for our country and for our people, especially for our little ones, too young, too weak to fight for themselves. We must demonstrate our solidarity with the brave pioneers who dream of a Jewish national homeland in Palestine, a refuge for all Jews everywhere but especially for our children who are our future. We have already established a transit camp in Algeria for endangered youngsters, but our work has just begun. Éclaireurs Israélites—Jewish Scouts of France—*enfants de la patrie*—are you ready to join us?"

A thunderous chorus of affirmation answered his question. "*Oui!* Yes! We are ready. We stand with you," they shouted.

Robert Gamzon smiled yet again, his face aglow with pride. He waved them into silence and continued, his voice calmer now.

"We will now hear the words of a brave leader of the

Blau-Weiss, our brother Jewish scouts in Germany. He will share with you the sad happenings in his community. Let us welcome our courageous comrade Leo Cohn!"

A man as tall as Robert Gamzon, his gaunt face wreathed in sadness, strode to the podium and again the room reverberated with applause. The scouts sprang to their feet and sang their welcome. They linked arms and swayed back and forth. Claude gripped Madeleine's hand, and her heart beat wildly. Transfixed, Samuel and David Hofberg moved closer to the podium, the better to hear the man who had led their troop in Berlin. His magical appearance in Paris impressed upon them the intrinsic unity of all Jews.

He began to speak, his French awkward but adequate, his accent thick. The French scouts shifted uneasily, glanced at each other quizzically, but within minutes, they no longer noticed his accent but listened raptly to his words. He had been eyewitness to the nightmare that haunted their dreams.

"I was in Berlin on Kristallnacht," he said. "I saw an old man being beaten by a squad of Hitlerjugend—a pregnant Jewish woman thrown to the ground. I saw a rabbi forced to scrub paving stones, his white beard first pulled and then cruelly cut. I walked through streets covered with broken glass, the remnants of synagogue windows, Jewish homes, Jewish shops. In every glittering shard I saw our people's terrible future. No—not their future but their present. It was happening now! There were arrests, transports to concentration camps. I raced to our Blau-Weiss headquarters and saw that our office had been ransacked, our books and pamphlets burned, the Jewish flag ripped to shreds."

He leaned forward, an ironic smile flitting across his face. "What did they hope to find in the meeting place of Jewish scouts?" he asked. "Our dangerous compasses? Our lethal songbooks? Our toxic Hebrew primers?"

The French scouts laughed bitterly. Madeleine saw Samuel Hofberg grip his brother's hand. Leo Cohn's words, she knew, triggered their own memories of their family's experience on that night of terror, their very last night in the city of their birth.

"We learned that night that the Jewish people are in terrible danger," Leo Cohn continued. "And we scouts must react to that danger. We must help all those in need of refuge. We must train for danger and learn the skills that will help us—and those who depend upon us, especially our children—to survive."

The young *éclaireurs* sat very still. They had loved their hiking excursions into the mountains, the adventure of filling their canteens with water from free-flowing streams, the playful harvesting of wild greens and berries for improvised picnics. But those joyous treks were now vested with new importance, new urgency. Leon Cohn had spoken the ominous word *survival*, and with that utterance they felt the first stirrings of fear.

He stared out at them, and sensing the darkened mood, he lifted his arms and raised his voice to a triumphant charge.

"Do not be afraid, my young friends! We will not allow Adolf Hitler to triumph. The people of Israel will endure. The Jewish scouts, the Blau-Weiss, the Éclaireurs Israélites, will endure! Our children will endure!"

Their voices joined his in a thunderous shout of affirmation.

"*Oui! Oui! Certainement. Certainement!*"

Robert Gamzon lifted the French flag, and Leo Cohn

waved the blue-and-white Jewish banner. The young people joined hands, their faces radiant. They sang as though their hearts might break. They sang in French. "La Marseillaise." They sang in Hebrew. "Hatikvah," the Jewish national anthem, the hymn of hope.

Claude's fingers dug into Madeleine's wrist, and she leaned against him. David and Samuel Hofberg stood beside Jean Louis and Etienne Levy, brothers all, French and German, united in their common faith and a recognition of their common destiny. Madeleine trembled with fear for them, for herself, for all those gathered so bravely in this room. Claude pulled her close and sang "Hatikvah" in Hebrew, his voice full and rich.

"*L'hiyot Am chofshi b'artzeinu,*
B'eretz tzion, Yerushalyim.
We will be a free nation in our own land,
The land of Zion, Jerusalem!"

Each word a promise, each word a pledge.

Tears seared Madeleine's cheeks. They would never give up. Hope would triumph as it had triumphed before. She remembered suddenly the words her grandfather had penned during the darkest days of his imprisonment. *Fight injustice with courage*, he had written.

That was exactly what she would do, she vowed. It was her birthday resolution. She smiled at Claude. He rested his hand on her head, the gesture a gentle gift. Yes, she thought, she and Claude would, like Simone and Anatol, eventually seize the day. They would seize many days. Always with courage. And with joy. Joie de vivre, the joy of life.

Still singing "La Marseillaise," Madeleine and Claude

joined the scouts exiting the synagogue. Their procession was orderly; their strong and melodic voices resonated bravely. Passersby paused and sang with them, their hands upon their hearts, tears in their eyes. France might be threatened, but its day of glory would arrive.

FOUR

Madeleine and Simone sat beside Anatol's hospital bed as he slipped quietly into death. Simone rested her head upon her young husband's silenced heart as Madeleine very gently closed his eyes.

"He was not yet thirty," Simone whispered. "It's not fair; it's not just."

Madeleine was silent. She had no words of comfort to offer her sister. Fairness and justice had vanished from their world, replaced by apprehension and uncertainty.

"Anatol is at peace," she told her sister and led her from the room.

There was much to do. A small girl to be cared for, a funeral to be arranged.

Once again the Dreyfus family gathered at Montparnasse Cemetery. Once again Pierre Dreyfus intoned the Kaddish, his voice breaking as Simone knelt beside the newly dug grave and dropped a sprig of lilac on the plain pine coffin. Once again, each mourner lifted a shovel overflowing with dark, moist earth and blanketed the pale wood.

They turned then to the nearby grave of Alfred Dreyfus, and one by one, each member of his family placed small stones upon it. Madeleine selected a pebble, sun blanched to the color of alabaster and wind polished to a fine smoothness. Simone, in turn, found a jet-colored stone. Their grandmother's lips moved in silent prayer.

"Sometimes I think our family is death haunted," Simone murmured to Madeleine.

"No," Madeleine protested. "We are a family in love with life, who want to make life better for those around us. Papa in his clinic, Maman and Grand-mère with their work in the Pletzl. And you and I as social workers and *éclaireurs*. Even Frederica with her laughter and games. We are life lovers all."

Hearing her name, the child smiled bravely and Simone held her in tight embrace.

"Yes. Our daughter is a wonderful child. But Anatol and I always worried that we were selfish to bring her into this dangerous world of ours. We worried that we would not be able to keep our Jewish child safe. Now I will worry alone."

"You are not alone," Madeleine countered. "We are together. Frederica will be safe. She will survive. We will all survive. It is actually possible that the German army will not invade France. Churchill has pledged assistance. Prime Minister Reynaud, in his broadcast only last night, said that an Anglo-French coalition has every chance for success. That will surely deter Hitler."

"I want to believe you, Madeleine," Simone said wearily. "But I think Monsieur Reynaud is cursed with false optimism. Since the German invasion of Poland, the question is not *if* the Germans will invade our France, but *when* they will invade."

Madeleine did not reply. In actuality, she shared Simone's ominous appraisal, which echoed Claude's own gloomy prognosis, but she refrained from admitting it. It did no harm to opt for hope, however elusive it might be.

They returned for the post-funeral meal of consolation in Lucie's home on the rue des Renaudes, newly aware of significant absences. Close Dreyfus cousins had already left France, their visas to different destinations that offered refuge, however tentative, bought and paid for.

Pierre and his family made a brief appearance. Their long-delayed departure for America was imminent, and they had preparations to complete before they left Paris to await their passage in Marseille.

There was subdued talk of days spent visiting one embassy after another in search of visas, only to realize that few countries would accept Jewish refugees.

The fear and tension in the room was palpable. Claude arrived as a Levy cousin described a futile visit to the American embassy. "The clerk there would not even accept my application. He advised me to go to the Costa Rican embassy. Where is Costa Rica?" he asked and laughed bitterly.

"That is why we need a Jewish homeland," Claude whispered to Madeleine. "If we had a homeland in Palestine, if England had kept the promise of the Balfour Declaration, no Jew would now be stateless."

She nodded in agreement. The creation of a Jewish homeland was no longer a distant fantasy. It was an urgent necessity.

"We will be talking about an escape route to Palestine at a meeting of scout leaders tomorrow night," Claude added. "Will you come?"

"I will try," Madeleine promised, although she cringed at his use of the word *escape*. She felt a flurry of anger at his despair. Did he not realize that she needed him to be strong and resolute, optimistic and hopeful? An impossible dream, she realized and cursed her own resentment.

She rose to greet the Hofberg family who had come to offer their condolences.

Madeleine's mother and grandmother frequently visited the Hofberg home on the rue Lascin, carrying welcome donations of clothing and food. Pierre Dreyfus had found employment for Herr Hofberg through a Jewish welfare organization, and Etienne and Jean Louis always accompanied Samuel and David to meetings of the *éclaireurs*.

But Madeleine took special pride in small Anna, who was the youngest member of Madeleine's own group of junior scouts. The little girl bore scant resemblance to the skinny waif who had once stood so wistfully beside the crepe vendor's cart. Her fair hair was now woven into a long, thick braid, her school uniform neat and clean, and her high-buttoned shoes sturdy, laced, and polished.

As always, she rushed into Madeleine's outstretched arms, bubbling over with exuberant tales of her adventures in school and her mastery of scouting skills.

"I can tie all the knots now, just as you taught us," she proclaimed proudly. "Will I get a new badge, Madeleine?"

"Of course you will," she responded. "Well done, *petite soeur*, little sister."

She felt a strong attachment to Anna, even fantasizing that the little girl was the younger sister lost to her so many years ago when Jeanne, her mother, then pregnant, had assured Madeleine that the child would be a girl.

"A little sister for you, Madeleine," Jeanne had said. "Just as you are Simone's little sister."

The baby had indeed been a girl, a breech delivery, stillborn and cyanotic, her tiny, blue-tinged face glimpsed for the briefest of moments by Madeleine and Simone, who had huddled beside their mother's bed.

Madeleine had been bitterly disappointed and wept for the little sister she would never have. Anna, she acknowledged, had somehow filled an enduring lacuna in her life. Her attachment to the child was irrational, she knew, but it was an irrationality she allowed herself. It did no harm. It caused no pain.

Claude rose to leave.

"Please try to come to the meeting. We have urgent matters to discuss. Matters that will involve you. Please try to be there," he said.

"Of course." Her smile was a promise.

Madeleine recognized the importance of the meeting as soon as she entered the small room in the rear of the synagogue that served as the scouts' office. Every seat was taken and Robert Gamzon, who visited only during times of crisis, sat behind a battered desk puffing nervously on a Gauloise as he shuffled through a sheaf of papers and selected a pale-blue aerogram. He motioned for quiet and shared its message in sad and sonorous tones.

"We have a communique from Palestine," he said. "The

British are intent on enforcing the White Paper, which severely limits Jewish immigration, so the scouts there are finding clandestine points of entry. Bribes must be paid and money must be raised. All intelligence indicates that France will soon be attacked by Germany. If the German invasion succeeds, the Jews of France will be in great danger. We know what has happened to the Jews of Germany. We too will see roundups, incarcerations, concentration camps. We anticipate that there will be French citizens collaborating with the Nazis."

"But that will not happen. Not here in France. Prime Minister Reynaud has promised that our community will be protected," a tall youth protested.

"Prime Minister Reynaud has lost faith in his own promise," Robert Gamzon replied. "He now realizes that it cannot be kept. We then must hope for the best and anticipate the worst. We are scouts, and we will do what scouts have always done. We will prepare. Prepare to save the Jewish children of France. We must rely on our own ability to survive and to help our children to survive. We must train to help them escape from France and find safe passage to Palestine. We must, all of us, be strong of mind, strong of body. Do you understand, my Éclaireurs Israélites?"

"We understand!" A chorus of assent rang out.

Madeleine clutched Claude's hand and listened intently to the ensuing discussion of how such training would be organized. She feared missing a single word, and gratefully, she saw that Claude was taking careful notes which he would pass on to her. Her hearing loss, slight as it still was, would not impede their efforts.

A committee was selected to create maps detailing escape

routes through the Alps and the Pyrenees. Contacts had been made in Switzerland and Spain. Safe houses had already been established in those countries. A cadre would be formed to undertake the forging of documents. Passports, identity cards, visas. They would need skilled calligraphers.

"Simone," Madeleine whispered to Claude. Her sister's elegant hobby, her graceful pen, would now be aimed against evil.

"Of course," he agreed.

"We will need weapons," Robert Gamzon continued. "Pistols. Grenades. Knives. Whatever we can find. We pray that violence will be avoided, but we must be ready to defend ourselves and defend our children if need be."

Madeleine shivered. There would be violence. There would be death. She thought of her grandfather's military sword, which her grandmother now and again removed from its scabbard and polished to a high gleam. She chastised herself. A ridiculous idea. Gamzon was in search of weapons that could be carried clandestinely or easily concealed. She remembered that the pistol her father had used in the Great War remained in the bottom drawer of his desk. Could she remove it? Should she? Would he allow it? She struggled with the thought even as her name was called.

"Madeleine Levy, will you be responsible for training some of the younger children?"

The question startled her. She had not realized that Robert Gamzon knew her name or recognized her capabilities.

"Yes," she said. "Yes, of course."

She sat back and wondered what such training would entail.

But she would learn. And she would teach. There was no other choice.

She and Claude left the meeting together. As always, they made their way across the Pont de l'Alma and paused to stare down at the waters of the Seine, silvered by the moonlit sky.

"How peaceful it is," she said. "Can war really be coming to Paris, Claude?"

He turned to her but did not answer, a frown creasing his face.

"Is something wrong?" she asked hesitantly.

He nodded and handed her the sheet of paper on which he had taken the notes on Robert Gamzon's directives. The scout leader had spoken rapidly, and Claude knew that Madeleine's hearing loss occasionally prevented her from grasping words spoken too swiftly.

"I am worried," he said.

"Of course. We are all worried. These are dangerous times," she replied too flippantly.

"But it is you I am worried about. Did you hear Robert Gamzon stress that we must be strong? Strong of body?"

"Yes. I heard him."

"I worry about your weakness." He spoke slowly, hesitantly, and she stared at him in confusion.

"My weakness?" she asked angrily, grasping his meaning.

"Your difficulty in hearing. It is a weakness that might prove dangerous," he continued, impervious to her ire.

"But I do hear. I am hearing you now, am I not?"

Her lips were pursed, and he flinched at the fury of her words. But he would not retreat.

"Yes. You hear me now because I am facing you and if my

voice does not reach you, you can read my lips. But there are times when you cannot hear nor see the lips of the speaker. That inability might threaten your safety. And the safety of those in your care. Our children."

"Do you think I would ever endanger the children?" She stared at him in disbelief.

"I know that you would not. But unpredictable things happen. Unforeseen dangers occur. I think it is important that you see an audiologist who might be able to help you," he continued.

"A ridiculous idea," she said. "Nothing can be done to help my hearing. The physician who cared for me after my recovery from scarlet fever told us that. And my own father is a doctor. Don't you think he would know if there was a remedy?"

She spat out each word, but Claude's reply was softly phrased, temperate and caring.

"You were eight years old when your hearing was damaged. Surely there has been much research since then. I have the greatest respect for your father, but he is an internist with a busy practice. I doubt that he has had the time to read the latest literature on audiology. It would do no harm for you to meet with a specialist in the field," he insisted.

"I don't have the time for such a meeting," she retorted.

He nodded. He knew that every hour of her day was crammed with obligations. Her daily routine as an *assistante sociale* was overwhelming as the influx of Jewish refugees from Germany increased. Her free hours and weekends were reserved for meetings with the younger scouts who relied on her leadership. Precious time was spent helping Simone, who was already in a cadre of *éclaireurs* training to forge the documents that would create new identities for Résistance fighters. Madeleine's rare leisure hours were often reserved for brief outings with Anna Hofberg. "Invite Anna to accompany you," he suggested. "I have made an appointment for you with Dr. Levin, an audiologist who is the father of one of our scouts. His office is not far from the café that you and Anna love so much."

"Very sly of you, Claude," Madeleine said.

She feigned irritation even as she reluctantly acknowledged that his concern pleased her. She smiled and placed her hand in his. Side by side, they leaned against the railing that rimmed the Pont de l'Alma and stared down at the silver-fringed waters of the Seine.

FIVE

The very next week, Anna accompanied Madeleine to Dr. Levin's office and sat patiently in his waiting room while the gentle, soft-spoken doctor conducted his examination. He was very thorough, shining his scope into each of her ears and then testing her hearing.

He sighed.

"I assume that it is difficult for you to hear when you are not directly facing the speaker," he said. "Is that so, Mademoiselle Levy?"

"Yes. I have grown skilled at reading lips, but I wondered if a hearing aid might help me."

He shook his head regretfully.

"I am afraid not. The scarlet fever that you suffered as a child caused nerve damage, and we have not yet developed instruments to remedy that. Research is ongoing, of course, but for now there is no relief that I can offer you."

"Will my hearing grow worse?" she asked hesitantly.

"We cannot say. Actually, you have been fortunate to retain the auditory capacity you have, but we cannot predict the progress of a deficit like your own. There is some anecdotal literature indicating that stress may impact negatively. My only advice to you would be to avoid tension and stress," he said.

He smiled bitterly, aware of the absurdity of his own advice. Madeleine shook her head wearily.

"I appreciate your words, but how does one avoid tension in today's Paris? Stress is in the very air we breathe. Still, may I call you now and again to ascertain if there is any progress in audiology research as it relates to my difficulty?" she asked.

He shook his head.

"I am afraid not. I am leaving Paris very soon. My wife has relations in Australia, and they have arranged visas for us. I fear that Jews are no longer safe in France," he said sadly.

Madeleine nodded and glanced toward the door, which was slightly ajar. She caught a glimpse of Anna's face, her eyes wide with fear, her lips trembling. The child had heard the doctor's words, his dark prediction. Madeleine turned to him and extended her hand.

"I wish you and your family bonne chance, good luck," she said.

"The Jews of France will need more than luck. I worry about the children. If only we could secure the safety of our children," he murmured.

"We in the *éclaireurs* are working hard to protect the children, to prepare them for what may come," she assured him.

She did not add that she herself was putting all her energy into that effort. Anna and the other children in her group were being carefully schooled to assume the new identities that might save their lives. They were taught to memorize the catechism in the event that they might have to pass as Christians. They went on long hikes in preparation for anticipated treks over the mountain passes of the Alps or the Pyrenees. They were small hostages to a destiny fraught with danger and uncertainty. Madeleine could not, would not share that knowledge with Dr. Levin. Like all scout leaders, she was pledged to secrecy. Trust was a rare commodity. They had been warned that everyone was suspect.

"Betrayal may come from anywhere, even from our own people," Robert Gamzon had said.

"I wish you well," Dr. Levin said, and he handed her a sealed envelope.

"A small check. For the *éclaireurs*. I know that you need funds," he said, and she smiled her gratitude.

She and Anna left the office, Anna visibly upset. She gripped Madeleine's hand too tightly, and tears glinted in her blue eyes.

"I heard what the doctor said," the child whispered. "But promise me that I will be safe. Promise me that you will protect me, Mademoiselle Madeleine."

"Of course I will. You are my *petite soeur*. Come, let us have an ice cream. June will soon be here, and that is the month of your birthday so we must celebrate." She forced herself to smile.

"Yes. In June I will be ten years old," the child said importantly.

"Then let us pretend that today is your birthday," Madeleine teased.

It was wise, she thought sadly, to push all celebrations forward. They were in a race against history. Every moment of joy was a goalpost successfully passed.

"And when is your birthday?" Anna asked as they sat in a café eating generous servings of chocolate glacé.

"The eighteenth of November. I am a child of winter," Madeleine replied.

She did not add that she had been born exactly a week after the celebration of the armistice that had ended the Great War. There was a family picture of the Dreyfus men still in uniform, gathered about her bassinet, each of them raising a glass in celebration.

"What were they toasting?" she had asked her mother once.

"Peace, of course. The end of the war to end all wars," Jeanne Dreyfus Levy had replied, and Madeleine had never forgotten those words, uttered with such optimism.

It was ironic, the thought that a scarce twenty-two years later, the German army hovered on the French border. The war to end all wars had instead birthed an even more dangerous conflagration.

"Perhaps we should celebrate your birthday early," Anna said happily.

"Yes, perhaps we should," Madeleine agreed. "But it might not be necessary."

November, after all, was many months away, and spring was the season of hope.

SIX

ANDRÉ, HER YOUNG FLOWER-VENDOR FRIEND, CHASED after Madeleine as she hurried home after a workday that had begun too early and extended into the early evening. But that, she knew, would be the pattern of her days, given the grimness of current events. Germany had turned hopeful spring into a season of despair.

She smiled at the boy who always reminded her of happier days.

"I saved my best lilacs for you," he shouted.

She broke her stride and examined the flowers in his panniers.

"How kind of you, André. Of course. The lilacs of June. Even this June."

Staring up at the cobalt-blue sky, she shivered against the impact of the harsh, unseasonable wind that had assaulted Parisians throughout the past week. The unpleasant weather, she thought, was an apt accompaniment to the sad news from Dunkirk and the terror that had gripped the city since the advent of the first horrific German bombing raid. War, unofficial undeclared war—decried as faux, false, by the government, but recognized as all too real by the vulnerable civilian population—had come to Paris. Lives had been lost; hospitals struggled to cope with the wounded. Madeleine's father and Jean Louis kept the doors of their clinic open throughout the night. And yet, despite the turmoil and the destruction, the tenacious lilacs continued to bloom. She envied the lovely blossoms.

"Such brave and foolish flowers," she whispered as she buried her face in the bouquets André had thrust at her and inhaled their fragrance.

"You must hurry home, André. You know that Prime Minister Reynaud has asked everyone to go indoors before darkness falls," she instructed the boy.

The prime minister's curfew, she knew, was a wise and necessary precaution. The Nazis, those creatures of darkness, waited for nightfall to launch their murderous raids on a city in love with light.

"I am not afraid of those stupid *Boches*," André announced scornfully as he wrapped her flowers in damp pages of *Le Monde*.

"Of course you're not. But you don't want your mother to worry."

She handed him three franc notes and watched him sprint through the gathering darkness, pausing to hand his only remaining bouquet to a beggar woman who clutched it to her breast.

She decided that despite the curfew, she would visit her grandmother that evening. Lucie Dreyfus loved lilacs, and Madeleine longed to see her smile.

She was surprised then, that when she arrived home, it was her grandmother who opened the door and motioned her to enter quickly. Her surprise turned to concern at the sight of her entire family assembled, an unusual gathering on a weekday evening. Simone, pale and sad-eyed, looked up from the labels she was writing, and Madeleine, bending to embrace her sister, read them with a sinking heart. *Cooking Utensils. Linens. Books.* It was a family custom to label the cartons of possessions they transported to their holiday homes, but she knew of no plans for a holiday. What was Simone doing? What was happening?

Even her uncle Pierre and his family, who would soon leave for the United States, were seated at the dining room table, removing one document after another from a file box, reading each carefully and consigning them to separate stacks.

Her brothers, Etienne and Jean Louis, stood before the bookshelves that lined the wall of the salon, methodically removing volumes, placing some in open cartons and discarding others.

"Only medical books," her father called. "We will transport only medical books."

"And anything by Zola and those about *l'affaire*," her mother added.

Lucie Dreyfus nodded her agreement.

"Of course. We do not want to leave our family's history behind."

Madeleine stared at her grandmother, who deftly razored open the hem of a long skirt and passed it to Pierre's wife, Marie. Her aunt then folded currency and jewelry into the open seam and stitched it closed. Madeleine remembered Frau Hofberg telling her that she had done just that before the family's hasty departure from Berlin. Perhaps such skill at hiding gems and money was embedded in the collective memories of Jewish women, she thought, a genetic heritage assuring survival.

"What has happened?" she asked, her voice trembling. "Why are you doing all this?"

She tightened her grip on the bouquets of lilacs, suddenly dizzied by their scent and the unexpected chaos that pervaded her usually orderly home.

All had been calm when she departed for work that morning. Yes, there had been sadness because of the air battle over France, but her father had insisted that the English would send additional squadrons. German troops were indeed advancing on Rouen, but Rouen was at a distance from Paris. They had offered each other reassurances and breakfasted in calm, their baguettes warm and slathered with butter, second cups of café au lait generously poured. Madeleine wondered what had occurred in the intervening hours to precipitate this burst of frenzied activity, the dismantling of their home, the concealment of their valuables.

It was her father who paused in his examination of papers passed to him by Pierre to answer her.

"The French army requisitioned our apartment this afternoon," he said gravely. "Our soldiers are being evacuated from Le Havre and Cherbourg. The army is being driven back across the Seine. The officer who came to order the requisition informed me that our apartment will be used as a planning base for operations in defense of Paris and advised us to leave the city at once. We are doing just that, of course. We will move south, to my family in Toulouse. We will be safer there, and hopefully, our family will not be separated."

Madeleine nodded. "Of course. I understand," she murmured.

La famille, unified and together, had always been their mutual priority. It was a Dreyfus coda.

"Will you be able to come with us, Madeleine? Can you arrange a leave of absence from your work?" Lucie Dreyfus asked anxiously.

"Yes. I will inform my superiors at once," she said.

Her reply was instinctive. Her first obligation was to her family, to her parents, her brothers, and Simone, with whom she had shared every day of her life. The Bureau of Assistance Sociale would manage without her for a short while.

But the interruption of her work with the Jewish Scouts was of greater concern to her. It had been decided that if the German army occupied Paris, the scouts would begin to activate plans to smuggle their youngest charges, most of them the undocumented children of refugees, across the border to safety in Switzerland or Spain. Her own small cadre of such children included Anna Hofberg.

Madeleine had trained them for what was certain to be an arduous and hazardous pilgrimage to safety. They were accomplished stealth marchers, aware of every subterfuge, accomplished students of Catholicism able to recite the Hail Mary and to deny their Jewishness if necessary. They had been drilled and drilled again in the techniques of survival. Each of them had a set of underclothing that concealed cloth wallets wrapped in waterproof covering, containing the identity cards Simone had forged with consummate skill. Compasses and maps were hidden where they could be redeemed only by a select group of leaders. Madeleine and her comrades had placed their hands upon their hearts in a secret meeting and pledged an oath of allegiance. The words were etched into her memory.

"I pledge to fight on until the total collapse of Nazi Germany. For honor, liberty, and the right to a Jewish life."

Claude's voice had melded with her own as they repeated the words, a duet of commitment and loyalty, binding them ever closer. Claude and Madeleine, comrades and friends. She dared not think beyond those two words. *Camarade. Ami.* All beyond that was in abeyance.

It was Claude, she knew, who would take her place if her small group of children were endangered in her absence. Struggling for calm, she assured herself that she would not be away from Paris for any length of time. She would accompany her family, help them to establish a safe haven in the south, and return to the capital as soon as possible. But still, in her mind's eye, she saw Anna Hofberg's narrow face, pale with fright, and remembered her promise to the child.

"I will always protect you," she had said.

It was a promise she would try, with all her might, to keep.

Simone handed her a pen and a sheet of notepaper.

"Write to Claude," she said softly.

But even as Madeleine lifted the pen, there was a knock at the door and Claude strode into the room. His chestnut-colored hair tumbled from his student cap in a mass of damp curls, and his avian face glistened with sweat. She understood that he must have run through the deserted streets of the city, never looking up at a sky dark with danger.

"I just heard that your apartment has been requisitioned,

and I came as quickly as I could. I was afraid you might have already left," he gasped.

"I would not have left without contacting you," she said. "You must know that."

"Of course I do. You must not worry. I will take care of your troop of children until you return," he said.

He did not ask when that would be. He understood that she had no reply to offer him. All plans for the future had been wrested from their grasp.

"Claude, please tell Anna that I will see her very soon, that I will buy her a birthday present in Toulouse."

A foolish promise, she knew. Would there be toys for sale in a city bracing itself for war? Still, she would find something, anything. She did not want Anna to fear that she was being abandoned.

"I will do that, of course," Claude said. "Her brothers are in my troop. I will see them tomorrow."

"Tomorrow," Madeleine repeated and wondered where she herself would be when the next day dawned.

Claude remained, assisting her family with the packing. Later that evening, he accompanied Lucie Dreyfus back to her apartment on rue des Renaudes and helped her fill cartons with whatever staples remained in her pantry.

"There will be very little food on the road to the south," he said. "So many Parisians are fleeing Paris, fearful because Reynaud has moved the city government to the Loire Valley. It will be very difficult to find food and shelter on the way to Toulouse."

"I know that, Claude," Lucie Dreyfus replied calmly. "This is not the first difficulty I have encountered in my life."

She spoke with a calm born of her long familiarity with danger and difficulty. She would confront and survive the Nazi threat, horrific and evil as it was, even as she had confronted and survived the horrific and evil attacks on her husband and her family all those years ago.

Methodically, she selected whatever she thought might be useful during the difficult days ahead. She and Claude ripped bed linens into strips.

"We may need them for bandages," she explained.

She wadded her jewels in newsprint and concealed them in containers of flour and sugar. She handed him a large diamond ring.

"Sell it," she instructed. "You will need the money for the children."

He understood then that she knew of the dangerous rescue program in which he and Madeleine were involved. He marveled that she had not argued against it, given how fiercely protective she was of her family, but then, of course, she was a woman conditioned to courage. He took the ring without protest.

"And please," she added, "take very good care of my Madeleine."

"Always," he said. "Ever and always."

His friend Marcel arrived, driving a battered Citroën, and the two young men carried the cartons to the car. Lucie turned briefly and stared up at the window of her abandoned dining room. She had left a small lamp burning, and she smiled at the golden light that glowed so gently in the elegant room where her family had spent so many happy hours. She was comforted. The room was unimportant. She had her memories. She had her family.

They returned to the Levy home, where Madeleine had taken control, dashing from one room to another, energetically directing her younger cousins so that the desperate packing became a game.

"She's so wonderful with children," Simone said, glancing at her sister.

"Yes. I know," Claude agreed.

He thought to add that he hoped that one day she would be wonderful with her own children, perhaps even *their* children, but he was silent. The thought had come unbidden and he banished it, angry at himself that he might think such a thing at such a time. He and Madeleine had an unspoken agreement. Even as they were aware of their growing closeness, they would not discuss the future. Planning was dangerous. Disappointment hovered in a darkening shadow.

He smiled wistfully at Simone and joined Madeleine and her brothers as they went through their father's medicine cabinets, laughing at the instructions on each bottle.

"Here's a good one," Etienne called. "One pill every hour with a clear, hot drink. We'll just have to tell the Germans to hold off while we brew a clear, hot drink."

They laughed, grateful for anything that relieved the grimness of their preparations.

Madeleine's parents studied ledgers, their faces tight with tension. Patients owed money to Dr. Levy, but there was no hope of collection despite their need for funds. They might be able to access their bank accounts from afar. This was not a time to worry about money. Jeanne slammed her household account book shut.

Pierre looked up from the documents he was sorting.

"My friend at the United States Embassy might yet be able to arrange visas for you and your family, Jeanne. Won't you consider it?" he asked.

She heard the plea in his voice. She and Pierre had been best friends, as well as brother and sister, from their childhood on, mutually protective of each other. It was Pierre who had calmed and reassured her when she learned that Madeleine's hearing had been damaged.

"Do not worry about our beautiful little Madeleine," he had said. "She is a Dreyfus. She will have the courage to overcome whatever difficulty comes her way."

And he had been right. Nothing had ever proven too difficult for Madeleine. Pierre had been prescient then, but his advice was irrelevant now.

"I cannot leave our country, our France," Jeanne said. "Do you think our father would have left?"

"Our father is dead. We must each decide for ourselves. I believe that I can do more to help our people, to help France, by arguing for them in the United States. American Jewish leaders have written telling me that they believe that as the son of Alfred Dreyfus, I might be able to influence President Roosevelt to at least lift the visa restrictions and admit more Jews, to join the fight against Hitler. I must follow my conscience, Jeanne," he replied.

"You mean you must protect your children," she retorted.

"As you surely will protect your own," he said. "But be assured: I will not leave until I am sure that Maman and your family are safely settled."

They both turned toward Lucie, who was using a double thread to sew her wedding pearls into the cuffs of Etienne's trousers.

"I was never fond of these pearls," she murmured, and Jeanne and Pierre smiled at each other in happy complicity, peace between them restored.

Claude left, and Madeleine walked with him to the outer gate. They stood together, moonlight silvering their upturned faces as they stared at the star-spangled sky. A soft wind soughed, and the air was suffused with the scent of lilacs.

"Nature, at least, is at peace," Madeleine observed wistfully.

"We too will know peace one day," Claude responded. "You and I. Do not be afraid, Madeleine."

They stared at each other, locking away the words they dared not say, the gestures that they had refused to allow each other. Regret overwhelmed them, and suddenly he held her close, buried his fingers in her thick, dark hair, and with great gentleness, kissed her.

"Are you all right, my Madeleine?" he asked.

"Better than all right," she replied, reading the words upon his lips.

With his arms about her, he spoke very softly, knowing her eyes would register the words her ears might not receive.

"When this war ends, we will go to Alsace and climb our pear tree."

"And pick its golden fruit," she added.

"And we will cook a wonderful sweet compote."

They smiled at their own words murmured in unison, their shared promise of hope uttered on a night of leave-taking when hopelessness held sway.

"*Á bientôt, chérie,*" he said.

"*Á bientôt, mon cher.*"

He pressed a slip of paper into her hand.

"A phone number," he said. "Use it only to assure me that you are safe."

She nodded and watched him walk down the road. At the corner, he turned and waved. She smiled even as tears streaked her cheeks. She willed herself to calm and returned to where her mother had set out a pot of fragrant tea and her family was gathered around the table in a room they would never see again.

SEVEN

THEY LEFT PARIS IN AN ODD CONVOY, EACH FAMILY VEHICLE laden with trunks and cartons, oversize valises, hampers of food, and containers of water. The Levys and Lucie Dreyfus in one car, Pierre and his family in another, their Mercier and Reinach cousins crowded into the large estate van that had, in happier times, carried them to their Alsatian country homes. They drove through the milky light of dawn, passing slowly through the familiar, prosperous arrondissements of the city, still untouched by the threat of war. But all semblance of urban order and peace vanished as the sun rose and they reached the Hôtel de Ville close to the Pletzl. The poor Jewish quarter had been assaulted by confusion and chaos.

Rumors of the imminence of the invasion of Paris had ignited fear and triggered an explosion of desperation among the Jewish refugees from Nazi Germany. They had seen their relatives, their friends, their neighbors arrested, the windows of their homes and businesses shattered, their synagogues destroyed. They had wept when their holy Torahs were burned and their books tossed onto bonfires. They had fled Hitler's reign, had fled Germany, but they knew all too well what those Jews who had been unable to escape had suffered—the mass arrests, the humiliations, the concentration camps. Terror informed their memories; death haunted their dreams. They were, once again, racing toward survival, intent on fleeing Paris before German soldiers goose-stepped their way through the City of Light.

Throngs of men and women rushed out of the city, their possessions crammed into clumsy burlap sacks hoisted onto their shoulders. Trunks were uneasily balanced on battered perambulators and rusted bicycles. Women carried babies; men cradled sobbing toddlers. The elderly and the ill were shuttled down the cobbled streets in wheelchairs. Householders stood in their doorways, their faces grim masks of defeat and uncertainty. Should they stay, should they leave?

Madeleine watched a group of bearded men, wearing the long, black frock coats and the high skullcaps of the Chassidic community, prayer shawls about their bent shoulders as they walked at a leisurely pace to a small synagogue. Her father stared at them, his lips twisted in contempt.

"They have no fear because they rely on divine protection. They are on their way to the morning service where they will pray to their God who neither hears nor cares," he said bitterly.

"He is our God as well, Pierre Paul," Lucie Dreyfus countered as their car inched its way out of the city.

He did not answer. He considered himself a proud and secular Jew, but he would not argue with Jeanne's mother who, despite all that she had endured, had never abandoned her faith.

"I'm hot," Etienne complained as they at last exited the city and followed the southbound caravans of weathered trucks and ancient taxis, new cars and old, every luggage rack laden with suitcases and rucksacks.

Madeleine opened the window just as two motorcycles streaked by, their engines roaring, their mufflers spurting noxious fumes that caused her to choke. Still, she smiled at the sight of a small blue auto that followed them, a wheelchair and a baby carriage tied to its roof.

"No generation left behind," Jean Louis muttered sarcastically as he pointed at the laden vehicle.

"We should be proud of that," she cautioned him. "We are different from the Nazis. We care for both infants and the aged."

"The voice is the voice of Madeleine Levy, but the words are the words of Claude Lehmann," Etienne teased.

Madeleine blushed. Yes, she was quoting Claude, but she would not tell her brothers that she was happy to repeat his words, nor would she tell them that the very mention of his name comforted her. She sat back, grateful that the air cleared as they reached an open country road.

Their small convoy halted in a small wooded glade. As they ate their long-delayed breakfast, Pierre located a news station on his car radio. They listened to the faint transmission, briefly elated at the news that England had increased its air support. That elation was swiftly deflated with the new bulletin that followed. Winston Churchill had denied Prime Minister Reynaud's impassioned plea to send ground troops to assist in the defense of Paris.

"Churchill has no choice," Pierre insisted. "England needs all its fighting men. If the British are defeated, then France will surely be lost."

"France is still free. She will remain free," Madeleine's father insisted.

Madeleine shivered. The dissent between her uncle and her father unnerved her. A divided family, like a divided people, lost its strength. She glanced at Simone, who nodded and held her small daughter close.

A blue-winged butterfly settled on the child's golden hair for the fraction of a second. The sisters sat very still and watched it soar beyond their view. They smiled. War might threaten, arguments might erupt, but the delicate beauty of a blue-winged butterfly endured.

Hand in hand, they returned to the car and the arduous journey southward was resumed. Now and again, Madeleine, who was a new driver, took her father's place at the wheel. She was grateful for his gently offered corrections of her navigation, a skill which they recognized might prove essential in the troubled times soon to come.

"By the time we reach Toulouse, you will be an excellent driver," he assured her, never mentioning that she braked too quickly when she failed to hear the urgent siren of an ambulance or the warning bell of a cyclist. Someone would alert her, he assured himself, unwilling to undermine her confidence by mentioning her hearing difficulty. It was minor; it was of no importance, he assured himself.

They stayed at wayside inns but even as their journey progressed, the news worsened. Holland fell. French troops retreated from Belgium. Rommel's army advanced. Hitler had abandoned the Chateau-Thierry-Metz-Belfort triangle as his next objective and directed his troops to Paris. The Dreyfus family stopped listening to the radio. They bought no newspapers. They took shelter in their ignorance.

On a sun-swept day, they parked their vehicles in a meadow and gathered for the picnic that had become essential to their routine. It afforded them the illusion of normalcy. Food was still relatively easy to obtain in the countryside, and Lucie spread raw vegetables, fruit, and fragrant cheese on a worn blanket.

Madeleine sliced the apples they had bought at a farm. She had asked for pears, but the farmer's wife had said regretfully that pears were not yet in season.

"No matter," Madeleine had replied and told herself that she would have a surfeit of pears when the war ended. She and Claude would hike through Alsace, and once in Mulhouse, they would climb their tree and pluck the golden fruit, allowing the juice to run free so that they might taste it when their lips met. She smiled. Why should she deny herself the luxury of dreaming on this radiant day? Surely she was entitled to her fantasies.

Her brothers and her younger cousins tossed a ball to one another.

"I think it would be wise for us to listen to the news," Pierre said reluctantly.

Jeanne nodded and they sat side by side in the one car with a working radio as Pierre turned knobs and at last elicited a transmission. They opened the windows so that the newscaster's voice could be heard by the others. Madeleine and Simone drew close and strained to listen as the transmission faltered and then regained strength.

They conditioned themselves to remain unafraid of the snippets of news. The Germans, they heard, were in Dijon, but that they had known. Reims was occupied, but that too they had known. Verdun, where Pierre had fought with such courage in the Great War, was once again in jeopardy, but that too they had known.

It was the sudden announcement that the German army was marching into Paris that caused them to cling to one another in a paroxysm of terror, to listen, frozen in disbelief, to the news. Their worst nightmares were their new reality.

"France has fallen!" The newscaster's voice trembled and drifted into silence.

The airwaves went dead. Static spurted from the radio. Choked by grief, the family could not speak.

"What is today's date?" Simone asked.

"*Juin, Quatorze.* The fourteenth day of June," Madeleine replied.

It was a date they would never forget.

Transmission resumed. The newscaster continued to speak, but he stumbled over each word that he uttered. They feared that he might weep before he completed his broadcast.

"Marshal Philippe Pétain, the deputy prime minister, speaks of forming a new government. He calls for an armistice with Germany."

"Never!" Pierre shouted. "What a betrayal an armistice would be. France cannot submit to the Nazi bastards. We must resist."

"And from where will you resist, Pierre? From the streets of New York? From the halls of Washington? Will Roosevelt hear you? Will your words save your country?" Madeleine's father asked angrily.

Madeleine turned from her father to her uncle.

"Let us not quarrel," she said quietly. "This is our precious time together. It is not a time for anger."

"It is a time to pray," Lucie added. "A time to pray for France, to pray for our people and for all who suffer in this terrible war."

Standing between her son and daughter, Lucie took their hands in her own, and one by one, the rest of the family joined them, forming a circle bathed in the golden light of the noonday sun. With their eyes closed, silent prayers were offered, their love for each other and for their country affirmed. The future might be threatening and uncertain, but they were together, pledged to keep each other safe.

Madeleine looked up at the cloudless sky and wondered what Claude was doing at this moment. She hoped against improbable hope that he was with Anna Hofberg on this sad day when France, the child's promised land of refuge, had become a war-haunted nation, a haven abandoned and under siege.

EIGHT

EAVYHEARTED, SADDENED BY THE IMAGE OF GERMAN boots thumping insolently beneath the Arc de Triomphe and down the Champs Élysées, they traveled on. The roadway teemed with cars and motorcycles. Petrol was in short supply, and there were long delays as they scavenged for fuel. Lucie plucked franc notes from her bustier and handed them, damp and fragrant, to scowling farmers who agreed to sell the fuel they hoarded for their tractors at exorbitant prices.

"Now we know that we are actually at war," Pierre said wryly, as he passed a wad of currency to a taciturn woman who, with great reluctance, sold them eggs and cheese.

They reached Bordeaux and found rooms in a small pensione owned by a Jewish family. Madeleine placed a call to Claude at the number she had committed to memory. The phone rang again and again, then drifted into an ominous silence. Her heart sank. Had Claude been arrested? Had he been hurt or forced to flee Paris? Then what of Anna, whom he had pledged to protect?

Dire possibilities crowded Madeleine's imagination, and to dispel them, she walked through Bordeaux which had so swiftly become a fortress city. Food shops were shuttered, cafés and bistros deserted. Blackout cloths covered the windows of the elegant homes on the Grand Boulevard. The night fliers of the Luftwaffe would encounter a darkness that obscured their targets. Road signs had been painted over with lampblack in an odd attempt to deny German invaders directional assistance when they entered the city. The French Résistance had begun its work. Madeleine felt herself lost in a wasteland of war and hurried back to the pensione.

Once again, with little hope, she dialed the number and gasped with surprise when Claude answered after the very first ring. Her heart soared as she heard him say her name.

"Madeleine. Is it really you?"

"Claude. Claude."

She smiled and listened to the swift intake of his breath, his sigh of relief, startled that she heard them with such clarity. It had long bemused her that she found phone conversations easily audible. Something to do with brain wiring and nerve endings, the soft-spoken audiologist had explained, but she could not remember his words. It was enough that she could hear Claude so clearly.

"Was the journey difficult? Is everyone all right? And your uncle Pierre. Is he safe? Here in Paris, we have been concerned about him."

"We are all well. But why are you so worried about my uncle?"

Claude paused and then lowered his voice, as though fearful that their conversation might be monitored.

"Can you hear me?"

"Yes."

"You know that your uncle was on the board of many Jewish

organizations, including the Éclaireurs Israélites, the Jewish Scouts. He kept his files of such organizations in his home. Before he left for the south with your family, he gave me the key to his flat on the rue l'Alboni so that I would have access to the *éclaireurs* materials. There were rosters of names, meeting places, financial records. It was important that such confidential information not fall into the hands of the Nazis.

"I rushed to the rue l'Alboni when the Germans entered Paris, but as soon as I opened the door, I saw that I was too late. Everything was in disarray. File cabinets overturned, books and papers scattered, every drawer opened, even foodstuffs tossed on the floor. The damn Fascists had searched the pantry and the icebox for hidden documents. They had moved swiftly and seized every file of any relevance to the Jewish community."

"But how could they have known of his involvement? And how did they find his home so quickly?" Madeleine asked, her heart pounding.

She imagined her uncle's elegant apartment, its windows looking out on the quiet, tree-shaded Square de l'Alboni, fresh flowers always in tall vases, thick carpets covering parquet floors. All now sullied. All contaminated by senseless hatred.

"The Dreyfus name has long been all too familiar to French Fascists. History has a long arm and an even longer memory. The Jew haters in Berlin and in Paris know that the son of Alfred Dreyfus is deeply involved in Jewish affairs. Your grandfather's old enemies and their descendants, the anti-Dreyfusards, are today's haters and are eager to collaborate with the Nazis. They have been waiting patiently for the German occupation, and their propaganda machinery is in place. Their journalists fill the pages of *Le Matin* with anti-Semitic garbage as vile as what appears in *Der Stürmer*. Gamzon believes that French Fascists may in fact be worse than the Germans."

His voice grew faint as though his very words had weakened him.

"French Fascists?"

The words were alien. Of course she knew that French Fascists existed—she had, after all, heard their shouts in the theater, seen their graffiti scrawled in Metro stations—but she had thought them harmless, immature pranksters. She had refused to believe that the minds of French citizens—ever inculcated with the ideals of liberty, equality, and fraternity—could so easily be poisoned by the irrational hatred and cruelty of Fascism.

"Yes. French Fascists," Claude responded, his voice trembling with comingled impatience and anger. "Given the information they found in your uncle's papers, the Gestapo now have the names of every Jewish activist in Paris, including yours and mine."

"And the names of everyone in my family," she acknowledged. "Perhaps they will target Simone's little daughter. The great-granddaughter of Alfred Dreyfus, although she is still a baby, must surely be a threat to the Third Reich and its French collaborators."

Madeleine laughed, relieved to hear Claude's laughter in return. Absurdity was a potent weapon against despair.

"But you do understand that we must now be more careful than ever. Share this news with your uncle, your parents," Claude continued, his voice betraying a new and frightening tone. "Paris is dangerous for Jews. Robert Gamzon has moved most Jewish Scout bases to the south and has dispatched several groups to Algeria. But our work will go on."

He hesitated, and she understood that even on this very secure phone line, he would not speak of their highly secret rescue program, of their vigorous training of the children they were determined to smuggle to safety in Switzerland and Spain and then, hopefully, to Palestine.

"Yes. Of course. It must go on," she agreed and thought of Anna Hofberg, her face pale and her blue eyes awash with tears as she was once again forced to flee for her life.

"Your little Anna is fine. She misses you, but she is fine," Claude assured her, and she marveled that even across such a distance with only a fragile phone line connecting them, he read her thoughts. Was that unique to lovers? She banished the thought. She and Claude were loving friends, not lovers, she reminded herself. Not at a time like this when their future was rimmed with uncertainty and their present was not their own. Friendship was possible; love would overwhelm. That, they accepted. That, they understood. Despite that farewell kiss in a darkened doorway, a memory she would not abandon.

Was she wrong to resent that understanding, that acceptance, to think of herself and her feelings when the world was engulfed with suffering? she wondered. Not wrong, she decided. She was not, after all, a saint, only a young woman with a yearning heart.

I am allowed, she thought defiantly.

"Madeleine, when do you think you will be able to return to Paris?" Claude asked, a new urgency in his tone.

"As soon as my family is settled. They say that the south will remain an unoccupied zone for now. My father's relations in Toulouse are trying to find an apartment for us. And I want to see that my grandmother is safely placed. When that is accomplished, I will return."

"I worry that your journey back to Paris will be dangerous," he warned.

She heard the concern in his voice and was grateful that he did not urge her to remain in the relative safety of the south.

"Everything is dangerous. But I am not afraid," she assured him.

"Of course. I know that. So until I see you, *á bientôt, m'amie.*"

"*Á bientôt, mon ami,*" she rejoined.

"*Ma chérie,*" he added, and her heart soared.

"*Mon chéri,*" she echoed.

She gripped the receiver, but the call had ended. The silent phone lay heavy in her trembling hand.

An hour later, she sat beside Pierre Dreyfus in a café and shared Claude's sad news with him.

"Havoc in your beautiful flat," she said. "I am so sorry, Uncle."

"I don't give a damn about the flat. Sticks of furniture. Paintings. Carpets. What do they matter? But I never should have left my files. I thought there would be time enough for me to return and retrieve them, but of course, I was wrong. I knew that our family had to leave Paris at once. We are Dreyfuses, which means our lives were in danger, so I took a risk."

Sadness and regret wreathed his voice.

"Our name has not been forgotten," he continued. "Those

who hated your grandfather for the crime of being Jewish fed that hatred to their children, their grandchildren."

"But I cannot believe that any of our countrymen will collaborate with the Nazis," she protested.

"Madeleine, we must be realists. The danger must be confronted. There are Frenchmen who may speak of patriotism and who believe that they actually protect their country by joining forces with the Nazis. And there are others who are simply venal and greedy, interested in their own gains. Pétain is an old man but still ambitious. He has lost no time in selling himself to our enemy. The hero of Verdun has chosen a new banner. He aspires to be the ruler of what he calls 'the new France.' I will expose him when I am in the United States, where I will advocate with all my strength for a free France even as you and your Claude, Simone, and your brothers will continue to resist the evil that has thrust itself upon us. We will, all of us, fight and we will prevail. Truth will triumph."

He sat back, exhausted by his own words, drained by the knowledge that the door to his home on the rue l'Alboni was closed to him forever.

Madeleine sat very still.

"*Your Claude*," her uncle had said.

She laid claim to his words. She would not forget them.

"Let us wish each other bonne chance, good luck, Uncle," she said and slid into his strong embrace.

That evening the family gathered in the salon of the pensione and heard Charles de Gaulle address his nation from London.

"France has lost a battle, but France has not lost the war," he declared defiantly. "Our *patrie*, our beloved nation, is in mortal danger. Let us all fight on to save it. *Résistance* is our battle cry."

Lucie nodded.

"Charles de Gaulle is a brave man," she said. "His father's son. I knew his father. He defended Alfred even when such a defense was dangerous. Like his father, Charles de Gaulle is pledged to truth, devoted to saving France," she said. "We must follow his lead."

"Will we be able to save France?" Etienne asked, his voice quivering.

Madeleine knelt before her younger brother and struggled to reassure him, speaking with all the calm and certainty she could muster.

"We will all work hard, and our country will be saved. We will protect our children. Remember that we are all *éclaireurs*. Scouts must always be brave and prepared to fight for justice, to do what is right."

"I am brave," Etienne said. "I'm at least as brave as Jean Louis."

"Well, perhaps you will be by the time this stupid war is over," his older brother said laconically, and the family laughed, grateful for the teasing banter that relieved the tensions of the evening.

There was no laughter the next morning as they gathered in the garden of the pensione for an alfresco breakfast. Lucie, as always, had worked her magic and secured scarce delicacies— freshly baked croissants and baguettes that she slathered with the butter and jam she had coaxed from the grocer's wife. They spoke without pleasure of the lodgings that relations in Toulouse had arranged, and sadly, sorrowfully, Pierre told them that he and his family were leaving for Marseille that very day.

They ate in silence, overwhelmed with the sad knowledge that this might be the last meal that they would all share.

Lucie did not weep as her son lifted her hand to his lips and kissed each of her trembling fingers.

"Au revoir, Maman," he murmured, the same words he had whispered all those years ago when he left to fight in the Great War that was to have ended all wars. On this spring morning, a scarce quarter century later, he worried that this new war might actually end the world, their beautiful world.

His sister, Jeanne, held him close, and he and Pierre Paul Levy embraced, their brotherhood affirmed. Their loves were mutual, their commitment to family and country shared.

As he said farewell to his nephews and nieces, Pierre Dreyfus's eyes burned with unshed tears. He loved his sister's children, and he feared for them. His hand rested for a very long moment on Madeleine's head, his fingers briefly entwined in her thick, dark hair. He did not deny that she was his favorite, as she had been his father's favorite. Perhaps he favored her because she shared his passion for truth, his tenderness of heart. Perhaps simply because she was Madeleine, so beautiful, so gentle, courageous, and generous, ever true to herself and sensitive to others.

"Au revoir, Madeleine," he murmured.

"*L'hitraot*, Uncle," she replied in Hebrew.

"Yes. *L'hitraot*. Perhaps in Palestine, my dreamer."

She smiled. He smiled.

"We may yet see each other again in Marseille," she said.

He motioned to his wife, Marie, and his children to settle themselves in the car. He drove swiftly away, never daring to look back.

NINE

THE ROUTE FROM BORDEAUX TO TOULOUSE WAS FAMILIAR to the Levy family. Pierre Paul had been born in Toulouse, and they had lived there for some years before moving to Paris. But Madeleine's pleasant memories of childhood days in that peaceful city were dispelled as her father swerved and braked, driving slowly down the narrow streets. She stared out the window at weary wanderers who moved aimlessly from one corner to another, stooped beneath burdens strapped to their backs, squinting through eyes blinded by sunlight and sorrow. Crowds of desperate refugees swarmed across the broad boulevards in search of lodging and food. Toddlers slept on park benches, their parents crouched on the ground beside them.

A cacophony of languages drifted toward them. Vegetable hawkers, pushing makeshift wagons, shouted in Spanish, their voices soaring over the cries of mothers calling to their children in Dutch and Walloon. The German invasion had triggered a surge of fear and sent frightened masses streaming into France from Holland, Belgium, and Luxembourg. Toulouse, so fortunately located in the "unoccupied zone" and with relatively easy access to the Pyrenees Mountains and the Spanish border, was a destination that offered hope, however faint, to fugitives from the Low Countries.

Her father braked to avoid a family who moved down the road, indifferent to oncoming traffic, and Madeleine looked southward and toward the distant rise of the Pyrenees. She thought of Robert Gamzon's daring plan to have the scouts guide groups of Jewish children across those forbidding mountain passes into Spain, and her heart sank. It would be a daunting enterprise. Daunting and perhaps impossible. But, of course, it was an effort that she would never, could never abandon. She had taken an oath. She had pledged herself to hope.

She glanced at Simone, whose gaze was also fixed on the distant peaks.

"It will be difficult," Simone murmured as though reading Madeleine's own thoughts.

The sisters required neither words nor gestures to understand each other.

"We will manage. Somehow we will manage," Simone added.

"What will you manage?" Jeanne asked.

"A silly private joke, Maman," Simone replied.

Madeleine smiled. She and Simone were complicit in protecting their parents from additional stress. They were aware that Jeanne and Pierre Paul, already haunted by anxiety, would be overcome with terror if they knew that their daughters were placing themselves in danger.

Her father paused the car to allow a funeral cortege to cross the rue de Périgord.

"Is death following us everywhere?" Jeanne asked.

Madeleine ignored her mother's question as she opened the window and negotiated the purchase of shining, celadon avocados offered by one of the many Spanish vegetable sellers who thronged the streets.

That evening, Madeleine asked Simone the question that had troubled her since she had heard the proliferation of Spanish that was spoken in the streets of Toulouse by Republican emigrants from Spain.

"If so many Spanish Republicans are seeking refuge here in France, will our Jewish children be safe in Franco's Spain?"

"I asked Robert Gamzon that very question," Simone replied. "He told me that although Franco himself is a Fascist, he has a mysterious sympathy for the Jewish people. The rumor is that he himself is of Jewish ancestry. Perhaps that is true, perhaps it is not. We must take our rescuers where we find them."

"Beggars can't be choosers," Madeleine agreed wryly.

"Especially Jewish beggars," Simone added, and they laughed in uneasy unison.

How good it was to laugh, Madeleine thought. She had almost forgotten how.

Their first days in Toulouse were fraught with difficulty and disappointment. The house her father's relatives had secured for them was too small to accommodate the entire family, and they were forced to separate. Simone decided to travel across southern France to Grenoble, where Anatol's parents were eager to welcome their son's widow and their granddaughter. Madeleine herself found a small room in an apartment rented by group of scouts.

Still, she considered herself and her family fortunate. The smallest hovels in Toulouse were snatched up by exhausted refugees. In the chaos of transit, families were separated and children were lost. Her heart turned as she saw the long lists of the missing plastered on the walls of buildings. She feared to read them, obsessed by the irrational fear that she might find her own name scrawled on the tattered sheets of paper.

The separation from her family afforded her guilty relief. Away from their constant concern, her privacy reclaimed, she could give way to her sadness, submit to her loneliness and the fatigue that clung to her like a gossamer shadow every waking hour of the day.

I am tired, she thought, as she lay awake in the darkness of a moonless night. *I don't want to do this anymore. I can't do this anymore.*

She wanted to weep, but tears would not come. She had not earned the right to weep. Instead she pummeled her thin pillow and sought a respite in fantasy. The war would end, peace would come, she and Claude would stare up at a sunlit sky.

But sunlight remained elusive as the news progressed, ineluctably, from bad to worse.

Marshal Pétain moved his nascent government to Vichy, designating that resort city the capital of the Unoccupied Zone. Once known as the hero of Verdun, he now blatantly sought an armistice with Germany. It was a betrayal that invoked the fierce wrath of Charles de Gaulle and his followers in London; it reinvigorated the Résistance in France.

Madeleine listened to de Gaulle's fierce condemnation of the Vichy government on Radio Anglaise and thought of a favorite Kipling poem she had memorized during her student days at the Lycée Moliére. She remembered vagrant phrases.

"Triumph and disaster must be confronted even with worn-out tools," she said aloud.

The words pleased her. She was, after all, an Éclaireur, a scout, prepared for both triumph and disaster, which she would confront with whatever "worn-out tools" came to hand. It occurred to her that she would have to teach that poem to Claude, and the thought caused her to smile. Yes, one day they would recite their favorite poems to each other.

He called the next day, using the clandestine phone line in the Toulouse *éclaireurs* headquarters.

"Madeleine, it is important that you return to Paris. The Nazis are now threatening to close the northern sector. Please come while it is still relatively safe. We need you."

She trembled to hear the plea in his voice.

"We?" she asked teasingly.

"Yes. The scouts. And Anna Hofberg, of course. She asks for you whenever I see her. The Résistance leaders have an urgent need for a qualified social worker."

She remained silent.

"And, Madeleine, I need you," he added ruefully.

She smiled. She had waited for those words, waited to hear them spoken with a tenderness of tone, even as he raised his voice so that she could hear without difficulty, forgetting her ease with phone conversations.

"Yes. Of course I will come as soon as I can, as soon as I can leave Toulouse. My family is still unsettled, and I want to be sure that the program I have organized for the Jewish refugee children from the Low Countries is in place," she said.

"I understand. Of course you must assist your family, and

your work with Les Éclaireurs Israélites du Sud, the Jewish Scouts of the South, is important. But you are much needed here in Paris. Do you understand?"

"I understand. I will come as soon as I can."

He was silent. She knew that he could not say more. They had been warned that even calls on their own clandestine line might be intercepted. Claude's reticence was self-explanatory. She was urgently needed for a specific secret project.

"*Á bientôt*," she said softly and replaced the receiver.

She wondered then why she had not told him how much she herself needed him, how she missed him.

"Claude, my friend, *mon cher ami*, my very dear friend, I miss you. I need you."

She sighed and repeated to herself the words she had not spoken. She would give them voice one day. Yes, of course she would.

Because she knew how urgently she was needed in Paris, Madeleine raced through the days that followed, working tirelessly to complete the projects she had set in place in Toulouse. She assisted her father in the organization of a clinic and dispensary, organizing programs for newly arrived Dutch and Belgian Jewish children. She met with the scout leaders dispatched to Toulouse by Robert Gamzon. The Union of French Jews was sponsoring his efforts to create a network of children's homes and workshops in southern France. They achieved their goals with astounding swiftness. Plans discussed at an evening meeting were executed the very next morning.

It was now common knowledge that the Vichy government was openly and unashamedly allied with Nazi Germany, which meant that time was of the essence. The Jews in France were in the same mortal danger that German Jewry had already suffered. Dread words were uttered in somber tones. Drancy. Pithiviers. Beaune-la-Rolande—internment camps from which Jews who were arrested in indiscriminate *rafles*—sudden, unprovoked roundups—were sent eastward. There were whispers of the existence of "concentration camps" and speculation about their locations and what happened within their dark confines. "Slave labor" was one ominous murmur, "death camps" another— words too dangerous to be given full voice.

Madeleine moved through the marketplace of Toulouse, amazed by the stunning swiftness with which France had become a divided nation. Shoppers avoided each other; merchants declined the custom of those who did not share their views. Sides had been chosen. Résistants who supported de Gaulle and the Free French were pitted against Fascist collaborators. Neighbor suspected neighbor. Families were sundered. Scouts from the south told Madeleine that the populations of the smallest hamlets, the most isolated market towns, were divided by deceit and distrust.

She and her brothers stood on a street corner and watched a brigade of acne-pocked teenagers, wearing bottle-green uniforms and armed with clubs, march across the Grand Boulevard.

"Le Garde Française Jeune Front," Etienne said derisively. "Such a long name for a group of copycat thugs, stupid imitators of Hitler Youth."

"Dangerous imitators," Madeleine retorted worriedly.

It was known that the Fascist youths rampaged through the streets of the city, attacking refugees, bullying school children, overturning vendors' carts, and scrawling *Entreprise Juive* across the windows of Jewish-owned businesses. It was said that these youths were encouraged to betray their own parents, their neighbors and relations, bribed with small amounts of francs, tin medals, and abridged copies of *Mein Kampf*, translated into crude French.

Pétain had decreed that the French motto of *Liberté, Égalité, Fraternité* be replaced with *Travail, Famille, Patrie*—Work, Family, Country! The new slogan was printed on posters, blared from the radio, and shouted by the Vichy-backed *gendarmerie* as they strutted through the streets.

"The Nazi lexicon translated into French," Madeleine's father said bitterly. "*Travail—Arbeit*. It is said that the words *Arbeit macht frei*—work will make you free—are inscribed on the gateposts of Auschwitz. Perhaps Pétain wants them etched across the Arc de Triomphe."

The entire Levy family accompanied Pierre Paul to the banks of the Garonne River on the day that Vichy officials declared the Francisque, Battle Ax of Gaul, engraved on the medals he and those who had served with him had earned during the Great War, was now the official insignia of their rogue Fascist government. Dr. Levy had worn that medal with pride, but he would never wear it again. He stood with a group of other veterans as they tossed their beribboned medallions into the slowly flowing waters, after which they stood in military formation and sang "La Marseillaise." Madeleine was proud to see a group of Jewish Scouts adding their vibrant young voices to the patriotic chorus.

The Éclaireurs Israélites du Sud, Scouts of the South, worked closely with the highly organized Résistance. They joined units trained to rescue downed RAF pilots and guide them to safety. They attended workshops on the workings of explosives, the construction of incendiary devices. Acts of sabotage were acts in defense of freedom. Madeleine added attendance at such workshops to her harried schedule, cycling furiously from one demanding meeting to another, yet managing to deliver the needlework her mother crafted to the small boutiques that sold it. The family's funds were dwindling, and they needed the francs such small sales earned.

Claude phoned yet again.

"When?" he asked, the question now a plea.

"Soon," she promised, her answer a pledge.

But doubt plagued her.

"Who will sell Maman's work when I return to Paris?" she asked her brothers one evening.

"We will," they replied in unison.

"No boutique owner could resist us," Jean Claude added, winking at Etienne, who bowed with pretend elegance from the waist.

Madeleine laughed. Her brothers, as always, delighted her. The war had spurred Etienne into new and charming maturity, and it had not hampered Jean Claude from pursuing his medical studies, mentored by their father. Both of them were talented and dedicated scouts. She knew that they could assume many of her own obligations. Yes, it was time to return to Paris. But she could not leave the south without traveling to Grenoble and seeing Simone. She smiled at the thought of her sister. Was it possible that they shared one soul? She laughed at her own foolishness and made plans for the journey.

A request from Jeanne altered her arrangements.

"My mother insists that she go to Marseille so that she might spend a few days with Pierre and his family before they leave for America. Could you arrange to travel back to Toulouse with her?" Madeleine's mother asked hesitantly.

"Of course," Madeleine replied, struggling not to betray her annoyance at the request. Her reaction shamed her. Of course she would always do whatever she could for her beloved Grandmother Lucie. Family first—a Dreyfus credo.

TEN

M ADELEINE'S JOURNEY TO GRENOBLE WAS DIFFICULT AND exhausting. There were military checkpoints, at which she had to produce her *carte d'identité*, state the reason for her journey, and confirm her sister's address and the names and addresses of every member of her family.

"Why is such information important?" she asked one young gendarme.

"We are at war," he replied indignantly.

"Of course," she replied apologetically and wondered if the war would be hampered or helped by the knowledge that her brothers were named Jean Claude and Etienne and her mother was a housewife.

But it was wonderful to see Simone, wonderful to sit beside her in the garden, wonderful to play with Frederica, now a cheerful, red-cheeked toddler who babbled incessantly as she chased butterflies in her grandmother's garden. Happily, she plucked a bouquet of wildflowers and presented them to Madeleine.

"*Fleurs, Tante* Madi," she chirped happily, and Madeleine held her close and tickled her neck with a long-stemmed bluebell. The child erupted into laughter.

"*Chantez!* Sing!" she commanded.

Madeleine nodded and sang the lullaby that had been her grandfather's favorite.

"*Entends-tu le coucou, Malirette?*" Pursing her lips, she imitated the call of the cuckoo bird until her small niece clapped her hands and dashed off to chase a rabbit who had wandered in from the meadow.

"You are so good with children. You will make a wonderful mother, Madeleine," Simone said.

"Do you think so?" her sister asked wistfully and turned away.

Simone's words filled her with the sadness that often came upon her as she lay in bed alone, reflecting that she had not yet known tender intimacy, a lover's breath mingling with her own, his touch, sensual and soothing, upon her body. The war had delayed her entry into fulfilling womanhood. Marriage and motherhood seemed distant and, perhaps, unlikely. Inevitably, when she descended into such a mood, her thoughts flew to Claude. Inevitably, too, thoughts of him deepened her dangerous melancholy.

Fighting that threatening sadness, she asked Simone if she might see her basement studio, which Anatol's parents had made available to her. In that windowless area, at an improvised worktable covered with boxes of paper, neatly arranged pots of ink, pens with a variety of nibs, tubes of glue, and tablets of watercolors, Simone forged the documents so essential to the Résistance. Her calligraphic talent was a vital weapon in the war against Fascism.

Simone proudly explained the intricacies of her work. A Résistance member who owned a stationery supply company provided her with stressed paper. Photos for forged passports and identity cards were easily obtained from Photomaton machines but she had not yet found the chemical immersion that would render the photos blurred but passable.

Simone opened a locked cabinet.

"Here are the documents I prepared for you," she said. "There are also papers for Claude and the Hofbergs. Passports, identity cards, health certificates, ration cards, all with Christian names."

"But surely the names can be traced," Madeleine said, examining her sister's handiwork.

"Not very likely. Groups of scouts go to church graveyards and copy down the inscriptions on tombstones. Those are the names I use. The Christian dead are saving Jewish lives."

"But don't you have papers for Jean Claude? Etienne? And our parents?" she asked.

"Their names are not on the list I received from Robert Gamzon's headquarters," Simone said regretfully. "I must follow instructions."

"Of course."

She understood that Simone had been instructed to prioritize documents for those who would soon undertake the mountainous treks to freedom. For the very first time, Madeleine felt a flicker of fear. Would Anna and her brothers have the stamina to endure such a dangerous and arduous trek? If Claude led them, would he return safely? She shivered at the questions she dared not ask.

Riffling through the documents, she took note of the variations in ink and the quality of the paper. She frowned. An astute border guard might examine them too closely and become suspicious.

Simone sensed her uneasiness.

"I know that my work is not perfect," she said apologetically. "I do my best, but I need more training. There are chemical techniques for altering ink and creating stamps that I must learn. I want to go to Paris for a workshop being conducted by Adolfo Kaminsky, a master forger who shares his secrets. Anatol's parents will care for Frederica, but I don't know how to make travel arrangements."

"I do. We will go to Paris together," Madeleine said and her spirits soared.

"When?" Simone's excitement matched her own.

They laughed with anticipatory pleasure. For the briefest of moments, the war was forgotten and they were simply two young women planning a holiday in their country's capital.

"I must first to go to Marseille," Madeleine said. "I promised Maman that I would see Grand-mère Lucie safely back to Toulouse. When I return, you must meet me in Toulouse and then we will travel to Paris together."

"Excellent," Simone agreed.

That night the sisters sat together, ripped open the hem of Madeleine's coat, and fashioned pockets in her camisoles, in which they hid the forged documents.

"It is fortunate that Grand-mère taught us to sew," Simone said wryly as they stitched the seams with double thread.

Madeleine left the next morning, covering her small niece with kisses and embracing Simone. The sisters were, as always, the closest of friends, readers of each other's dreams. Tears streaked their cheeks as they clung to each other, but the knowledge that they would soon walk the streets of Paris together sustained them.

ELEVEN

ADELEINE REACHED MARSEILLE AND SAW AT ONCE THAT the port city was in turmoil. Throngs of refugees crowded the streets and stood impatiently in queues to purchase small amounts of food, desperate mothers breaking a single baguette into small pieces to be fed to hungry children too weak to protest. Families slept in parks, in squares, on the steps of buildings, heads resting on valises and rucksacks. Crowds gathered outside the Hôtel Splendide, clamoring for admission to the offices of the American Relief Center whenever it was rumored that visas might be obtained. Wails of disappointment resounded down the street when the doors were slammed shut. Madeleine winced at the choruses of pain and sorrow, resonant enough for her to hear them clearly.

Would that I were totally deaf, she thought bitterly as she rushed to the small flat near Montredon that Pierre had managed to rent while he and his family waited for the ship that would carry them to the United States.

Her uncle was delighted to see her and was oddly imbued with optimism. Lucie watched as he showed Madeleine the sheaf of letters he had received from America. His sponsors in the Jewish community there were eager to welcome him and his family. An apartment in New York City had been rented for them.

"We hope it will suit the family of the great Alfred Dreyfus," a sponsoring philanthropist had written.

Madeleine refrained from asking why such a powerful philanthropist did not advocate more strongly for the Jews of Europe, who wept at the doors of the American consulate in Marseille.

Invitations to speak had come from every city, Pierre boasted. He and Madeleine studied a map of the United States, frightened by the vastness of its territory, although the names of the cities amused them. Milwaukee. Walla Walla. Peoria. They struggled with pronunciation, laughed at each other's efforts. Their laughter masked their fear; it was an anodyne to their sadness, their uncertainty.

Pierre had written to the *New York Times* and other newspapers suggesting feature articles on the desperate situation of European Jews but had received a reply only from the editor of a Jewish journal who had asked him to contribute an eyewitness account of the impact of the Nazi occupation of France.

"'It is hopeful that such an article, with the byline of the son of Alfred Dreyfus, whose story is well-known in America, will influence our Congress and President Roosevelt to take a more active role in fighting Hitler,' the editor wrote. 'At the very least, we think that it will convince the State Department to issue more visas to endangered Jews.'"

"But every Jew in Europe is endangered," Madeleine observed wryly. "Will the United States issue six million visas?"

"To be hoped for but unlikely," Pierre replied. "Although look at this map. The country is so vast that it could without difficulty absorb every applicant."

He pointed to the State of South Dakota and read its coordinates aloud.

"Look, Madeleine, South Dakota measures 77,000 square miles and has only 600,000 residents. It has room for the entire Jewish population of France."

"Especially since its capital is already named Pierre," Marie Dreyfus observed and they laughed.

Madeleine and her cousins reminisced about the happy times they had shared as children. They were resigned to the knowledge that they might never see each other again, but they struggled to contain their sadness, offering one another wistful assurances that all would be well.

"Perhaps you will indeed be instrumental in influencing President Roosevelt, Pierre," Lucie said.

As always, her faith and confidence in her son never faltered.

"Of course you will, Papa," his children shouted.

Madeleine and her cousins clung to fragile threads of hope, even as the muffled voices of the *Radio Anglaise* newscaster reported an increase in *rafles*. The brutal and random round-ups of Jews by the Gestapo throughout northern France were now a daily occurrence. A Jewish man might leave for work in the morning and never return home. Women were arrested in markets, wrenched away from their children at playgrounds. Children disappeared, their whereabouts unknown, their parents bewildered and bereft. There were mothers who committed suicide, fathers who went mad with grief.

"You dare not venture into Paris," Pierre warned his mother and Madeleine.

Lucie nodded but Madeleine said nothing. She would not

tell her uncle that she and Simone would soon travel to the occupied city.

The day of departure dawned with a teasing brightness. At the pier, Lucie bravely struggled to conceal her anguish as her grandchildren and her daughter-in-law, Marie, kissed her.

Pierre held her close.

"*Ma mère*," he murmured, his voice breaking. "My mother."

"*Mon fils, mon coeur.* My son, my heart."

Madeleine read the words on her grandmother's lips. She struggled to hold back her tears as she embraced her uncle, her aunt, and her cousins.

"We are young. We are strong. We will be together again, Madeleine," Pierre's oldest daughter, Françoise, assured her.

"Of course we will. That is why we say au revoir," she replied. "*Revoir.* We will see each other again."

The words rang hollow even as she uttered them. They defied belief. Anything might happen. Anything would happen.

Pierre Dreyfus did not wish her au revoir.

"Adieu," he murmured. "Go with God. May He bless you."

He repeated the words in Hebrew.

"*HaShem y'vorach otach.*"

Standing together on the pier, the sea-scented wind brushing their faces, uncle and niece wept.

"Shalom," she whispered.

She saw his lips move in answer, but his words were lost to her as the ship's horn blared its harsh final warning.

TWELVE

S IMONE WAS ALREADY IN TOULOUSE WHEN MADELEINE
and Lucie returned. Together, the sisters helped the family
move into a flat obtained by the distribution of a profusion of
bribes. It was very small and on the fourth floor of a building
without an elevator, but it was on the rue de la Dalbade, and the
elderly concierge, Madame Leonie, was known to be sympathetic to the Résistance. Jeanne was relieved that there was a
large storage unit adjacent to the bedroom.

"I can store the clothing that I collect for needy children
there," she said and at once thrust a carton of donated sweaters
into the empty space. Such garments would be needed when
small trekkers followed escape trails across the snow-topped
mountains. Hypothermia was as lethal as the Mausers of the
Nazi troops.

The flat was, they all agreed, ideally located. Because of its
proximity to the eastern bank of the Garonne, Dr. Levy and Jean
Claude could walk to their clinic, Etienne to his school, and
Jeanne to the market and the boutiques that bought her elegant
embroidery. Her needlework was an important source of income
for the family. Their resources had been sadly depleted by the
Vichy government, which had decreed that French Jews were
mandated to pay a fine of one billion francs as a punishment

for attacks on German soldiers in the north. The full amount was to be raised by the Jewish Council. Failure to pay would be punished by public hangings. The Jewish Council, fearful of draconian reprisals, had moved swiftly.

Twenty thousand francs from the Paris bank account of "the widow Madame Lucie Dreyfus" and a similar amount from the account of "the Jewish doctor Pierre Paul Levy," is forfeit, their edict read.

"It seems that our family name is well remembered by both the Jewish Council and the Vichy traitors," Lucie averred with a sadness she did not mask.

"Still, there are many who stand with us," Madeleine countered reassuringly.

She comforted herself with the knowledge that members of the Résistance and Charles de Gaulle's Free French forces in London supported the Jewish Scouts. She did not speak to her grandmother of the Vichy spies who haunted the markets and cafés, treacherously scavenging scraps of information which they offered for sale. She knew that the slightest changes in routine were entered into dossiers. The family conspired to protect Lucie from all anxiety.

They agreed that given her age, Lucie would have difficulty climbing the stairwell to the new apartment, so Madeleine found a room for her grandmother with central heating in a boarding house near the Church of Saint Etienne.

"I want you to be warm, Grand-mère," she said. "Warm and safe."

"Ah, Madeleine. You worry about everyone. Please take some time to worry about yourself."

"I will be fine, Grand-mère," she said, the reassuring lie falling too easily from her lips.

She dared not speak of how often she seethed with resentment because her own needs were so subverted by her responsibilities to others. This was not the time to worry about herself. But would such a time ever come? Would she ever have the ease to think only of Madeleine Levy? *Madeleine Levy and Claude Lehmann.* She took an odd clandestine pleasure from the mental coupling of their names as she hurried back to the rue de la Dalbade.

An autobus to Paris was due to leave within the hour. Simone and Madeleine embraced their parents, and Jean Louis and Etienne carried their bags to the bus station.

"Take care, Madeleine, Simone," Jean Claude said.

"We love you."

Etienne's voice was very faint, but Madeleine pressed her fingers to his lips and felt his caring words tender upon each trembling digit.

The sisters shivered under the winds of danger throughout the long journey north. The forged papers Simone had prepared were within easy reach in their portmanteaus, and they had committed every detail of their false identities to memory. It was a necessary precaution because an ordinance issued by the German Occupation Authority had closed the entire northern sector of the country to Jews. The bus was stopped at every Gestapo checkpoint, papers were given cursory glances, and the passengers endured the searing glances of officers who stomped through the vehicle. Madeleine feigned sleep and Simone did not lift her eyes from the open book on her lap during such searches. But at Bourges, three members of the Feldgendamerie, the military police, boarded, brandishing their batons and shouting at the frightened passengers.

"*Documents! Cartes d'identité!*" they demanded, pushing their way from one row of seats to another, indifferent to pleading mothers and crying children. Two families were ordered off the bus, and through the grime-encrusted windows, Madeleine and Simone saw them herded into a waiting truck, the mothers holding the hands of their terrified children, the fathers tight-lipped and pale, their shoulders hunched in the shame peculiar to men who were powerless to protect their families.

Tentacles of fear tightened around Madeleine's heart as the soldiers approached their seats. Her breath came with difficulty, but Simone very calmly shifted in her seat and handed her a small pouch crammed with cosmetics.

She understood. As Simone had done only seconds earlier, she combed her hair, applied rouge to her cheeks, and outlined her lips in heavy red lipstick. Holding a miniature mirror, she studied her newly made-up face. Never vain, for the very first time, she rejoiced in the power of her own beauty. She practiced a smile and slipped surprising easily into her new identity.

She was no longer Madeleine Levy. She was Adele Valheur, a chambermaid at a pensione in Neuilly. The story she and Simone had contrived was a simple one, and she told it well as she handed her papers to an officer so young that acne sprouted on his very pink cheeks.

She explained that she and her friend Emilia, asleep beside

her, who unhappily was a mute, were returning to work after a brief holiday in the south. They had been the guests of some very important Gestapo officers. She giggled. She had promised not to reveal their names, but if pressed she might do so.

"*Non. Non.*" The young officer declined the offer as he scanned her work permit.

"Read the address of my employer carefully," she said. "Remember it. Come visit me some evening. Ask for Adele. I will know how to please you."

She moved forward and thrust her face close to his so that she could see his lips and be certain of his reply, certain that she and Simone, whom he had studiously ignored, were out of danger.

He nodded and replied in slow, coarse French.

"Perhaps I will do that, Fraulein Adele."

He smiled lasciviously and handed the documents back to her.

"You must get a new photograph. The one on your work permit does not do you justice."

"I will try. But all the good photographers have left Paris."

"Only the Jewish ones. But German photographers will soon arrive and take over their studios. Be patient. Perhaps I will accompany you to have a new photograph taken. There are many poses I could suggest."

He grinned, his teeth glistening with saliva, yellow pus oozing from the pimples on his too-pink cheek.

"That would be most pleasant," she said, struggling against the bilious nausea that soured her throat. She batted her eyelashes and returned the documents to her purse.

"I will not disturb your friend's sleep," he said.

"How kind you are."

She retained her false smile as he moved on, harshly interrogating an elderly couple whose papers fortunately were in order.

It was only when the bus was on its way that she leaned back, exhausted and depleted.

Simone smiled at her.

"You are becoming an excellent actress, Madeleine," she said. "But the quality of that photo might have betrayed us. I must learn how to doctor those Photomaton copies so they look more authentic. I hope this Adolfo Kaminsky who is said to be a master forger can teach me to do that."

"I hope so too," Madeleine replied vaguely, still dizzied by the fear she had struggled to suppress during that brief and dangerous encounter. Cold sweat coated her body, but clutching Simone's hand, she willed herself to calm. Somehow she had dissimulated, and somehow she had survived. She marveled at the role she had played so well, marveled that her fake sensual smile had fooled that stupid *feldgendarme*, marveled that she had heard him so clearly. How disappointed he would be when he discovered that there was no Pensione Royale on the rue des Rois in Neuilly. In fact, there was no rue des Rois. Newly revived, she stared out the window and watched a caravan of German lorries lumber clumsily down the narrow roadway.

The sisters separated when they arrived in Paris, arranging to meet that night at the small hotel in the rue Jacob where they had arranged to share a room. Simone hurried to the Left Bank where Adolfo Kaminsky, the expert Résistance forger, was conducting a workshop, while Madeleine went to meet Claude at the office of the *éclaireurs*.

The new scout headquarters was above a café on the rue des

Grands Augustin favored by the painter Pablo Picasso. It was said that when a contingent of Germans entered the café, the painter bellowed a demand for *crème caramel*, an agreed-upon warning to the scouts on the upper floor to cease all movement and conversation.

Claude was overjoyed to see her, but he was more angered than amused when Madeleine told him about her interrogation on the bus.

"What if he had realized that your papers were forged? You might have been arrested and sent to Drancy. Why did you place yourself in such danger?"

"What else could I have done?" she asked, her eyes flashing, her anger matching his own.

She understood that his fury masked his concern. She knew that there was no need to remind him that danger was now their constant companion, that every step they took, every word they spoke had to be vested with caution. *Because they were Jews. Only because they were Jews.* It was irrational, absurd, an absurdity and an irrationality that she and Claude acknowledged, even as they recognized the danger it imposed.

The brief anger between them subsided as swiftly as it had been ignited. She took his hand and pressed it to her cheek in a gesture of forgiveness. He had been right to speak of danger, and she had not been wrong to react with ire.

"Vichy spies are everywhere," he said softly. "They haunt the cafés, eavesdropping in the hopes of gleaning any scrap of Résistance information. We must be very careful."

"I am always careful," Madeleine assured him. "But is there any reason to be particularly fearful now?"

"There is," he replied. "We have been asked to undertake a difficult and important mission. You and I. Are you ready?"

Her heart beat faster. Her breath came in uneven gasps. She closed her eyes and struggled for calm. But when she spoke, her voice was steady.

"If we are to be together, Claude, then I am ready," she replied and leaned back, surrendering at last to the exhaustion that had haunted her throughout the long and danger-darkened day.

"We will be together," he replied. "That is all I can say now. We must wait for instructions."

She nodded. She asked no questions. He offered no answers. A voice sounded through the silence between them.

"*Crème caramel!*" the artist shouted, his Spanish accent immediately recognizable.

They waited. Claude peered through the window and watched the German soldiers stride across the road. They sat motionless until the bald artist leaned back in his chair and lifted his sketch pad, an agreed-upon signal that the danger had passed.

Hand in hand, they left the *éclaireurs* office and walked through the fading twilight radiance. At the rue Jacob, Simone waited for them in the hotel's small garden café, her face lifted to the slowly gathering darkness. They followed her gaze. A single star had appeared, and they did not look at each other as their separate wishes floated skyward.

THIRTEEN

THE NEXT MORNING, THE SISTERS LEFT THE HOTEL AND walked swiftly toward the boulevard adjacent to the rue Jacob. Passersby glanced at them, moved by their grace and beauty. Simone, slight and fair, looked wonderfully cool in a light-blue, wide-sleeved cotton summer dress that swirled about her knees. Madeleine, dark-haired and strong-featured, wore a rose-colored linen sheath that accentuated her high color. They both wore broad-brimmed straw hats that protected them against the harsh sun that streamed across the unshaded cobblestoned street. They smiled, their pace unhurried, their faces turned to each other as they chatted happily. They were adhering to their grandmother's tutelage. Lucie had often said that cheerful, well-dressed young women never aroused suspicion. They paused at a busy corner and waited patiently for traffic to ease, hoping that Lucie's advice was vested with validity.

They flashed flirtatious smiles at the gendarmes who stood guard at the Metro station and hurried to catch the train that carried them to the Left Bank. Simone had insisted that Madeleine accompany her to the workshop Adolfo Kaminsky was conducting, and Claude had thought it an excellent idea.

"Forgery is a convenient talent," he had said and Madeleine, although protesting her ineptness, had agreed. Any small scrap of knowledge might prove to be ammunition in the terrible and unconventional war they were fighting. She wondered if it would be of any use for the mysterious assignment they were to undertake but knew that it would be dangerous to speak of it. Simone's ignorance was protection in these strange and treacherous times.

Exiting the Metro, she and Simone wandered from street to street, assuming the role of tourists, gazing into shop windows and sipping coffee at a small café, until they were certain that they were not being followed. At last, they entered an apartment building surrounded by scaffolding. Following Simone up the debris-strewn stairwell, Madeleine was overcome with nausea, assaulted by an overpowering stench that grew stronger with each ascendant step. She paused and gagged.

"The odor is from the chemicals that Kaminsky, our master forger, uses," Simone explained. "He operates a laboratory here. Acids. Powders. Compounds. Forgery can be very complicated. And, unfortunately, very noxious."

"How do the other tenants stand the stench?" Madeleine asked.

Simone shrugged.

"They think he's a painter and the smells come from his tubes of oils. They assume that all his visitors are artists. In Paris, artists are routinely forgiven. And, of course, in occupied Paris, no one asks too many questions."

They entered the room where two young men and a woman huddled over a Bunsen burner as a dark-haired youth explained the elements of a compound to them. The young instructor was slight of build, a teenager who spoke with both authority and dedication in an accent Madeleine had difficulty identifying.

She flashed a questioning look at Simone.

"Yes. That is Adolfo Kaminsky, our guru forger. He is an Argentinian," Simone explained in a whisper. "His parents are Russian Jews who left France for South America and then returned when he was a small boy. The family was so poor that even though Adolfo was just a child, he found work, first doing odd jobs at a dairy and then at a dry cleaners where he managed to learn a lot of chemistry. He bought secondhand chemistry textbooks and studied them, experimenting on all kinds of stains, analyzing inks. When the Germans invaded Paris, he and his parents were arrested by the Germans and sent to Drancy."

"Drancy."

Madeleine shivered at the very mention of the dreaded transit camp from which Jews were inevitably deported to Auschwitz. She had known Drancy in another life, her now-so-distant childhood. On a long-ago sunny afternoon, Alfred Dreyfus had taken her on a surprise outing to a suburb then under construction called Drancy, conceived as a self-contained community with every social amenity It was ironic that such an idealistic undertaking was now the dreaded internment camp.

"But I thought that Drancy was a place of no return," she said. "How did the Kaminskys manage to free themselves?"

"They were released because they had Argentinian passports. That is when Adolfo realized the importance of documents and how his knowledge of chemistry could help the Résistance by perfecting our forgeries. He has been working with us ever since. There is so much I can learn from him," Simone continued as she shrugged into a stained smock and joined the group huddled around the young Argentinian at the makeshift laboratory table. Madeleine followed her.

They watched as he poured the contents of a test tube into a jar. They observed how its tint was slowly altered. One by one, each observer repeated the same process.

Madeleine hesitated briefly and then imitated her sister. She did not have Simone's talent for calligraphy, but she might yet learn something. Overcoming her revulsion at the odors that permeated the narrow room, she observed closely and took careful notes in her moleskin notebook.

She studied the array of items ranged on every surface—quill pens, pots of ink, rubber stamps, reams of paper of all sizes, unstopped jars of noxious chemicals. She watched as used passports were skillfully altered, their cases stressed. Lactic acid erased blue ink. Rubber stamps were scraped and pierced with the tines of a fork, then pressed onto pads of ink that had been blanched so that their imprints on documents were faded to an impressive authenticity.

Adolfo Kaminsky described what he called "the magic of color" and demonstrated how dyes could be altered with the use of different compounds.

"I learned about lactic acid when I worked in the dairy," he said. "When a bride asked my dry-cleaner boss to remove a blue ink stain from her wedding dress, I told him to soak the dress in milk. It worked on the wedding dress, and now it works on ration cards and exit visas."

He laughed, the contagious laughter of a boy young enough to be amused by magic tricks and old enough to know that such tricks might save lives. Madeleine watched as he showed the small gathering how a steam iron could be passed across sheets of covering to stress the vellum, how quills could be sharpened and photos treated. By blending chemicals heated to boiling on an electric hot plate, he demonstrated how brown became black, how green became purple. He showed them the bicycle wheel he had transformed into a centrifuge machine that altered the texture and color of parchment.

His students clapped. His skills became their own. They would carry the tricks he had taught them back to their Résistance cells in Lyon and Lille, in Rouen and Avignon. Simone would practice them in the basement of her in-laws' home in Grenoble. Lives would be saved by the magic of colors altered, paper transformed.

Madeleine swelled with pride at the skill and courage of the small cadre of forgers, all of them so diligent and heroic, all fired by the knowledge that the documents they prepared would rescue men, women, and children they would never know. Their selflessness astonished. She realized with surprise that the odors of the chemicals no longer sickened her.

She watched Simone step forward, take a document across which the word *JUDE* was scrawled in huge, ugly letters, and erase them with a brush heavy with a mysterious oil. There was a small round of applause, and Simone smiled proudly and wiped her ink-stained fingers on her smock, portions of its fabric already eaten away by acid.

The groups of acolytes dispersed, clutching bags of the chemicals and other supplies offered by Kaminsky. He waved them out but scarcely looked up from the small pile of papers he was busily doctoring. Word had come that documents were urgently needed for a small group of Jewish children who had been hidden in a convent and were in danger of being sent to Drancy. He would, he explained, have to work through the night. The documents had to be ready by dawn if the children were to be saved.

Simone left for Grenoble late that afternoon, foregoing the brief Paris vacation she and Madeleine had planned because of her eagerness to practice her new skills. She and Madeleine embraced.

"My very first project will be to create a new photograph for Adele Valheur," she told Madeleine laughingly. "Unless of course you wish to choose a new name."

"No. I will remain Adele," Madeleine replied. "I would not want to waste all those beautiful ration cards you created for her."

The sisters laughed. They did not dare to weep. Tears were a luxury.

FOURTEEN

C LAUDE WAITED FOR MADELEINE IN THE GARDEN CAFÉ, and she saw at once from the seriousness of his gaze and the rigidity of his posture that their mysterious instructions had arrived. He managed a thin smile as he motioned her to sit beside him. Aware that they were being watched by a Vichy police officer who nursed an absinthe at a neighboring table, she flashed Claude a demure look and kissed him on both his cheeks.

"Have you been waiting long, *mon cousin?*" she asked, her voice pitched high.

The officer frowned. A meeting of two cousins did not interest him, but he remained in his seat, lifted his glass lazily, and moved his chair closer to their table.

"Not too long," Claude said, and now his smile was wide and welcoming. But when he spoke, he kept his voice low, even as he passed an envelope to her.

She nodded and opened it, removing several Photomaton snapshots of small boys and girls.

"My mother wanted you to see the newest pictures of my brothers and sisters," he said, and now it was he who spoke loudly enough for the Vichy officer to hear. "Leonie has lost a tooth. Marc has a new haircut."

"Oh, how sweet they are," Madeleine said, spreading the photos across the table.

The officer yawned, placed a franc note on the table, and left the café. Photographs of small children with missing teeth interested him not at all.

"We have our instructions," he said quietly. "What we must do is not as complicated as I had feared. There are five children, Jewish children from Poland, their parents seized in a *rafle*, who are now hidden in a small convent near the Palais Royale. They speak no French; they have no documents. The nuns learned from their own informant that a plumber they had hired, a man dependent on the Gestapo for small bribes, revealed the children's presence to the Germans. The nuns believe that they are to be removed from the convent tomorrow morning and sent to Drancy. We are assigned to rescue them, and that is what we must do," Claude said.

"But how?" she asked. "Five children. Without papers. Where will we take them?"

"They will have papers," he assured her. "Whatever is needed. *Cartes d'identité*, ration cards, even travel permits. The documents are being prepared, and the nuns arranged to have their pictures taken at Photomaton so that we can attach them."

"Ah, the photos that you showed me," she said and thought of Adolfo Kaminsky, bent over his worktable. She understood that, by odd coincidence, he had been preparing the documents for the very children she and Claude would, somehow, in some way, spirit to safety.

"Yes. Those photos. We are to be the *convoyeuses*, the escorts of those poor children. We will arrive at the convent before dawn, carrying the documents. I have been given a list of addresses of householders who will each hide a child in the city as well as two farmers who will shelter able-bodied boys in the countryside," he explained.

She sighed.

"Five separate journeys. Five dangerous journeys."

"We are Parisians," he countered. "We know the city well. We will follow the pathways beneath the bridge. We know every alley, every vacant field. I have directions to each address in the city, and we will have access to a car when we travel to the countryside."

"And if we are stopped, how do we explain what we are doing with five children?" she asked.

"That is the sweetest deception of all. We explain that we have been asked by the Vichy government to train them to be members of Le Garde Française Jeune Front, the Hitler Youth of Paris. I even have badges for each of us identifying us as leaders of the movement. A good idea, isn't it?" he asked proudly.

"Only if it works," she replied, but her smile of agreement matched his own.

"It will work," he said.

At midnight, there was a knock at the door of Madeleine's hotel room. She opened it, and a youth thrust a large manila envelope into her hand and scampered away.

"The documents," Claude said and smiled. "All goes according to plan."

"Yes," she agreed and wished she shared his certainty. His courage and his certainty. But that would come, she assured herself as she helped him sort through the documents, both of them marveling at Kaminsky's expertise.

It was still dark when they made their way across the city to the Palais Royale. The convent was without light, but at their approach, the heavy door opened and a young nun beckoned them to enter. Five children, three small girls and two boys, huddled in the vestibule, gripping each other's hands, their faces pale masks of fear. The Mother Superior stood beside them, speaking softly, and Madeleine realized that she was praying and that the murmured Latin comforted the terrified Jewish children.

"Thank you for your prayer and your concern," she told the nun, and her words were rewarded with a weary smile.

The children were introduced, and she and Claude, using the fixative Kaminsky had included, busied themselves attaching the photographs to the requisite documents. They then pinned the badges of the Garde Française to their jackets. Madeleine cringed as her fingers traced the red and black swastika on the cheap pieces of felt.

"I shall burn this as soon as I can," she said.

"Keep it. You may need it again," the Mother Superior said, smiling although there were tears in her eyes as she embraced each child in turn.

"Stay safe," she instructed them. "Remember that God is with you."

"Your God or ours?" the taller of the two boys asked in broken French.

"We have only one God," she replied. "And He is with all of us."

They left then, Madeleine walking ahead of the children, Claude behind them, *convoyeuses* committed to the safety of the youngsters in their care.

They navigated their way through the darkened streets, selecting little-used roads and obscure pathways. Before the sun rose, they had managed to escort all three of the little girls to the families who had volunteered to keep them safe. The sweet-faced children did not weep as Madeleine kissed them goodbye.

"They have no tears left," she said sadly to Claude as they hurried to the dirt road beneath the Pont de l'Alma that led to the deserted street where a Résistance car awaited them.

"It is only an hour's drive from the city to the farm," Claude assured her as the boys scrambled into the back seat.

"I'm all right," she said.

Claude nodded, his gaze fixed on the road. He took her hand in his own and held it for the briefest of moments, a silent acknowledgment that the most dangerous stretch of their daring enterprise confronted them. Gestapo troops were stationed at every entrance and exit to the city, and they would have to drive through every checkpoint without arousing suspicion. The two boys, as though sensing their tension, clung to each other, not even daring to stare out the window.

They drew up to the exit that led to the road that would carry them southward to the farm located near Sainte-Savine. As they had anticipated, a Gestapo guard blocked their way and ordered them to pull over.

"*Papiers*," he demanded.

Claude handed him the driver's license Simone had prepared so carefully, including at least one citation for speeding. ("To lend it authenticity," she had said laughingly. "No self-respecting Frenchman has a totally clean license.")

"*Carte d'identité*," the German barked.

Claude smiled, searched through the glove compartment, and smiled again as he held it out.

"Couldn't remember where I'd put it. You would have had a problem," he said apologetically.

"No," the guard replied. "You would have had a problem."

He studied the document carefully, turning from the photograph to Claude, looking straight at his face and then studying his profile.

"And your girlfriend? Where are her papers?"

Madeleine shrugged impatiently, undid the buttons of her blouse, and withdrew the *carte d'identité* of Adele Valheur from her camisole, aware that it carried with it the warmth of her breasts, the scent of her skin, and noting that the German sniffed it appreciatively.

"And the boys?"

"Scouts. New to my Garde Française troop." He touched his badge, and Madeleine giggled flirtatiously and lifted a finger to her own. "We are taking them to a training camp. Do you want to see their parents' permissions?"

"No need," the guard replied briskly, and still holding their papers, he went to the pill box and conferred with another officer, both of them gesticulating and nodding.

Madeleine's heart sank.

"He doesn't believe us. He is going to arrest us," she muttered.

"Quiet," Claude ordered. "Put on lipstick. Smile."

Obediently, she did as he said, thinking that her face might freeze.

The officer returned. He handed them their papers and added a small package.

"Two knives for your new recruits," he said. "My own son is in Hitler Youth, and it is good to see French youngsters eager to help Germany. This is their reward." He smiled broadly.

"Merci," Claude said, accepting the package. "How good of you. We wish your son well. Our boys will put these knives to good use."

"Tell them to use them slice a few Zhids," the German said and waved them on.

Madeleine sat back. The smile left her face, her heart beat less rapidly, and her breath came with ease. They had passed through. They were safe. The small boys laughed and clapped. Claude stepped on the accelerator, and within an hour, they had reached their destination. The farmer and his wife welcomed them warmly.

"Are you hungry? Will you stay for breakfast?" the motherly woman asked, her arms already resting on the shoulders of the boys.

Madeleine glanced at Claude. Of course they were hungry. They had eaten nothing since the previous evening. Nor had they thought about food. She laughed.

"Not just hungry, madame," she told the smiling woman. "But famished."

The meal they ate at the scrubbed wooden table in the farmhouse kitchen was, she thought, the most delicious *petit dejeuner* of her entire life.

FIFTEEN

CLAUDE SUGGESTED THAT THEY CELEBRATE THEIR SAFE return to Paris with dinner at a bistro. It would be a defiant gesture of normalcy, he explained laughingly. Entering the small eatery, Madeleine was surprised to see German officers mingling freely and easily with French patrons. The uniformed soldiers spoke politely to waiters, rose to offer seats to the elderly, and smiled benignly at the few small children. Commandant, his epaulettes emblazoned with the death's head symbol of the SS division, opened the door for a pregnant woman.

"Paris is suffused with a surreal calm," Claude explained wryly. "Everyone is playacting. Germans and French alike. A halcyon time, but the storm is just over the horizon. The Nazis move slowly. They are courting the French, but very soon the honeymoon will end. Today they warned that anyone associated with the Résistance will be executed. Slowly, they are making their power known, unmasking their cruelty, reminding us that we are a captive people. They smile in our bistros and then issue our death warrants in their headquarters. Next winter, all of Paris will shiver because French coal is being shipped across the border to warm homes in Berlin. And every day we see new threats to the Jewish community. They have created what they call *un Commissariat Général aux Juives*, an agency to deal with Jewish affairs. All Jews are required to report there and register."

"Register?" Madeleine asked. The very word confused her.

"Yes. An order of André Tulard who has created what we call the *fichier Tulard*, a filing system that lists all Jews by profession and includes their addresses and other details. If you are to remain in Paris, you too must register. I have already done so. And when I completed the process, I was given this obscene badge and told that I must wear it," he said.

He glanced nervously around the smoke-filled room before opening his jacket to show her the felt yellow Star of David pinned to his shirt.

"I do not wear it on my outer garment, but if I am stopped, I can open my jacket and show that I am obeying their hateful law. It is my silent and foolish protest," he said ruefully.

"But such a file, such registrations, will make it easy for the Nazis to find Jews and arrest them at will," Madeleine protested.

"That is their intent, of course. We know that, but we must comply. Failure to register is a crime punishable by hanging. And such a punishment has already been enacted. A father and his young son, one of our very own *éclaireurs* boys, were hanged right next to the Arc de Triomphe. A symbolic warning, we know, and one which we take seriously. We scouts cannot take the risk of failing to register." He fell silent and lifted the menus.

"So much for this surreal, superficial calm," she said bitterly and watched a Gestapo officer spring to his feet and open the door of the bistro for an elderly French couple.

"But remember, our compliance is also superficial. We wear the yellow star, but we also wear the blue-and-white bandanna of the Jewish Scouts. We register but we plan. We comply and we resist."

He smiled and showed her his own bandanna, tucked beneath his collar.

"I am too modest to show you mine," she retorted teasingly.

As always, the soft blue-and-white cotton square was nestled between her breasts, in the folds of her camisole.

He grinned.

"One day you will be immodest and daring enough to show it to me," he teased.

"I think we will have to wait for peace to be restored," she said, a tacit reaffirmation that their feelings remained hostage to the clear and present danger that dominated their lives.

Not fair, she thought angrily, childishly, even as Claude nodded and ordered two glasses of *vin ordinaire*. They toasted each other, their glasses clinking.

"*L'Chaim*," they whispered. "To life."

"*À France*," they said together in full voice, impassioned and audible.

The pledge to their country was heard through the bistro, and other patrons echoed them in a proud and defiant chorus. The German officers sat in a brooding silence, all pretense of courtesy abandoned. Madeleine and Claude smiled at each other. A very small battle in an overwhelming war had been won.

The next morning she accompanied him to the offices of the *Commissariat General Aux Juives* so that she might register, obedient as Claude himself had been to the repellent mandate of the repellent German occupiers of their beloved city.

As they walked through the second arrondissement, the

streets grew more and more familiar. She stared up at a street sign.

"La Place des Petits," she said. "Of course. I came here often as a child."

"The Germans requisitioned that building to house their damn Commissariat," Claude said, pointing to an imposing redbrick edifice in the center of the street.

"How ironic," Madeleine said. "This building belonged to our family. The Dreyfus name is on the facade."

They drew closer, and she traced her finger across the letters of her family name, elegantly carved onto a marble pillar.

"Wasn't it generous of my great-uncle to erect a building for the use of the Gestapo?" she asked and laughed.

Her question was edged with sarcasm, her laughter laced with fury.

Hand in hand, they entered the building. The bloodred Nazi banner, a black swastika in its center, hung over the heavy walnut reception desk that dominated the ornately paneled lobby. The hem of its cheap synthetic fabric brushed the Dreyfus name so expertly etched into the dark wood.

Madeleine took her place in a line of elderly Jewish men and women who clutched worn leather portfolios that contained the documents that validated their very existence, certificates that proved that they had indeed been born, deeds that confirmed their ownership of a home, certificates for grave sites that assured them a resting place in death. Perhaps diplomas. Perhaps professional certifications. All that defined their lives. As French citizens. As Jews.

A white-bearded man, leaning heavily on a cane, had

pinned the Croix de Guerre to his suit jacket. She remembered Frau Hofberg telling her how the Iron Cross she had placed in the window of her home on Kristallnacht had been stolen and thought to warn the old man of the futility of his gesture but she remained silent.

Her turn came at last. Claude stepped aside as she stood before the harsh-voiced, overweight Frenchwoman who wore the bottle-green uniform of the Vichy police. The interrogator's thick fingers stroked the swastika pin on one lapel and then moved to caress the Vichy medal engraved with the Battle Ax of Gaul, the Vichy emblem plundered from the brave veterans of the Great War, on the other. She barely glanced at Madeleine who leaned toward her, the better to read her lips as she asked her invasive questions in staccato spurts.

"Name?"

"Madeleine Levy."

"Place of birth?"

"Paris."

"Religion?"

"Jewish."

"Are both your parents Jewish?"

"They are."

"How many of your grandparents were or are Jewish?"

"All four of them."

Madeleine hesitated, then daringly amended her answer, choosing the condescending tone which her grandmother reserved for rude tradesmen.

"You may know the name of my maternal grandfather, Alfred Dreyfus. He was a Chevalier de la République, a hero of the

Great War, as was my uncle, Pierre Dreyfus. Our family name is famous in France. In fact, it is on the facade of this very building and carved into the wood just above your own desk," she said.

The Vichy policewoman shrugged indifferently. She did not look up. The name Dreyfus was foreign to her and of little interest. She had never noticed that it was etched above the desk at which she sat each day. Reference to the Great War was lost on her. It belonged to a vanished era. She merely lifted her pen, filled out a series of forms, and shoved a new *carte d'identité*, a pamphlet of regulations, and a yellow felt Star of David at Madeleine.

"Given that all four of your grandparents were Jewish, then under the Statut des Juifs, the statute relating to Jews, you are a Jew," she muttered.

"Of course. I am proud to be a Jew," Madeleine replied, maliciously pleased to note that the woman's pen had leaked and her meaty fingers were ink-stained.

"Take careful note of the entry on page six of the regulation pamphlet. It tells you that as a Jew, you are forbidden to work in the fields of education, civil service, and military communication. There is a quota system limiting the number of Jews who are allowed to practice law or medicine."

She spoke robotically but with sadistic pleasure.

"Do you understand, Mademoiselle Levy?" she asked, spitting out the patronym contemptuously.

"I understand," Madeleine replied.

She glanced at the card that identified her as a Jewess, resident in the fourth arrondissement of the city of Paris, and slipped it into the waterproof envelope in her purse that contained her own documents and those of the nonexistent Adele Valheur. Both sets of papers would be within easy reach should she need them, as she knew she would. She wondered how she might transmit the new registration card to Simone so that copies might be forged, but she reminded herself that of course the shrewd teenaged master forger Adolfo Kaminsky had probably done that already.

"Do not forget to wear the Star of David on your outer garment," the officer barked as Madeleine turned to leave.

She turned and smiled laconically.

"I certainly will. I will wear it with pride," she said, but her words went unacknowledged. Her interrogator was already spitting her questions at an elderly woman who answered in a voice that quivered with fear.

Walking swiftly, Madeleine and Claude left the building.

"At least Jews are not barred from social work," she said bitterly.

"It is fortunate that you were certified before the occupation," he said. "The reason why your return to Paris was a matter of urgency is because you are a trained social worker. Madame Danier will explain the details tomorrow. You are fortunate. My situation is very different. Jewish students are no longer welcome at the Sorbonne. A reasonable act, I suppose. If Jews are forbidden to work as lawyers, why should they be allowed to study law?"

"Oh, Claude. I'm so sorry."

She knew how much he had sacrificed in pursuit of his law degree.

"What will you do?" she asked.

"We have brave professors at the Sorbonne. They hold

secret seminars for Jewish students and smuggle law texts to us. There are Frenchmen who still believe in *liberté, égalité, fraternité*," he said.

"Of course there are."

When she had an address for her uncle Pierre, she would write and tell him of the efforts of the Sorbonne professors, of the goodness of the farmer who had welcomed two Jewish boys into his home, of the nuns who sheltered Jewish children in their sequestered convent. She wanted Pierre to know that not every Frenchman had capitulated to Pétain.

Pierre Dreyfus had sent no word since his arrival in New York, a silence the family attributed to his overwhelming schedule of writing and speaking. It was possible, of course, that he had indeed written but that his letters had been in the mailbags of international liners torpedoed by German U-boats. It was another worry that Madeleine hugged to herself, fearful of frightening her parents and her grandmother.

She sighed and wondered why it was so important that she meet with Madame Danier, although she was pleased that she would see her wise and compassionate mentor again.

The dean of the Institute of Social Work was delighted to welcome Madeleine back to Paris. She greeted her warmly, happily recognizing that her former student, once so shy and hesitant, had blossomed into a confident and beautiful young woman. Madeleine's brown hair, thick and silken, fell smoothly to her shoulders. Her dark eyes were flecked with gold, her smile generous. The dean speculated that Madeleine Levy's new confidence and self-assurance had in all probability been forged by her experiences as a Jew in Nazi-occupied France.

She motioned Madeleine to a seat and poured coffee for both of them from the carafe always present on her desk.

"More chicory than coffee," she said apologetically. "Most of our good coffee seems to have found its way to the dining quarters of German officers who have developed a fondness for our café au lait."

She waited for Madeleine's smile and continued.

"I am so pleased to see you. You have been much missed. We feared you might be unable to return, given these absurd restrictions against Jews," she said.

Her mentor's choice of the word *absurd* pleased Madeleine. She sipped the bitter brew and nodded.

"Yes. Absurd," she repeated. "And wicked."

"We are living in an era of absurdity and wickedness," the dean agreed, and she added a spoonful of sugar to her cup as though to sweeten the bitterness of her utterance.

"But we must each fight wickedness and absurdity," she continued. "We at the Institute of Social Work are committed to undertaking projects that are modest in nature but important to those they benefit. I think of such projects as lighting small candles against the darkness of the Occupation Authority. Many small candles can give forth a mighty glow. Do you agree?"

Madeleine turned the words over in her mind.

"But a single small flame is easily extinguished by the slightest wind," she replied.

"Does that mean we should cease lighting it?"

"No. Of course not."

She waited, growing impatient with the circuitous introduction to the agenda she knew the dean would soon propose, but she was aware that this was Madame Danier's pedagogic method. Her social work students had always been taught to weigh assignments for their abstract worth as well as their immediate practicality.

"I am prepared to light a candle, however small," Madeleine added.

"Excellent. That was what I hoped to hear. Your comrades in the *éclaireurs* assured me that you would say just that. That was why it was important that you return to the north, despite the danger. Such a small candle has presented itself. And we hope you will agree to light it. The Institute has received a grant from an anonymous Résistance supporter to organize an educational and recreational program for the children of conscripted workers in an armament factory in Gentilly. It is a cruel situation.

"The Nazi authority has forcibly recruited men and women, most of them Jewish. They have uprooted entire families and resettled them in a crude barracks near the plant. It is part of the program that they call Service de Travail Obligatoire, Obligatory Work Service to the State. To the State of Germany, of course, not the State of France. The children of those workers have been deprived of both education and recreation. There are no facilities for them, no health care, inadequate food. They are malnourished and depressed. They rarely see their parents. As social workers, we understand the impact of the trauma of separation on youngsters. We cannot ignore such a situation."

She spoke with the certitude and conviction of a professional pledged to respond to an urgent need.

"Of course not. It cannot be ignored," Madeleine echoed.

"We know that you have a special talent for working with young children and a gift for organization. It was an official of the Jewish Scouts who suggested that you be placed in charge of our program in Gentilly. We want to establish programs for the children. It is our wish that you agree to undertake this operation."

"I do agree," Madeleine said without hesitating.

"Excellent. Public transportation to Gentilly is a problem, but I have been told that the Jewish Scouts can arrange that. Am I correct?"

She flashed Madeleine a complicit smile, and Madeleine nodded. The dean obviously knew that the Jewish Scouts, with the support of the Union of French Jews, had managed to commandeer an odd armada of vehicles—ancient cars, rusted lorries, battered vacation caravans. They did not rival the German tanks and the Vichy police cars, but they were carefully maintained and easily available.

"I will have no difficulty traveling to Gentilly," Madeleine said.

Claude would arrange it, she knew. She herself was a novice driver, although among Simone's forged documents was a license for Adele Valheur. She had assured her sister that, because of her hearing deficit, she would only drive in an emergency. Claude would take the wheel, she decided, and felt a guilty thrill of pleasure. Their togetherness on the journey to the suburb would be an unexpected gift of precious shared time.

Madame Danier handed her a folder.

"This is a roster of the children who will be in your charge. I think you will be relieved to see that little Anna Hofberg and her brothers are listed. I know you have a special affection for her."

"I do," Madeleine said.

She did not add that she had in fact planned to seek out Anna, her fantasy little sister, that very day. "The situation of the Hofberg family is worrisome," Madame Danier said. "Not only are they Jewish, but they are refugees without any legal status in France. No documents of any kind."

Madeleine was silent. She longed to tell Madame Danier that she carried with her Simone's forged documents for the Hofberg children, but that knowledge could not be shared. Like all scout leaders, she had taken an oath of secrecy. What was not known could not be revealed.

"Is the Vichy government aware of the Institute's efforts in Gentilly?" she asked.

"We sent a memo to what they call their Social Service Bureau. Since such a bureau is almost certainly nonexistent, we can be certain that it was never read, but the copy in our file may offer us some protection."

Her answer did not surprise Madeleine. It was necessary that the Institute shield itself with a wall of pretense. Robert Gamzon had impressed upon scout leaders that their courage did not mandate suicide.

"I assume that my name did not appear on that memo," she said.

"Of course not." The reply was indignant. "We are careful, not stupid, Madeleine."

"I just wanted to be sure that danger will be minimal," Madeleine said defensively.

"These days we awaken with danger and await danger even in our sleep. I can offer you no guarantee of safety. But of course you are free to decline the assignment," Madame Danier said.

It was Madeleine's turn to be indignant.

"It has not occurred to me to decline," she replied, and they smiled at each other in mutual understanding of the risks and obligations they shared.

Madame Danier walked to the door with Madeleine and took her hand.

"Adieu, *ma fille*," she said softly.

"Au revoir, *ma maîtresse*," Madeleine replied.

With those words, so somberly uttered, with that touch so tentatively offered, they acknowledged that it was entirely possible that a *revoir*, a reunion, might never occur. The war had robbed every leave-taking of the certainty of return.

SIXTEEN

CLAUDE COMMANDEERED AN ANCIENT SEDAN, AND ON A bleak October day, they drove southward from Paris to the industrial compound in Gentilly. Madeleine, her heart pounding, presented her credentials as an accredited social worker to a gruff Milice officer. The Milice was a Vichy French police force, partnered with the Nazi SS, sharing both their toxic prejudices and their vicious methods. She was relieved that the officer barely scanned her documents and ignored her proffered explanation that she was on official assignment to assist "the children of the patriotic workers in the Führer's industrial operation."

Madame Danier's words were both false and well chosen. *A more accurate description would have been "the children of the Führer's slave laborers,"* Madeleine thought caustically as the officer tossed the papers back to her.

"Those children are delinquent scum. Jewish trash," he muttered. "Your driver?" he asked, barely glancing at Claude and not bothering to question him or ask him to provide documents. He was an important man with no time to spare for underlings like drivers.

"Yes, my driver," Madeleine said, and she and Claude followed him to a dilapidated outbuilding.

Its windows were broken, the rough floor encrusted with filth. Spiderwebs dangled from a cracked and weatherworn ceiling, and the stink of animal excrement fouled the air.

"You may have the use of this building," the Milice officer barked. "Good luck to you. You will need it. You are trying to tame wild animals. Lepers. *Untermenschen*."

He left, slamming the door behind him.

Madeleine trembled, although neither his words nor his attitude surprised her. The hostility of the Milice to the Jewish community was common knowledge. She surmised that large bribes had been paid to the Milice commandant for the modest program she was organizing.

Claude placed a reassuring hand on her shoulder and ran his fingers through her dark hair, brushing away the ash-colored grains of asbestos that rained down upon them.

"Forget about the bastard," he said. "Let's start to clean this place up before we are asphyxiated."

With his usual prescience, he had thought to fill the trunk of the car with cleaning supplies, and they went to work at once, mopping the floor, washing down the walls, and covering the broken windows with slabs of cardboard. As they worked, small groups of children wandered over and watched. One by one, the boys and girls began to help. Within minutes, the Hofberg children appeared.

"Madeleine, is it really you?"

Anna rushed up to her, thin arms outstretched, her face aglow with sudden happiness. Madeleine hugged her and kissed her on both cheeks, relieved to see that despite her pallor, the child did not appear to be ill.

"And is it really you, my Anna?" she asked in turn and was rewarded with a giggle.

"It is really me," Anna replied. "We hate this terrible place, but at least our family is still together."

Samuel and David held out their hands in welcome. Their *éclaireurs* training had transformed the shy and frightened boys into confident troop leaders. They looked at her gratefully, and she understood that her very presence offered them a modicum of hope.

They swiftly organized the assembled children into units with defined tasks. One group helped Claude cover the windows, while another rid the area of accumulated rubbish. A contingent of girls joined Anna in fashioning decorations using the crayons and construction paper Madeleine had scavenged from teacher friends. Swings of rough wood were attached by frayed ropes to the leafless branches of deadened trees. With effort and energy, a playground was created, and the joyous shouts of children swinging through the air and bouncing on improvised seesaws shattered the somber silence. By the end of the day, the grim and forbidding area had been transformed into a welcoming space. The parents of the children, wearied by their long hours of hard labor, smiled gratefully to see their children restored, however briefly, to happiness as they trudged back to their barracks.

The German soldiers and Milice officers shouted angrily and raised their batons menacingly when one child or another scrambled out of the play area.

"Our Fascist compatriots are surprised at what the children of *untermenschen* have accomplished," Claude said.

"Our children are wonderful," Madeleine agreed. "They are our future."

"Yes. Our future."

They smiled at each other. *Future* was a word they rarely uttered. Any length of time beyond their dark present was forbidden territory, undefined, amorphous. They dared not think of what might happen during the next day or the next week. Their tomorrows were shrouded in uncertainty, limned with danger.

On the drive back to Paris after that first strenuous day, Madeleine rewarded herself by resting her head on Claude's shoulder. They savored the silence of the dying day, the melancholy pastel hues of the setting sun. It was a respite from the anxiety and activity that consumed their waking hours and haunted their sleepless nights.

"Wouldn't it be wonderful to run away? Just the two of us," she murmured sleepily.

"Don't say that; don't think that," he retorted angrily. "Don't even think it. Our duty is to our people. To our children. You must remember the pledge that we made."

"I remember and I'm sorry," Madeleine said even as she acknowledged to herself that she was not sorry. She reserved the right to indulge in vagrant fantasies, as cowardly and shameful as they might be.

During the weeks that followed, Madeleine worked tirelessly to create a pleasant ambiance for the children in the factory complex. She enlisted Jewish teachers whom the Vichy government had fired and arranged for them to organize a school, paying them with small stipends from the grant the Institute had obtained.

Each morning, she and her newly recruited staff, crammed into a battered vehicle, its license plates deliberately made illegible by coatings of mud, and drove to Gentilly. The once-quiet suburb, transformed into an ugly industrial zone by the Germans, was only kilometers south of Paris, but the journey was suffused with tension. Stopped at checkpoints by the Vichy police, Madeleine and her crew pointed to the yellow stars on their jackets and offered forged documents that identified them as Jewish workers reporting to a road-clearing detail. They prayed that the boot of the car, crammed as it was with school supplies, children's clothing, and food, would not be opened. Surprisingly, it never was. Her more optimistic colleagues attributed their daily escapes to the sympathy of the Vichy police.

"They are Frenchmen after all. Sons of France who stand with us," one teacher argued.

"No, they don't bother stopping us because they are lazy," another countered. "Lazy in peace, lazy in war. Who joins the Vichy police? The scum of Paris alleyways. Bullies without hearts. Lousy anti-Semites all."

Madeleine shook her head warningly.

"I prefer to think they allow us to pass the checkpoints because they secretly believe in a free France," she said.

She did not, of course, believe her own words, but she spoke them to discourage her companions' outbursts of fear and anger. She knew that their safe passage, of course, was because of bribes discreetly paid and greedily accepted.

Within months, the Gentilly project was a recognized success, spoken of with admiration by the staff of the Institute of Social Work and the leadership of the Résistance. Madeleine was exhausted but gratified. She thrilled to the sounds of the children's laughter, and her heart soared when Anna rushed toward her with a welcoming hug each morning.

Anna was playing; she was studying. She and her brothers slept in their parents' cramped one-room cubicle in the barracks. But crowded and depressing as it was, Anna thought their togetherness a miracle.

"And you," she informed Madeleine happily, "you are the miracle worker."

The warmth of the emergent spring filled Madeleine with a hopeful serenity. One April morning, ablaze with sunlight, she was the designated driver because Claude had another assignment. She stopped the car beside a forsythia bush that blossomed in a wild, neglected garden.

"Let's bring our children some flowers. They should have some beauty in their lives," she told the teachers who were traveling with her.

"Flowers will not keep them safe," Edith, an emaciated teacher whose young husband had been caught in a *rafle*, said bitterly.

Madeleine recognized Edith's disparaging tone. She did not disagree. She could not offer her children security, but they were, at the very least, entitled to the scent and touch of the first harbingers of spring. Edith remained in the car as Madeleine and the others filled their arms with flowers.

She parked the car in a secluded area, studiously avoided by both the Germans and the Milice. Clutching her wild bouquet,

eager to show the long-stemmed, golden flowers to Anna, she
hurried to the playground which, even at that early hour, was
usually crowded with noisy laughing, singing children. But
there was neither laughter nor song.

Her heart stopped. Silence prevailed. The area was deserted.
The swings dangled in forlorn emptiness. There were no clamor-
ous queues for the seesaw, no carefree games of tag. Madeleine
paused and looked around, fighting the chill of fear that caused
her to shiver despite the warmth of the morning. A hawk flew
low, an ominous warning. She hurried into the building.

Small groups of children were gathered around their teachers, but no classes were in progress. The children were subdued,
staring nervously each time the door swung open. A large group
of youngsters who usually attended the early-morning classes
was missing, including Samuel, David, and Anna Hofberg.

"What has happened?" Madeleine asked.

The bouquet of forsythia fell from her hands and dropped
soundlessly onto the rough floor, scattering yellow petals shaped
like tears.

François, a tall boy, stepped forward. Madeleine knew him,
knew that he had turned thirteen only a few months earlier.
She had danced at his bar mitzvah at which a courageous young
rabbi had officiated, having smuggled a Torah scroll into their
improvised school. François's mother, newly pregnant, had been
aglow with pride as he chanted his Torah portion.

He took her aside and spoke slowly and loudly, and
Madeleine understood that Anna must have told him about
her hearing deficit.

"They came last night," he said. "A *rafle*, a mass arrest. It was the Gestapo who came. Not the Vichy police. Not the Milice. Germans. They rounded up refugees. People without papers. They took people who were ill. Pregnant women. My mother." His voice broke. "My father. My brother."

He shuddered and fell silent.

Rina, a small girl, Anna's special friend, whose father had been deported weeks earlier, hurried to his side, and glancing up at him and seeing that sorrow had stilled his voice, she took up his story, speaking very softly.

"They had trucks. The Germans. They pushed people onto those ugly, big trucks. They had guns, those soldiers, those Nazis. They had batons. They hit my mother when she tried to hug me, to say goodbye to me. Why did they hit her? Why are they so cruel? I am all alone now. Who will take care of me?"

Rina's small voice escalated, became a wail. Tears streaked her pale cheeks. Madeleine held her close, smoothed her matted hair, and murmured words she knew to be lies.

"You will see your mother again. But now we will take care of you. We the Éclaireurs Israélites, the Jewish Scouts. We will keep you safe. You can depend on us, little one."

Slowly, the child grew calmer.

"Anna Hofberg? Her brothers? Their parents? Were they taken?" Madeleine asked François.

"Her mother and father were pushed onto the very first truck. I heard her mother call Anna's name. I heard her father shout that they should hide. Anna and her brothers. They listened to their father, and they ran. It was dark but they found a place to hide," François said. "They are in great danger. They have no papers. And now they have no mother, no father."

"Do you know where they are?" Madeleine asked.

"I know. I will take you to them. Come with me."

She marveled at the firmness of the boy's tone, the clarity of his command. His recent bar mitzvah had made him an adult member of the Jewish community, but it was the cruelty of the Nazis that had thrust him into manhood. His own parents, his brother, had vanished but he stood ready to help the Hofberg children.

"Take some food," he advised.

Madeleine crammed her pockets with rolls and fruit and followed him across the playground where children now feared to play. He sprinted to the rear of the building and Madeleine kept apace, her breath coming in painful gasps, her heart racing. He paused at an abandoned storage shed, barely visible between pyramids of factory waste. Discarded metal shards and fragments of broken glass glinted in the sunlight. Francois kicked away rusted barriers, scraps of wire, and knocked sharply on the door. Three taps, a pause, another tap. A code, Madeleine realized, and she smiled bitterly at the canniness of children who planned for their own escapes, lessons she had not thought to teach.

The door opened. They entered quickly and closed it behind them. Her eyes adjusted to the darkness, and she saw the Hofberg youngsters huddled in a corner, their pale faces masks of terror. Anna was curled into the fetal position, her frail body blanketed by a gray overcoat that Madeleine recognized. It had belonged to her brother Jean Louis, and her mother had given it to David Hofberg.

"Madeleine, you came," Anna whispered.

"Of course I came," she said and forced herself to smile. "Let us pretend that we having a picnic."

She distributed the food she had brought, but there were no smiles. Anna and her brothers would not be deceived into gaiety. They stared at the food but made no move to eat. At last Madeleine handed each of them a roll, an apple.

"We don't know what we must do, where we will be safe. What has happened to our parents? Our mother was crying," Samuel said.

"I have no answers," Madeleine said, kneeling beside Anna and holding her so close that the crumbs from the roll the child was eating fell onto her lap. "I can only tell you that those arrested in *rafles* are often taken to Drancy, a transit camp just north of Paris. I imagine that your parents are there."

"Transit. Where will they go from there?" David asked.

She hesitated. She feared to tell them the truth, but neither would she lie to them.

"Most of the internees at Drancy are transported east. To Poland."

"Poland."

They whispered in unison, their eyes closed. *Poland* was a word in their lexicon of terror. They had heard of a concentration camp there called Auschwitz. Another called Treblinka. They knew what happened to Jews in Poland, the land of Auschwitz and Treblinka, the kingdom of death.

"Drancy is so close to Paris. They can be rescued. Can't the Résistance rescue them? Can't the scouts do something?" Samuel asked, his voice hoarse with desperation.

Madeleine shook her head.

"We *éclaireurs* are not magicians. We cannot liberate a camp protected by heavily armed German soldiers and the Vichy military. But we can save you. All three of you. We can help you escape from the Occupied Zone, from the Nazis."

"How will you do that? We have no papers. We have no money. No relations. We are Jews, refugees without refuge. We will be hunted by the Vichy police, by the Gestapo," David protested.

Madeleine glanced at François. The tall boy understood her silence.

"I will leave. It is best that I have no knowledge of your plans," he said.

It was apparent that he knew that each and every member of the Résistance was pledged to secrecy about discrete operations. That which was not known could not be revealed. It was known that after hours of horrendous torture, even the staunchest Résistance fighters had been compelled to divulge secrets.

"You must listen to Mademoiselle Levy. You must trust her," Francois advised the Hofberg youngsters.

He bent to pat Anna's head, to shake hands with each of her brothers, and left the shed. Madeleine again marveled at his restraint and his courage. Not twenty-four hours had passed since his own parents and his brother had vanished from his life, but he expended no time on sorrow. Grief was a luxury that had been denied him. Courage had taken its place. He closed the door behind him.

"What is your plan?" Samuel asked Madeleine.

She opened her purse, unzipped its lining, and removed the waterproof oilskin folder that contained the forged papers Simone had prepared for the Hofberg children.

"These papers will grant you safe travel to Paris. You will

be with me. The Vichy police at the checkpoints know my car. They have been bribed, and they will probably not even glance at your documents. In Paris you will be hidden in an Éclaireur safe house with other Jewish boys and girls. You will receive training that will prepare you for the trek across the Alps to safety in Switzerland."

"The Alps? Switzerland?"

The boys stared at her, fear in their eyes, tremors in their voices. They were, she knew, imagining snow-covered mountain passes, hostile border guards, rough terrain, an unwelcoming population.

"You are frightened. Of course you are," she said gently. "It will be dangerous but you will be well trained, well protected. The *éclaireurs* have engaged *passeurs*, Swiss guides. A senior scout will be with you throughout the journey. We have excellent maps, reliable contacts. Enough money to bribe border police. We are hopeful. And you must be brave enough to share our hope. If you remain in France, you will face great danger. But once you are in Switzerland, a route will be found to bring you to safety in Palestine."

"But what about Anna?" David asked. "She is so little. She would not have the strength for such a trek."

"Anna will remain with me. I will take her to my family in Toulouse. When she is stronger, when she is ready, she and I together will join another group. We will escape across the Pyrenees into Spain. If I am safe, she will be safe. And, of course, I mean to be safe."

She smiled, and this time they returned her smile. Sadness lingered, but she had ignited a spark of hope.

She handed Samuel the packet of documents. "Memorize the names and dates. Take very good care of these papers. They are your insurance policies."

"We will," they promised.

"If God wills it, they will carry you all the way to Palestine. And Anna will join you there," she added.

"If God wills it," they echoed, despair in their voices, disbelief in their eyes, but a new determination in their posture.

When the long day ended, they scrambled into Madeleine's car. Anna sat between her brothers on the journey to Paris. Subdued by grief, trembling with fear, the small girl nevertheless summoned the courage to smile brightly at the Gestapo officer who stopped their vehicle at a checkpoint.

"*Guten Abend, mein Herr,*" she said, and he smiled to hear the language of the fatherland spoken by such a pretty blond child. He assumed her to be the daughter of a Gestapo officer traveling with household servants. He handed her a piece of chocolate and waved the car on.

"Well done, Anna," Madeleine said, but Anna was asleep, her hand resting on David's shoulder, her small hand clasped around Samuel's, a trio of siblings who might soon be separated forever.

Madeleine focused on the road, its new darkness silvered by a pitiless moon.

SEVENTEEN

C LAUDE LEARNED OF THE *RAFLE* IN GENTILLY IN AT *éclaireurs* headquarters in Paris, but there was no news of Madeleine. He knew only that she had left for Gentilly that morning with a group of teachers, all of them unaware of what had occurred the previous evening. He worried that the Gestapo had still been there when they arrived, which might mean that they had all been arrested. He shuddered at the thought of what such an arrest might entail. Torture. Deportation. Horror. Inconceivable horror. Bile surged up in his throat. He vomited out his anxiety, struggled to remain calm, repeating her name as though it was a mantra of comfort: *Madeleine, Madeleine. Madeleine.*

He thought ruefully of the news he had been so eager to share with her. Given her success in Gentilly, the national Résistance leadership wanted her to take on an important assignment in Toulouse. He knew that she would be overjoyed to be reunited with her family, but would such a reunion ever occur? Was she free and unharmed? Had she managed to avoid interrogation? Would he ever see her again? He shivered. His entire body was bathed in cold sweat. Throughout the long day, hour after hour, he grew convinced that she was lost to him, that she would disappear from his life.

Grim imaginings obsessed him. He thought of her in a Gestapo prison. He thought of her frightened and alone. He blamed himself for encouraging her to undertake the Gentilly project. He blamed himself for never speaking of the depth of his feelings for her, for maintaining their tacit agreement that all tenderness for each other would have to be shrouded in silence until the danger of war had passed. She had deserved more. He should have offered her more.

Late in the afternoon, he left the scout offices and wandered through Les Halles. Excursions to the produce market had always diverted him from descents into melancholy. Impulsively, he purchased a cluster of cherries because they were Madeleine's favorite fruit.

He carried them back to his room and arranged them in an amber-colored glass bowl, all the while thinking of how the confluence of colors would delight her. She had a keen eye for beauty, often pointing out visual nuances lost to him. That talent, he thought, was a compensation for the auditory appreciation that was denied her.

He went to his window and stared down at the narrow street, empty of all traffic because the German Occupation Authority prohibited all vehicles except their own and those of Vichy collaborators. Bustling, cosmopolitan Paris had become a silent ghost town. Fearful of RAF bombing raids, the Germans had ordered that the bulbs of streetlamps be painted over with cobalt coloring. Eerie shafts of the resultant blue light slithered across the rain-darkened cobblestones. Now and again a police van cruised by. A drunken clochard leaned against a fence and sang a song that Claude did not recognize. Sadness overcame him as he stood there, hypnotized by the ominous darkness. He thought to light a lamp but he remained motionless, reluctant to abandon his vigil.

A sudden knock at the door startled him. He hesitated. His heart pounded. Unexpected visitors were too often the bearers of bad news. He stood very still, paralyzed by fear, cursing his own cowardice. Another knock sounded, stronger, insistent. He knew he could delay no longer. He opened the door, braced to confront whatever disaster awaited him.

Madeleine, her face blanched, fell into his arms.

He held her close, relief coursing through him, his heart surging.

"I was so worried," he said. "I was mad with worry. I thought you were lost to me, lost before I had even claimed you."

The unmonitored words rushed forth in a torrent. He kissed her, his cheek pressed against hers, their tears comingling.

She wept in mute acceptance of his words, words that reflected her own thoughts. Feelings that had remained too long concealed had at last emerged. He had given voice to all that she herself wanted to say.

He took her hand and led her into the darkened room. Madeleine lit the lamp, and they sat side by side on the battered sofa in a circlet of golden light. She reached out and touched the amber bowl filled to the brim with the shimmering crimson cherries.

"How beautiful," she said. "I sometimes forget that there is still beauty in our world."

She remembered the forsythia, the beautiful flowers she had thought would bring a smile to Anna Hofberg's face, and sighed to think that even that small gift of beauty had been lost to the child. Leaning into Claude's embrace, she recounted the events of the day, the tragedy of the Gentilly *rafle,* the hazardous journey to Paris, and then their journey to the safe house on the Left Bank.

"I'm sorry to have worried you," she apologized. "But time was of the essence. The children had to be taken care of. I myself was never in any real danger. The one gendarme who stopped me only wanted a match. But I am exhausted and I am famished."

He smiled.

"That is a problem easily solved. We will go out and have a wonderful meal. You are safe. We are together. We must celebrate."

"And how does one celebrate in occupied Paris?" she asked, plucking a cherry from the bowl and allowing its sweet juice to run down her chin.

Gently, he wiped it away.

"We will have dinner at that bistro you like on the Champs-Élysées."

"A very good idea," she agreed.

A few scant hours of happiness would offer compensation for the long and terrible day. They would pretend that they were an ordinary young couple enjoying a spring evening in the city of love. They had earned the happy pretense. Claude shrugged into his jacket, and she was dismayed to see the yellow felt Jewish star sewn onto the pocket.

"I now obey the edict of our German friends," he said wryly. "Résistance orders. We cannot risk arrest."

She nodded, but her own yellow star remained in her purse.

Hand in hand they walked slowly down the hushed city streets. Blackout shades hung at every window. The headlights of the few cars that passed them were covered with lampblack, the streetlamps painted blue. Passersby spoke in hushed tones and walked too swiftly. A miasma of fear hovered over the dark and silent city.

They reached the bistro and stood hesitantly in the doorway. Almost immediately they were aware of the cold stares and the unsmiling faces of the other diners that turned toward them, all staring openly at Claude's yellow star.

Madeleine smiled at Maurice, the head waiter, who had always been solicitous with her family. Invariably, when she and her grandfather entered, he had led them to the choicest table, never failing to crown her usual *chocolat* with a double dollop of whipped cream.

"*Bonsoir,* Maurice," she said, but he offered neither recognition nor a greeting. He pointed them indifferently to a table in a darkened corner next to the water closet.

Two Gestapo officers seated nearby leered at them and pressed their fingers to their noses. The overdressed Frenchwomen who sat beside them giggled maliciously. Madeleine realized that the false amity of the early days of the German occupation, of *la guerre faux,* the false war, had vanished. The real war had begun. Enmity was in the air.

"Soon Jews will not be allowed in bistros," Claude muttered.

"It is of no importance," Madeleine said. "Let's leave."

Hostile glances followed them as they exited, weaving their way past tables shared by German officers and very young *demoiselles* suggestively dressed. Their laugher shrilled and their voices were so loud that Madeleine had no difficulty hearing them.

"*Juden!*"

"*Juives.*"

She ignored them, although her heart pounded. She held her head high, walked slowly, smiled, and touched Claude's yellow star as though it were a valued adornment.

"You see now that Paris has changed. More rapidly than I had realized," Claude said sadly as they made their way toward the river. "What happened in Gentilly, *rafles* and deportations, is happening here in the heart of the city. You must leave the Occupied Zone and return to Toulouse. An assignment awaits you there."

She asked no questions and they walked on, savoring the quiet of the evening, striving to reclaim the joy of their togetherness.

They purchased crepes from a vendor's cart and nibbled at them as they made their way to the Pont de l'Alma, their favorite of all the bridges of Paris. Leaning over the balustrade, as rays of moonlight drifted across the dark water of the river, Claude handed her a cluster of the cherries he had plucked from the amber bowl as they left his room.

"Dessert," he said. "The first fruits of the season. I remembered how you love cherries."

He would not tell her of the fear that had impelled their purchase. She smiled and popped a plump fruit into her mouth, savoring the taste of spring upon her tongue. She tossed the pit into the silver-spangled river and turned to him.

"But I must remain in Paris. There is my work in Gentilly. My obligations to *les éclaireurs*. I belong in Paris."

And I belong with you, she thought but dared not speak the words.

He shook his head.

"You have done wonders in Gentilly. Your program will run smoothly, and we have others in place who will continue it. But the Résistance feels that you will be even more useful in Toulouse. We are launching a major rescue operation there, and you have been selected to lead it. Your profession provides you with excellent cover, excellent entry. A position as a senior social worker has been arranged for you in the Secours National, the government social service network."

"The Secours National?" Madeleine asked indignantly. "I will not work for such a treacherous agency. It calls itself a welfare organization for the French State, but we know that it is funded by the Vichy government. It uses money stolen from liquidated Jewish property, money stolen from my own family. Do you expect me to work for Pétain and his Vichy Nazis?"

Her eyes were ablaze with fury, her cheeks almost as red as the cherries she clutched. He thought that she had never looked more beautiful, and he wished he could tell her so. But this was not the moment. There were more important things to be said, vital plans to be shared. He sighed.

"Listen carefully, Madeleine," he said with a calm he did not feel. "You will not be working for Pétain and Vichy. You will not even be working as Madeleine Levy. You will be leading other scouts in the Résistance. Our people have infiltrated the Secours, and our secret operatives are safe. Social workers are not suspect. As a Secours employee with Vichy documents and clearance, you will have safe passage throughout the south. Escape routes from France are being planned in the Unoccupied Zone. Maps, forged papers, currency—all must be transmitted. You will be a courier, unlikely to be challenged. You will be able to travel from one Résistance cell to another."

Madeleine trembled.

"It sounds a great deal more dangerous than my work in Gentilly," she said.

"But didn't you just say that you are not afraid of danger?" he teased and popped a cherry into her mouth.

"I did," she agreed. "I am not afraid of danger but..."

She hesitated.

"But what?" he asked gently.

"I am afraid of not seeing you. I am afraid of our lives being at a distance from each other."

She had the courage, he realized, to say the words he denied himself.

"But we are never really separated, are we, my brave Madeleine?" he murmured.

He held her close and kissed her very gently, tasting the salt of her tears as it mingled with the sweet red juice that stained her lips. His own eyes overflowed. He wept with relief that she was safe and his arms. He wept with grief that they would soon be apart.

She lifted a finger to his cheek and wiped away a tear. She understood the source of his sorrow and matched it with her own.

"We are always together in mind and heart. And yes, one

day we will be truly together always. We are young. We have time," she whispered.

I will fight my fear, she told herself.

"World enough and time," he agreed, but she had turned away. She did not hear him and could not see his lips.

They walked on in silence.

"I do not deny that there will be danger," he said.

"Yes. I worry about the danger. But mostly I worry that I will not have courage enough to meet the challenge," she replied, rewarding his honesty with her own.

"You will," he said firmly. "You are Alfred Dreyfus's granddaughter."

"Yes. I will try."

A new determination seized her. She would claim the courage that would sustain her. She would battle the fear that weighed upon her heart. Oh, she would try. Of course, she would try.

"Then you agree to go to Toulouse?" he asked quietly.

"You know that I will," she replied. "You know that I will do anything you ask." She placed her trembling fingers upon his lips so that they would capture the words he next spoke.

"*Je t'aime*," he said.

There was no need for her to reply. Her heart soared. Joy had surprised her at the end of a day wreathed in sadness.

TOULOUSE

EIGHTEEN

THE VERY NEXT MORNING, CLAUDE REQUISITIONED A battered Citroën from the Résistance's clandestine armada of vehicles, and he and Madeleine drove to the safe house on the Left Bank where Anna Hofberg awaited them. They looked away as Anna and her brothers parted, their faces wet with tears, their voices coarsened by sorrow. They spoke softly of their parents so newly vanished from their lives. They spoke with subdued hope of their future. Samuel and David embraced Anna.

"Palestine," they whispered. "We will be together in Palestine."

"Palestine," she repeated, struggling to contain her sobs, her narrow shoulders quivering.

Madeleine tried to find words of comfort but realized at last that all she might offer was her own embrace. Anna slept in her arms throughout the journey to Toulouse, where the entire Levy family welcomed them.

Madeleine was overjoyed to greet Simone, now returned from Grenoble. The Résistance leadership had asked her to train a select team of forgers in Toulouse, using Adolfo Kaminsky's unique methods. Documents establishing false identities were urgently needed as German reprisals intensified. It was said that Kaminsky himself often worked through the night. There were nights, Simone confided to Madeleine, that she herself worked until daybreak.

The apartment on the rue de la Dalbade was a hive of Résistance activity. In the small kitchen, forged passports were piled up next to sacks of potatoes; identity cards, the ink still wet and shining, shared counter space with newly baked baguettes. The salon, a frequent gathering place for regional underground fighters, was now and again transformed into a clandestine clinic where Pierre Paul and Jean Louis Levy, father and son, tended to ill and wounded. Résistants.

Jeanne spent hours in the bedroom storage area where she sorted through the donations of warm outer clothing and sturdy footwear for children. Given the freezing temperatures of the mountain passes of the Pyrenees during the winter months, Jeanne wanted to be certain that each small trekker was protected. She maintained a careful and orderly inventory, cartons labeled, every item recorded in the ledgers she kept beneath her bed.

Anoraks. Ten children's. Twelve adult, she wrote.

Hiking boots. Four size six. Two size eight. Six size twelve.

There were columns for sweaters, for mittens, for heavy socks. She kept careful count, ever aware that the clothing she collected and dispensed might save young lives.

Madeleine was greeted with great enthusiasm by the concierge of the building, Madame Leonie, a dour elderly widow who had enlisted in the Résistance on the very first day of the German Occupation.

"My husband did not die in 1917 so that *les Boches* could march into France in yet another terrible war they incited," she said grimly.

Claude was surprised and pleased that his close friend Serge Perl, a renowned Résistance leader now in charge of Résistance units in Toulouse, was a guest of the Levys and a frequent visitor.

"*Un fils de maison*," Jeanne whispered. "A son of our household."

Craggy featured, tall, and muscular, Serge, like many men of powerful build, moved with leonine grace. His voice was gruff, but his laughter was contagious. His long-lashed gray eyes softened when he looked at Simone.

Madeleine was quick to notice that her sister blushed and smiled whenever Serge entered the room. Simone was careful to reserve a place for him next to her when he joined the family for a meal. He, in turn, sprang to his feet and accompanied her when she took her small daughter for a walk.

"Now with Madeleine and Simone home, we Levys are the four musketeers," Etienne proclaimed.

"Can't I be a musketeer also?" small Anna asked and then frowned. "What is a musketeer?" she asked.

They all laughed as Jean Claude offered her a garbled and wholly inaccurate reply and laughed again as they assured her that four musketeers had now become five.

Madeleine winked at her.

Listen, she wanted to say. *This is what laughter sounds like. You must not forget how to laugh.*

It was bad enough, she thought, that Anna had lost her family, that the war had robbed her of innocence. She should not, would not, be deprived of the legacy of laughter.

And Anna, ever resilient, did laugh and planted a very wet kiss on Madeleine's cheek.

"I am so happy to be a musketeer, whatever that is," she said.

"It doesn't matter. What matters is that we are all one family," Madeleine replied, and Claude smiled at her.

"The day will come," he told her that evening as they walked along the banks of the Garonne River, "when we will truly be one family."

"Soon. Let that day come soon," she said and clutched his hand.

The next day he returned to Paris and her new life in Toulouse began.

Her masquerade was launched, her costume the dark suit and white blouse deemed suitable for a social worker on the Vichy payroll. She wore her thick, dark hair twisted into a tightly wound chignon. Following instructions, she met with officials of the Secours National and pledged her allegiance to the benevolent government of Márechal Pétain. She herself was surprised by how effortlessly she slipped into the role of double agent. She was a Résistance fighter who, with great efficiency, followed the instructions of her Vichy superiors.

As a senior qualified social worker, she was charged with the responsibility of seeing to the welfare of indigent children. She supervised all requisitions, daringly adding requests to routine submissions. She demanded supplies, appending explanations for the additions, none of which was ever questioned.

She insisted that a dozen pairs of boots be issued, explaining that the children in her district walked long distances to school and the boots would prevent damage to their feet which might incur medical expenses. The boots were issued and immediately went into Jeanne Levy's inventory for the children making their way to freedom across the forbidding Pyrenees.

Madeleine's brother Jean Louis submitted a list of medical supplies which she added to her requisitions, explaining to her Vichy masters that having such supplies in local clinics meant fewer visits to hospitals and thus saved money. She was congratulated on her attention to economy, and the Vichy bureaucrats happily pocketed the money ostensibly saved. The salves, pills, and bandages were bundled into the rucksacks of the Spanish guides and the *convoyeuses*, the Éclaireur escorts who accompanied each group of children.

She invented a bevy of Suzannes and Maurices, Brigittes and Andrés and inserted their names on the rosters of orphans in need of assistance. Simone, in turn, forged identity cards, permits, ration stamps, and other documents for them. A score of vulnerable, undocumented Jewish children were suddenly under the protection of the Vichy regime itself.

The Toulouse forgers also created ration cards, using Kaminsky's unique dyes, and cheerfully dispensed them to their Résistance comrades. The multicolored coupons authorized single liters of wine, renewable every ten days, packets of Gauloises and pouches of tobacco, all of which were consumed at impromptu nocturnal parties. They did not apologize for their happy gatherings. These were, after all, their salad years, the days of their youth. They would not allow the Germans to rob them of their brief, too brief, hours of gaiety. Why should they not drink a glass of wine, smoke a cigarette, and dance in each other's arms? Soon, very soon, all laughter would be stilled. They could not dance across the frozen terrain of mountain trails.

A pilot effort to test the feasibility of such escape routes was planned. Serge Perl told Madeleine that Claude had been chosen to lead that first group of escapees.

"It will be a very small, well-trained unit. All boys, trained in survival skills in Paris. Claude and a Spanish courier will guide them through secret passes in the Pyrenees to a border encampment in Spain. Tsofim, Scouts from Palestine, will be waiting there, and Claude will then make his way back to France. I share this with you because Simone has told me that Claude is your special friend."

Madeleine smiled at him gratefully.

"Yes," she said. "Claude is special to me."

"Simone thinks highly of him," he said. "As do I."

His gruff voice softened when he spoke her sister's name, Madeleine smiled gratefully. She knew that Serge was revered in the Résistance for his courage and his strength. She had watched him with small children, and she understood that his gruffness disguised a tenderness. Humor erupted unexpectedly, as when he spoke of a German absurdity, such as the Gestapo mandate that Jewish veterinarians could not treat pets owned by non-Jews.

"Even parrots and parakeets are honorary Aryans," he said. "We must be careful not to contaminate them with our Jewish ointments."

Simone had told Madeleine that Serge was the son of an orthodox family, an ardent Zionist. Heroism and loyalty, knowledge and commitment were second nature to him, Simone had said proudly.

Thinking of her sister, Madeleine breathed deeply and added daringly, "Am I wrong to think that you and my sister are special to each other?"

He smiled shyly.

"No. You are not wrong. And I must ask if you would welcome me as a brother?"

It amused her to see that he blushed although his gaze was steady.

"I would be honored to be your sister," she replied and took his hand in her own. She rejoiced for her sister. Simone had been a widow for long and lonely years, weathering privation and loneliness as she cared for her daughter and worked tirelessly creating the forgeries that saved so many lives. Her fingers were ink stained, her skin scarred by the chemicals that too often overflowed on her arms and wrists as she worked.

"I forge documents in my sleep," she had confided to Madeleine. "I dream that I am drowning in a flood of ink, that I float to safety on rolls of parchment."

"And do you dream of Serge?" Madeleine had asked.

Simone nodded.

"I dream of him. I think of him. Anatol is in my memory, but Serge is in my heart."

Madeleine had listened in silence. She did not tell her sister that Claude lived in both her memory and her heart. She said, instead, that she thought it a miracle that, surrounded as they were by hatred, Simone had been surprised by love. She hugged to herself the jealousy that overcame her on evenings when Simone and Serge went walking hand in hand while she herself sat alone, longing for Claude's touch, for the reassuring sound of his voice.

Lying awake, she struggled to organize her thoughts. Of course, Simone and Serge would marry. They had the courage to lay claim to a life together despite the dangers that confronted them. Could not she and Claude to the same? Weren't they entitled to some happiness?

Immediately, she thrust her fist against her pillow and chastised herself for the thought. Things were different for them. Serge and Simone were both based in Toulouse, while Claude worked in Paris. They had mutually agreed that, despite their deep feelings for each other, their obligations to the Résistance had first claim on their lives. Patience would be their lot as long as war raged, but the future was theirs. Peace would come. *La Paix. Peace.* And with it, love. *L'Amour.*

"*Paix. L'amour,*" Madeleine whispered into the darkness.

But even as she repeated that mantra of reassurance, she sank into a sadness she could not control.

"It is not fair! It is not fair," she added and fell into a dreamless sleep.

It was Serge who told her of Claude's imminent arrival in Toulouse. He and his contingent of children would begin their hazardous journey from there.

She gasped with excitement. She choked on her fear.

Within days, Claude entered her parents' apartment, his narrow face bronzed, his body lean and muscular, testimony to the long weeks of physical training. Wordlessly, she moved into his arms.

"We have so little time," he said. "I leave tonight."

"We are fortunate to have any time at all," she murmured.

They spent a brief, precious hour in a small café, talking

softly, their hands lightly touching across a small table covered with a red-and-white-checkered cloth. She told him that Serge and Simone had decided to marry as soon as possible.

"How fortunate they are," he said wistfully.

"We are young. Our time will come," she reminded him, aware that her words rang false even as she spoke them.

She was young, very young, she told herself. Of course, both her mother and her grandmother had been married and mothers when they themselves were very young. But then, war had not intruded on the years of their young womanhood. She and Claude lived in the shadow of danger and uncertainty. It was foolish of her to compare their pasts with her present.

"Our lives will soon be our own," she assured Claude, and he lifted her hand to his lips.

At midnight, the hour at which he was to meet his young charges, they walked together to the secret rendezvous at the southern border of the city.

"I want to go with you," she said. "Why can I not go with you?"

"Because the work that you are doing here is too important," he replied patiently. "The Résistance du Sud, the Resistance of the south, relies on your efforts. As do I."

"You will come back?" she asked plaintively. "You must come back," she insisted.

He held her close, hoisted his rucksack onto his shoulders, threaded his fingers through her thick, dark hair, then turned and disappeared into the night. The squadron of children whose faces she could not see trailed behind him in ghostly procession.

She realized, as she walked back to the rue de la Dalbade, that he had not answered her question.

One week passed and then another. She stopped counting the days. She thought the worst. She willed herself to think the best. And then, returning home one evening, she saw Serge awaiting her outside, his hand outstretched.

"What?" she asked and feared his answer.

He smiled.

"Comb your hair," he said. "Claude is here."

Pale with exhaustion, he sat in the salon and Madeleine, weak with relief, sank down beside him and kissed his callused fingers one by one.

That evening, he described his experience to the assembled Levy family.

"It was not easy," he said. "From the first the weather was against us. Two fierce rain storms flooded the *filieres*, the mountain passes, but our couriers, our brave Spanish guides, led us to shelter in caves and crevices. We waited out the storms and continued on to Tarbes, where a group of Résistants were waiting with supplies of food and clothing. One of our boys was ill with fever, and we waited for two days in a mountain village until he recovered. Then we hiked to Perpignan and crossed the border into the Spain. As arranged, we met three *tzofim*, scouts from Palestine, and they took over. I slept, I think, for two days and two nights straight, in a Perpignan safe house, and then began the trek back. As you see, I have arrived, safe and even sound."

He smiled; he laughed.

"But waiting for that sick boy to recover placed you and your charges in great danger," Dr. Levy said.

"I could not have left him. We are pledged to protect all the children in our care. And that sick boy was David Hofberg, Anna's brother."

"Then David is safe," Anna cried.

"David and Samuel both. Soon to arrive in Palestine."

Anna leapt onto his lap and flung her arms around his neck. "Merci, Claude. Merci." She trilled her gratitude, her face radiant with relief.

Claude smiled and stretched out on the sofa. Almost at once, his eyes closed and he fell asleep. One by one, the family left the room. Madeleine remained and knelt beside him. She saw that his breath came in small puffs, that he smiled as though teased by a pleasant dream. That quiet intimacy filled her with tenderness. Never before had she seen him lost in sleep. She dimmed the lamp, placed a pillow beneath his head, covered him with a blanket. It was important that he rest. He was to leave at daybreak for Paris, yet another journey fraught with danger. But for these few hours, he was safe and they were together. She stretched a blanket across the floor and lay down beside him.

They slept through the night and wakened together in the milky light of dawn. He enfolded her in his arms until, reluctantly, they arose and, without speaking, accomplished the morning routines. She heated water, and he washed and shaved. She handed him a clean shirt, found him a warm sweater in her mother's storage closet. They shared a hasty breakfast. The coffee brewed with chicory was sour, the baguette dry and stale, the margarine rancid. Food was increasingly difficult to obtain, but the sparse meal pleased them. It was enough that they were eating it together. She placed a packet of bread and cheese in his rucksack. He heard a car slow down on the street below. The bells of the Basilica of Saint-Sernin struck the hour. 6:00 a.m.

"I hear the bells. I must leave," he said.

"How fortunate it is that I cannot hear them," she said and held him close.

Clinging to each other, they walked to the door.

"Adieu, *ma chérie*," he said.

His lips brushed her cheek.

"Adieu, *mon cher*," she replied and traced the dark arch of his eyebrow with trembling fingers.

"Shalom," she whispered as the door closed behind him. The bells, in teasing tintinnabulation, continued to ring and she realized that she heard them, however faintly.

NINETEEN

A LETTER ARRIVED FROM LUCIE DREYFUS, ITS DETER-
minedly cheerful tone masking a sadness which her family
discerned. It was Jeanne who suggested that Simone and
Madeleine visit their grandmother. It would, she thought, give
her daughters a brief respite from their dangerous and exhausting work and offer her mother comfort and reassurance.

Lucie, who now called herself Madame Duteil, because
the Dreyfus name was too easily identifiable, had been given
refuge in the retreat house of the Sisters of Valence, a courageous order of Catholic nuns. She was delighted to see Simone
and Madeleine and whimsically apologetic about her newly
assumed identity.

"It is my second nom de guerre," she said. "During *l'affaire
Dreyfus* I called myself Madame Valabregue, and your mother
and your uncle Pierre also used that name so that they would
not be bullied by the children of anti-Dreyfusards. History
repeats itself. The Dreyfus name once again makes us vulnerable. Alfred is dead, but the Vichy Fascists will persecute all who
bear his name. I have followed the advice of Résistance leaders
and am now known as Madame Duteil. A pleasant name and
bit easier to pronounce than Valabregue, *n'est pas?*" she asked her
granddaughters, smiling mischievously.

"Certainly easier to lip read," Madeleine assured her. "The Levy name is also considered dangerous, too identifiably Jewish, so our entire family is now called Dupuy. We managed, with Madame Leonie's help, to circulate the rumor that the Levy family fled Toulouse and it is *la famille Dupuy* that resides in the apartment on the rue de la Dalbade. Madame Leonie complains to anyone who will listen that they have too many visitors, that she does not know what to do with mail that still comes for the Levys. Her complaints, as well as the wonderful new documents Simone has created for us, keep us safe."

She showed Lucie the documents Simone had forged so skillfully.

"I even created a new medical certificate for our father, complete with a gold seal and the signature of the Préfecture des Médecins. Pierre Paul Levy has been replaced by Monsieur le Professeur André Dupuy. A Gestapo general actually visited his surgery last week. He said he was relieved that a non-Jewish doctor had taken over the practice of the Jew, Levy. He would never have trusted that Jewish *untermentsch* to treat his hernia. Our father was pleased to tell him that his hernia was actually a cancerous tumor that would be best treated in Berlin. He left the very next day, so now there is one less Gestapo officer in Toulouse," Simone said.

Lucie laughed.

"Good for our Pierre Paul," she said. "And what name have you assumed, Simone?"

"I call myself Madame Dupuy. Simple enough. I say that I am a widow and that my late husband, Anatol, was a distant relative of our family," she said, and Madeleine noted that her sister could now speak Anatol's name without the wrenching melancholy of his sad and untimely death.

"Today you call yourself Madame Dupuy, but I hope that very soon your real name will be Madame Perl. When you and Serge last visited me, I saw how very close you were. I hope that you will soon marry," Lucie said.

The sisters stared at each other in surprise. Their grandmother, always supportive of their decisions, seldom offered direct advice.

Simone hesitated, and when she spoke, her voice was very soft, her reply tentative.

"You are right, of course, Grand-mère. Serge and I do care deeply for each other, and if these were normal times, we would surely marry. But because of the war and the dangers we face, we feel it may be prudent for us to wait."

Lucie shook her head.

"Life is never free of danger. It is *because* of the war that you should marry and seize what happiness you can, while you can."

She covered Simone's ink-stained hand with her own.

"*Ma* Simone, *ma* Madeleine, remember that the Dreyfus name has a special place in French history. Your grandfather's story belongs to the past, but the future is yours. Mold it as you will," she said. "You and your Serge should claim that future."

Simone sighed.

"How can we even think of the future? When we awaken in the morning we are not certain that we will be alive at the end of the day. The young wives in my Résistance cell are determined to avoid pregnancy. They do not want to bear children who may not survive, who may be orphaned. Only last week my friend Charlotte had an *avortement*—an abortion. Her husband had been deported, and she could not imagine going through pregnancy and raising a child alone. Also, she knew that she herself was in danger of arrest. We know that pregnant women are sent to their deaths in concentration camps so that the Nazis can end two Jewish lives. Serge and I are involved in dangerous work. We too fear arrest, deportation. Death. It would be foolish, even selfish, for us to think of marriage, of creating a family," Simone protested.

"Not foolish. Not selfish. Courageous. Selfless. And hopeful. Hope sustains us. It sustained me throughout my Alfred's ordeal. I trembled. I wept. I could have filled buckets with my tears. But I remained hopeful and I willed myself to courage. That is what you must do, Simone. Have the courage to marry your Serge. Have the hope that if you have children they will live lives of peace in a better world than the one we know. Do you agree, Madeleine?" Lucie asked and turned to her younger granddaughter.

Madeleine hesitated and then nodded. She understood why Lucie spoke only to her sister. Simone and Serge expressed their love openly, his hand reaching for hers, her head resting on his shoulder, their voices gentle in greeting and parting, their lips meeting in sweet softness. They were senior Résistance leaders, both assigned to Toulouse, their daily lives melded. They shared their days and talked softly, tenderly in the quiet of the evening. Their present was a portent of their future. She thought of them as already married.

Her own situation was very different. She and Claude concealed their closeness, avoided any display of their ever-intensifying affection, fearful of crossing into a treacherous reality already rife with danger. They lived in different cities, Claude in Paris, she in Toulouse, both pledged and trained to rescue Jews, to guide them to safety. Their treks would be undertaken separately, the terrains they would follow equally hazardous. The mountain passes of the Pyrenees and the forested trails of the Alps were both fraught with difficulty and danger.

Her grandmother spoke of the unborn children of the future, but Madeleine's life and Claude's were focused on the threatened children of the present, children like her blue-eyed, small surrogate sister, Anna Hofberg. Their future, hers and Claude's, was mortgaged to history. They dared not think beyond the day that would dawn when the sun next rose. Every hour of their separate lives was a gamble, dangerous and unpredictable.

Madeleine sighed, but her voice was strong when she turned to Simone.

"I agree with Grand-mère, Simone," she said. "You have every right to happiness today. And we all must live in hope of happier tomorrows. That is what you must tell Serge."

Simone eyes were bright, her color high.

"I will speak to Serge," she said quietly. "The decision must be his."

But there was a lilt in her voice and Madeleine nodded. She knew how Serge would decide, and she knew that his decision would be swift. None of them had any time to waste.

Two weeks after the visit to the convent, Simone and Serge stood beneath a marriage canopy fashioned from their father's prayer shawl and held by Etienne and Jean Louis. Madeleine, wearing a pale-blue linen dress, her dark hair floating to her shoulders, stood beside her sister and held her small niece's hand.

"I have a new *père*," the child whispered happily.

"And I have a new *frère*," Madeleine replied in turn.

Serge was more than a brother to her. He was her comrade, her loyal and caring friend.

The room was dimly lit, but the faces of the bride and groom were radiant with joy. Madeleine leaned close so that she might more easily read the lips of the elderly rabbi whose wispy voice was too faint for her to hear. The intoned prayers entered her heart. Tears came to her eyes as Serge turned to Simone and murmured the ancient oath.

"Behold, you are consecrated unto me according to the laws of Moses and Israel."

He crushed the traditional glass, a symbol of Jewish loss and longing, beneath his boot and shouts of "*L'Chaim*" rang out. Madeleine added her voice to the joyous chorus, flushed with pride in her tenacious community of friends and relatives. Pursued as they were by hatred, confronted each day with danger and death, they retained their love of life and their hope for the future. The mandate of Moses would outlive the foul edicts of Adolf Hitler.

"*L'Chaim*, to life," she repeated and joined the circle of women who danced around the bride, their skirts swirling as they celebrated peace and happiness. "*Hava Nagila*," they sang. "Let us be joyful."

Small Anna gripped Madeleine's hand and laughed as she trilled the song that had become the optimistic anthem of the Jewish Scouts.

"*Anu banu artza, livnot ulhibanot ba. We will go up to the land to build and be built by her.*"

"And so we will, Anna, so we will," Madeleine promised the child whose graceful steps matched her own.

Lucie Dreyfus, leaning heavily on her cane, kissed Madeleine on her cheek.

"Today belongs to Simone, but your turn will come," she said.

"I hope so, Grand-mère," Madeleine said as she fixed her gaze at the door, willing it to open, willing Claude to enter.

She had sent him news of the wedding with a Résistance courier but had received no reply. His silence had been worrisome, but his absence was ominous.

How could he not have come? How could he not at last have sent word to me? she thought, torn between anxiety and anger.

She reproached herself. She had no right to either emotion. War raged, people were dying, and yet she was stupidly immersed in self-pity.

"*Stop!*" she commanded her inner self, but anger and anxiety persisted.

She went to the window, lifted a corner of drapery, and peered down into the street. The rue de la Dalbade was deserted except for the occasional Vichy police vehicle that lumbered down, its headlights covered with lampblack, its invasive loudspeakers silenced. Such patrols had neither purpose nor destination. Their presence was simply a hectoring reminder that France was a country under Nazi occupation.

Pedestrians sheltered fearfully in doorways when police vehicles passed. A battered auto with Paris plates parked in a space often claimed by Claude. Madeleine's heart soared, but it was an elderly man who emerged from the vehicle. He glanced furtively around and hurriedly ran around the corner.

She did not avert her gaze. Claude might yet come. There could be many reasons for his delay, she told herself but even as she stood there, Serge Perl moved to stand beside her. She smiled at her new brother-in-law.

Serge was an instinctive leader, emanating quiet author-ity. His muscular body rippled with strength and his voice, although often harsh, was oddly reassuring. He was now the leader of an elite group known as "The Sixth," a sobriquet for the "Jewish Army," created by Toulouse Zionists to coordi-nate all Résistance efforts involving the Jewish community. His network extended from villages near Castres to Toulouse and the Mediterranean coast. He was one of the very few leaders entrusted with the details of every Résistance opera-tion in France. He, of course, would be able to explain Claude's absence. Madeleine was seized with fear, certain that he had news and certain too that it was news she did not want to hear.

He took firm hold of her trembling hand and led her away from the window.

"Claude will not come, Madeleine," he said. "He is leading a group of children across the Alps to Switzerland. He sent a radio message from a safe house en route that he is halfway there. The weather cooperates and the trek goes well. So we believe he is safe. You must not worry."

He enunciated carefully, making certain that whatever eluded her ears would be captured by her eyes. She read his lips; she felt his kindness.

"Thank you, Serge." She dredged up the strength to utter those few words. "I will try not to worry."

It was, she knew, a promise that she could not keep. Worry was her constant companion, shadowing her days, haunting her nights.

She kissed his cheek and turned away, wondering what it might be like to live without worry. She thought of the reassuring words he had offered, turned them over in her mind, spoke them aloud.

"The weather cooperates. The trek goes well. We believe he is safe."

The words brought comfort but anxiety adhered, pressing hard upon her heart.

"Let him come back to me. Let him be safe."

Her whispered prayer offered solace, however brief and transitory.

"Are you all right, Madeleine? Why are you not dancing?"

Anna stood beside her, her hand outstretched.

"I am fine, Anna. Come, let us dance."

She willed herself to smile. Sadness was a luxury she could not afford. It was also contagious, and she would not allow it to infect Anna, whose life was now so oddly intertwined with her own.

Hand in hand then, they rejoined the circle of dancing women. Simone, the bride, drew Madeleine into the center, and the sisters whirled in a lively *depka*, a dance of joy, a dance of hope.

TWENTY

O NE WEEK PASSED. THEN ANOTHER. WORRY TRAILED
Madeleine through the days and morphed into terror as
daylight died. Dreams became nightmares in which she chased
through darkness hoping to catch a glimmer of light. But just as
hope faded, Claude returned. Pale and drawn, he arrived at the
Lévy apartment and stumbled into Madeleine's outstretched
arms. It saddened her to see how pale and depleted he was, but
her spirits soared when he told her that he had been assigned
to coordinate Résistance efforts in the Unoccupied Zone and
would be based in Toulouse.

"The south is in turmoil," he said. "The Germans are focusing on this area."

"We have noticed," she replied wryly, and he laughed.

"Of course you have," he said and held her close. "It would
have been difficult not to notice."

German troop movements had accelerated, *rafles* occurred
daily, and deportation camps were established in obscure rural
provinces throughout the zone. Barracks, surrounded by barbed
wire and studded with searchlights, had been swiftly erected
at Gers, Noe, and Recebedou, all hamlets that were gateways
to the Pyrenees. Similar encampments sprang up along the
Mediterranean coast. It was clear that Berlin had instituted a

determined effort to block all escape routes in their wild and irrational determination to imprison and deport every Jew in France.

The Résistance leadership moved swiftly to counter that effort. Courageous volunteers undertook dangerous operations, ignoring life-threatening risks. Jean Louis and Etienne Levy led a team of Jewish Scouts on nocturnal missions of sabotage. Their targets were the trains that transported German troops as well as the railroad tracks across which those troop trains thundered. Jeanne Levy's kitchen became a laboratory for the creation of explosives. She fried an abundance of onions and garlic to mask the odor of death-dealing chemicals.

The increase of *rafles* left more and more Jewish children without parental protection and with a desperate need for new documents and hiding places. Simone worked through the night, creating new identity cards and passports, her quill pens dancing across stressed paper, rubber stamps wet with doctored ink adding illegible authenticity. Madeleine cycled through the countryside, seeking refuges for the vulnerable young-sters, the forged documents concealed in her undergarments. She carried large amounts of money, solicited from mysterious sources, which she offered to farmers and householders who, with great courage, agreed to shelter a Jewish child. The hiding place offered might be in an attic, a cellar, a hayloft, even a chicken coop, and the francs she distributed were used to buy food, supplies, and silence.

At a scattering of convents and monasteries, nuns and monks offered protection, furnishing the children with school uniforms and teaching them the catechism. Every small Jewish girl carried a rosary. Every small Jewish boy was cautioned to shield his penis with his hand when urinating so that his circumcision would be concealed. No one could be trusted. Anyone might inform on a Jewish friend if it bought a family an extra ration card or a liter of *vin ordinaire*.

Lucie Dreyfus knew that the Mother Superior of the Sisters of Valence, ever smiling, ever calm, concealed a knife within her robes even as she spoke with disarming courtesy to the Vichy police who now and again appeared at the convent. The nun would not stab the officers, she confided to Lucie, but she would sooner kill herself than divulge information about those she had sworn to protect.

"But doesn't the church teach that suicide is a mortal sin?" Lucie asked.

"God will forgive me. I am protecting His children," the nun replied.

Madeleine and her combat group of elite Résistance fighters packed cartons of food, clothing, and soap, which she requisitioned from the General Service Unit, to be smuggled into Vichy prisons and transit camps. The drivers of milk trucks, bakery vans, and grocery lorries were willing accomplices. Hidden within packaged bread and sacks of cereal were Simone's forged documents.

The Résistance prepared parcels of clothing which reluctant International Red Cross workers and somewhat more acquiescent Quakers agreed to distribute to internees. Wire cutters were concealed in the sleeves of sweaters, metal files thrust into the folds of knitted scarves. Apples were sliced open and razors inserted into them. Madeleine cut her finger on such a razor and sucked her own blood, pleased that the tiny weapon was so sharp. It might earn a prisoner freedom; it might save a life.

"How much did it cost us in bribes to get the Red Cross to cooperate?" Serge asked her bitterly after her return from a pleading visit to the international charity's offices.

"A few thousand francs. But in the end they agreed. They themselves are frightened," Madeleine replied, wondering why she made excuses for aid workers so reluctant to offer their aid to Jews. "The Fascists have threatened them."

"The Fascists threaten all of us," he said impatiently even as he flashed her an approving smile. He and Claude were both aware of Madeleine's daring and persistence. It was known that when she was stopped by Vichy police, she stared them down and produced her credentials as a social work supervisor for the Secours National.

"How dare you detain Madeleine Dupuy who is on a special mission for Márechal Pétain himself?" she would ask haughtily before speeding away on her bicycle, never waiting for their response. She gripped the handlebars so tightly that her fingers were white-knuckled. Her eyes were always riveted to the road because she could not hear the warning sounds of traffic. It was a small but manageable impediment, she assured herself even as she trembled with a fear that she struggled to control.

"You must be more cautious," Claude shouted one night, and she shrugged, pleased by his concern but indifferent to the words which she tossed back at him.

"And you too must be more cautious," she retorted.

"We will be cautious together," he told her. "Tomorrow you and I will cycle to Gers."

Her heart soared. She did not ask why he had been ordered to accompany her. It did not matter. All that mattered was the brief journey that would grant them precious hours of togetherness.

The very next day, both of them wearing the uniform of Red Cross relief workers, they cycled side by side down country roads. The soft winds of autumn brushed their upturned faces, and their hands touched now and again as they pedaled slowly eastward, toward the distant mountains on which crowns of ice already gleamed. The sun was high when they reached Gers and approached the grim prison camp.

Claude daringly and authoritatively presented the guards on duty with documents embossed with the seal of the International Red Cross. One such document stipulated that he be allowed to personally deliver the parcels to specific addresses. The other was a demand that Madeleine be allowed to speak with female prisoners and distribute items necessary for feminine hygiene.

The guards looked at each other in bewilderment, then summoned their commandant. The overweight, red-faced Gestapo officer stared at them angrily.

"Why is such a request being made? Does the Red Cross believe that soldiers of the Third Reich are dishonest enough to pilfer the packages they send? Do they think that Hitler's army does not know how to treat women—that pure-blooded Aryans would mistreat or molest Jewish and Roma women— women who are beneath our contempt? These requests are outrageous. We will not comply," he shouted and waved his swagger stick threateningly.

Claude replied calmly, his gaze steady.

"A news conference will be held tomorrow in Paris, and the assembled journalists will be informed of your decision. They will wonder why you refuse the request of the Red Cross, a recognized international humanitarian organization. They will, I am sure, demand to know what you are hiding. The Paris correspondents of the *New York Times* and the *Herald Tribune* will be attending and will surely report your intransigence. I do not think Herr Hitler will be pleased to see such stories on the front pages of American newspapers."

The commandant glared and studied the proffered documents again. He turned away, turned back, dropped his swagger stick, and cursed angrily at the guard who did not hand it to him swiftly enough.

"Very well. You may carry out your instructions. You have exactly one hour," he spat out at last.

Claude nodded. Within an hour he had completed the distribution of unexamined parcels of contraband to Résistance leaders, and Madeleine had met with a small group of woman Résistantes. She had handed each of them packets of gauze-wrapped cotton pads stuffed with forged identity papers, maps, and currency. Few words were exchanged. They contented themselves with whispers of hope.

As the autumn sun began its slow descent, Madeleine and Claude left the compound, ignoring the muttered curses of the guards who slammed the gates behind them. They cycled back to Toulouse through the gathering darkness.

"Will they escape?" she asked Claude as they paused to rest at a wayside inn.

"They will have more of a chance tomorrow than they had yesterday," he replied. "Thanks to your courage."

"*Our* courage," she corrected him gently.

"*Notre courage*," he agreed and pressed his lips to hers.

Claude left Toulouse again the next day, embarking on a mission he could not discuss. Madeleine resumed her frenetic and lonely life. Every free hour that she scavenged was devoted to the small group of children, Anna among them, whom she was training for their escape through the Pyrenees to Spain. She taught them to march single file, maintaining absolute silence. She taught them a hymn that they were to sing as they marched through mountain hamlets. They would be masquerading as a church-sponsored hiking group.

"His eye is on the sparrow, and He also watches me," they sang, and she prayed that that much at least was true.

All the children had memorized the Hail Mary, dubious protection but it would have to suffice.

"Will we leave soon?" Anna pleaded.

"Soon," Madeleine lied.

They braced themselves for winter. Madeleine raided her mother's storage closet for warm clothing for Anna. She found a heavy sweater and an anorak to give to Claude on his return.

"He is always cold, always exhausted," she told Simone worriedly.

Light snows fell but ceased before the city could be blanketed in wondrous whiteness. A slippery gray frost covered the streets of Toulouse, and ill-shaped glaucous clouds drifted through a darkening sky. It occurred to Madeleine, as she maneuvered her bicycle down ice-coated intersections, that Nazi malevolence had robbed the world of winter's alabaster beauty.

TWENTY-ONE

O N December 7, as harsh winds wailed across France, Japanese aircraft rained bombs on American naval vessels in Pearl Harbor. One day later, Adolf Hitler declared war on the United States. In London, Charles de Gaulle and the Free French celebrated America's entry into the war. The airwaves trembled with the sounds of "La Marseillaise" and "The Star-Spangled Banner" played in rapid succession, twin anthems of solidarity. Madeleine, both elated and apprehensive, listened to conflicting rumors.

Speculation was rampant, hope and fear colliding. American military would be turned on Germany. France would soon be free, but not before many battles would be fought, many lives lost. Loyalties shifted from one day to the next.

Allegiance to Vichy was much diluted as Pétain's shocking duplicity and his submissive obedience to his German masters became apparent, all subterfuge abandoned. He swore revenge against any group that defied him. His methods were now as cruel as those of the Nazis, his anti-Semitic pronouncements and edicts as harsh and relentless. But his governance was no longer submissively accepted. Scores of volunteers besieged Résistance networks.

The Résistance symbol, the Cross of Lorraine with two

bars, beneath the inscribed motto *Vive de Gaulle*, was newly prominent. Scrawled on colored paper, the symbols littered Metro platforms in Paris, dangled from the railings of bridges, appeared on the counters of *boulangeries*, and were concealed within the pages of *Le Monde* and other newspapers. Daring children drew them in colored chalk on the pavement of narrow streets and broad avenues, scurrying away to avoid the wrath of the Vichy police.

"France is experiencing a somewhat belated surge of patriotism," Claude said bitterly to Madeleine as they met in a small café on one of his infrequent visits to Toulouse where he was based. "Suddenly I am asked to find guides for an army of volunteers who claim they want to join the Free French in North Africa or reach de Gaulle in London or form guerrilla units to fight the Nazis in the borderlands. They need papers, they need money, and they turn to the Jewish Scouts for help. One such latecomer had the nerve to tell me they turned to us because Jews always know how to get money. The chutzpah!"

"Yes. The chutzpah," Madeleine agreed, suppressing a yawn.

She struggled against the fatigue that had overwhelmed her all that week. There had been a spurt of new arrests, and she had been warned that despite her false papers and her cover as a Vichy social worker, she was not immune to danger. She was advised to stay on the move and avoid her parents' home. She heeded such advice and scurried from one nocturnal refuge to another, one night sleeping on the sofa of a sister scout's rented room and the next night on a cot in Serge and Simone's apartment or her friend Hélène's guest room.

"Who are these volunteers?" she asked Claude.

"The problem is we're never certain. We try to vet them. We've learned that some of them are soldiers who are fed up with the Vichy regime and want to desert. Others are escaped prisoners from the camps in the southwest. There are teenagers who fear being conscripted to work in German munition plants. We don't know what to believe, whom to believe. We worry that the local Milice, the French police who work with the Nazis, are trying to infiltrate our ranks. We worry about preserving our security. We know that we must prioritize our primary goal," he said grimly.

"Our primary goal?"

"The rescue of our children, of course. Anything that places children in danger must be avoided."

"Yes. I know that. But are there new dangers I should be aware of?"

A foolish question, she knew. Each day brought new dangers.

Claude hesitated and then shook his head wearily. His words came slowly, his voice weighted with sadness.

"I do not want to frighten you, but yes, we have reason to be concerned. There may be informants among these new volunteers. And the news from Madrid is troubling. We are told that the Spanish are tightening their borders and we will soon be unable to use our escape routes through the Pyrenees. That leaves us only the Swiss who, it seems, are more reliable than the self-proclaimed veterans of the Spanish Civil War. The Swiss pretend to no humanitarian motive. They simply want to be paid. It now costs three thousand francs to get one Jewish child over the Alps, and there have been times when the Swiss guides threaten to abort a mission unless we offer more money. The mercenary bastards."

"I'm not surprised." Madeleine added sugar to her ersatz coffee but did not drink it. "My uncle Pierre negotiated escape routes with Spanish *passeurs* before he emigrated. He told me that one of them actually said that the Spanish wanted Jewish refugees to pass through their country as light passes through a glass. It was the Swiss who wanted their efforts to be bought and paid for. One day they sell their assistance to the Jews; the next day they may sell it to the Germans. And then they go on manufacturing their cuckoo clocks and watches."

She remembered her uncle's anger as he spoke, and she wondered if she would ever see Pierre Dreyfus and his family again. His letters arrived infrequently, but he had written of his meeting with Eleanor Roosevelt who was very sympathetic to the plight of European Jews. Her husband, he had added, was much less concerned, indeed, not concerned at all.

She thought to tell Claude about Pierre's letter just as a winter wind swept through the café. The door swung open and two Gestapo officers entered. They commandeered a table, shouted too loudly at the waiter, their French guttural, their voices rasping.

"*Deux café. Gâteaux. Chocolat. Vite!*"

Claude stood and closed the door, which they had left open. The Germans stared at him contemptuously and turned away.

Claude drew his chair closer to Madeleine.

"Toulouse will soon be totally under German control," he said, speaking very softly. "The danger grows. As you see. Turn around but don't stare."

She turned and was careful not to stare.

The Germans were now arguing loudly with the frightened waiter. Their coffee was not hot enough. Their cakes were stale. Still, they ate. They drank. They slammed plates down and left without paying the bill.

"You must take precautions," he murmured.

"What can I do?" she asked.

He hesitated, and she read both the love and the fear in his eyes.

"The Résistance thinks you should move to a safe location," he replied.

"There is no safe location for a girl named Madeleine Levy, although she may call herself Dupuy. And where can I be more useful to the Résistance than here in Toulouse, where I have friends, where I masquerade as a Vichy employee? Would you want me to leave my parents, my brothers, Simone and Serge?" she asked.

"I would not want you to do anything you yourself would not want to do. But I worry about you being in Toulouse," he replied.

"And I worry about you wherever you may be."

They exchanged wry smiles. Their mutual fear for each other was testimony to their love.

Claude left Toulouse the next day. As always, Madeleine did not know where he was going or when he would return. Depressed but resigned, she continued her nomadic life, darting into her parents' home to reassure them that she was safe and to speak briefly with Anna, whom Jeanne Levy protected and coddled.

Madeleine sought out various nocturnal refuges, a small canvas bag containing a toothbrush, a nightdress and a change of underwear always concealed in the pannier of her bicycle. An urgent encrypted warning had been issued by combat headquarters advising that there was extreme danger and all militants were to change residences immediately and often. They further stipulated that there be no meetings in restaurants and cafés, that no one was to be trusted.

Madeleine knew the validity of such warnings. Many Résistance leaders and Jewish Scout leaders had already been arrested. She felt safest staying with her friend Hélène, a midwife and avid Résistance worker who also delivered the babies of German women and French prostitutes. That dual role offered her information as well as immunity, however fragile.

Strong, competent Hélène was indifferent to all warnings of danger and death.

"My job is to bring life into the world," she told Madeleine as they relaxed over small glasses of anisette, obtained by using Simone's expertly forged ration stamps. "Let us forget about death."

"I will try," Madeleine promised, but she knew that it was a promise she could not keep.

Her false identity as a supervising social worker for the Secours National brought her into close contact with the Gestapo Français, French collaborators who were willing accomplices to German interrogators in the torture chambers of the rue Maignac prison. She hid her contempt for them and maintained casual flirtations.

Leon, a Gestapo Français lieutenant was a persistent suitor, contriving to escort her to meetings and holding her hand as they crossed a busy intersection.

"These Résistants are dangerous. They would think nothing of running you down. Did you know that there are Jews among them?" he said.

She nodded, thanked him for his concern, and flashed him a beguiling smile. But when he bent close and whispered an endearment in her ear, she shook her head.

"I cannot hear you," she confided. "I see that you didn't realize that I am somewhat deaf."

"I am, in a way, relieved to know that," he replied.

That relief translated into invitations to accompany him to cafés where he met with both his superiors and his subordinates to discuss the names of suspects and locales that would be raided. All secrets might be revealed because he assumed that Madeleine was unable to hear the conversations, and he shared that knowledge with his comrades.

Madeleine, of course, had exaggerated her hearing deficit. She read lips, listened attentively, and memorized every scrap of information to pass on to Serge, who moved quickly. New identities were created, meeting places and safe houses abandoned, lives preserved.

She was relieved when Leon was transferred to Paris and consoled him at their parting with the promise that she would join him there.

"I know a wonderful hotel in Neuilly," she said and struggled to remember the name of the hotel she had invented when she played the role of Adele Valheur. It was of little importance.

He would not try to find her. Paris was full of beautiful young collaborators.

The weeks of winter passed slowly. Claude was rarely in Toulouse, and Madeleine treasured the hours she spent with Simone's small family. Her time with them was a respite from her own frenetic existence and the loneliness that never left her. She fantasized that her sister's incandescent happiness, undiminished by the darkness of the times, was a portent of her own future.

"Your day will come," her grandmother Lucie had whispered to her on Simone's wedding day. Madeleine hugged the words. Her wise grandmother was seldom wrong.

As a Résistance leader, Serge maintained a radio. Hidden in a kitchen cabinet beneath an uneasy pyramid of onions and potatoes, it was equipped with a frequency powerful enough to receive broadcasts from London. The French language Radio Londres offered the only credible news of the actual progress of the war. Radio Paris blared anti-Semitic diatribes, and both Radiodiffusion Nationale and Radio Jeunesse were Vichy controlled, their newscasts blatantly false.

The kitchen was darkened during broadcasts and the volume kept low because listening to the BBC was deemed a serious crime punishable by imprisonment or death. Madeleine huddled with other Résistance workers to listen to the news. She heard the first notes of Beethoven's Fifth Symphony followed by the tapping of a single letter in Morse code. Dot-dot-dot-dash—the letter V—V for Victory. She moved very close because the voice of the Free French newscaster was barely audible to her. Still, she grasped the words. "*Ici Londres. Les Français parlent aux Français.* London here. French citizens speaking to French citizens."

The news was never good. With sinking hearts they learned of the deportations of Jews from every European country under German occupation to infamous destinations. Treblinka, Sobibor. Chelmno, Belzec. Auschwitz, Birkenau.

"Death camps." Serge spat out the words, his fists clenched. His own family was somewhere in Eastern Europe, wandering through the killing fields or perhaps already murdered.

On a dreary March evening, Madeleine joined her brothers in Simone's kitchen. Jean Louis and Etienne, pale and exhausted, stretched out across the floor. She did not ask them what had caused their fatigue. Tongues of frost licked the grimy windows. Serge slammed down blackout shades, unscrewed the weak electric bulb, and lit a small candle that flickered and died, leaving the room in darkness. *A bad omen*, Madeleine thought.

Sipping the bitter coffee Simone brewed from chicory and acorns, she heard the newscaster's dull, almost unbelieving voice report that a "special train" had left Paris for Auschwitz with 1,112 Jewish prisoners, many of them Résistance fighters. Her throat tightened, her hands trembled. She dropped her mug, indifferent to the dark stain that spread across her skirt.

"Claude," she whispered and shivered with fear.

Serge, who knew the movements of every Résistance operative, moved swiftly to her side. He spoke very softly. He was, she knew, breaking Résistance protocol.

"Claude was not in Paris," he said and she leaned against him in gratitude and relief.

"Where?" she asked but that was information he could not share.

He turned back to the radio and dialed a secret frequency on which a Résistance operator was issuing coded messages.

"My call letters," he said grimly.

He copied everything onto a slip of paper, decrypted the code, and memorized it, his lips moving slowly, silently. He then shredded the paper, opened the darkened window, and tossed out the tear-shaped fragments that were carried away by the wild wind.

He turned to Jean Claude and Etienne, their fatigue now replaced by grim determination. They stared at him, knowing that a mission would soon be undertaken. They were ready. They were willing.

"We have learned that the Gestapo are awaiting a shipment of arms to be delivered to the Castres train station sometime tomorrow. We do not know exactly when, but we know where and we know what we must do."

He opened the icebox and removed a carton thrust in the rear and marked *Beurre*. It did not contain butter but a compact transmitter. He worked quickly, his fingers racing across the keys as he tapped out a coded message.

"I have told combat headquarters that we will make certain that such a shipment will never arrive because by tomorrow morning Castres will not have a train station."

He motioned to his young brothers-in-law. Wordlessly Jean Louis and Etienne darkened their faces with the sticks of charcoal Simone handed them as Madeleine pulled heavy socks over their boots to soften their tread. Their mission and intent was clear to her. She and Serge, both her brothers, and other scout leaders had spent long hours in the basement of a darkened schoolhouse where an instructor from England had conducted a workshop on the use of explosives.

Smuggled across the Channel, the diminutive Cockney engineer with a ready laugh and horrific French had managed to teach them the secrets of effective sabotage. Their targets would be bridges, ports, trains, and terminals; dynamite and gelignite their weapons of choice. Primers were easily available. Heavy rope made excellent fuses. Serge, Madeleine knew, had more than once translated that clandestine training into action, often assisted by Jean Louis and Etienne.

She watched as they pulled burlap sacks of equipment from beneath the beds. Serge kissed Simone, the brothers embraced their sisters, and they all disappeared into the night.

Simone sighed.

"The Gestapo will not receive this shipment, but they will send another one tomorrow and another the day after that. We are shooting arrows at machine guns."

"We are doing what we can," Madeleine said quietly.

"I know. But I know too that Hitler will not rest until every Jew in Europe is dead." Simone stared at the documents spread across her kitchen table, at the pile of photos she would affix to them, Photomaton snapshots that she had learned to doctor. Shrugging, she opened a pot of paste and turned to the task at hand. Madeleine also took up a brush. This much they could do. This much they had to do.

At last, the completed documents were boxed up and Simone went to the window where she would stand vigil throughout the long night, waiting for her husband and her brothers who might or might not return.

Madeleine, in turn, crept into the narrow bed where her small niece slept and tried to think of a prayer that might offer solace. Words did not come and she fell asleep, soothed by the rhythmic rise and fall of the child's breath, dreaming dreams now threaded with terror, now threaded with joy.

As the first light of dawn streaked across the wintry sky, the three men returned. Madeleine heard Simone's cry of joyous relief, and she was suffused with gratitude.

"Thank you," she murmured, and realized that the words were a prayer.

TWENTY-TWO

THE CRUEL WINTER SLOWLY DRIFTED INTO SPRING. TENDER new grass covered the meadows, and wildflowers grew in colorful profusion. Golden forsythia and violet masses of grape iris waved in the gentle wind. Riding through the countryside to meet with her Vichy supervisors, Madeleine leapt off her bicycle and gathered up sheaths of bluebells and clumps of lavender. She smiled and offered them to a rotund Vichy officer who accepted them gratefully. He threaded a bluebell through his epaulette so that it rested against the burnished pin on which the Battle Ax of Gaul, the official Vichy emblem, was engraved. She flinched, angered by the contiguity of the sweet, small flower with the emblem of betrayal and hatred.

She discussed the incident with Claude later that night as they shared a hasty dinner on one of his brief and infrequent visits to Toulouse.

"And of course I advised him to put the flowers in water," she concluded. "He thanked me profusely. That might earn me some protection."

"Foolish, Madeleine," Claude murmured, and she understood that he refrained from saying that protection of any kind was transitory and unreliable.

Summer swept in with a burst of warmth. Wild roses

bloomed along the banks of the Garonne and forced their way through the hedges of country roads in a riot of color. Lucie Dreyfus favored wild roses, Madeleine remembered, as she clipped sprays of red and white blossoms and lilacs of a vivid blue. *A Bastille Day bouquet*, she thought as she inhaled their fragrance. A memory of Bastille Day 1935 came to her with startling clarity.

Seven years had passed since her grandfather's death. Standing in a circlet of sunlight, holding the flowers close, she thought of all that had happened during that span of years. War and occupation. Painful separations. The Dreyfus family scattered, friends vanished. Death and danger. Her dreams were an amalgam of visions of smoke curling darkly skyward from chimneys of death in Poland and roses that burst into blossom. She smiled, marveling at their beauty and their imagined fragrance.

She was grateful, she assured herself as she inhaled the scent of those red, white, and blue blossoms, for the companionship of her comrades, of Simone, her brothers and parents, for Claude's protective tenderness. Hope was alive, memory endured. Bastille Day offered both sadness and solace.

She decided, impulsively, that she and Simone would visit their grandmother at her convent retreat, her most recent hiding place; together they would light a memorial candle and mark the anniversary of Alfred Dreyfus's death.

She cycled swiftly back to Toulouse. The *boulangerie* was open, and she purchased the last remaining apple tart, Simone's sweet of choice. *A good omen*, she thought happily.

Clutching the white bakery box and the flowers, she entered

her sister's home. She was surprised, at this unlikely hour, to find a small group of Résistants in the kitchen, listening attentively to the radio. The room was dimly lit. The shades had been drawn again, and the air of the small room was heavy with the smoke of Gauloises and unwashed bodies. No one turned to greet her. A grim silence prevailed. Simone looked up at last, her eyes red-rimmed, her face a mask of unbelieving grief.

Madeleine set the flowers and the cake down.

"What has happened?" she asked, but Simone lifted a finger to her lips and motioned her to a stool close to the radio. Madeleine sat and leaned forward, but the volume was even lower than usual and she could glean only a few words. *Vél d'Hiv*, she thought she heard, although the newscaster's familiar voice was muffled, his words emerging slowly, sorrowfully.

"Vél d'Hiv." She heard the words again. A name she knew. The accepted abbreviation for Vélodrome d'Hiver, a Paris landmark. Situated on the boulevard de Grenelle, not far from the Eiffel Tower, it was an imposing structure. Her grandfather, who was so in love with Paris that he knew the history of every building of note, had told her that it had been built for the track cycling event of the 1924 Olympics and had become the venue for fencing, boxing, and weight-lifting competitions. Its glass dome, he had claimed proudly, was the envy of all of Europe.

Why, she wondered, had mention of the velodrome created such anguish in the room? Why was Simone holding her daughter close as tears streaked her face? Madeleine cursed her inability to hear and bent her head to the radio.

She caught another word. *Rafle.*

Vél d'Hiver. *Rafle*. She struggled to piece them together, to vest them with meaning, but they remained a jagged puzzle, captured words that she could not fit together. The radio fell silent. Simone turned to Madeleine and took the bouquet of roses and lilacs, pressing it to her cheeks, Her tears fell like dewdrops onto the soft, bright petals.

"Simone, what has happened?" Madeleine asked.

Her sister spoke slowly, clearly.

"In Paris, very early this morning, even before daybreak, the Nazis rounded up thousands of Jews and Résistance fighters. They arrested entire families. They took small children. Infants. The elderly. No warnings, no explanations. They shouted that each prisoner could take one blanket, one sweater, one shirt. No food. No water. No medical supplies. No nappies for the babies. They were herded onto buses and trucks. Families were separated without rhyme or reason. Some were taken to Drancy, but most were transported to the Vél d'Hiv. We've now had reports on conditions there. Horrible. Inhuman," Simone said, her voice breaking as she spoke. "A Quaker volunteer who went in to try to care for sick babies choked up when she tried to describe the horrors she saw there."

"Babies. Why would they imprison babies?" Madeleine asked and immediately recognized the absurdity of her question.

Why, indeed, would they imprison anyone? Mothers, fathers, the elderly, the infirm? She knew the answer, of course. Because all were guilty of the crime of being Jewish. There was no rational answer to her why. Hatred defied reason.

Dizzied with sorrow, Madeleine clutched Simone's hand.

"What will happen?" she asked.

"We don't know. Serge is in touch with Résistance leaders, with Claude in Paris and Robert Gamzon in Algeria."

"Then Claude is safe," Madeleine said.

She forgave herself for the relief she felt. It did not diminish her sorrow.

"Yes. Serge has been in radio contact with him. He is in a safe house where he has some contact with the Red Cross and the Quakers, who seem to be the only source of information," Simone replied.

She glanced across the room where Serge sat at the kitchen table, studying a large-detail map of Paris.

He was, Madeleine knew, searching for a possible escape route although he surely knew that for the prisoners in the Vél d'Hiv, no escape was possible. She looked up as her brothers burst into the room.

"The Nazi bastards, the rotten Vichy traitors," Jean Louis muttered. "They waited until the Bastille Day celebrations were over to turn on their own people. French Fascist scum betraying French Jews, French Résistance fighters, their own neighbors. Give them a few francs, a bottle of wine, and they'll sell their own parents to Hitler. *Incroyable.* Unbelievable."

"Bastille Day has no meaning for the Vichy French," Etienne added. "They are the shock troops for the Nazi occupiers. Do you think that the mobs who follow Pétain and Laval, who pledge allegiance to Hitler and wear swastika armbands and the Battle Ax of Gaul on their lapels believe in *liberté, égalité, fraternité?*"

"Try to remember that we have many friends who fight Vichy," Simone reminded her brothers quietly. "Our comrades in the Résistance, the Christian scout troops from L'Oratoire du Louvre who work with the Éclaireurs Israélites, rescuing and hiding Jewish children. There are courageous householders and farmers who hide our children and the children of Résistance fighters at great risk to their own lives. Not every victim of the Nazis is a Jew."

"But every Jew is a target," Serge reminded her, his voice echoing ominously across the room.

He folded his map, acknowledging that the search for an escape route was an exercise in futility. He turned to the radio again in an effort to reach Radio Londres but there was no transmission. It seemed, Madeleine thought, that the horrors in Paris had choked the Free French in London into silence. Her bouquet of red, white, and blue flowers lay on the table in a wilted mass. No one had thought to put them in water.

Days passed and news from Vél d'Hiv filtered in, each report, each rumor, more horrific than those that had preceded them. Quaker volunteers and Red Cross workers abandoned their guise of neutrality and spoke bitterly of the inhumane conditions. The famous glass roof of the Vélodrome had been painted dark blue as camouflage against the RAF bombers that made sorties over Paris. The dark color raised the daytime summer heat to unbearable temperatures. Because the windows were bolted shut to prevent escapes, no air circulated.

There were only five lavatories for the estimated thirteen thousand prisoners, no nappies for infants, an inadequate supply of buckets for human waste. The stench of excrement, urine, vomit, and unwashed bodies sickened even the guards. Rust-colored trickles emerged from water taps. It was said that those who tried to escape were shot on the spot. Their blood congealed on the concrete surfaces where once brightly costumed cyclists had raced. There were stories of suicides. Death by self-imposed starvation. A man strangled his wife with his necktie and then choked himself to death. A desperate mother, driven to distraction, suffocated an infant who would not stop crying.

Simone wept. Madeleine's grief rested heavily upon her heart. They listened to the threatening radio address of Pétain's vice premier, Pierre Laval. His words increased their despair.

"No one and nothing can deter us from the policy of purging France of undesirable elements, without nationality," he proclaimed.

They stared at each other. Their families had been resident in France for generations, yet now they were "without nationality." They were the "undesirable elements." Nazi policy was now French policy. Their worst fears had been realized.

Serge held Simone close, his hand resting tenderly on the almost imperceptible rise of new pregnancy. Madeleine cycled to the rue de la Dalbade, embraced her parents, and held Anna too tightly.

Within days, the Vélodrome was emptied. Radio Londres reported that its prisoners had been transported to Drancy, Beaun-la-Rolande, and Pithiers, the way stations leading to Auschwitz.

"The way stations leading to hell," Serge amended bitterly.

TWENTY-THREE

THE TRAGEDY OF VÉL D'HIV IGNITED A NEW URGENCY. THE country was haunted by the fear that the cruelty enacted in Paris might occur without warning in Toulouse, in Lyon, in the smallest villages of the Unoccupied Zone. All equivocation ended. The leadership of the Jewish Résistance knew that they were in a race against time. As *rafles* increased and mothers and fathers disappeared, there was a desperate search for additional hiding places for abandoned Jewish children. Madeleine and her comrades worked endless hours in search of any possible refuge. Sleep was a luxury. Meals were snatched on the run.

She lived a double life. Her Vichy employment provided her with excellent cover for her Résistance activities. She wore the lapel pin of the Vichy Battle Ax of Gaul. In the eyes of her supervisors, she was Madeleine Dupuy.

But she knew herself to be Madeleine Levy. The blue-and-white scarf of the Jewish Scouts was tucked into her camisole. When exhaustion overcame her, she slept at her parents' home, dismissing Jeanne Levy's insistence that she be aware of the need for caution.

"I am very careful, Maman," she told her mother, the reassuring lie uttered with ease.

She offered Claude no such reassurance. During their brief

and breathless phone conversations, they spoke guardedly of the dangers they confronted, speaking in a code of their own invention.

"A good day is over," she might say, which meant that she had survived and was safe.

"Lonely here," he murmured which meant that he missed her, that he loved her.

"Lonely here too."

She never knew where his "here" was. Résistance secrecy transcended lovers' needs.

She thought herself to be a skilled thespian, performing on an unsteady stage. She greeted her Vichy coworkers amiably on her routine visits to the Secours National offices, her smile masking the hatred in her heart. She completed her official duties and sped on her bicycle down unfamiliar roads and across rural pathways in a desperate effort to find hiding places for endangered boys and girls, always moved by the courage of those who offered assistance, always angered by those who refused to help.

"I cannot risk putting my family in danger," the owner of a small inn said regretfully.

"All of France is in danger, monsieur," she retorted wearily but did not add that the situation of Jewish children was the most dangerous of all.

She was very careful, aware that there were those who volunteered assistance and then surrendered the very children they had offered to shelter to the Vichy police, claiming the rewards on constant offer. A betrayed Jewish child might yield a bonus of extra ration books, perhaps even several liters of petrol. She asked pointed questions, consulted with parish priests, explained her rejections circumspectly.

The news that the SS Commandant, Klaus Barbie, had been assigned to Gestapo headquarters in Lyon dismayed the Résistance leadership. It was yet another indication that the Southern Zone would soon be entirely under Nazi control. Any pretense of French governance would soon be abandoned.

"But of course we do not have a French government. Pétain and Laval are Hitler's puppets," Serge said bitterly as he read aloud from *Le Matin*, the leading collaborationist newspaper. Pétain had written an article accusing the Résistance of "a betrayal of the fatherland."

Serge ripped the newspaper into shreds which Simone gathered up.

"Serge, please do not destroy this excellent *papier de toilette*," she chastised him laughingly.

Madeleine and the other Résistants gathered around the Perls' kitchen table joined in the laughter.

The smallest of successes reassured her. She found refuge for twin brothers in the basement of a tavern. The abbot of the Lavour monastery took in three boys who had miraculously escaped a *rafle* that had entrapped their parents. Three lives saved. Four.

She waited impatiently for Claude's phone calls, which grew more and more infrequent and then ceased. Serge told her that Claude was traveling a great deal but could say no more.

Madeleine understood that he was obedient to Résistance protocol. His silence was her protection. Claude's journeys would have to remain impenetrable mysteries for his safety and for hers. She imagined him in danger. She imagined him safe. She imagined herself in his arms. She wakened from a nightmare, tears streaking her face, because she had dreamt that he was dead.

At last a courier handed her a letter from him. Weak with relief, her hands shaking, she read it. He wrote cryptically, aware that the courier might be intercepted, but she deciphered his carefully worded message with little difficulty.

He wrote that he was in good health, fully recovered from a lingering infection. She understood that to mean that he was out of danger after a long ordeal. He boasted that his store had held a successful sale with all merchandise sold and delivered. That, she knew, meant that a rescue mission had been completed and the children in his care were safe in Switzerland.

"We really should plan *un vacance*, a holiday, in the very near future," he wrote in conclusion. She smiled. The word *vacance* had disappeared from their personal lexicon. He meant only that they might soon see each other, possibly in the near future.

She committed those carefully chosen words to memory, newly optimistic. The war had transformed each shared hour into a burnished gem of time.

"The near future," she repeated to herself as she cycled to a rendezvous in the countryside with the owner of a granary who had agreed to hide two Jewish boys in his silo.

"They must be very small, these boys," he stipulated as he counted out the money she handed him. "The space is very narrow."

"I understand," she replied and wondered if she should caution the youngsters that they must not grow. Another inch in height, another ounce of weight might betray them. Ever the actress, she smiled at the man who was, after all, risking his life and that of his family. His words were foolish, but his courage was manifest. She arranged for the two boys, orphaned cousins whose parents had disappeared in the Vél d'Hiv, to be transported to the granary the next day. Each month, she cycled there, smiled at the owner, and thrust an envelope of twelve hundred additional francs into his hand. The agreed-upon price for sheltering a child was six hundred francs a month, sums which the Résistance raised with great ingenuity and great difficulty.

Madeleine waited. The "near future" of Claude's message was increasingly illusory as days and then weeks passed. She continued her nomadic, nocturnal wandering, no two nights in the same place, staying too often with Serge and Simone. She no longer listened to Radio Londres. The news had become unbearable. Exhausted, she slept, her sleep punctuated by dreams woven of memory, threaded with hope.

She dreamed she was in her girlhood bedroom, reclining on a chaise longue upholstered in rose-colored velvet and singing her favorite lullaby, "Entends-tu le coucou, Malirette?" She awakened, still humming the simple and soothing tune. But later that morning she remembered that there had been no such chaise longue in her bedroom. It had been a promised birthday gift, forfeited when her parents' home had been requisitioned. Her bedroom, she was certain, had been stripped of its rose-colored draperies and transformed into a sterile military office.

"No chaise longue," she murmured and winced at the foolishness of the thought.

On another night, she dreamed that she wore a simple white dress. Organdy. White roses were threaded through her long, dark hair and she stood beneath a leafy canopy in a sun-spangled forest, holding a beribboned bouquet of bluebells. She was happy because she was waiting for Claude. It was the "near future" of his letter. But all too soon, the light faded, the flowers wilted. Shadows fell. She remained alone. The dream ended and she wakened, weeping, calling his name.

"Claude! Claude!"

Her desperate dream wakened Simone, who rushed to her side.

"Hush, Madeleine. He will come. Soon. Very soon. Tomorrow perhaps. The next day."

Her sister's voice was very soft, its cadence reassuring, and Madeleine fell back and slept a mercifully dreamless sleep.

She awakened, angry at herself for the despair that had come upon her unbidden. She would have to be stronger. She would have to learn patience. He would come.

He did not come, either the next day or the day after that. Defeated, she did not dream of him again. Either of his presence or of his absence. Hope, she decided, in a burst of cynicism, was treacherous and had to be abandoned. Disappointment weakened resolve. She would concentrate on her mission, on the children she was charged with protecting. She needed every milligram of strength. Dreamless sleep became her refuge, muted optimism her sustenance, irrational anger at Claude's absence and his silence a secret source of strength. And yet her dreams persisted, chasing after her, twirling rainbows of hope, briefly banishing despair.

TWENTY-FOUR

A s the German occupation became more onerous, the Toulouse Résistance was overwhelmed by a multitude of volunteers. Serge and Madeleine interviewed applicants considered suspect. Betrayal was feared. The Milice offered tempting rewards for the smallest scraps of information and it was known that there were those who traded rumors and scant intelligence for a carton of Gauloises or several bottles of *vin rouge*. No risks could be taken. Possible Vichy infiltrators were rejected with elaborate excuses.

Still, so many young men and women were welcomed as fighters for a free France that the Jewish Scout camp near Moissac, slightly north of Toulouse, could not accommodate them. Secret barracks were established in Villefranche and Muret, where those newly admitted to the Résistance were trained.

As Allied air sorties increased, special stress was placed on operations undertaken to assist downed RAF pilots. The rescued airmen were provided with new clothing and new identities and transported to safety. Simone worked late into the night, gripping her quills tightly, boiling inks and dyes that stained her fingers, transforming a Welsh navigator into a Paris shopkeeper, a Scots mechanic into a Grenoble schoolmaster.

Madeleine navigated her way through a maze of uncertainty, trusting and untrusting in equal parts, reassuring the children in her care, distributing money and gratitude to those who agreed to hide the frightened youngsters, some in attics and barns, one small boy in a church steeple and another in the basement of a village library. She seized on any available locale as long as her children were safe.

Her only fear was her awareness that her hearing was steadily deteriorating. She relied increasingly on reading lips and asking those who spoke to her to repeat themselves, pretending inattention.

"Sorry. I wasn't really listening," she said again and again.

"Too much noise. Could you speak louder?" she asked in a strategic meeting held in a room too close to a heavily traveled roadway.

She did not want her Résistance comrades to fear that her disability might compromise their efforts. And it would not, she assured herself. She would simply be more careful, more observant.

"Let your excellent eyes compensate for your poor ears," the kindly audiologist had recommended.

Remembering that brief consultation so many years ago, she wondered idly if he and his family had indeed reached safety. It was possible, she supposed, to defy destiny with initiative. That, after all, had been her uncle Pierre's belief when he left for America, determined to keep his own family safe. But she could never have made such a choice. France was her home. The daring fight for its freedom was her obligation.

"*Vive la France*," she said loudly, pleased that she could hear the sound of her own voice.

It had long been a Dreyfus family custom to celebrate the arrival of a new year together. It was Simone who suggested that she and Madeleine follow tradition and spend the last day of 1942 with their grandmother.

"Grand-mère must be very lonely," Simone said. "Serge will be traveling, and I do not want to be alone."

Madeleine nodded. She understood that Simone, ever sensitive to her sister's every mood, her every thought, had in fact perceived Madeleine's own loneliness. There had still been no word from Claude. His absence was ominous, his silence frightening. Madeleine did not tell her sister that she felt herself to be beyond loneliness. She had drifted into the season of terror.

"Of course. Let us go to Valence," she agreed, grateful for the distraction of the journey, eager for her grandmother's comforting embrace, her reassuring serenity.

Lucie Dreyfus, her pale skin papery, her thinning silver hair swept into a neat chignon, embraced her granddaughters, her blue eyes glinting with sapphire brightness. Isolated and alone, despite the attentiveness of the kindly nuns, she hungered for news of the family.

The sisters, speaking too rapidly and coating their words with an assumed optimism, assured her that everyone was safe and well. They told her that their mother had received a letter from Pierre, who was traveling across the United States pleading the cause of the Jews of Europe. Eleanor Roosevelt herself had offered assistance, he had written. The mayor of New York, Fiorello La Guardia, had pledged support.

"Pierre can be very persuasive," Lucie said proudly, and glanced at the framed photograph of the son whom she knew she might never see again.

Simone did not speak of Serge's disappointment that Pierre made no mention of petitioning President Roosevelt to bomb the railroad lines leading to Auschwitz. She did not want to cast aspersions on Pierre's efforts, nor did she want Lucie to learn about the fate of Jews sent to Auschwitz in the cattle cars that rattled their way across the steel arteries of the besieged continent. Instead, she spoke of their family's efforts to resist, of the clinic Pierre Paul had established in their rue de la Dalbade home, her forgeries and Madeleine's work with children in need of refuge.

Determined to amuse Lucie, Madeleine contributed anecdotes about her brother Etienne's newly acquired juggling skill, her small niece's progress at the underground school established by the Résistance, and her own culinary failures as she tried to prepare meals in Simone's cluttered kitchen.

"I almost poured the dyes Simone was boiling for her rubber stamps into my soup," she said.

"It might have improved the taste," Simone added, and they laughed as they sipped the weak coffee and nibbled the dry, sugarless biscuits a shy novice offered. The war briefly forgotten, they were, for that precious moment, simply a grandmother and two granddaughters enjoying a relaxed and intimate evening hour.

"I remembered to bring you the Résistance newspapers, Grand-mère," Madeleine said. "I managed to get both *Défense de la France* and *J'Accusé*."

Lucie reached for them gratefully.

"*J'Accusé*," she murmured. "The very title Emil Zola used in his appeal on your grandfather's behalf."

"The paper is well named," Madeleine said. "We too make accusations. Against the Germans. Against Pétain and Vichy. Against those who will not help our people."

"Yes. *Nous accusons.* We all accuse," Lucie said as she scanned the lead article. They could not protect her from the news that two thousand Jewish children had been sent east in sealed cattle cars. The attached editorial, addressed to French mothers, was both plea and accusation. It was a passionate plea stating that "these horrors happened with the complicity of the French government collaborating with those who hold our people hostage… Do not by your silence become accomplices of these murderers."

The message, which Madeleine had helped to draft, had been designed to encourage French mothers to hide Jewish children. Very few French mothers had actually answered the call, but even a few was better than none.

As the darkness deepened, Lucie served wine made from the pale-green grapes cultivated in the convent's small vineyard.

"The Nazis cannot prevent grapes from blossoming," she murmured, turning to the window that overlooked the vines, barren now and trembling in the wintry breeze.

Simone laughed but Madeleine offered no response.

Lucie looked at her searchingly.

"Did you not hear me, Madeleine?" she asked, speaking loudly now and leaning close so that Madeleine could read her lips.

"Now I can hear you, Grand-mère," she said, her affirmation a reluctant admission.

"Has your hearing grown worse, *ma chérie?*" Lucie asked.

Madeleine nodded, relieved to answer honestly.

"A little worse, I think. I am not surprised. It was bound to happen. The audiologist I consulted warned me that such worsening might result from tension."

She glanced at Simone, who nodded in helpless agreement. Tension never left them. It accompanied their every breath, their every thought, their every movement.

"You must be very careful," Lucie warned, her voice gentle but her words laced with fear.

"I try," Madeleine replied, but her own words were lost to her. Only weeks earlier she could hear the sound of her own voice, but slowly, almost imperceptibly, that ability had faded. How much time did she have, she wondered, before she would be surrounded forever by a wall of silence? She trembled.

Simone gripped her hand, and they sat quietly in the circlet of lamplight, the lingering taste of the wine sweet upon their tongues.

Madeleine, grateful for that gentle pressure, turned to Simone. She saw, with a burst of joy, the new radiance of her complexion. Of course. Simone was pregnant. That certain knowledge both startled her and filled her with pride. Simone and Serge, who fought death and confronted danger every day of their lives, had the courage to bring a new life into the world. They defied the darkness of the present, never losing faith in the brightness of their future. She smiled at her sister who smiled back, a wordless exchange that confirmed their secret sharing.

There was a sparse dinner, and once again they sat together in the tiny salon, talking softly, trading memories, telling stories as the convent bells tolled away the last hours of 1942 in melodic tintinnabulation.

"I am not sorry to see this sad year end," Lucie said.

They nodded in agreement. It had been a year of darkness and defeats, of familial separations and the horrors of Vél d'Hiv, a year of desperate days and lonely nights.

Somewhere in the building, the benevolent Sisters of Valence sang hymns to the newborn year, their voices sweet with hope, vibrant with faith.

Ten o'clock. Eleven o'clock. The bells tolled. Lucie refilled their wineglasses and reached for the calendar on the small table beside her chair. Twelve o'clock. The bells rang out. The nuns' voices soared with heartbreaking tenderness. She tore off the last page. 1942, with all its sadness, had ended. She held the calendar up. They stared at the picture of an angel holding a banner that read *January 1943*.

They stood and raised their glasses.

"To the New Year," Lucie said. "To 1943. May it bring peace."

"Peace!" they echoed as the voices of the nuns grew stronger. "Shalom," they added in a whisper.

"Hallelujah!" the nuns sang in loving chorus.

"Hallelujah," the three Jewish women echoed in unison and drank deeply, hands linked, eyes locked in love.

TWENTY-FIVE

ANUARY BROUGHT A BLIZZARD THAT TRANSFORMED Toulouse into a gleaming white fortress. Ice coated every road, rendering the city isolated and inaccessible. Phone lines were dead. Mail could not be delivered. Madeleine was oddly grateful for the wintry siege. It spared her the disappointment of Claude's continuing silence. The Milice and the Vichy police avoided the icebound streets, which meant that she could safely remain for consecutive nights in her parents' home. But very late one evening, someone knocked lightly, perhaps too lightly, on the door of the rue de la Dalbade apartment, and Madeleine was gripped by fear. Her father motioned the family to remain silent as he opened the door to allow the merest sliver of light to slide through from the hallway.

"Who is it?" he asked, but there was no answer.

A white envelope was pressed into his hand, and they heard the sound of steps retreating hurriedly down the stairwell. Madeleine went to the window and saw a man jumping into a lorry, its heavy tires already plowing silently down the icebound street. It was, she knew, a vehicle from the motor pool accessible to Résistance fighters. Her heart stopped. Such transport was used only by daring nocturnal messengers who relayed the news of a Résistance fighter's injury, arrest, or death to his family.

Claude, she thought. *Claude is lost. Claude is dead.*

Dizzy with fear, she remained frozen at the window as her father held the envelope out to her. She opened it, removed the single sheet of paper. She stared at it and recognized Claude's distinctive handwriting. Weak with relief, she sank into a chair and read it through.

It was brief. He had to write quickly, he explained, because a courier would be driving a lorry through Toulouse, and this was a magical opportunity to tell her the good news. He himself would be arriving in Toulouse within the week.

"I could not contact you earlier because I was unavoidably detained," he wrote cryptically.

She thought that might mean that he had been arrested. Why? How had he escaped? Was he still in danger? She was flooded with suppositions, atremble with fear. Could he be "unavoidably detained" again?

Let him come soon, very soon, she prayed silently.

He had signed it *avec amour*, "with love." *Love.* How foolish her anger at his absence, his silence. How unworthy her sadness. How treacherous her dreams. His life was not his own. His fidelity, his allegiance, like hers, was to the Résistance. How could she have been so selfish, so self-involved, to descend into a dangerous melancholy, to doubt him, to doubt herself? He would come soon. They would be together. That would be enough.

It was Serge who told her the next day that Claude would be meeting with Robert Boulloche, the head of the Résistance throughout the Unoccupied Zone. Serge himself would be joining them at the Toulouse Résistance headquarters.

"Boulloche," Jeanne Levy murmured. "Our family knows that name. His father, Judge Boulloche, advocated for my father during *l'affaire*."

"Isn't it strange that Grand-père's story recurs now and again? It casts a shadow across history as we are living it," Madeleine observed.

"Not a shadow. A light," Simone countered.

"Yes. A light," Madeleine agreed.

The thought comforted her.

Claude arrived on a morning when sunlight at last broke through the gray skies that had canopied Toulouse since the onset of winter. He and Madeleine clasped hands and stared skyward. They saw the new brightness as a happy omen, and they spent a joyous day following the sunlit path that bordered the Garonne. Those brief hours were an enchanted respite from the anxiety they had suffered during the long weeks of their separation. He did not speak of the dangers he had faced, of the evil he had seen. She did not speak of the darkness of her dreams, of the fear in her heart.

The optimistic owner of a small riverside café had placed a table in a ribbon of pale sunlight, and they lay claim to it. They ordered croissants and bowls of café au lait and ate very slowly, pretending that their world was one of peace, that sharing a meal at a sunlit table was an ordinary event rather than a wintry miracle.

"Perhaps we will come here again tomorrow," Madeleine said wistfully.

Claude nodded but they both knew that another span of carefree hours was unlikely.

His stay in Toulouse was punctuated by urgent meetings at which agreements were forged to coordinate the efforts of diverse groups. The Éclaireurs Israélites, Combat, Sixième, and the Maquis would be integrated into one united Résistance dedicated to undermining the German occupiers and their Vichy puppets.

It was understood that time was of the essence. Vichy collaborators were moving with terrifying swiftness. Paris was newly ruled by Kurt Lischka of the German Security Police, a brutal commandant responsible for deporting Jewish prisoners to Auschwitz. With merciless zeal, he had unleashed the dread Sicherheitsdienst, Gestapo-trained operatives, on a defenseless Jewish community paralyzed with fear. Men, women, and children, the aged and infants in arms, were herded into cattle cars and beaten with truncheons, their belongings wrenched from their hands. Résistance leaders knew that the horrors taking place in Paris would soon sweep through Toulouse and every other city in the Unoccupied Zone. Escape routes through the Pyrenees would have to activated sooner rather than later.

Madeleine and Claude were sharing a meal with Simone and Serge when an encrypted message from Brussels was transmitted. Serge deciphered the code and turned to them, his face grim, his voice a monotone of sadness.

"The Gestapo made a series of arrests. Résistance prisoners were tortured in the Fresnes Prison. Some poor creature, who knew what he should not have known, talked. The Germans now know about our Comet escape route through the Pyrenees.

It is totally compromised. They have already posted sentries and established checkpoints. We can no longer use it."

Madeleine stared at him in disbelief. The Comet escape line was the route through which she had hoped to lead her children. All their months of planning had been wasted. A new escape plan would have to be devised, a near impossible undertaking given the increased vigilance of the Milice, that brutal French military unit known to execute anyone who harbored a Jew. Milice operatives had invaded a farm near Castres only a few nights earlier and shot an elderly farmer and his invalid wife who had hidden a Jewish boy in their barn. The child had been arrested, beaten, and sent to Drancy. She shivered to think of what the Milice might do if they intercepted the contingent of children she thought to guide to freedom. What if Anna were to fall into their hands? *Anna!* The child's name came to her unbidden. What would they do to her Anna?

Sensing her fear, Claude drew her close. He spoke slowly, enunciated clearly. Her eyes were riveted to his lips.

"It will be all right," he assured her. "There is another route. More difficult but manageable. We will make our way through the Irati Forest to Pau, and we will then be only thirty miles from the Spanish border."

"*We?*" she asked.

"*We.* You and I. Leading the children together. Yes. I will do everything I can to make that happen," he said.

Serge nodded.

"It is possible that you and Claude can work together," he agreed. "We will try to make it probable."

Madeleine breathed deeply. If Claude was with her, all her

fears would disappear. He had promised to do whatever he could to make that happen. She repeated his words and Serge's reassurance to herself. She fought back her tears as he smiled at her and took her hand in his own, caressing each of her very cold fingers until warmth returned to them.

"We must all be very careful," Serge warned.

That need for caution was paramount as the news grew more and more ominous. Thirty Jewish children who had been hidden in an orphanage in Marseille were seized and deported to Sobibor. In that dread camp, they were almost certainly sent to the gas chambers, their fragile bodies incinerated in the crematoria. It was said that the smoke rising from the chimneys of Sobibor obscured the light of the sun and darkened the moon.

Lucie Dreyfus learned of the fate of the children. She wrote that she had lit a candle for them and said Kaddish. The compassionate Sisters of Valence sang a requiem mass in their memory.

The voices of the nuns were sad and beautiful. They wept as they sang, she wrote to Madeleine and Simone.

The sisters turned to each other, repeated her words aloud, and like the nuns, they too wept but they could not sing. Their voices were stilled by sorrow.

Claude's brief stay in Toulouse came to an end. He would soon leave on another secret mission, but he and Madeleine were determined to snatch a few precious hours of togetherness.

"Just a few normal hours," Madeleine said. "A meal, perhaps in a bistro where there are linen cloths on the tables."

"White cloths," he agreed. "And we'll share a bottle of wine."

"*Vin blanc*," she insisted, smiling, although they knew that the Germans had plundered every wine cellar in Toulouse leaving only *vin ordinaire* that tasted of vinegar. But of course they would settle for that and consider themselves fortunate.

They went to a quiet bistro on the rue de Peche and, as was their habit, sat at a table near the door, so that they might exit swiftly if they sensed any danger. A guitarist strolled through the small room, singing very softly. They swayed to the rhythm of the gentle melody and tried to remember the words to his song.

"*Je ne regrette rien.* I regret nothing."

Madeleine sang along, having at last retrieved a single verse, grateful that her hearing loss had not impeded her memory.

Suddenly, without warning, all serenity was shattered by the blaring horn of a Citroën Traction Avant, the official Gestapo vehicle. It had been parked just outside the bistro, and two Milice officers stood guard beside it. A Gestapo commander, the wintry sun glinting on the death's head emblem affixed to his epaulettes, emerged, bullhorn in hand, and shouted an edict in harshly accented French. His oppressive voice was loud enough for Madeleine to hear him without difficulty.

"All Frenchmen between the ages of eighteen and twenty are to report at once to precinct authorities. Under the new order, Service de Travail Obligatoire, you have been granted the privilege of working in Germany for a period of two years. This is mandatory. No exemptions. This is the order of Márechal Pétain himself. Failure to report for service to the Führer will be severely punished by the Márechal!"

Pedestrians stood frozen in silence. Shopkeepers shuttered

their windows. A woman hung the tricolored flag over her doorway.

"*Vive la France! Vive de Gaulle!*" she shouted.

"*Vive la France! Vive de Gaulle!*" Isolated voices on the street echoed her words.

A Milice officer moved toward her, his truncheon raised threateningly, but the German commandant shook his head.

"We don't want a riot. Ignore the Bolshevik anarchist bitch."

Events on the rue de Peche were clearly visible through the large glass windows of the bistro. The diners stared at each other, shocked into silence, their wineglasses lowered. Cutlery clattered to the floor. The proprietor lowered the window shades and the guitarist played "La Marseillaise." Madeleine, Claude, and the other patrons stood and sang as though their hearts would break.

"*Allons enfants de la République—le jour de gloire est arrivé...*"

The Citroën rolled on, its horn bleating, the red-and-black swastika banner and the French tricolor fluttering from its antenna in an obscene twinning.

Madeleine turned to Claude.

"Two years. They will conscript our boys for two years. Two years as slave laborers. They will take my brothers. Jean Louis. And perhaps Etienne."

Tears flooded her eyes, bile rose in her throat. She feared that she would vomit out her despair and hatred.

"Madeleine, my Madeleine."

His gentle voice calmed her. Determination replaced anguish. She would not allow her brothers to be sent to Germany. She had resources. She knew about hiding places.

She had confederates. She and Claude, Simone and Serge would keep Jean Louis and Etienne safe.

"We must save my brothers," she said.

"Of course we will save them. They will not go to Germany. We will protect them. We will protect as many of our boys as we can." He spoke directly into her ear, his breath soft, each word clearly heard.

Claude left Toulouse that same evening. A delay of even a few hours would be dangerous. Etienne and Jean Louis Levy sat beside him in a battered auto that carried a Vichy license plate. They all wore jackets stolen from Milice officers who had made the mistake of getting drunk in a bar owned by the mother of a Maquis fighter. They each carried identity cards and *Ausweises*, passes issued by the Gestapo, which Simone had hurriedly forged and thrust into the oven to hasten the drying of the ink used for her elegant calligraphy.

Madeleine kissed her brothers and pressed packets of sandwiches wrapped in greased paper into their rucksacks. She tried not to weep, but stray tears escaped her eyes.

"Do not worry, Madeleine," Jean Louis said. "We will see you soon. Very soon. The Americans are in the war, and they will soon bring it to an end. The *Défense* reported that Churchill and Roosevelt sent a telegram to Stalin assuring him that they will bring Germany to her knees in 1943. And this is 1943."

His angular young face radiated optimism. She would not tell him that the *Défense*, a newspaper published by the Free French, was often overly optimistic for propaganda purposes. She would not extinguish his hope with her fears. She wanted to believe him. She willed herself to believe him.

"Yes. This is 1943. This is the year it will end," she agreed.

She and Claude stood together, their faces turned to each other, his hand on her shoulder.

"Take care of my brothers," she said.

"I will. And you, *chérie,* take care of yourself. Be careful. Very careful."

"Do not worry, Claude."

Her voice was strong, reassuring, his parting embrace tender, but they dared not meet each other's eyes.

Madeleine remained alone until his car turned the corner. Only then, as she walked to the nearest safe house, did she allow herself to weep. She wondered if her tears would morph into slivers of ice as they coursed relentlessly down her cheeks.

TWENTY-SIX

WEEPING WINDS HAUNTED THE EARLY DAYS OF FEBRUARY. Snow fell, blanketing the roads with glittering and treacherous frost. Unable to ride her bicycle, Madeleine trudged on foot or, reluctantly, drove one of the Secours National cars. Frigid air permeated every home in Toulouse because all available coal heated German barracks and offices. Any surplus fuel was shipped to Berlin.

I do not think I will ever be warm again, she wrote to Claude. It was a letter she would not send. She had no address for him. Still, she filled page after page, easing the heaviness of her heart with the words that she yearned to share with him.

France remained under siege but the Résistance was heartened by news of distant events. The Allies had consolidated their hold on North Africa, and before February ended, the German endured a defeat in the battle for Stalingrad. The war was turning, Simone and Madeleine assured each other.

"We must celebrate," Simone insisted.

Madeleine offered a farmer ration coupons from Simone's stock of excellent forgeries in return for a very scrawny chicken. Simone transformed it into a tasty stew, Serge produced a bottle of *vin ordinaire*, and they held a celebratory dinner at which they toasted the Allied victory and dared to become slightly drunk.

"The road to peace is open. Russia has rid herself of the Nazis. France will soon be rid of *les Boches, à la victoire*," Serge shouted. "To victory!"

"*À la Victoire!* To Victory!"

The voices of the small group of Résistance fighters resonated with hope. Serge played his balalaika, and the tiny room was suffused with the laughter of slightly drunk dancers happily bumping into each other, newly certain that victory and peace would soon be theirs.

Madeleine sipped her wine and wondered where Claude was. There had been no word from him for weeks. Her brothers, she knew, were safe. A Gentile friend of her father's had hidden them in the attic of his home, but Claude once again was mysteriously and disturbingly silent. She conditioned herself against pessimism and stared hopefully at the door. She imagined him entering the crowded room, imagined him sweeping her into his arms, imagined the warmth of his body pressed against her own as they danced. She stared at the dregs of wine in her glass and sat back, sadly aware that her tender imaginings were unlikely to ever morph into reality, but still, they comforted her, however briefly.

It was sad, she thought, that she had never danced with Claude. Was a dance too much to ask for? It was even sadder, she reflected, that they had never spent a single night together, that they had never wakened in each other's arms. She shrugged off the regret and replaced it with gratitude. It was enough that their caring friendship had blossomed into a sustaining love, surviving distance and danger. Her dreams would have to suffice.

She smiled at the thought, and rising from her seat, she danced alone, moving with solitary grace to the gentle rhythm of Serge's balalaika.

*

The euphoria over the Allied victories in Russia and North Africa was short-lived. Germany, clearly fearing the opening of a second front, tightened its hold on France and imposed draconian measures against the Résistance. There were summary executions of the families of Résistance fighters. *Rafles* occurred with increasing frequency. Brutal deportations of Jews to the death camps in Poland accelerated, and arbitrary curfews were imposed.

"Hitler cannot decide whether he wants victory for Germany or the extermination of every Jew in Europe," Serge said bitterly.

"He wants both," Madeleine said wearily. "But we will give him neither."

The Résistance fighters persisted, weathering infiltrations, flinching at defeats but never flagging in their efforts or their commitment.

We are like ants, Madeleine wrote to her uncle Pierre. *If you step on an anthill, the survivors of the colony rush to rebuild. And that is what we do. If one cell is betrayed, we organize another.*

Because it was known that all correspondence was read by the Germans, she gave her letter to a courier who would see that it was mailed from Italian-occupied Marseille.

"The time will come when we will not be afraid to mail a letter," she told Anna Hofberg, who had accompanied her to her meeting with the couriers.

"And will there come a time when we can share an ice cream?" the child asked teasingly.

"The time is now," Madeleine said.

Ice cream was, of course, a casualty of the war, but she purchased two oversize waffles, which they munched as they walked back to the Levy home on the rue de la Dalbade. She hugged Anna and, relieved to see that the roadway was clear of ice, she mounted her bicycle and raced through Toulouse to yet another secret meeting.

"I too am an ant," she told herself smiling.

Her responsibilities in the Résistance now included a leadership role in the newly organized BRCA, the awkwardly named Central Bureau of Information and Action, which supplied Allied intelligence units with military information on German positions throughout France. In return, the Allied agents were smuggled into the country by plane, boat, and even submarine to train Résistance members in sabotage techniques and rescue efforts.

Madeleine was one of a small elite cadre charged with coordinating secret operations. Night after night, exhausted as she was after long days of masquerading as a loyal Vichy employee and then snatching a few hours with her troop of children, she crouched in open fields and along the banks of the Garonne to lead newly landed agents to safety. Because of her excellent cover as a Vichy employee, she was assigned to the most dangerous operations.

She was, she boasted to her amused sister, an accomplished actress, donning a variety of costumes for a variety of roles. She spoke in throaty tones to the Milice officers who now and again stopped her. Always cognizant of danger, her jacket open to reveal her tight-fitting bodice, she smiled seductively as she supplied monosyllabic answers to questions that she could barely hear, conscious that her interrogators were more interested in the steady rise and fall of her breasts than the words she spoke. Still, she trembled uncontrollably when she was waved on, relieved to have evaded arrest and imprisonment.

She served as a courier, cycling from one Résistance unit to another, caches of forged documents concealed beneath the hillocks of produce in her paniers.

"Sabotage is our most important weapon," Robert Boulloche, the head of the Toulouse Résistance, told her as he handed her a package deceptively wrapped in gaily patterned paper.

"You must give this to Serge as soon as possible," he said. "It contains important information, including all our plans to deactivate Gestapo phone lines and strike railroads and bridges."

She was both surprised and flattered that he trusted her enough to reveal such closely guarded secrets.

"A strange gift for my brother-in-law," she said hesitantly. "You must know that he and Simone are expecting a child. Such operations are extremely dangerous."

Her words were a warning that she knew he would not heed, but she could not resist the impulse to protect her sister. Of course, Boulloche knew that danger might lead to death. What if Serge were apprehended? What if Simone, now in the late stage of her pregnancy, were widowed for a second time? How would Madeleine herself cope with the death of Serge, whom she had come to treasure as a brother and a protector?

All that was irrelevant, she knew, even as she spoke. Loyalty to the Résistance was their paramount obligation.

"Yes. Such operations are indeed dangerous, but Serge is well prepared, well trained. He is our best operative. We depend on him. As we depend on you, Madeleine. You know what you must do if the Milice or the Gestapo stop you," Robert Boulloche replied.

"Of course," she replied. "I too am well trained, well prepared. I will do what I have done before. I will smile, reach into my pannier and offer the officer a fruit. I will tell him that this package is a birthday gift for my old grandmother. Perhaps I will ask him if he has an old grandmother. Perhaps I will bite into the fruit before I hand it to him, leaving a rim of lipstick." Her voice rose and fell in a flirtatious lilt, her tongue moving slowly across her moistened lips.

She curtsied, her elegant recital ended. She marveled that Robert Boulloche did not hear the rapid beat of her heart, that he did not inhale the scent of her fear.

"What an excellent actress you have become. We have nothing to fear. Who would suspect a beautiful, confident young woman like yourself?"

The Résistance commander grimaced at the absurdity of his own question. They both knew that everyone was suspect, that neither youth nor beauty offered protection when every street and byway was haunted by collaborators.

"We are grateful for your efforts, Madeleine Levy," he said with studied formality, all levity abandoned.

"May I ask if my friend Claude Lehmann is safe?"

She whispered the question and waited tensely for his answer.

"As of today, he is safe," Robert Boulloche replied cautiously. "I wish I could tell you more, but you understand that I cannot."

She nodded, grateful for that small nugget of reassurance. She would have to be content with that.

She rode swiftly to her sister's flat and delivered the package to Serge. He unwrapped it, scanned the documents it contained, and concealed them beneath a kitchen floorboard. Madeleine watched as he hammered it back into place. His task accomplished, he stood, smiled at Simone, and placed his hand gently on the rise of her pregnancy.

Madeleine turned away, shamed by the envy that came upon her as she witnessed that simple gesture. She did not deceive herself. She acknowledged, she envied the sister whom she loved so dearly. She envied Simone because she slept each night in her husband's arms, because she was already a mother and would soon have another child, while she herself lay sleepless and alone on narrow cots, pledged to patience and resigned to loneliness. *Yes*, she thought bitterly, *I am stupidly envious.*

That envy shamed her. It was wrong of her to begrudge her sister the comfort of her husband's touch, her child's laughter, the swell of the new life she sheltered. Of course she did not begrudge Simone her happiness. She simply yearned that such small joys might one day belong to her.

"Let me prepare dinner," she told Simone, her offer an apology for thoughts she could not share.

They ate the sparse meal hurriedly, and Madeleine and Serge left to attend a meeting in the basement of a *boulangerie*. An exhausted English engineer, newly smuggled into Toulouse in a parachute drop, instructed a small group of Résistance saboteurs in techniques to be used in the demolition of bridges. His answers to their questions were terse and direct.

Serge, always aware of Madeleine's hearing deficit, took careful notes which he handed to her. Lying awake that night, she committed each instructive phrase to memory, then shredded the flimsy sheet of paper and tossed the fragments from her window. They floated like ghostly snowflakes through the windswept darkness.

TWENTY-SEVEN

THE CHILL OF WINTER LINGERED THROUGH THE EARLY DAYS of spring. Tensions rocketed as new fears erupted. Sabotage operations by Résistance units proliferated. German trucks exploded, fires broke out in the billets of the Vichy police, Molotov cocktails were tossed at Milice patrol cars. The Gestapo responded with draconian measures, declaring that for every German soldier killed or wounded, ten Résistants or innocent citizens would be put to death. Their threats were ignored. The Résistance continued the programs of sabotage, and collaborators continued to play sycophant to their German masters.

Madeleine heard conflicting rumors repeated in whispers. It was said that a second front would soon be opened. It was said that British planes were flying nocturnal sorties over Brittany. A shopkeeper reported that plans for a second front had been abandoned. An editorial in *Le Matin* speculated that Roosevelt was focused on the war in the Pacific and uninterested in the European theater. Hope and despair did battle with each other, rising and falling with each conflicting newscast.

Children taunted schoolmates, spouting their parents' conflicting ideologies. Neighbors were estranged, families divided. Distrust shadowed every household, poisoning friendships, creating unease between lovers.

Over dinner one evening, Madeleine's father spoke of an incident at his clinic.

"My very first patient was Guillaume Gerard. You may remember him, Madeleine. He was your brother's classmate."

"Of course I remember him," Madeleine said. "Was he ill?"

She did not tell him that she knew Guillaume well. He was a leader of the Maquis, a demolitions expert and a courageous saboteur who was often at her BRCA meetings. Such information could not be shared, not even with her own father, although he himself was allied to the Résistance and routinely treated her comrades.

"Not ill but badly burned. An accident with explosives. I was able to admit him to the burn unit at L'Hopitale Generale, explaining that his burns were the result of a kitchen fire. Fortunately, Madame Roget, the admitting clerk, asked no questions."

"She wouldn't," Madeleine murmured.

She wondered if her father knew that Madame Roget was a member of the Résistance, although she deliberately wore the Vichy lapel pin of the Battle Ax of Gaul. Perhaps he knew, perhaps he didn't. Deception, Madeleine thought wryly, was the watchword of their times.

"I then rushed back to the clinic where two Milice officers were waiting with a Vichy policeman who had been stabbed by a *Résistant*. The wound just missed the jugular. I sewed him up. Seventeen stitches. It was only nine thirty in the morning, and I had already treated both a comrade and an enemy," he continued and laughed harshly.

"Papa, why must you treat collaborators? Vichy? Milice?" Madeleine asked angrily.

"I am a doctor. I treat anyone who needs my help," Pierre Paul Levy replied calmly.

She blushed, ashamed of her question, ashamed of her anger.

Later that same evening, she glanced out of the kitchen window and noticed a Citroën parked just outside their building. Two men leaned against it and stared up at their apartment. She lowered the shade and dimmed the light.

"Maman, you must be careful," she said.

"I am careful," Jeanne replied. "I rely on Madame Leonie, our wonderful concierge who sees everything and hears everything. We know that the rue de la Dalbade swarms with informants and collaborators. But that is true of every street in Toulouse and probably of every street in every French city. And, of course, although we no longer call ourselves Levy, there are those in Toulouse who know that we are Jewish, and some who also know that I am the daughter of Alfred Dreyfus."

"We worry, Simone and I," Madeleine said.

"Everyone worries. We live in a world of worries," Jeanne replied.

She did not tell Madeleine that she no longer shopped in her own neighborhood. The greengrocer asked too many questions; the butcher's assistant, impoverished and elderly, recorded the comings and goings of residents in a barely concealed copy book. It was known that such scribbling earned her small sums and even the occasional bottle of *vin ordinaire* when she submitted it to the Gestapo.

Strangers lurked, now and again following Pierre Paul when he left for the clinic. Jeanne took circuitous routes when she visited Simone and repeatedly cautioned Anna Hofberg never to speak to strangers. A padlock was affixed to the storage closet that contained her precious inventory of winter clothing. "We are extremely careful," she repeated.

"As we are," Madeleine assured her.

Before leaving that evening, she held Anna close and reminded her to hurry home at the end of each school day.

Daffodils blossomed in April, pushing their way up through the dark, rain-soaked earth. Sunlight spangled the city streets and the pathways of the countryside. The comingled scents of jasmine and lilac filled the air. Golden forsythia grew in profusion along the banks of the Garonne. Madeleine, indifferent to the Vichy squad cars with their screaming sirens that sped past her, paused to watch the laden branches sway in the gentle breeze.

Housewives flung open their windows, washed their curtains, waxed their floors, beat their rugs so fiercely that dust motes danced through the sunlit air. War or no war, the homes of Toulouse would sparkle for Easter, for Passover.

A group of Jewish women gathered each day in the kitchen of the synagogue on rue Palapret to bake matzoth for Passover seders. Madeleine thought it amusing that this was the year that her self-proclaimed secular parents had decided to host the holiday dinner.

"It seems that Nazi hatred has inspired your parents with a love of their Judaism," Serge said drily.

"Better late than never," Simone retorted, flashing her husband a conspiratorial smile.

The sisters helped their mother prepare the food, following Lucie's recipes for the Alsatian delicacies served at Dreyfus family seders in Mulhouse.

If you want to eat the seder foods of your childhood, come to Toulouse for the holiday, Madeleine wrote to Claude.

She gave the letter to a courier, but she knew that it was doubtful that Claude would receive it and even more doubtful that he would manage the journey to Toulouse. Résistance fighters, newly arrived from Nice, reported that the Germans had increased their surveillance of even minor roadways. Travel to the south would be extremely hazardous.

"But even the Nazis could not prevent anemones from blossoming so early in the meadows of the Riviera," the same courier said. "Never before have they appeared so early in the season."

"Perhaps they hurried to bloom because they were afraid the Germans might invade and trample them. Or perhaps because they are wise flowers and understood that it was important that they come to life in time for Passover so that they might decorate the seder table," Simone commented without looking up from the identity card she was forging.

"I wonder if I'll ever see an anemone again," Madeleine said wistfully. She had always loved the velvet-petaled crimson flowers.

Serge smiled.

"Perhaps you should look on your bed," he said.

"My bed?" she repeated and hurried into the alcove where Simone always had a cot made up for her. A small bouquet of anemones lay on the thin pillow, a note nestled amid the scarlet petals.

Pour toi, Madeleine, she read and her heart soared. Claude's handwriting. Was it possible that he was actually here in Toulouse? She closed her eyes, pressed the fragrant bouquet to her breast, and turned to the doorway. Unseeing, she felt his presence. Unhearing, she imagined his voice. Moving blindly she glided across the floor and stepped into his outstretched arms.

"I have come for the foods of my childhood," he said, holding her close, breathing each word into her ear so that not a single syllable was lost.

Walking hand in hand toward her parents' home, he spoke more seriously and explained that it was a special assignment that had bought him to Toulouse.

"I am here because the current of the war has shifted and the priorities of the Résistance must also change," he said gravely. "Especially for those of us who are involved in child rescue efforts."

"And of course, especially for Jewish Résistants," she added knowingly, and he nodded.

Like all Résistance leaders she had seen the latest intelligence reports. She knew that Hitler, frustrated by the German defeats in North Africa and Russia, was now focused obsessively on his war against the Jews. Infuriated that the Finnish and Bulgarian governments refused to deport their Jews to his network of death camps, he now threatened Switzerland, demanding that the Swiss close Alpine escape routes or risk his wrath.

"The good Swiss have decided that their fear of the Luftwaffe outweighs their greed for Jewish bribes, or perhaps the Germans have offered them more money than we can raise. We know only that they have made their mountain passes inaccessible to us. A group of Jewish children led by our *éclaireurs* was denied entry at the border just last week. Somehow they did make their way across, but we must now rely only on getting our youngsters to Spain through the Pyrenees. Even there, many of our routes are no longer viable. Still, Toulouse is our gateway, and I have been sent to recruit new couriers and to find new pathways," he said. "We already know of the Irati forest, but there are other possibilities. Our Spanish friends have topographical maps. Their goatherds know how to cross unmarked areas. I have a list of contacts, veterans of the Catalonia battlefield, who are prepared to help us."

"It will be dangerous," Madeleine protested. "Some of the Spanish couriers have already been exposed as double agents. An innkeeper in Pau whom we trusted was secretly working against us and revealing our operations to the Gestapo."

"We know that. I will have enough time in Toulouse to vet the loyalty of every new *passeur*," he assured her.

"How much time?" she asked.

"A week."

She gasped. A week. Seven days. Seven nights. A gift of hours, an expanse of time they had not known since the onset of the war. For seven days she and Claude would be in the same city, walking down the same street, looking up at the same sky. Of course, they would both be working hard, but there would be scavenged moments of shared laughter and ease of touch, a precious togetherness to be sealed and stored in tender memory.

"Then you will be here for the seder," she said, suffused with happiness.

"Of course. For the seder. For the food of my childhood, according to your promise."

He laughed. Pulling her into a circlet of sunlight, he kissed her lightly on the lips.

The Dreyfus women, during that pre-Passover week, concentrated their energies on seder preparations. Jeanne traded cigarette and tobacco coupons for potatoes and onions. Madeleine bartered her mother's embroidered lace collars for a basket of pears, and Simone daringly forged ration cards to be used for the clandestine purchase of kilos of sugar and flour, trays of eggs. Madeleine's face was flushed as she stirred fruit into simmering syrup to prepare the famous Alsatian pear compote that Claude claimed he could taste in his dreams.

A grateful patient presented Pierre Paul with two chickens, and the nuns of Valence gave Lucie a duck.

"For your holiday," the Mother Superior told her and Lucie wept, moved by the enduring goodness and courage of the Catholic sisters.

The comforting scents of the traditional foods of the festival of freedom wafted through the apartment. Soup boiled, poultry roasted, sweet fruit simmered as they stirred and chopped, grinding spices, mixing apples and nuts for charoset, cutting through bulbs of horseradish, grimacing as they sneaked tastes of the bitter root. Their faces, rosy from the steam rising from the stove, their eyes bright with the sheer pleasure of their efforts, they dared to feel the onset of joy.

Madeleine set the table. She spread Lucie's elegant embroidered white linen cloth across the wobbly trestle tables in the Levys' shabby salon. She found a small blue vase for the bouquet of crimson anemones that became their centerpiece. *Vin ordinaire* filled the glasses at each place setting. Anna Hofberg and Frederica arranged the seder plate, happily chanting the name and purpose of each symbolic food.

"Parsley for spring. Shank bone for remembrance. Maror for bitterness."

"Surely we don't need maror this year," Pierre Paul murmured. "We have an ample abundance of bitterness."

"Papa," Simone said reprovingly. "No cynicism. This is meant to be a happy night."

"And so it will be," Madeleine assured her, glancing nervously at the door.

Guests were arriving. Members of the *éclaireurs* who were on Claude's team drifted in, but although he had promised to be on time, he had not yet arrived. Madeleine willed herself to calm. She reminded herself that he had scheduled a late-afternoon meeting with Robert Boulloche, who had a receiver strong enough to receive transmissions from Poland. Jewish Résistance leaders understood that Nazi operations in Warsaw set the barometer for what might happen in France. It was important to monitor those distant events carefully.

There was no danger in Claude's meeting, Madeleine assured herself. Robert Boulloche, the Résistance leader for the entire province, had excellent security. Perhaps the newscast had been delayed. Still, she was unnerved by Claude's lateness. As he himself often reminded her, danger lurked everywhere in Toulouse.

Battling her anxiety, she went into her parents' bedroom and peered at herself in her mother's long mirror, smiling approvingly at her own reflection. Simone had trimmed her long, dark hair so that it fell in thick silken swathes about her shoulders. The spring sunlight that brushed her face as she cycled through the countryside had burnished her skin to a rose-gold glow. Glints of green danced in her hazel eyes, and her floral-patterned cotton dress clung to her body in soft folds.

"Madeleine, we are beginning the seder," her father called, and she turned away from the mirror and went into the dining room. She slipped into the seat Simone had saved for her. The empty chair next to her own was reserved for Claude.

"Where is he?" Simone whispered.

Madeleine shook her head and willed herself to calm, although her palms were damp and biliousness soured her throat.

"He'll be here soon," she assured her sister although her own thoughts spiraled, fear alternating with hope.

He had to come. Why had he not come? He would come. He was safe. He could be in danger. No. Of course he was only delayed. Traffic. A punctured tire.

She sat quietly as Lucie Dreyfus lit the candles and recited the benediction over the flickering flames. She added her voice to their small chorus of gratitude as they intoned the traditional prayer of thanksgiving that they had reached this hour of celebration.

"*Shechiyanu, v'higyanu, v'kimanu l'zman hazeh*. We have been supported and sustained to reach this happy day." Their voices rose in grateful unison.

Song filled the room. The four questions were asked, the children's lyric sweetness pierced their hearts. The adults nodded sadly.

Yes, they agreed silently, this night was different from all other nights even as this year was different from all other years, and this war was different from any other war. The song of ancient explanation began, but Madeleine was silent, her gaze never leaving the door, willing it to open, willing Claude to enter.

"We were slaves unto Pharaoh in Egypt," they sang but their voices froze into silence. With force and suddenness, the door was flung open and Claude, his brow beaded with sweat, his eyes burning, his face pale, strode into the room.

"Warsaw," he gasped and they stared at him in fear and bewilderment.

All gaiety vanished. Something had happened, they knew. Something terrible.

"The radio. Turn on the radio," he thundered and stumbled toward the empty chair beside Madeleine.

Madeleine, her heart pounding, held a glass of wine to his lips, stroked his cheek, felt its burning heat as though his very flesh had been seared by misery.

Jeanne hurried into the kitchen to retrieve the hidden radio and placed it on the seder table. Serge connected it and raised the fragile antenna, turning the dial until he found the frequency that would tell them the truth. They heard the familiar voice of the Free French newscaster, broadcasting at an unscheduled hour, which in itself, they all knew, meant darkness and danger.

"*Ici Londres. Les Française parlent aux Français.* This is London. Frenchmen speaking to Frenchmen."

Mute with fright, they waited for the code. Dot-dot-dot-dash—V for Victory, followed by dot-dot—H for Honor.

"*Vive l'honneur*—long live honor," they murmured as the introductory notes of Beethoven's Fifth sounded. Another code. They braced themselves as the newscaster spoke, his voice rising and falling in the cadences of grief.

"This is an emergency broadcast that will be repeated every hour on the hour. There has been a tragic turn of events. The Warsaw ghetto is surrounded by the Waffen-SS. German tanks are plowing through the streets, shooting methodically, the barrels of their guns aimed at every doorway, every window of the Jewish quarter, hospitals and schools alike. Houses and factories are burning. Sirens and screams, a chorus of terror, sound throughout the ghetto. The Nazis use their powerful weapons, machine guns and howitzers, on the ghetto fighters. They herd defenseless women and children into trucks." The announcer paused, his voice breaking.

Lucie Dreyfus clasped her hands in prayer, but only a sob escaped her lips. Tears streaked Jeanne's cheeks. Serge clenched his fists, and Simone held a finger to her trembling lips as the newscast continued.

"But the Jews of Warsaw are fighting back. Yes, the brave Jews of Warsaw are fighting back. They throw their handmade grenades at invading tanks. They pour buckets of boiling water onto patrolling soldiers. Molotov cocktails sail through the air.

Yes, the ghetto fighters struggle *avec courage, avec espoir*, with courage and with hope."

His voice was choked with sorrow. In London, the announcer for the Free French radio service, in contact with his Polish counterpart, wept for the Jewish fighters, the embattled Jewish martyrs of the Warsaw ghetto.

Claude clutched Madeleine's hand and she, in turn, placed her arm protectively around Anna Hofberg's quivering shoulders.

"I don't want to hear any more," Anna whispered.

But there was no more to be heard. The radio emitted a burst of static and was silent. Reception had ceased. It was possible that the Vichy police had honed in on their transmission signal and jammed the line. If the signal was traced to the Levy apartment, they would all be arrested. Swiftly, Pierre Paul unplugged the radio and thrust it back into its kitchen hiding place.

"Tonight Warsaw. Tomorrow Paris. Then Toulouse," he muttered bitterly and returned to the table where the family sat blanketed in sadness until Lucie's trembling, sweet voice broke through.

"We were slaves unto Pharaoh in Egypt," she sang, her voice growing stronger as she continued, "but we were delivered with a mighty hand and an outstretched arm."

One by one, they added their voices to hers and chanted the ancient chronicle of the triumph of hope over despair, freedom over slavery. This was a night when their remembered history sustained them. They had, in generations past, escaped catastrophe. Hitler, like Pharaoh, would be defeated. On this seder night, the Jews of Warsaw were fighting back, resisting. The Jews of France would do no less. Résistance to evil was their credo, their pledge.

Their hearts were heavy but their voices gathered strength. They continued reading the Haggadah. They laughed as the Hebrew was mispronounced, as red wine formed circles of stains on the white cloth, as serious answers were given to foolish questions. They grimaced as they ate the bitter herb. They swirled sprigs of parsley in salt water and fed them to each other. The food was served and complimented. "Such wonderful soup." "Such delicious chicken." "Such succulent duck."

Madeleine ladled the compote onto Claude's plate.

"The food of your childhood," she reminded him and he, tasting its sweetness, slowly emerged from his melancholy. He smiled.

"Do not be frightened," he said. "We will prevail."

She read his lips, she touched them, as though each word he uttered might be imprinted upon her fingers. What she could not hear, she could feel.

"The Jews of Warsaw are very brave," she murmured.

"As are the Jews of France," he agreed. "As is my Madeleine of Toulouse."

She looked across the table, her eyes resting on Serge, who sat back, his large hand stroking Simone's slender wrist. She thought it wondrous that in this death-haunted world, on a night when the wails of Jewish infants trebled through the Warsaw ghetto, Simone and Serge, daring and optimistic gamblers, awaited the birth of their child with loving tenderness.

Sitting beside Claude, Madeleine willed herself to be a

secret sharer, a committed chaser of their dream. Yes, she dared to believe, to dream, that her sister's unborn child, conceived in a time of raging war, would grow up in a world of peace.

She sipped the last glass of wine and joined in the singing of the final blessing.

"May God who makes peace in the firmament grant peace unto his people. Amen."

Their voices swelled as the candles flickered and slowly burned down, dropping waxen tears onto the wine-stained cloth, canopying the room in a soothing dimness.

TWENTY-EIGHT

CLAUDE LEFT TOULOUSE. THEIR PRECIOUS WEEK OF togetherness was over. He had managed to find new routes, to recruit a new cadre of Spanish guides. He was now assigned to an operation in a distant city, he told Madeleine.

"Where?" she asked although she understood that he could not, would not, tell her.

"But in France?" she persisted.

He did not answer. He lit a Gauloise and blew a smoke ring. He twisted a ringlet of her dark hair about his finger.

"Not Poland?" Her voice trembled.

"No. Not Poland."

That much he could tell her. She breathed a sigh of relief. The scraps of news that drifted in from Warsaw continued to be disheartening. The BBC reported that the ghetto battle against all odds still raged and would, in all probability, continue for several weeks. The Germans were intent on murder and destruction but Jewish resistance continued. Madeleine had heard rumors that Jewish French Résistants might be smuggled into Poland to join the ghetto fighters.

"That is what they say," she told Claude.

"Such rumors are ridiculous," Claude replied tersely. "French Jews are not going to Poland. Robert Gamzon himself has said that it is not our duty to go to the slaughterhouse. It is our duty to escape it. We did not join the Résistance, we did not become *éclaireurs*, to die. We joined to save lives."

She nodded, prepared a packet of food for his journey, and leaned into his embrace as they stood in the doorway of her parents' apartment. He touched her hair, pressed his lips to one cheek and then the other, rested them on the yielding softness of her mouth.

"I will write," he promised.

She did not reply but placed his hand upon her breast, felt its tender pressure, the tactile pledge of his love and her own.

She did not weep until he left the building, until she heard the muffled roar of the engine as he drove the Citroën down the rue de la Dalbade. She did not see which way it turned. It did not matter. Danger lurked in every direction. She allowed her tears to run their course and then returned to her work. There were forms to be filled out, children to be spirited to hiding places. Life would go on. Of that much, at least, she was certain.

April drifted into May. The days grew longer. Warm winds rustled the golden wands of budding forsythia. Madeleine gathered the graceful sprays and bought bouquets to her mother, her grandmother, to Simone. Flowers, as always, brought her comfort, a small relief from the oppressive sadness she felt as the news went from bad to worse.

The uprising in Warsaw ended. The ghetto was in ashes. Seven thousand Jews had been murdered; seven thousand Jews had been deported to Treblinka. The numbers overwhelmed. Memorial candles for the martyrs of Warsaw flickered in the homes of the Jewish Résistance fighters of France.

"*Sept mille*, seven thousand," Simone murmured as she lit a candle, careful to place it out of view of the window. "One memorial candle for seven thousand lives."

"We would need a forest of flames to honor them all," Madeleine said sadly.

She imagined a huge expanse of fire, a conflagration that would incinerate all evil, all hatred. She sighed and saw that a troop of Vichy shock troops, the dread Milice force, was marching robotically down the narrow street. Evil persisted; hatred endured. She stared at the bravely flickering flame of the memorial candle and braced herself for the dark days to come.

And they came. In May. In June. The sunlit days of spring brought only news that grew increasingly dark. As the Germans suffered continual losses, they increased the arrests and deportations, an odd and distorted compensation for their defeats on the battlefield. Venomous attacks assailed the Jews of France. The Résistance responded.

The Jewish leadership in Paris formed an umbrella organization, the Jewish Union for Resistance and Support, which would operate throughout the country. Madeleine and Serge were named leaders of the Toulouse unit. Recognizing the imminent danger to Jewish children, they increased their efforts to spirit the youngsters to safety.

"We must do even more," Serge insisted.

She agreed. Three groups of Jewish youngsters in her roster had already crossed the Pyrenees, following the new routes Claude had mapped out, guided by Basque mountaineers and *éclaireurs* with whom she had worked. She yearned to lead the next such group, which would include Anna Hofberg, who had survived a bout of pneumonia during the chilly days of early spring and was now recuperating. Madeleine was determined to save the small girl, the surrogate sister of her fantasies. But Serge voiced valid objections.

"Anna is not ready," he said. "Her health is too fragile. The other children in her group need more preparation. And you are needed here. Your cover as a Vichy employee is important. No other Jew can cycle through the south with impunity. Your skills are vital. The Résistance family relies on you, Madeleine."

He paused.

"As does your family," he added.

She heard the plea in his voice and knew she had no choice. Of course she would remain in Toulouse. Because of her family. Because Anna was not strong enough for the arduous trek. Because the Toulouse Résistance needed her. And, she admitted, because it was in Toulouse that Claude would find her. It was from Toulouse that he and she, working in tandem, would lead her small group of children across the Pyrenees to freedom. That had been his promise to her. She invoked his words, however tentative, at moments when she felt herself sinking into melancholy.

I will try to be with you, he had said.

"Of course I will stay in Toulouse," she told Serge.

"You are very brave, Madeleine," he said.

"Do I have a choice?"

The bitterness in her voice startled him. He stared at his young sister-in-law and saw the sadness and yearning in her eyes.

"Nor do I," he replied. "Resistance is our only option. There is no other choice. Not for you and me. Not for Simone."

"Or for Claude," she added. The very mention of his name comforted her.

Serge nodded.

"Or for Claude," he agreed.

"You remember that we go to Lyon next week," Serge reminded her and she understood that he wanted to distract her, to prevent her from sinking into the quagmire of dangerous sadness. How kind he was, her gruff and daring brother-in-law, her sister's loving and beloved husband.

"Of course I haven't forgotten," she assured him.

The Lyon meeting involved all regional leaders. It would be a dangerous gathering, made even more dangerous because it had been initiated by Jean Moulin, a Free French official. His courage was legendary. He was Charles de Gaulle's own special envoy, endorsed by Britain's special operations executive, and had been smuggled into France in a covert high-risk operation. His vulnerability made all who met with him vulnerable. The Lyon meeting, fraught as it was with peril, evoked a visceral fear which Madeleine fought with determination. She knew that the journey itself would be hazardous, but her attendance was mandatory. As Serge had reminded her, they had no choice.

Cycling to a safe house beneath a starlit sky, she wished herself away from danger and sacrifice. With the soft night wind brushing her face, she imagined herself safe in Claude's arms.

"Why can I not have even one hour of happiness?" she shouted into the darkness as she cycled ever more swiftly. A light spring rain began to fall, the soft, cool drops brushing her cheeks as though in answer to her plaintive plea.

Their journey to Lyon was, surprisingly, without incident. The meeting convened in the basement of a church, and Madeleine, glancing around the dimly lit room, realized that she and Serge were the only Jews present.

"It does not matter," she told herself. "We are all Résistants, Jewish and Gentile alike."

She tried not to think of the stories that had emanated from Warsaw of non-Jewish partisans who had refused to assist the Jewish ghetto fighters. The French were not Poles, she assured herself and concentrated on Jean Moulin's words.

He was a ruggedly handsome man, charismatic and soft-spoken, at once authoritative and reassuring.

"My base will be the Southern Zone," he said. "But my aim is to unite all Résistance forces throughout France. All. Jewish units and non-Jewish units alike."

His gaze rested deliberately on Serge and Madeleine. There was a murmur of agreement, of approval.

"*Les juives. Les Juives. Nos camarades.*"

Serge and Madeleine relaxed. Jean Moulin nodded, smiled approvingly, but all pleasantness vanished when he spoke of the Nazi regime. He made no effort to conceal his fury at the Nazis' cruelty, his contempt for all they represented.

"They are cowardly, those *doryphores*." He spat the word out, and the assembled leaders laughed at its aptness.

A *doryphore* was the green and greedy potato bug, hated by

French farmers because it devoured their crops. Yes, Madeleine thought, the Nazi occupiers in their despised green uniforms did resemble the vermin of the fields. They would devour all who loved freedom. Thinking of the Nazis as vermin diminished the fear they inspired. She added her voice to the chorus of Résistance leaders.

"*Doryphores*," they shouted and snapped their fingers as though to crush the disgusting beetles that haunted their land.

"Our weapon against the *doryphores* is sabotage. We will exterminate them, deny them life and power, by cutting their communication lines, derailing their supply trains, blowing up their ammunition stores. We will destroy bridges, railroad tracks."

He unrolled one topographical map after another, spreading them across a trestle table. With a pointer, he specified targets in each area of the Southern Zone. When he reached the Toulouse area, Madeleine and Serge leaned forward, their eyes never leaving the unfurled map. Jean Moulin spoke tersely.

"The Toulouse train station must be hit. The police headquarters. But most important of all, the bridges must be destroyed or, at the very least, rendered impassable."

His pointer rested on the Ponts Jumeaux, the three bridges that spanned the banks of the Garonne River—the Pont St. Pierre to the north, the Pont St. Michel to the south, and the Pont Neuf at the center.

Serge and Madeleine nodded. They understood the strategic importance of the bridges. They were essential to German troop movements, the conduit for the convoys of trucks that transported Jewish prisoners from Brens and other internment centers to the cattle cars at the Bobigny depot, that rattled their way to Treblinka and Auschwitz. The destruction, even the partial destruction, of the bridges would deter and, hopefully, terminate the deportation of French Jews to the killing fields of Poland. But they understood, too, how hazardous and fraught with danger any attempt to sabotage the bridges would be.

Serge stood, bent over the map, sighed deeply, and turned to Moulin.

"An attack on those bridges will be difficult, perhaps impossible," he said. "Our city is riddled with collaborators," he continued. "There is a huge Vichy and Milice presence. Informers are everywhere. Our Résistance fighters have little training in sabotage and limited access to *matérielle*. The risk is too great, the outcome too uncertain. I am not sure we can proceed." He spoke slowly, every word etched with regret.

"I know all that, of course," Jean Moulin said. "But you will be well trained. All that is needed for successful demolitions will be supplied. The risk may be great but the outcome will, I assure you, be certain. We, in the Free French, have faith in you, Serge Perl. In you and in Madeleine Levy. You must have faith in yourselves."

He lit another cigarette. Madeleine watched as he blew a smoke ring. The wispy halo drifted lazily through the window-less basement. That playful exhalation relieved her fear. Moulin's confidence, his ease, reassured her. She relaxed, calmed by the certainty he exuded.

"Are you and Mademoiselle Levy prepared to undertake this project?" he asked.

He spoke loudly, clearly, his loudness and clarity aimed at Madeleine, who nodded.

The assembled leaders stared at them expectantly.

Serge glanced at Madeleine. She met his gaze.

"*Oui*," she said, her own voice loud and clear.

"*Oui*," Serge echoed, and Jean Moulin smiled.

"*Bon*. While you are here in Lyon, you will be well trained in the techniques of demolition, the intricacies of explosives. This is knowledge you will share with your comrades in Toulouse, but experience has taught us that an act of sabotage, such as the one we envision for the bridges, is safest when only two well-trained and committed volunteers are involved. You two will coordinate the operation. You will appoint two operatives for each of the other bridges. Not now. Not yet. You will know when to act."

Serge nodded. Moulin's message was clear, his perception accurate. Serge and Madeleine were the designated leaders. Moulin understood that they represented an ideal partnership. They shared a mutuality of commitment. They were brother and sister, their bond sealed by both marriage and affection, their loyalty inbred.

The meeting continued, and when it drew to an end, Jean Moulin approached Madeleine. He leaned toward her, facing her so closely that she read his lips with ease. He enunciated each word clearly. Of course he knew about her hearing deficit. She wondered what else he knew about her.

"Please, Mademoiselle Levy, be assured that you will have everything you need for this important mission. Everyone will be of assistance. We are all dedicated to putting an end to the deportations of your people. The Free French stand firmly with the Jewish Union for Resistance and Support."

He turned to the others in the room, all of whom had

heard his words. Heads nodded. Assent was murmured. Smiles flashed. Madeleine felt a rush of gratitude. They were not alone. The Jews of France had comrades in arms. Jews and Gentiles together, all loyal to the *patrie*, jointly bound by the ideals of *liberté, égalité, fraternité*.

The meeting was at an end. They dispersed slowly to avoid suspicion. Serge and Madeleine were the last to leave, followed closely by Moulin. He touched her arm, drew her aside.

"I bring you greetings from your friend Claude Lehmann. He is safe," Moulin said.

She trembled. Questions raced through her mind, but she knew that they could not be asked.

"Merci," she murmured and followed Serge out. A faint light was trained on the street sign that read rue Juiverie. She smiled bitterly. They stood on a thoroughfare named for a synagogue and a community that no longer existed. How long would any *juiverie* endure in France? she wondered as they walked on.

The next several days in Lyon were spent with a pale engineer. Smuggled in from England at considerable personal risk and speaking in oddly accented French, he taught them the intricacies of booby traps, the advantages of long fuses and short sticks of dynamite, the virtues of petrol and glycerine. They learned the most effective methods of destroying iron rails, of bringing down great spans of bridges. He cautioned them not to be afraid of what he called "collateral damage." There was no guarantee that lives might not inadvertently be lost, but he assured them they were mandated to proceed.

"But we may be killing innocent citizens," a timorous Résistante from Avignon protested.

"Yes, there may be unfortunate deaths, but in the end you will be saving lives," he replied. "It happens in war that a few may be sacrificed to save the many. Compassion is a luxury we cannot afford. Conscience must be shelved until we win the war."

They were not surprised when the Avignon volunteer disappeared from the course.

Each day Madeleine grew more confident. She learned quickly, handling the *matérielle* with a deftness that surprised her. When the course was completed, she and Serge thanked the pale Englishman. He smiled bitterly.

"You have both done well. Consider yourselves accomplished saboteurs," he said. "Au revoir. Bonne chance."

He grasped Serge's hand and kissed Madeleine on both her cheeks.

"A strange graduation ceremony," she murmured to Serge as they began the journey back to Toulouse.

"All will be well," he assured her.

But all was far from well. Simone greeted them with her eyes red rimmed, her hands trembling as she handed Serge a flimsy copy of *Le Ferro*, a collaborationist tabloid.

He recoiled from the damning headline. In bold type and capitalized letters, it screamed out Madeleine's name. He read it and solemnly, reluctantly, handed it to Madeleine. She read it and swayed dangerously, overcome with faintness. She clutched her sister's outstretched hand. She had been betrayed, her identity revealed. The newspaper article placed her in the gravest of danger with the revelation that she was not Madeleine Dupuy, a practicing Christian and a senior social worker in the employ of the Vichy-controlled Secours National, but that she was, in fact, Madeleine Levy, a Jew, a Résistante, an Éclaireur leader. As Madeleine Dupuy, she had been protected from suspicion and arrest. That protection was now forfeit. It was now public knowledge that she was a Jew and a Résistante, an Éclaireur leader.

She read on. The crude reportage was laced with anti-Semitic taunts and Fascist-inspired hatred.

The Jewess who dares not speak her name... She who calls herself Mademoiselle Madeleine but she is Levy—the Jewess Levi—a granddaughter of that infamous traitor Alfred Dreyfus, the screed read.

"Our grandfather is resurrected," Simone said bitterly, and she handed Serge yet another broadsheet known for its crude Fascist orientation. He read it aloud.

"*She calls herself Dupuy but she is Levy—the grand pontiff of the Secours National. Had you missed that point, good Christians? Sweep her out! Sweep her out!*"

He snorted his derision.

"Full of misspellings," he said. "Grand pontiff indeed. What does that even mean?"

Madeleine shrugged. Its meaning was a matter of indifference to her. Her faintness passed, replaced by relief and, oddly, leaving her free of fear. From the very onset of her elaborate masquerade, she had known that she was surviving on sheer luck, that inevitably her true identity would be revealed. Anyone might have betrayed her. The Vichy bureaucrat who had sought sexual favors, the subordinate who had resented her seniority, the clerk whose incompetence she had cited.

She had played her part as best she could but uncertainty had haunted her every hour, every day. Now, at last, she could reclaim her own persona and emerge as Madeleine Levy, a proud Frenchwoman, a proud Jew. Her new vulnerability was her new strength.

"All right. The masquerade is over," she said quietly. "How do we proceed?"

"Much as before," Serge replied. "Simone and I are relatively safe. Vichy intelligence has always known that we are Jewish, but they have not yet decided to identify us as members of the Résistance although they watch us carefully. Simone's pregnancy has, in fact, been an excellent cover. They assume, I suppose, that no couple active in the Résistance, living in fear, would bring a child into the world."

"A pity that I did not become pregnant," Madeleine said and, despite themselves, they laughed. "So what do I do? How do I protect myself?"

"We always knew this might happen," Serge replied, "and we are prepared. You will go underground. We have safe houses throughout Toulouse and in the countryside. In Villefranche and Castres. Simone will prepare a set of documents—a new *carte d'identité*, new ration cards, a driver's license."

He spoke calmly, but his hand trembled as he held a match to the flimsy copy of *Le Ferro*, reducing it to ashes, willing it out of existence.

"The new documents are already prepared," Simone said.

"And our parents? And Anna?" Madeleine asked. "If my identity is known, so is theirs."

"They have already left Toulouse. They are farther south, in the country, staying with a farmer whom I know we can trust. I arranged that while you and Serge were in Lyon. I had to work quickly. When you were unmasked, so were they. It would be known that Maman's father was Alfred Dreyfus and that Dr. Dupuy, he who treats the Gestapo and Vichy bureaucrats, is actually Dr. Levy. In this city of collaborators and double agents, their lives would be in danger," Simone said.

Madeleine marveled that Simone had so swiftly and competently organized their parents' and Anna's escape.

"Our work together will go on. All that we learned in Lyon will be put to use," Serge assured her cryptically.

They could not speak, even to Simone, of what they had learned of what they would undertake, but Simone intuited that her sister and her husband had become skilled mechanics of death. She turned first to Serge and then to Madeleine.

"I understand that you must do what must be done," she said. "Whatever that might be."

Within hours, Serge escorted Madeleine to a safe house on the outskirts of the city. She carried with her only a hastily packed rucksack of clothing and the packet of Simone's expertly forged documents that validated her new identity.

She was welcomed by Edith and Roselle, veteran Résistantes who had been in her Paris *éclaireurs* troop. They embraced her, urged her to eat the food they had managed to prepare, and showed her the small cot hidden behind the false front of an improvised wall where she would sleep when she stayed with them.

"Not every night," Edith said. "There are other safe houses that will shelter you. We must be careful."

"I know," Madeleine said wearily.

The next morning she sat very still as Roselle cut her long, dark hair and then, using a noxious compound, dyed it blond.

"The Milice will be looking for a dark-haired woman," Roselle said. "This will deceive them."

"Hopefully," Madeleine agreed.

She stared at her new self in a mirror.

"Who are you?" she asked her reflection, struggling to recognize the young woman whose sleek helmet of corn-colored hair hugged her head. Would Claude recognize her? Did she recognize herself?

She shook her head, thanked Roselle, and dressed quickly. Discarding her own simple cotton dress, she shrugged into the emerald-green, close-fitting satin blouse and the very short black skirt that Edith handed her. Roselle hung a silver cross around her neck. It dangled on a flimsy chain that fell to the cleavage between her barely concealed breasts.

She shuffled through the documents Simone had prepared and memorized her new identity.

"Say bonjour to Denise Delacroix, nursemaid and aspiring actress," she told her friends. "Let us hope that her chances of survival are better than those of Madeleine Levy."

"You will be fine," Edith assured her even as she and Roselle exchanged worried glances. "Just be very careful, Mademoiselle Delacroix."

"I will try," Madeleine said. "Certainly I will try."

TWENTY-NINE

HER NEW LIFE BEGAN. SHE WAS CONSTANTLY ON THE MOVE, constantly on guard. She avoided all contact with her former colleagues at Secours National and visited Simone very late in the evening, slinking through streets she had once walked fearlessly. She slept in a different bed every night and scurried through darkened lanes and unfamiliar roads for her meetings with Serge and one or another of the newly trained Résistance saboteurs who were her comrades in arms. Like them, she was daring. Like them, she was cautious.

Twice in one week their explosives, set to timed detonators, exploded beneath German ammunition trucks. Madeleine raced away in one direction, Serge in another, disappearing just as Gestapo investigators reached the scene.

She sauntered down the Place Saint-Sernin and was stopped by Milice officers. She smiled at them, passing her tongue across lips reddened with a thick coating of scarlet lipstick, her eyelashes fluttering flirtatiously. Her heart beat rapidly, but her hands were steady as she handed them her *carte d'identité* and affirmed that she was indeed Denise Delacroix, an unemployed actress, now working as a nursemaid for the children of a ranking Gestapo officer.

"You may call him, but he will not appreciate being

bothered," she said. "He is not very pleasant when he is irritated."

It was a story they accepted without question and one which she told with surprising ease.

On another day, after dashing from the scene of the explosion, she approached a Garde Française Jeune patrol to report that she had seen a group of Résistantes running from the scene toward the railway station.

"Merci, mademoiselle," the youths shouted and gave chase as she walked calmly on.

After each encounter, each near escape, she congratulated herself on her good fortune. She was safe and she would stay safe because one day she would live a life blessed with love and serenity.

"Claude, I am waiting," she murmured each night as she struggled toward evasive sleep on a makeshift bed in one unfamiliar refuge or another.

Always, the very utterance of his name comforted her.

"Your friend Claude Lehmann is safe," Jean Moulin had said.

"Claude, stay safe," she commanded in a whisper, although she could no longer hear even the enhanced sound of her own voice. Her deafness, she knew, was proceeding into profundity.

The last days of June were even warmer than usual. Daringly, despite the danger, Madeleine and Simone visited Lucie Dreyfus, carrying with them a basket of plump scarlet cherries that concealed the Résistance journals inaccessible in Valence. The Vichy police had deemed that possession of such newspapers was a criminal act and would be severely punished.

"The absurdity of it," Madeleine said angrily. "The Nazis think that reading a newspaper is a crime."

Simone grimaced.

"Hardly the worst of their sins," she said.

Lucie was delighted with their visit, with the cherries and the newspapers. She led them to the walled garden and they sat on low chaises, grateful for the respite of a pleasant, sun-bright afternoon. Every scavenged hour of peace was precious, given the dangerous present and the precarious future. Madeleine stared down at the poppies, lupines, and daisies that stubbornly thrust their way earthward through the blue and gray flagstones that lined the garden path. The bright blossoms were tenacious as they fought their way into life. She plucked a blue-petaled lupine and smiled. The insistent flowers triggered thoughts of the children in her troop.

The Jewish youngsters were death haunted but life loving. Like the persistent flowers, they lifted their pale faces to the radiant skies and chased each other in joyful play. Their laughter radiated hope. She pressed the blossom to her cheek, taking comfort from its warmth.

Lucie turned to her granddaughters.

"Do not be frightened," she said serenely. "We are in the hands of God."

She touched Simone's abdomen, and at the lightness of her touch, the unborn infant moved ever so slightly.

"Ah, my great-grandchild is welcoming me," she said and Simone and Madeleine laughed. This was a moment they would remember.

Lucie turned the pages of *Liberacion*, the leading Résistance newspaper.

"Not very much news," she commented. "No bombings. Is the Résistance growing weary?"

"A strategic pause, Grand-mère," Madeleine said as she popped a cherry into her mouth.

She could not tell Lucie that she and Serge had decided on a brief suspension of the sabotage program as they readied themselves for the attack on the bridges. Jean Moulin's advice informed their actions. A pause in all sabotage activities would lull their enemies into a false sense of security and offer them a modicum of protection, he had suggested. Madeleine banished all thoughts of future actions and leaned forward so that the sunlight might brush her face. One day, she thought, she and Claude would sit quietly in a circlet of brightness. One day.

But when would that day come? When, when? Perhaps never.

She shivered, shamed by the pessimism of her own thoughts, angry at herself, angry at the dangers of her days and the loneliness of her nights. Still, she summoned a smile as she and Simone prepared to leave, each of them kissing Lucie on her withered cheek and promising to visit again soon. They parted at the gateway to the convent, and Madeleine went on alone to meet with Serge at a safe house on the road to Castres. She dreamed that night that she and Claude followed a ribbon of sunlight as they strolled down an unfamiliar path.

The Gestapo, reacting to the random acts of sabotage, announced what they called "a vast movement of repression," and the Résistance leaders swiftly changed their tactics.

"Moulin is right. Our inaction will catch them off guard," Serge assured Madeleine. "The Gestapo and their Milice collaborators will assume that they have at last frightened us into submission. We will resume operations when they feel confident that they are safe, that their so-called repression has frightened us into suspending acts of sabotage. We must wait for word from Jean Moulin. The order to attack the Ponts Jumeaux must come from him."

"I agree," she said. "But the collaborators seem to be gaining strength. Did you read the editorial in today's issue of *La Dépêche?*"

"I read it. Imagine a Frenchman, once a respected journalist, writing that the actions of the Vichy police should be carried forward with vigor. That bastard. That filthy Pétainist. 'The actions of the police,' indeed." Serge's voice quivered with anger.

"He meant of course 'the actions of the Gestapo.' Vichy, the Milice, the Garde Française Jeune, they are all one and the same. Fascists all. France may be the only nation in Europe to be complicit in its own occupation," she said.

"You go too far, Madeleine," he replied reprovingly. "Not all of France is complicit. There are de Gaulle, the Free French, the Résistance. Think of the mayor of Annemasse who arranged for a group of Jewish children to slip through a barbed-wire fence to safety in Switzerland. Like him, we will fight on against the occupation, against the Nazis. But why has there been no word from Moulin?"

He peered through the grimy window of the safe house, as though willing Jean Moulin to stride up the rutted pathway.

"Serge, go home. Simone is waiting for you. Jean Moulin will contact us when the time is right," Madeleine asserted reassuringly, despite her own fears and uncertainty.

But day after day passed, and Jean Moulin did not contact them. Nor was there any word from Résistance leaders in

Paris and Lyon. All coded transmissions had ceased. No couriers arrived. The *Résistants* of Toulouse felt the chill of abandonment.

During the last week of June, on a night when Madeleine daringly took refuge in Simone's apartment, a haggard Résistance courier stole in through a window at midnight.

Pale and distraught, seated rigidly on a straight-backed chair and clutching a mug of chicory coffee that Simone pressed upon him, he told them that Jean Moulin and eight key leaders of the Unified Résistance had been secretly arrested in Lyon ten days earlier.

"We were betrayed," he gasped. "There are double agents everywhere. Moulin was delivered to Klaus Barbie."

"Klaus Barbie?" They repeated the dread name in unison, their voices faint.

Klaus Barbie, the Gestapo chief in Lyon, was notorious, his cruelty unmatched, his torture methods barbaric. It was said that any prisoner subjected to his inhuman interrogations inevitably revealed whatever information he demanded.

"We are lost," Serge said despairingly. "Jean Moulin knew everything about our operations in Toulouse. He surely revealed all our details to Barbie."

"He revealed nothing," the courier insisted angrily. "Not Jean Moulin. He was a Résistant to the very end, choosing death over betrayal. We know for a fact that he was cruelly tortured and that he died in Barbie's dungeon without answering a single question. You are safe, *mes amis*. But our comrade Jean Moulin is dead."

A tear trickled down his cheek. He closed his eyes, and still seated so rigidly on that straight-backed chair, he fell asleep, the coffee cup falling from his hand and shattering on the hardwood floor.

Simone covered him with a blanket. Not daring to light a lamp, they sat around the table in the darkness and discussed their options.

"Actually, there is only one option," Serge said at last. "We remain the Jewish Union for Resistance and Support. We continue our program of sabotage. We have the names of all Moulin's contacts, the suppliers of *matérielle*, men and women who will assist us when we target the bridges."

"But, Serge, what of the children? We are pledged to rescue one last group," Madeleine asked. "Shouldn't they be our priority?"

The children were, of course, her priority. Her promises to Anna and her small troop of brave and hopeful youngsters were sacrosanct.

Serge nodded.

"Of course the children must be rescued, but that will be possible only if the damn Fascists are in disarray. We must throw the bastards into confusion, explode their fortresses, destroy their confidence. If the Milice and the Gestapo are in full operation, if the convoys of death continue to cross the Ponts Jumeaux, our own position is vulnerable. They will have the manpower to police our escape routes. But with the destruction of the bridges, they will be disorganized, frightened, their focus diverted. And then we can proceed with our plan to guide the children across the Pyrenees to safety. That was Moulin's blueprint, and it must be ours," he said firmly.

"Yes. Of course," she agreed reluctantly.

It was, she supposed, what Claude himself would advise. She wondered if the courier from Lyon, now snoring so gently, knew anything about Claude, but she knew that she could not ask him.

The Résistance operatives moved swiftly, defiantly, through the long days of early summer. The hiatus of restraint was over. The trained saboteurs moved with stealthy expertise and steely determination. The sun burned fiercely, its heat and radiance matched by the noxious fires that blazed throughout the city. The mysterious, destructive conflagrations were accompanied by sudden and deafening explosions. German armament depots were destroyed, many set afire in broad daylight. Others were incinerated in the dead of night. The occupying forces could discern no pattern. Their fire trucks raced from one end of the city to the other, warning bells clanging every hour and adding to the chaos. The odor of cordite mingled with the scent of newly blooming roses. A haze of smoke hovered over the sunlit streets of Toulouse.

The Gestapo, enraged and impotent, pursued perpetrators and witnesses but the citizens of Toulouse, many newly loyal to the cause of the Free French, were stubbornly uncooperative. There were those who reported that they had seen a redheaded woman run from the scene of a demolition. Others maintained that it was, in fact, men on motorcycles, two, perhaps three, revving away from that same scene. Perhaps a youth on a bicycle. No, a gang of boys on bicycles. In desperation and frustration, the Gestapo and their cadre of collaborators responded with roundups, incidents of torture, and random internments, but the sabotage continued unabated.

Madeleine, exhausted but invigorated by the success of the demolitions, moved through the city and the countryside, alternating hiding places and disguises. Each day she played a different role. One day, with her hair concealed beneath a kerchief, her arms balancing baskets, she masqueraded as a mute peasant woman. The next morning, wearing a stylish beret and steel-framed spectacles and shouldering a book bag, she was a graduate student at the Université de Toulouse. Dressed in the shapeless coverall of a cleaning woman, mop and pail in hand, she managed a visit to Simone. The Levy sisters giggled like schoolgirls at her successful deception, ignoring Serge's warning glances.

"As though you even know how to wash a floor," Simone said, laughing as Madeleine danced through the kitchen with the mop as her partner.

Simone, now in the last weeks of her pregnancy, was no less daring than her sister. The string bags she carried to the market each day were filled to the brim with ripe, red tomatoes and glistening purple eggplants, grenades concealed beneath the brightly colored vegetables. She carried back sticks of dynamite, packed between earth-encrusted carrots and stalks of celery. The farmers' barns and silos were, as Jean Moulin had assured them at that Lyon meeting, excellent hiding places for *matérielle*, and the farmers themselves were loyal confederates.

"Not all of them. There are those who are collaborators. We must not grow overconfident. We must be vigilant," Serge warned gravely.

Serge, Madeleine knew, was echoing de Gaulle's messages from London, transmitted through the BBC. The leader of the Free French, true to his military training, constantly emphasized that the Résistance had to follow protocol, a difficult command to obey during the hot summer days of 1943. Without warning, the SS, claiming that French officers had been too lenient, assumed responsibility for the arrests and deportations of Jews and made random and arbitrary arrests.

Terror and fury seized Toulouse as more and more families were victimized. Anger dulled caution. Revenge replaced forbearance. Acts of retribution became daily occurrences. The tires of German vehicles were slashed. Stinking pats of manure were tossed into the doorways of German barracks. French employees filled sugar containers in German military commissaries with salt. They spat into tureens of soup, and a baker whose son had been arrested urinated into a vat of dough. Garbage was hurled into the gardens of collaborators, their windows broken, swastikas chalked across their property. A girl who was known to consort with German officers was thrust into a car and driven blindfolded out to a field in the country where her head was shaved and she was stripped to her under-wear. Half-naked and weeping, she made her way back to the city, where she was scrupulously ignored. Madeleine, encoun-tering her by chance, draped a bedsheet plucked from a clothes-line over the trembling girl and led her to the shelter of the Cathedral of St. Cyprien.

"We cannot behave like the damn Nazis," Madeleine told herself. "We are better than they are."

She raced away as a priest approached the sobbing girl.

Neither the Germans nor the Milice were deterred by what they dismissed as futile acts of mischief.

"Idiots. What they do is of no importance," the German commandant scoffed and ordered that arrests and imprisonment be increased.

But, on a very hot evening, those acts that had been so casually called "mischief" exploded into violence.

The Odeon Cinema on the Grand Boulevard showed *Ohm Kruger*, an anti-British propaganda film, promoted by Goebbels himself. Enthusiastic German soldiers, many of them accompanied by overly made-up and underdressed very young French girls, flocked to the theater. They stood at attention as the swastika flag was raised and sang *"Deutschland über Alles"* in drunken revelry. They applauded wildly as the film ended and saluted each other with *Sieg Heil* salutes as they left the theater, laughing and talking as they swilled beer sold from street carts. Suddenly, one grenade and then another were hurled into their midst.

Panic and chaos erupted. Beer bottles were dropped, revolvers drawn; barrages of ill-aimed shots were fired at rapidly moving targets. Booted feet pounded the Grand Boulevard as enraged and frightened German soldiers, abandoning all their much vaunted discipline, jostled each other in their efforts to escape the scene.

Madeleine, cycling past the cinema at that hour, braked in astonishment. She realized that the barrage of grenades had not been authorized by the Résistance and was certain to incite a draconian reaction by the Gestapo. The perpetrators had been very brave and very foolish. She wondered who they were, and she hoped against hope that they would not be caught. She sought refuge that night at an *éclaireurs* safe house.

Serge arrived the next day, his face grim, his eyes red rimmed, his voice hoarse with fatigue and sorrow.

"They caught the perpetrators, of course. Three boys. Kids. Foolish kids. Brave, I suppose, maybe heroic, but definitely misguided. It was all for nothing. Not a single German was killed, and they were all caught. Only one of the boys was Jewish. Moshe Klausner. Nineteen years old. His parents and young sister were picked up in a *rafle* and deported. He was out of his mind with anger and grief. His little sister was diabetic, and without her insulin, she was probably dead even before the family was herded into the damn cattle cars."

Madeleine and Simone listened in silence, imagining the terror of a child whose life was slowly and painfully ebbing away.

Madeleine thought of Anna, and her heart sank. She had promised Anna that she would keep her safe always. A foolish promise perhaps, but one that she had believed even as she had believed Claude's assurances that, together, he and she would guide Anna and the other children to freedom. His assurance, her promise, were now casualties of the whirlwind of history.

She knew that rescue operations were increasingly dangerous, although daring feats were reported in the Résistance underground intelligence network. Near the Swiss border, Jewish children had been brought to a cemetery dressed as mourners, all of them draped in black veils. They then climbed a gravedigger's ladder, scaled a wall, and scurried to safety in

Switzerland. If only there was such a cemetery near the Spanish border, Madeleine thought wistfully as Serge rested, his large hands covering his eyes. She knew that he was weeping.

"What will happen to the boys they arrested?" she asked quietly.

"It has already happened. Today's edition of *La Dépêche* reports everything," he replied.

He glanced at the newspaper and read out the salient facts.

"There was no trial. They took the boys to the Vichy Interrogation Center on the rue Maignac, and all three of them were shot by a firing squad in the courtyard in full view of anyone passing by. Supposedly that was a lesson to us, a warning. Here is the quote from René Bousquet, the Secretary-General of the Police, his exact words."

Serge read aloud from the Fascist broadsheet.

"'We will crush the terrorist forces, the so-called Résistance.' Bousquet is letting us know that he will be relentless," Serge said, shredding the newspaper and trampling it beneath his feet. "We are forewarned."

"All right. We are warned," Madeleine said drily. "But we continue as before. Is that correct?"

"Yes. As before. But with increased caution."

"Of course. Always with caution," she agreed.

He turned to Simone. Her sister, Madeleine knew, would light three memorial candles for the three youths whose lives had ended that day. If only their deaths had been more purposeful, she thought. If only their rash act had had some small consequence.

I would want my death to mean something. The thought

fluttered unbidden through her mind, and she swiftly amended it. *But I do not want to die.*

She wrote to Claude that evening, another letter that she would not send, pouring out her loneliness, her yearning to see him, describing the fear that clung to her like a gossamer shadow.

It is not that I fear death, she wrote. *But I fear dying without having lived. Without realizing the dream that we shared, days and nights together, holding each other close.*

She folded the flimsy sheet of paper covered with the words that he would never read and went to the window. She held a match to it and watched it disappear into flecks of gray ash that fluttered onto the sere earth below.

THIRTY

J uly passed. August arrived. Despite Bousquet's
ominous warning, the Résistance remained undeterred.
Police officers were ambushed, collaborators exposed, and
acts of sabotage continued unabated. Each daring attack was
executed with great caution.

Madeleine, in her graduate student disguise, used a bolt
cutter concealed in her book bag to sever German communication lines on the road to St. Cyprien. She kicked the dead
wires aside and cycled swiftly away, waving gaily at the German
patrol cars that sped past her as she continued on to a safe house
not far from the banks of the Garonne.

Unsettled and desperate, the Germans and their Vichy
cohorts targeted the Résistance's secret radio broadcasts. Serge
learned that squad cars, camouflaged as repair trucks, used
homing devices to locate transmitters. Radio operators were
arrested and brutally tortured until codes were revealed. He
and Simone buried their own radios and transmitters in a fetid
compost heap and relied instead on couriers and illicit mimeographed broadsheets for information. Only sparse news from
the world beyond Toulouse reached them.

Madeleine plucked a copy of *La Terre Française*, a Fascist
propaganda tabloid, from a trash can. It contained a crudely

written report of a revolt at the Treblinka death camp. Five hundred Jewish slave laborers had been shot by SS and Ukranian guards.

"We have punished the Jewish scum," the commander of the camp exulted.

Tears blinded Madeleine. She wept for the murdered Jews. She wept at the cruelty of the murderers.

As she sat with a group of comrades in Simone's kitchen that evening, the newspaper was passed from hand to hand. Silence shrouded the room. Horror muted their voices.

Serge stood amid the shadows and very softly intoned the Kaddish. The small group of young fighters added their voices to his in a melancholy chorus of grief and affirmation.

The spirits of the Résistance fighters soared when they learned that the Allies were bombing Berlin and Hamburg. Surely that meant that victory was near. Learning of the American air raid on Regensburg, they lifted tiny cups of wine in celebration only to learn that the bombs that fell on the German city had killed a large contingent of French slave laborers.

"We are playing a game of chess," Madeleine complained to Simone. "We make a move. The Nazis counter us. Our pawns for their bishop. Our knights for their rooks. Our sadness for their joy."

"As long as they don't place our king in check," Simone retorted wryly and shifted position.

The weight of Simone's pregnancy this last trimester hampered her every movement, and though she did not complain, Madeleine knew that her sister was often uncomfortable. Still, despite Serge's objections and Madeleine's concern, Simone continued to visit the farmers markets and often worked late in the night, forging lifesaving documents. It was Simone, determined not to despair and to scavenge a few hours of gaiety, who organized a picnic reunion for their family in a low-lying meadow not far from the city.

The Levys and Lucie Dreyfus managed transport, and Madeleine filled a basket with cheeses, vegetables, and fruits donated by sympathetic farmers.

It was a happy day, golden hours of peace snatched from the unremitting darkness of war. Anna Hofberg tossed a bright-red ball to Simone's small daughter, and the assembled adults watched them in wonder. The sight of children playing in a grassy field was a miracle of a kind. They munched on the picnic food, grimacing at the cheeses that were too hard and the coarsely baked baguettes that crumbled at the touch.

"Never will I forgive the Germans for these baguettes," Dr. Levy said jokingly. "I accept invasion, I accept occupation, but the confiscation of butter and almond paste is truly unforgivable."

He laughed and, wiping the crumbs from his mustache, he passed his stethoscope across Simone's abdomen.

"I am just checking the heartbeat of my grandchild," he said. "And it is wonderfully strong."

Madeleine, watching her father, saw that despite his reassuring words, his eyes darkened with concern as he continued to palpate Simone's abdomen. She understood that his experienced fingers were assessing the position of the fetus, and she intuited his anxiety despite his reassuring smile.

"Is it not wonderful that a healthy Jewish baby will be born in Nazi-occupied Toulouse?" he asked. "A miracle. You are miracle workers, Serge and Simone."

"Miracle workers," they echoed happily and smiled, grateful for the brief moment of levity, grateful that they had managed to come together on a sunlit afternoon.

Letters were produced. The nuns of Valence had agreed to receive all the family's mail so that the dangers of censorship might be avoided. Madeleine had told Claude that it would be safe for him to send any letter meant for her to Madame Lucie Duteil.

Lucie read aloud a letter from Pierre Dreyfus. He was traveling throughout the United States, raising funds for the beleaguered Jews of Europe and the struggling Jewish community in Palestine.

"He misses France. He misses all of us, but his work in the United States is important. He has met with Eleanor Roosevelt, the wife of the president, and she has promised to do what she can for us," Lucie reported.

"Would that her husband had similar thoughts," Serge said bitterly. "If only he would direct one of his bombers to target the railroad tracks that lead to Auschwitz, so many lives would be saved. I hope Pierre has told that to Mrs. Roosevelt."

"I am sure he has," Lucie said as she handed Jeanne letters that Jean Louis and Etienne had sent from Paris.

Jeanne Levy's hands trembled as she ripped the envelopes open, but her face was aglow with relief as she read each closely written page.

"Our boys are safe," she said, her voice tremulous.

Jean Louis, now a qualified doctor, was working at a clandestine clinic, and Etienne was deeply involved with the *éclaireurs* in programs to hide and protect Jewish children. He was working closely with a courageous Christian pastor, Father Vergaras, who based his rescue operations in the Oratoire du Louvre. Etienne wrote proudly that he had accompanied the mime Marcel Marceau on a mission to spirit Jewish children into hiding places.

"Our sons make us proud," Pierre Paul Levy said. "As do our daughters. Is that not so, Jeanne?"

He spoke quietly, but Madeleine saw that his eyes brimmed with tears as he held his wife close. Jeanne trembled in his embrace.

"If only pride could conquer fear," she murmured.

Madeleine and Simone glanced at each other. They understood that their mother was never free of acute anxiety, the residue of her girlhood fear for her father and her young womanhood being scarred by the bloody battles of the Great War.

During the Battle of Verdun, Jeanne had wakened in the night screaming, her nightgown sweat-soaked, tears streaking her cheeks. She had dreamed, she confided, that her husband, her brother, and her father all lay bloody and dead on the battlefield.

The sisters knew that such nightmares had recurred. Instinctively, they moved closer to her; Jeanne's daughters had become their mother's protectors.

What strange reversals war causes, Madeleine mused.

Their grandmother's voice, now pleasantly light, pierced their brief, melancholy silence.

"Madeleine, this letter arrived only yesterday," Lucie said handing her a pale-blue envelope, double sealed with two bands of yellow wax.

Madeleine stared at it in surprise and disbelief. The stamps were Swiss. The postmark was Lausanne. The ink was so light as to be barely discernible. But the handwriting was Claude's. Her hand trembled. Her heart pounded. It was Simone who took the envelope from her and very carefully broke the seals. She read the letter, her lips moving silently, and then turned to Madeleine and summarized its message, enunciating each word carefully.

"Claude writes that he is well," she said. "He managed to lead a small group of Jewish children through the Alps and will soon return to France. He misses you. He thinks about you. He will be with you before the summer ends."

"Read it exactly as he wrote it," Madeleine said weakly. "Word for word."

She sat back and allowed her sister's clear and determinedly loud voice to wash over her, speaking Claude's loving words. She took the letter from Simone, read it herself, and lifted it to her lips.

"Before the summer ends," she repeated.

She would count the days and bless each passing hour because soon, very soon, Claude would make his way back to her.

The sky darkened. Rain threatened. The Dreyfus summer picnic was over. Regretfully, they exchanged embraces. Kisses dampened their cheeks, but their eyes were dry.

"Au revoir," they murmured. "Adieu. Shalom."

Lucie whispered a prayer, and although they did not understand the Hebrew, they bent their heads and said "amen" in unison. Messages would be sent. They would meet again. Of course they would.

Pierre Paul, Jeanne, and Anna climbed into his battered Citroën, the back seat crammed with his precious surgical equipment and his ever-shrinking supply of drugs. The Nazi occupiers had commandeered all medical supplies. Pharmaceutical warehouses had been emptied, their contents shipped to Berlin. Medicines were now more valuable than gold, bandages and disinfectants more precious than diamonds. Pierre Paul rummaged in the back seat and beckoned to Madeleine. He handed her a package wrapped in newspaper and secured with rough twine.

"Morphine," he said tersely. "For Simone. She may need it when she goes into labor. I did not want to frighten her, but when I examined her, I saw that the baby is badly positioned. If there is no shift, the birth may be a breech and delivery will be very painful. I will be too far away to help her."

Sorrow and regret limned his every word. He was a physician, a father, unable to relieve his daughter's pain.

"I understand," Madeleine assured him. "You must not worry. Our good friend and neighbor Hélène is an experienced midwife. She will administer the morphine if it is needed. And you must always remember that our Simone is very strong."

"Yes. She is strong. Both my daughters are strong," he said and held her close.

Madeleine clutched the parcel and struggled to believe her own words. Yes, Simone was strong but even her strength had its limits. Madeleine recalled assisting her father with a breech delivery many years ago in an emergency situation. Although that young woman had survived, Madeleine knew that breech births often threatened the lives of both mother and infant. She shuddered to think of her sister's vulnerability as she thrust the precious parcel of morphine deep into her rucksack. She sat beside Simone, gripping her sister's hand as they drove back to Toulouse.

At the approach to the Canal du Midi, the sun began its slow descent, casting the melancholy pastel shades of a late-summer sunset across the still waters. A vagrant wind brushed Madeleine's face, and she felt the first welcoming chill of autumn. Summer's end. Claude's arrival. She smiled and stared into the slowly gathering darkness.

THIRTY-ONE

DESPITE HER FRENETIC AND EXHAUSTING ACTIVITIES, her daily races from clandestine meetings with Résistance leaders to stealthy visits with the hidden children in her care, all of which drained her energy and left her weak with fatigue, Madeleine was haunted by insomnia. She lay awake hour after hour, tossing and turning on the narrow cots concealed behind the false walls of one safe house or another. A profusion of anxieties intruded on her nocturnal thoughts. *Simone. Claude. Anna. Her parents. Her brothers.* Each precious name triggered an explosion of fear and denied her any possibility of sleep.

As the Gestapo tightened its stranglehold on Paris and imprisoned cadres of Résistance fighters, she grew more and more concerned for her brothers. Dark imaginings teased and mocked her during the long hours of her very long nights.

She struggled to calm herself with reassuring news, the optimistic assessments of the battles being waged. It was true that the Allies were on the offensive. Berlin was being bombarded, and more than once, she had seen the lights of low-flying RAF planes winging their way across the Channel to home bases in England. Victory was on the horizon, she told herself, and with victory there would be peace.

"Blessed peace," she whispered into the darkness. She closed her eyes, but sleep did not come.

Unable to rest, there were nights when she left her bed, dressed in dark clothing, and cycled down the dark and deserted streets into starlit rural regions, following roughhewn paths illuminated only by shafts of silver moonlight. Now and again, she saw the lights of planes streaking across the sky in nocturnal sorties.

"Bonne chance," she called to the Royal Air Force pilots as they flew westward. They would need whatever luck could be mustered. She knew that three hundred RAF airmen had been killed and almost as many taken prisoner.

One star-streaked night, again beset by sleeplessness, she cycled deep into the countryside, her eyes lifted skyward as she pedaled. Hypnotized by the beauty of the sky, she searched out the constellations whose names her grandfather had taught her so many years ago.

"Ursa Minor. Ursa Major," she said aloud. "Ah, Cassiopeia."

She craned her neck.

"But where is my Andromeda?"

It was always Andromeda that she had greeted with enthusiasm, in love with the myth of Perseus's faithful wife, in love with the musical cadence of the name.

"Andromeda," she repeated as she cycled on.

She swiveled eastward, craning her neck, but it was not Andromeda that she saw. Searching the heavens, her gaze was, instead, riveted on the slow, almost balletic descent of a parachute. The argentine moonlight emphasized the stark whiteness of the chute's silken swell as it swayed gently in a vagrant breeze. She discerned a figure dangling from its cords, dark suited and motionless. It was a pilot, she realized, trained to submit to the choreography of the wind.

Madeleine watched intently as the plummeting parachute cleared a copse of young elm trees and barely avoided a narrow rivulet to fall to earth only meters from where she stood. The pilot lay supine and inert on the tall grass, and she thought for a brief and terrible moment that he might be dead. She watched intently and, at last, saw him move, slowly, almost imperceptibly. With a sudden spurt of strength, his arms reached up, and he struggled to release himself from the restraining straps.

She hesitated. She was not close enough to see his uniform, to read whatever insignias might be on his epaulettes. It was possible that he was German or Italian. Axis planes had been spotted flying over Toulouse, but that had not happened recently. It was far more likely that he was English or American. She moved quickly and rushed toward him. His nationality did not matter. He was a man, a human being, alone and perhaps wounded, in a deserted meadow in the dead of night, in need of help. She reached into her pocket for the small torch she always carried, and clutching it tightly, she knelt beside him and trained her light on him. She saw, with relief, that he wore the brown flying helmet of the Royal Air Force. She leaned closer so that she might see his face and hear him when he spoke.

He was a tall man, ruddy skinned, his blue eyes bright. He moved one leg slightly, then the other, one arm and the other, and smiled as though surprised to note that his limbs were undamaged.

"Who are you?" she asked, grateful for the basic English she had been taught at the Lycée Molière.

"I suppose it's all right to tell you," he said. "I'm Staff Sergeant Claude Sharple of Penzance, the most beautiful town in England's most beautiful county, Cornwall. And who are you, and where am I?"

Leaning on one elbow, he grinned at her and she smiled in return. That his name was Claude seemed to her a magical sign of a kind. A foolish thought, she knew, but she claimed it as comfort.

"I am Madeleine Levy, a member of the French Résistance. You are in France, on the outskirts of the city of Toulouse, a so-called unoccupied zone under the control of Germany and its Vichy puppet government. It is dangerous for you to be here. We must move quickly before you are discovered," she replied, stumbling over her words, speaking breathlessly.

She darted away, retrieved her bolt cutter from the pannier of her bicycle. Working together, they cut him free of his parachute.

"Where is your plane?" she asked.

"It was a fighter escort. It was shot down miles from here."

"They will be looking for you. The Germans."

"If they think I survived," he replied.

"They will be looking for you because they will not know whether you are alive or dead. They take no chances. And they must not find you."

He did not ask why. They both knew what happened to captured Allied airmen. The Germans treated prisoners of war with barbaric cruelty, ignoring any pretense of adhering to the laws of the Geneva Conventions. Torture was routine. There were summary executions. The bodies of the dead were often stripped of all identification, uniforms discarded. The corpses were incinerated, their weapons seized.

Madeleine studied the area, turning left, then right, finally pointing to a windbreak of young trees planted closely together.

"There. It is the safest place."

Together they pulled the downed parachute into the small grove.

"Now we must bury it beneath the leaves. Then you must stay here until I return. Lie very quietly on the ground and try not to move. I won't be away long," she said, scooping up foliage and piling it over the white folds of the parachute.

"But where are you going?" he asked, and for the first time she heard the slightest quiver of fear in his voice.

It did not surprise her. He was very young, perhaps not even out of his teens, very alone, wearing his country's uniform in an area controlled by a ruthless enemy. He feared execution. He feared death. She understood. After all, she too feared execution; she too feared death.

"I am going to get help," she said with a calm she did not feel. "My Résistance comrades will return with me, and we will help you to escape to safety. Please trust me."

His smile returned.

"Not that I have any choice, but I do trust you. How could I not trust a pretty lass who speaks English with such a charming accent?"

Obediently then, he disappeared deeper into the windbreak, and she mounted her bicycle and sped to the nearest safe house.

Within two hours she returned with a small group of Résistants. They worked feverishly, aware that before the sun rose, all traces of Staff Sergeant Claude Sharple would have to disappear. They dug a hole and buried the parachute and his flying suit, covered it with leaves and rolled a boulder over it. The downed pilot quickly dressed in the thick sweater and worn work pants they gave him. Serge ran toward them with a set of forged documents which Simone, roused from sleep, had hastily prepared, affixing a very blurred photograph to the *carte d'identité* and a medical certificate attesting that Girard Polyneaux, a shepherd, had unfortunately been born mute.

"Couldn't you have fitted me out with a name I might be able to pronounce?" he asked jokingly.

"Since you are a mute, that will present no difficulty," Serge countered, and they all laughed.

Laughter, Madeleine thought, was their sole relief, their claim to a briefly restored normalcy, a reminder of a time when humor was their constant companion and the sound of merriment was not alien.

A dark-haired young man stepped forward, Sancho, a *passeur*, a Spanish guide who had fought against Franco and now assisted the Résistance.

"Sancho, our loyal friend, will take you across the Pyrenees to safety," Serge told Claude as he shook his hand.

"Thank you," the young aviator responded.

He turned to Madeleine.

"And I will never forget you," he said, and awkwardly but tenderly, he kissed her on both her cheeks and then followed after Sancho to begin his long walk to freedom.

She stared after him.

"Adieu, Claude," she murmured, aware that the very utterance of the name he shared with her beloved friend imbued her with hope and with pleasure.

"Claude, Claude," she repeated as she cycled thought the milky light of a nascent dawn.

THIRTY-TWO

SEPTEMBER WINDS RUSTLED THE LEAVES OF TREES NEWLY ablaze with the fiery hues of autumn. Madeleine stared up at the arboreal crowns of russet and gold, scarlet and burnt orange, the favorite colors of her favorite season. Tall purple asters rimmed the banks of the Garonne, and jet-black caper berries shimmered on earth-hugging bushes. Now and again she plucked a flower and filled her panniers with clusters of late-blooming *fraises du bois*, the wild strawberries that basked in patches of pale sunlight. She crammed the sweet fruit into her mouth and tossed the residue as well as the wilting blossoms into the fallen foliage.

She had no vase for her small flowers, no bowl to fill with the plump red berries. She was a nomadic fugitive who lay wakeful on a different cot each night, yearning for sleep but fearful of her dreams. She allowed herself thoughts of Claude, repeating in a whisper the gentle promise of his letter that he would see her before the end of summer. But summer was coming to an end, and he had not arrived in Toulouse. Once again, she was weighted with anxiety. Once again, she feared to sleep because too often she dreamt of death and danger.

"Is he safe?" she asked Serge. There was no need to say his name.

"We have had no news of him. All we know is that the children he guided through the Alps are now in Italy, in the care of the *tzofim*, Jewish scouts from Palestine. Claude's orders were to return to France, and that is surely what he will try to do. But such a journey will not be without obstacles, which probably account for his delay. Try not to worry, Madeleine."

Serge spoke slowly, patiently, his tone revealing neither optimism nor pessimism, his eyes resting on a much-creased map spread across the kitchen table.

"What obstacles?" Madeleine asked.

"I will show you."

He plucked up a pen, allowed it to hover over the map, and rested it on the pale-green outline that was Switzerland.

"The last word we had from him was the letter he wrote to you. It was postmarked Lausanne."

The pen rested on the small dot that was Lausanne.

"Yes, Lausanne."

She did not tell Serge that the letter was always on her person, tucked beneath her camisole. Even as he spoke, she felt the thin paper brush her breasts.

Clutching the pen, he traced the route that led from Lausanne to Toulouse, his face turned to her, mindful of her need to read his lips so that not a word would be lost.

"He would have had to cross the Pennine Alps to reach Turin, and we know that Italy was dangerous and uncertain territory even in late summer. The Italians themselves were divided between the anti-Fascists and Mussolini's thugs, just as we in France are divided between Vichy and the Free French. Claude would have had to proceed slowly, cautiously. He had to make his way westward, perhaps crossing the border near Grenoble."

"Claude would be slow. He would be cautious," Madeleine said, moving her own finger across the map.

Simone leaned over her sister's shoulder and smiled.

"Claude is like this baby I am carrying then, very slow, very cautious. They are both traveling to Toulouse. Who will win the race—my baby or your Claude?" she asked mischievously.

They all laughed then, grateful to Simone for easing the tension.

"I will make tea," Simone said. "Grand-mère's solution to all problems, a cup of tea."

Madeleine watched her sister move across the room and noted the slowness of her gait, hampered as it was by the great weight of her pregnancy. Simone's condition worried her. Their midwife friend, Hélène, had examined Simone and told Madeleine that the baby remained in breech position. Madeleine thought gratefully of the morphine she had hidden in Simone's kitchen. Fervently now, she wished the birth to come swiftly. With equal fervor she prayed that Claude had managed to cross the Italian border safely.

"You must be patient," Serge said quietly, folding the map. "The Allies have begun the invasion of Italy. American troops are already on the beaches of Reggio. That should ease his journey through Italy. Do not despair, Madeleine. Do not give up hope."

She nodded. Despair was not an option, although she acknowledged that hope remained elusive.

But hope soared anew when Italy surrendered in the second

week of September. That surrender meant there would be no Fascist patrols in the Pennine Alps, no Nazi troops strutting through the streets of Turin. Claude's journey could proceed in relative safety. Serge assured her that he would now be able to avoid the dubious sanctuary of safe houses and move through Italy relatively free of threat and danger. Sleep came to her that night and a dream in which Claude strode toward her, his arms outstretched.

Newly energized, Madeleine, partnered with Serge, managed varied acts of sabotage. They severed communication lines, planted explosives at a Gestapo quartermaster station and scouted out other targets. She increased her visits to the scattered children in her care, cycling swiftly from one locale to another and reassuring each of them that their trek to freedom was not far off.

"*Quand?* When?" The question was increasingly insistent, but she had no answer on offer.

"*Quand?* When can I join my brothers?" Anna Hofberg wrote plaintively from her hiding place with Madeleine's parents.

"Soon," Madeleine replied. "Very soon, I hope."

She could not explain that she had to receive instructions from the Résistance leadership, that she was waiting for Claude's arrival, that she too was impatient, that she too asked "*Quand?*" When?

Cycling to a distant safe house, she lifted her eyes to the sky that darkened early in autumn's encroaching sweep. A flock of geese flew southward, and she marveled at how they soared with such beauty and grace across borders that for her were fraught with danger and destruction. She decided, impulsively, that their flight was an omen. Claude, too, would safely cross borders and return to her. A foolish thought, she knew, even as she waved to the birds who flew even higher and disappeared into the soft white pillows of wind-tossed clouds.

The optimism ignited by the Italian surrender dissipated as the Nazis tightened their noose around all of France. The position of Jews in the Southern Zone grew more tenuous with each passing day. An advisory issued by Résistance headquarters in Paris advised all Jewish Résistance leaders in the south to go underground immediately. Many operatives disappeared while others remained active, but it was clear that the ranks of Jewish Résistants were dangerously depleted.

"I am running out of disguises," Madeleine told Serge and Simone with bitter humor, removing the kerchief that covered her hair, newly dyed red. She shed the white smock worn by junior pharmacists and riffled through her packet of forged identity cards, each with a different name, a different address, a different birth date.

"Sometimes I forget my real name. I must remind myself that I am Madeleine Levy, not Danielle Durand or Arielle Maupin. Although I have grown rather fond of Arielle," she said. "Arielle will soon have a doctorate in pharmacology, and soon, too, she will marry her classmate Philippe," she said, amused by the identity she had created for her alias. "She and Philippe are planning to leave Toulouse very soon."

Serge shook his head bitterly.

"We should all leave Toulouse, but Simone and I must wait until our baby is born. She cannot travel in her condition.

It is a miracle that we have remained safe. Probably because the Milice is biding its time as it spies on us. We are more valuable to them here than in prison. And of course the bribes that I pay to their commandant are useful. Prisoners do not pay bribes, and Vichy and Milice officers have developed a taste for champagne and pâtés."

The few members of their cell who remained in Toulouse often clustered around Serge's clandestine radio. Huddled in the darkened room, they listened to the BBC broadcasts and learned that despite defeats in Italy and Russia, Hitler had not abandoned his war against the Jews. He was manically determined to see that all of Europe was *judenrein*, free of Jews. There were vicious deportations of Jews from Holland, Belgium, and France to death camps. Radio Londres reported that during the first weeks of September, two thousand Jews from Holland, fourteen hundred from Belgium, and one thousand from France had been sent to certain death in Auschwitz. There were reports of mass executions over mud-filled trenches. Those who were soon to be murdered were forced to dig their own graves.

"Hitler seems more focused on killing Jews than on winning the war," Serge said.

He turned to Madeleine.

"The time has come. We must do something to slow the deportations," he said.

She nodded. They could no longer rely on directives from Paris or Lyon. They were on their own.

"And we know what we must do," she agreed. "The bridges. Moulin told us that we must target the Ponts Jumeaux."

"He was right, of course," Serge asserted. "And that is what we will do."

Moulin, so prescient in strategic planning, had recognized the importance of the bridges and mandated that they be made inaccessible. The brave Résistance leader was dead but his advice endured, eerily relevant all these months later as the deportations accelerated and Nazi cruelty intensified.

The three bridges that spanned the banks of the Garonne River—Pont St. Pierre to the north, Pont St. Michel to the south, and Pont Neuf to the center—had to be destroyed so that Jewish lives might be saved.

The very next day, Madeleine cycled along the riverbank, concentrating intently on the structure of the three spans. It was clear that they had been built by masons of great skill. The serried gray fieldstone escarpments, threaded with rose-colored mica, were supported by concrete bases. They had been reinforced over the years with additional layers of cement, which rendered them a strong and formidable target. Formidable but not impossible. She made a swift sketch and then hid behind a tree and waited.

Within an hour, several open trucks crammed with prisoners lumbered across one bridge and then another. She counted the vehicles, monitored the intervals of their passage and took note of the motorcycle squads of SS officers that escorted them. She recorded all the information in a notebook that she handed to Serge when she met him in a designated safe house.

"We waited too long," he said worriedly, assessing each detail.

"No. We had to be certain of success," she said.

She reminded him that they had discussed targeting the bridge earlier but the summer days were too long. They needed the cover of darkness and time to accumulate a sufficient supply of more powerful explosives. That had meant cultivating both townspeople and farmers whose complicity would be vital to their success. Caution and patience had been their watchwords. But the time had come to abandon caution and patience.

Serge nodded his agreement.

"We have new intelligence," he told her. "The Germans are increasing the number of convoys. They pack the trucks with prisoners from the internment center of Brens and the transit camp at Drancy for transport to railroad depots. There the prisoners—Jews, Roma, political dissidents—are forced into cattle cars that carry them eastward to the slaughterhouses of Auschwitz and Treblinka."

He spat out the names of the death camps as though they were poisonous pellets lodged upon his tongue.

"We will need confederates, transport, funds. We will proceed but we need help," he added worriedly. "Where will we find the resources?"

Help came from an unexpected source.

A Parisian Résistance group, Defénse de la France, published a journal entitled "The Fruits of Hatred." It included photographs—somehow smuggled out of Sobibor, Auschwitz, and Treblinka—of emaciated men, women, and children, their pleading eyes sunk into skeletal faces. That publication was distributed throughout France. The truth of German inhumanity was now hideously validated.

The Toulouse Résistants stared in horror at the images

of malnourished children in ragged, striped uniforms, at half-naked women, gaunt faced, their bones jutting through skin scarred with ugly lesions. There were grainy shots of cadaverous men harnessed to carts laden with the corpses of small children. The Résistants closed their eyes as they viewed obscenities that could not be denied. Women wept. Men spewed vomit across the floor. They knew that the convoys that crossed the bridges carried men, women, and children to torture. To slave labor. To death.

The photos had been sent from the Gaullist network in London to Paris with instructions that they be published as soon as possible. It was a desperate effort to jolt the French public into recognizing Nazi barbarity. Such recognition, it was hoped, would weaken cooperation with Vichy and strengthen the Résistance.

That effort had success, however limited. It had an impact on French citizens known to be of stoic and pragmatic temperament, those who had opted to join neither Vichy nor the Résistance. The photos in "The Fruits of Hatred" penetrated that stoicism, that pragmatism. Many turned to the Résistance. In Toulouse, a contingent of volunteers found their way to Robert Boulloche. He vetted them carefully and directed them to Serge and Madeleine.

"Your help has arrived," he assured Serge. "These new recruits have access to *matérielle*, to transport, to hiding places, to money. There is no need to wait. There is no time to wait. Death sentences are being written as we speak."

Listening to his plea, Simone recalled her conversation in Paris with the master forger Adolfo Kaminsky.

"If I sleep for an hour," he had said, "thirty people will die."
She transposed his words.

"If we do not attack the Pont Jumeaux, if we wait for an hour, a day, a week, hundreds—no, thousands will die. Jews. Political prisoners. Gypsies. Innocents. We dare not sleep. We dare not wait."

Serge and Madeleine nodded their agreement. They needed no persuasion. Other Résistance comrades were summoned and arrived one by one, a stealthy parade of courageous warriors. Madeleine spread her drawings of the bridges across the table, and methodically, quietly, they planned the operation.

They worked through the night, covering every surface with lists scrawled on sheets of brown paper, topographical maps, inventories of available *matérielle*, coded lists of safe houses and hiding places. Names were discussed. Six saboteurs would be needed, two for each bridge. Serge and Madeleine, working together, would form one team, but who would the other four be? Stubs of half-smoked Gauloises and mugs thick with dregs of chicory-infused coffee were scattered throughout the room as decisions were made, discarded, reviewed, every detail considered and reconsidered. Agreement was reached. The operation would be difficult, dangerous, but neither the difficulties nor the dangers were insurmountable. Volunteers stepped forward, and at last two other teams were selected.

In the early hours of the morning, Madeleine lay down to sleep on the narrow cot Simone kept in readiness. She realized as she closed her eyes that this was the first time in many weeks that she had not thought of Claude. His absence did not trouble her. He was with her in spirit. She would do what she had to do.

She slept peacefully that night, her hand upon her breast, pressed to his letter sent from Lausanne all those weeks ago. It was worn to tissue thinness, its promise unfulfilled but its hope reignited. She had no need of dreams.

THIRTY-THREE

THE TEAM OF SABOTEURS, LED BY SERGE, PROCEEDED WITH meticulous attention to detail. An architect made intricate drawings of the bridges, and they were photographed from strategic angles. Every eventuality was considered. It was understood that unimaginable situations might arise, that their act of sabotage might itself be sabotaged. But they persisted. The three strike teams studied the photos, the drawings. Madeleine and Serge would be responsible for detonations at the Pont St. Pierre, the northern span, the most important crossing.

There was a clandestine meeting with members of the Toulouse Masons Guild who had volunteered their services. They were grizzled artisans, their eyes sharp, their hands calloused. They nodded with professional certainty as they discussed the construction of the bridges. They all agreed, with pride and regret comingled, that the stone formations of each bridge, built of boulders hefted into place by teams of master masons, were almost impregnable.

"But surely there are vulnerabilities," Serge said.

"There are always vulnerabilities," Maître Jean, himself a master mason, agreed.

He spread the architect's drawings and the photographs across the table.

"Take note of the arches beneath each bridge. Do you see how they are roofed with cement? Much patched cement. That indicates weakness. If explosives were attached at those locales and then detonated, the roadway above the arch would be so severely damaged that no vehicle could pass over it. It would be repaired, of course, but a repair of such extensive damage would take considerable time. If in fact, the Germans could find a single mason in Toulouse who would work for them," he added, smiling.

"And until the repairs are accomplished, German convoys will be unable to pass over the river," Serge said thoughtfully.

"Of course."

The masons erupted in laughter at the foolishness of his question. But they forgave it. He was a Jew. Jews did not understand such things. Still, this Jew was brave. And daring. As was the beautiful woman called Madeleine, who worked with him. That too they knew.

"Then we will target the arches, of course," Serge said decisively. "But how will we attach the explosives to the ceilings of the arches?"

A chorus of suggestions poured forth.

"Tape."

"Quick drying cement."

"Industrial glue."

"You must not worry about how the explosives will be attached," Maître Jean assured Serge. "We masons will manage it. It is not unusual for the *Corps de Metier des Maîtres Maçons*— the Guild of Master Masons—to inspect bridges and undertake repairs. We will explain to the Germans that our work is routine and that we are concerned for the safety of their vehicles. We will assure them that our fee for such labor will be moderate."

He laughed, pleased with his own plan, pleased that the Gestapo would pay for the demolition of the bridges. He himself had never officially joined the Résistance, but like many French citizens, he had long detested the Vichy government. His only son had been recruited under the hated Service de Travail Obligatoire and sent to Germany as a slave laborer. But it was seeing the photos of the concentration camp prisoners in "The Fruits of Hatred" that had spurred him to action. He had, he confided to Madeleine, shared the photos with his comrades in the Masons Guild who had been horrified and immediately pledged their support.

"We are grateful to all of you," Serge said and he circled the room, shaking hands with each mason.

"And we are grateful to you. We will work together to save our France, our *patrie*," a grizzled, elderly mason replied.

Serge and Madeleine worked tirelessly, ever aware of the dangers that confronted them. They assessed their supplies of *matérielle*. Whatever was missing could be improvised. They had not forgotten the instructions of the weary English expert who had led the demolition workshop in Lyon. They shared that knowledge with the rest of their team.

They gathered lengths of rope, piles of cotton wool, sticks of flint, long wooden matches. Local farmers ferried the explosives long concealed in their barns and silos to the green market, concealing them on their wagons and flatbed trucks beneath pyramids of harvest vegetables—golden squash, long green zucchini, sacks of new potatoes. They drove the contraband with great care to the marketplace in the heart of Toulouse.

Complicit housewives scooped up sticks of dynamite, accelerants that had been poured into vials labeled *olive oil*, canisters of lampblack. They crammed them into their baskets, beneath their produce and baked goods. Smiling and chatting, they waved to Milice officers and headed to Simone's kitchen. The collaborators, paid by the Gestapo to keep vigil outside the Perl residence, were not suspicious of such visits, seeing them as innocent coffee breaks, occasions for idle gossip. The women waved cheerfully to the surveillance team as they left. Behind the blackout curtains of her cluttered kitchen, Simone swiftly concealed the demolition *matérielle* in her pantry and her larder.

At night, in that same darkened kitchen, Simone, Madeleine, and the midwife, Hélène, working by the faint glow of an oil lamp, carefully, almost tenderly inserted detonating caps under the paper covering of each explosive. They filled milk bottles with cartridges, primers, and the precious vials of accelerators, then waited for the arrival of François, the dairyman, a Résistant with an excellent cover.

In predawn darkness, Francois loaded the bottles, concealing them beneath cases of butter and cheese. Driving through the half darkness, he deposited the laden bottles in a burrow close to the bridges and then proceeded to Gestapo headquarters where he cheerfully helped a German soldier unload the crates of dairy products.

"Bon appétit," he said, and the soldier waved as he drove away.

The jolly *boulanger* closed his bakery late in the evening and drove his truck to the shed that Serge supposedly used for woodworking. He and Serge heaved sacks of flour into the small enclosure. Hidden within the snowy mounds of finely milled grain were yards of coiled cord to be used as fuses.

Madeleine counted and checked every component, and Serge counted them yet again. They measured the cord and wrapped the wooden matches in surgical cotton wool against dampness. Everything was divided into three separate containers that the masons carried nonchalantly to the three bridges.

"Supplies for the repairs of the arches," they told the German unit that stopped them. They were waved on. The Gestapo understood that the bridges had to be kept in good repair. It was important that their convoys be able to proceed without difficulty. They wanted to be rid of those damn Jews, those filthy gypsies, the lousy Communists. They wanted to be done with the long, cold nights of standing guard. They hoisted their rifles and thought of the warmth of the beer cellars in Hamburg and Berlin, the brightness of the coal-fed stoves, the peppery taste of the wurst.

"*Schnell.* Work quickly," they instructed the masons who nodded amiably and did indeed work quickly. They finished in record time and assured the German guards as they left that their work had gone well, that the bridges would now pose no problem.

"*Alles gut,*" they said and drove quickly back to the city.

"Stupid *Boches,*" Maître Jean said an hour later, as the guild members gathered in a bistro and toasted their success with oversize glasses of *vin ordinaire.*

It had been determined from the onset that the operation would be carried out under the cover of darkness, preferably on a moonless night. The pattern of nocturnal activity on the road leading to the bridges was diligently recorded. It was noted that the road was sparsely patrolled in the late evening and almost totally without any traffic or surveillance after midnight. They knew, of course, that the Germans relished their beer and submitted happily to the pleasant drowsiness that followed their drinking.

"We will wait for two, perhaps three hours after midnight, when they will be dead asleep," Serge decided. "It is good that our enemies have such fondness for their Lowenbrau."

"And for their cognac," Madeleine added drily.

Clothing was prepared for the saboteurs. They would wear close-fitting black trousers and jackets and rubber-treaded boots coated with black polish. Deft needlewomen sewed pockets into the jackets to contain small knives, torches with the slenderest of beams, miniature tools, and long wooden matches.

"In case," Serge said cryptically, flicking a knife open to reveal a deadly blade.

Madeleine did not ask him to finish the sentence. "In case" meant a multitude of dangers too frightening to contemplate.

"Time is passing," she said. "When do we act?"

"When?" the other team members asked.

They were impatient but Serge would not be rushed.

"It depends on the moon," he said. "And on Babette."

Pretty Babette, long a Résistante, was a barmaid in a local bistro favored by the Germans. She had, for some weeks, flirted teasingly with one Ludwig, a German corporal who stood guard at the approach to the bridges. A tedious duty, he told her. No one ever appeared.

"I stand there for no reason. The Résistance has lost all energy. They live in fear of the Führer's army. Still I must follow orders, foolish as they are."

Babette sympathized. Résistants were stupid, she agreed. She confided that she knew that the autumn nights were chilly. Surely he grew cold. And for nothing. The bridges were not in danger. And her room, which was so close to his post, was so very warm. Especially beneath her quilt. She longed to be with him beneath her quilt.

"I will keep you warm. I will make you happy," she promised. "Why should you stand guard night after night for no reason? When will you come home with me?"

"We must wait for a moonless night," he said. "On such a night I will not be missed. The officers rarely patrol when it is so dark. Coddled cowards that they are."

"Of course. A moonless night," she agreed happily and reported the news to Serge.

"Fortunate corporal," he said.

"Not really." Babette giggled mischievously. "*J'ai le gonorrhee.*"

Serge's laughter was without humor, but his gratitude was sincere.

They waited. Nights passed. They stared up at a full moon that cast a silvery light, then at a half-moon, less radiant but still aglow, then at a graceful crescent just luminous enough to be dangerous. Uneasy and restless, they studied the ink-dark sky until midmonth, when neither moon nor star appeared. Their time had come. Babette loosened her hair, applied fresh lipstick, winked at Serge who stood in a corner of the smoke-fogged bistro, and disappeared from her station.

Serge hurried home and ascertained gratefully that the surveil-lance team of Vichy spies beneath his windows had abandoned their posts, as they had begun to do on most cold nights. Like Babette's Ludwig, they had grown bored and thought their assignment foolish and futile. They drank and then they slept.

Madeleine waited for Serge.

"Tonight," he said tersely. "We strike tonight."

She nodded, relieved that small Frederica was sleeping at a friend's house. She would be safe if the act of sabotage was traced back to Serge. Madeleine dared not think of what would happen to Simone and Serge if they failed or were betrayed. She did not contemplate her own fate. She was neither wife nor mother. She had no hostages that might be surrendered to misfortune. She would not think of Claude.

The entire team assembled, and in silence they donned the black outfits and darkened their faces with lampblack. One by one they slipped out of the back door and disappeared into the velvet darkness of the night. In concentrated silence, they would move single file, at a distance from each other, until they reached the bridges. There the select duos would work together, swiftly and soundlessly. As each fuse was ignited, as the flame crept slowly toward the explosives, but before the conflagration, they would sprint away in different, well-planned directions to scattered safe houses located at a distance from the bridges. It had been mutually decided that given the locale of the Pont St. Pierre, Madeleine and Serge would be the last to leave.

Simone, who had been strangely quiet all evening, handed Serge and Madeleine their jackets. With her usual attention to detail, she checked that the torches in their pockets emitted steady beams of light. She stood beside Madeleine in front of the sliver of a mirror and applied the lampblack to her cheeks. Madeleine paused, aware that her sister's reflected face was drained of all color, that her lips were clenched and her eyes were dangerously bright. Simone was terrified, Madeleine knew, and that terror was justified. Both her sister and her husband, the two people nearest and dearest to her, were leaving on a mission fraught with danger.

Madeleine struggled to find words that might soothe her and swiftly abandoned the effort. It was best to say nothing. It was best to offer comfort with a swift embrace.

She turned, her arms outstretched, only to see that Simone's mouth was twisted in pain, that her legs could barely support her. She stumbled clumsily across the room and sank into a chair, making no sound, although her breath came in stertorous gasps. She gripped the armrests, her knuckles white, flecks of spittle dotting her lips.

Madeleine knelt beside her.

"Simone, what is it? Are you in labor?" she asked.

A bilious reflux soured her own throat as a flow of clear, odorless fluid poured out of her sister's body and puddled the floor. Her question required no answer. They were doctor's daughters, certified social workers who had completed a course in basic midwifery. They understood that the membranes containing the amniotic fluid had ruptured and the birth process was launched.

Simone groaned, biting her lips so hard that drops of blood dripped onto her chin.

Serge rushed to her side, wide eyed with concern, with fear.

"When did the contractions begin?" Madeleine asked.

"Perhaps an hour ago. So mild that I ignored them. False labor, I thought. But now…" Simone's voice tapered off and she writhed in pain.

Gently, Madeleine and Serge eased her onto the floor. Madeleine dashed into the kitchen, placed a large pot of water on the gas ring, plucked up towels, and rushed back to Simone. Serge knelt beside her, massaging her abdomen with his black-gloved hand. He glanced at his watch. Madeleine stared at hers. Their thoughts merged, their twin concerns heavy upon mind and heart. *Simone. The Pont St. Pierre.* Their double urgencies, their double obligations. *What would they do? What should they do? What could they do?*

"I must get Hélène," Madeleine said and hurried out, not waiting for Serge's reply.

She ran down the street to Hélène's room and pounded frantically at the door. Hélène opened it.

"Simone?" she asked and seized her bag. The two women raced down the street and burst into the room.

Simone had shifted position. She lay on her side, her head resting on Serge's lap, biting down on a strip of cloth.

"She is in terrible pain," he said, and Madeleine saw that her brother-in-law, renowned for his strength and courage, trembled with fear, his face drained of all color.

Hélène's trained hands moved across Simone's abdomen, then placed her stethoscope on its distended rise and adjusted the earpieces. She listened, moved the scope, frowned, and moved it again. At last she nodded and managed a thin, reassuring smile.

"The baby's heartbeat is strong," she said as she loosened Simone's clothing, pulled her undergarments off, lifted her legs, and examined her internally.

"She's almost fully dilated," she murmured.

Madeleine bent close and Hélène whispered.

"I can feel the baby's shoulder but not the head. It's a dangerous positioning."

"A breech," Madeleine said. "My father feared as much."

She remembered suddenly that a breech had caused the death of the infant her mother had carried to term and then lost, the phantom younger sister she had never known. She banished the thought as Simone was seized by another stronger contraction. She screamed, writhed in agony, and clutched Serge's hand.

Madeleine rushed into the kitchen, retrieved the package of morphine from its hiding place beneath a sack of onions, and handed it to Hélène.

"Thank God," the young midwife said and administered the narcotic. For a brief and blessed moment, Simone lay quietly.

Serge turned to Madeleine.

"What must we do?" he asked, his voice trembling, the decisive Résistance leader now confronting indecision. "We cannot abort the attack on the Pont St. Pierre, not after all our planning, not with so many relying on us."

Even as he spoke, Simone was assaulted by a new onset of pain, unmitigated even by the narcotic.

"Serge! Serge! Don't leave me," she wailed. "Serge, I need you."

She was a woman in labor, the agonizing pain of childbirth canceling out all other concerns.

He knelt beside her, stroked her hair, whispered words of comfort, of assurance.

"I am here. I will not leave you," he promised and stared beseechingly at Madeleine.

"Of course you cannot leave her," she said firmly. "Nor can we abort the operation. I will proceed without you. It will be all right. I know exactly what to do. Everything is in place. We have practiced it so many times."

"But we have always worked together. How will you manage alone? You will have to deal with the fuses, the accelerants."

"I will contact the rest of the team. They will have finished their work at Pont Neuf, at Pont Michel. They will help me. We will cope. We will succeed. You must not worry. Simone is your concern tonight. Only Simone."

Madeleine spoke with a calm she did not feel and glanced at Hélène, whose hands were moving deftly across the rise of Simone's abdomen.

"I am trying to manipulate the baby, to change its position. I think it will work but it will take time, a long time. There is nothing more you can do here, Madeleine. Go to where you are most needed. Where I myself need you."

Madeleine understood the import of her plea. Hélène's fiancé, Edouard, was interned at Brens. The demolition of the bridges would prevent his deportation and perhaps save his life.

"Yes. That is what I must do," she agreed.

She kissed her sister's forehead and felt the saline moisture of Simone's sweat upon her own lips. It met the tear that drifted down her cheek. Salt upon salt, sorrow upon sorrow.

"Be strong, Simone," she whispered.

There was no answer. Speech was impossible. Simone's small store of energy was in reserve to battle the pain that consumed her.

"And you, Madeleine, you too must be strong," Serge said, his voice resonant enough for her to hear echoed the words she herself had offered his wife.

She left then, closing the door behind her. She did not hesitate as she raced through the moonless darkness to the Pont St. Pierre.

THIRTY-FOUR

B REATHLESSLY, MADELEINE RAN ACROSS FIELD AND meadow until she reached the route that she and Serge had chosen for their approach to the bridge. It ran through rough terrain but offered the cover of random copses and wild hedges. They had hiked it together again and again, memorizing the natural landmarks, the trees and ravines, the thorn bushes and conifer windbreaks, so that the path would be familiar to them even under the cover of darkness. Moving swiftly and confidently now, she followed it, crossing the fields strewn with bracken and weaving her way through copses of birch and elm. The fallen leaves were slippery beneath her feet, and she slowed her pace.

"Caution, caution," she reminded herself.

She avoided a narrow stream, but even as she moved forward, she caught her foot in a tangle of root and fell to her knees. She cursed softly and stood, relieved that she was bruised but uninjured.

She would take no more chances. She lit her torch and followed its narrow ribbon of light through the familiar landscape, passing a rutted shepherd's crossing redolent with the stink of manure, the underbrush flattened by herds of goats and sheep. She increased her pace and suddenly, without warning, the rough pathway vanished and she sank into the boggy soil of a treacherous marsh.

Dizzied and bewildered, she gasped and dropped her torch. She bent and combed through the muddy surface, tossing aside weeds and branches until at last her fingers closed around it. She swiveled its weak beam, uncertain of which way to turn. With palpable relief, she spied a landmark she and Serge had taken note of, a copse of young birch trees, their white bark shimmering in the darkness. Just past it, she knew, was a gradient that led directly to the bridge. She walked swiftly toward it, newly aware of her vulnerability.

"Left foot up," she murmured to herself. "Right foot down."

"Important not to fall."

"Almost there."

"Only a few more meters."

"Left foot up."

"Right foot down."

The rhythmic repetition of the chant that she could barely hear steadied her. She stared upward, hoping to see the lights of the bridge, and at that moment of distraction, she did not see the lichen-encrusted log in her path. She tripped over it and hurtled forward, tumbling facedown onto the ground. The scent of damp earth filled her nostrils, grit invaded her mouth. Her eyes burned but she did not weep. Instead, she lay motionless, briefly overwhelmed by a paralyzing fatigue, a suffocating sadness.

She moaned. Oh, she was tired. So terribly tired. Tired of hopes shattered, of disappointments compounded. Tired of being alone. So alone. She felt herself smothered in a cloud of self-pity, weak with longing. How tired she was of being a heroine, of denying her own desires, riveted to a cause that all too often seemed doomed to defeat. Writhing on the wet earth, she chastised herself for the unbidden thoughts that shamed her.

"Claude." She wrenched his name from the depths of her misery.

"Claude!" she repeated loud enough that she could her own voice. Perhaps, she thought, a vagrant wind might carry her summons to him. *Magical thinking, stupid imaginings,* she protested mentally. Annoyed at her own foolishness, she forced herself to stand. Once again, she had escaped harm. No fractures, no sprains. She moved on, her every step vested with caution.

She peered across the dark expanse and saw the flutter of dim lights. Suffused with relief, she realized that they emanated from the lamps that lined the causeway of the Pont St. Pierre. She was so close, very close.

She turned her gaze southward to the other bridges, but they were completely dark. There would be no help from the teams at the Pont St. Michel and the Pont Neuf. The distance was too great, the darkness impenetrable, contact impossible. She would have to manage alone. And as she had promised Serge, she would cope. She would more than cope. She would succeed. The storm of weakness and indecision had passed.

Newly energized, she followed the lights of the bridge, moving slowly, and then with a spurt of adrenaline, she dashed to the burrow blanketed with fallen branches, beneath which she and Serge had concealed the cache of *matérielle* needed for the demolition. Thrusting the ground cover aside, she saw at once that nothing had been disturbed. She could proceed.

Swiftly, she pulled out one length of coiled rope to serve as an improvised fuse. Removing the small knife from the pocket of her jacket, she cut the coil and spread the rope across the muddied earth. Clutching one end, she crawled through the wild grass and pulled it toward the arch, stopping only when she was within its confines and directly beneath the bridge. The air in the partial enclosure was fetid and stagnant, smelling oddly of tallow. Candle stubs littered the earthen floor across which empty wine bottles were scattered, the remnants of lovers' clandestine meetings, she supposed, left in place by the wise masons when they affixed the explosives.

They had cemented the sticks of dynamite to the crenelated surface, then covered them with a thick coat of paint, leaving the detonating caps untouched. Gently, she placed the rope directly beneath the explosives and sped back across the field, straightening the rope as she ran, remembering the English instructor's somber warning that any unevenness might impede the progress of the flame. Satisfied that one fuse was in place, she pulled out the second loop of coiled rope, but as she knelt to cut it free, she saw the outline of fresh footprints in the muddied earth.

She froze. She had been discovered. Bitterly, silently, she cursed her deafness. The slightest sound would have alerted her, but of course she could barely hear her own voice, never mind the tread of a footstep, the rustle of a branch.

She stood very still and saw a figure move through the darkness and lurch toward her, arms raised threateningly.

Terrified, she gripped her knife. Her lips parted but the scream died in her throat, stifled by the black-gloved hand that covered her mouth while another hand wrenched the knife from her grasp.

She could not see her captor, but she smelled the sourness of his breath and the malodor of his unwashed body. Overcome with nausea, she struggled to free herself. She felt that repellent sour breath warm against her ear, but then she heard his voice, a familiar, tender voice, enunciating each word so clearly that she could hear without difficulty.

"Madeleine. Hush, my Madeleine. You must not scream. *C'est moi.* Claude. I am here, *ma chérie.* I am here to help you."

His hand left her mouth and she turned to him, weak with relief, tears streaking her cheeks.

"Claude. Oh, Claude. You heard me call your name," she gasped.

Her magical thinking had morphed into miraculous reality.

"Heard you? No. I heard nothing. Only the wind."

"Where have you been? I waited and waited. And how did you know where to find me?" she asked, a confusion of questions melding anxieties of the weeks past to the events of this night of danger and daring.

He told her then, speaking rapidly and clearly. He knew that there was no time to be wasted, that the hour was crucial, but he snatched a precious few minutes to reassure her, to explain his long silence and his puzzling absence. There was time enough for that.

"My trek though the Pennine Alps was difficult. Yes, the Italians were defeated, but I knew that pockets of *fascisti* remained. I walked at night, scavenged for food, slept when and where I could until I reached the headquarters of the Italian Jewish scouts in Turin. They gave me maps, money, and forged papers that got me across the border to Grenoble.

"I walked, day after day, from Grenoble to Toulouse because I knew it was too dangerous to use public transport. Vichy and Gestapo police were everywhere. But today a farmer in Villefranche let me ride in his wagon all the way to Toulouse, and I went at once to your sister's home. I knew that Serge would know where you were, and I could not wait another moment to see you. Not a moment."

He held her close and she pressed her fingers to his lips, as though to capture words as yet unspoken. He kissed her hand and spoke even more rapidly.

"Once there, Serge told me of the plans to sabotage the bridge and why you had to proceed alone. He was desperate that I find you and help you, and I was desperate to make sure that you were safe. He gave me his gloves, his boots, his jacket and told me how to reach the Pont St. Pierre, how to find you."

She nodded, suffused with gratitude, impelled by urgency. They had little time and precious minutes had been forfeit.

"I am safe. But now we must work quickly."

"Tell me what we must do."

He was her lover. He was her confederate. He would obey any order she issued.

"This rope," she explained. "It is our igniting fuse. We must get it into the arch. The incendiaries are in these milk bottles. I will pull the rope, and you will carry the crate of bottles. Then everything will be in place for the detonation."

In silence they moved through the darkness. She crawled once again across the ground, so drenched in nocturnal dew that moisture saturated her dark clothing. Claude hoisted the crate of bottles packed tightly with bullets and primers. In the shelter of the arch, he followed her hissed directions and set the crate down at the correct angle. The necks of the bottles were directed toward the cemented and camouflaged sticks of dynamite on the ceiling. She placed the rope accordingly. Moving quickly, she thrust a long candle, the wax at the wick scraped away, into the lethal contents of the milk bottles. She removed the wooden matches and flint from the pockets of her vest, lit a match, and handed it to Claude, who held the flickering flame to the candle. The wick burned slowly, emitting an odd fragrance. She lit a second match, held it to the end of the rope, watched the flickering flame crawl steadily across the hemp. Satisfied, she gripped Claude's hand and together, never turning, they raced out of the arch, away from the flame, now fiercely burning.

They dashed across the field, never slowing their steps until they reached the burrow. They flung themselves into it, lying prone and shuddering as the thunderous explosion shattered the nocturnal stillness.

They sat up and stared. Blazing crimson and golden arrows of flame shot skyward and cascaded in a fiery torrent across the night scape. The boulders fell with cacophonous thuds.

"It's done," Madeleine whispered.

"You did it, my Madeleine," he said.

"No. *We* did it."

Together then, hand in hand, they raced away, aware that

within minutes, armies of Vichy police, Milice brigades, and Gestapo troops would swarm the Ponts Jambeaux.

Only when they were at a safe distance did she ask the question that had haunted her every hour of that night of doubt and danger.

"Simone? When you were there, when you spoke to Serge, was she all right? Had the baby been born?"

He hesitated.

"I did not see Simone," he said quietly. "But I heard her. A whimper. Not a scream. Serge only said that the labor was progressing, that Hélène was optimistic. I would have wanted to bring you better news, but that is all that I know."

"Yes," she said. "All right."

She would have wanted better news but she was grateful that he had not dissembled. He had said enough to offer her some relief, however vague. Her sister was alive. Hélène was not one to offer false predictions. She would know soon enough. For the moment, hope, fragile hope, would have to suffice.

She leaned against Claude and they walked on, at last pausing to rest beneath a tree in a meadow at a distance from the bridges. The tall wild grass swayed in the gentle predawn breeze. Exhausted, they lay side by side on the moist and fragrant ground. Claude drew her close. She stared up at the gathering light of the new day, grateful that they were together, and that together, they had managed a small triumph for the Résistance, for their people. Their patience had been rewarded.

His lips found hers. His hand rested tenderly on her head. They were quiet, entwined in each other's arms. Their embrace was a pledge. The golden rays of the nascent sun brushed their faces and they closed their eyes, laying claim to a brief, precious hour of silence and solitude.

At last they began their walk back to Simone's home, careful to avoid the main roadways already crowded with squad cars and earthmovers, repair trucks and even the occasional tank.

"Can a tank repair a damaged bridge?" Madeleine whispered and they laughed.

It was full daylight when they arrived. The Perls' windows were dark, and an ominous silence prevailed. They hesitated, as restrained by fear as they were impelled by hope. At last, Madeleine thrust the door open and, not daring to look at each other, they entered.

Joy burst upon them as the plaintive wail, peculiar to newborn infants, penetrated that fearful silence. Happiness came with a burst. Their hearts grew light; laughter lingered on their lips. Across the room, Simone smiled at them, her baby swaddled in a soft white blanket and pressed to her breast. Madeleine rushed to her side.

"A girl, Madeleine," Simone said. Her voice was hoarse with exhaustion, but her face was aglow with happiness.

"She's beautiful," Madeleine murmured as she very gently stroked the infant's feathery wisps of hair. "And her name?"

"Yael. Grand-mère suggested it. It means 'glory to God.'"

"Yael," Madeleine repeated.

She understood that Lucie Dreyfus would choose that name for a Dreyfus infant, a name that was an affirmation of the faith that had sustained her through all the years of her life, years of war, years of peace.

She smiled gratefully as Simone handed her the baby. She

looked down at the newborn's tiny face, her skin lucent, her eyes tightly closed. Serenity took her by surprise. The anxieties of all those long weeks and months evaporated. All her fears were erased. Simone had survived her difficult pregnancy. A healthy baby had been born. Claude sat beside her. The strike against the Ponts Jumeaux had succeeded. A miracle. Many miracles.

Their daring act would bring reprisals, she knew. She and Claude would face new dangers, new challenges. But on this sun-bright morning, after the long night of terror and uncertainty, she felt only gratitude. Her infant niece rested in her arms, and tears came unbidden. Tears of joy.

"Yael," she murmured. "Yael. Glory to God. Glory to God in the highest."

THIRTY-FIVE

REPRISALS DID COME, FIERCE AND IMMEDIATE. DETERMINED to arrest and punish the saboteurs of the bridges, the Milice, the Vichy police, and their German masters combed the city, arresting dozens of suspects and subjecting them to harsh interrogations and torture. Despite their draconian efforts, they obtained no information. The disciplined teams responsible for the demolition at Pont St. Michel and Pont Neuf were gone from Toulouse, having fled to distant safe houses in Arles and Avignon.

Serge was arrested and questioned, but he remained stoic. His alibi was incontrovertible.

"My baby was born that very night. I was at my wife's side throughout her long and difficult labor. You have spies who keep watch on my house. They themselves will confirm that I never left. And of course the midwife was with me."

The surveillance team, not daring to reveal their dereliction, insisted that he had not left the house.

Hélène, summoned to Gestapo headquarters, calmly confirmed Serge's account.

"Were any other witnesses present?" the Gestapo interrogator asked.

His face was turned away from her, but Hélène recognized

his voice. She had delivered his baby only months earlier and saved his wife from toxemia by plunging her hand into the gaping cervix to remove the placenta.

"Only the newborn infant," she replied sardonically, unintimidated by the man who had wept and pleaded for her help when he thought his wife might die. His tears had made him vulnerable to her. That she had saved his wife's life placed him in her debt.

"Your sarcasm does not impress me, mademoiselle," he said angrily.

"It is not my intent to impress you," she continued daringly. "But then you yourself know that a worried husband does not leave the side of his beloved wife at such an hour. It is said that even in the animal kingdom, the male hovers near the laboring female. The lion stays with the lioness. Perhaps even your Führer would not leave his wife at such a time. But then, of course, Herr Hitler has neither children nor a wife. I have heard that he never cries, that he thinks tears are unmanly. Perhaps he does not know that even his Gestapo officers have been known to weep."

"You go too far, mademoiselle," her interrogator shouted. "Get her out of here!" he commanded to the soldier at the door.

"I leave. I hope your little son is doing well. And your wife."

He did not reply. His debt was paid. The Jewish bitch was entitled to no further demands on him.

Hélène smiled, but she did not stop trembling until she left the building. Serge waited for her on the corner.

"Thank you, Hélène," he said quietly as they walked on, passing convoys of *Citroën Traction Avants,* the official Gestapo vehicles, their sirens blasting as they headed toward the Ponts Jumeaux.

With each passing day, rumors proliferated. The damage to the bridges was extensive, beyond repair. No. The damage was minimal. Repair groups were at work. No. It seemed that skilled workers could not be found. The masons of Toulouse had mysteriously disappeared. Crews would have to be brought from Paris.

The pursuit of the saboteurs continued unabated. The Secretary General of the Police issued adamant announcements.

"Every suspect will be arrested. Anyone with any information must come forward," officers shouted from loudspeakers mounted on the trucks that traversed the city.

"Death to the perpetrators! Death to the Maquis, death to the Résistance! Heil Hitler!" blared for hours on end throughout the city.

Madeleine and Claude were spirited out of Toulouse on a farmer's cart, hidden beneath rough blankets that reeked of manure. They traveled southward to Carcassone, and in that small village, Madeleine was given refuge in the modest home of Madame Fauchere, a widowed seamstress, while Claude found shelter in a monastery.

It surprised them to learn that neither Madame Fauchere nor Père Louis, the abbot of the monastery, had been members of the Résistance during the early period of the Occupation. Each had felt called to action only after seeing the horrifying photographs in "The Fruits of Hatred." The Gaullists in London had been prescient when they gambled that when confronted with the incontrovertible photographic reality of German cruelty, even the most pragmatic French citizens would experience a crisis of conscience and join the battle against Nazi cruelty.

"I must atone for my silence," Madame Fauchere told Madeleine when she expressed her gratitude. "You must not thank me. I am proud that you are a guest in my home."

"We should have acted sooner," the abbot confided regretfully to Claude. "We might have saved the children whose photos we saw in 'The Fruits of Hatred.' I will never forget their faces, their poor little faces. Those photographs of horror. God Himself, and Christ our Lord, must be weeping."

"We are grateful that you are acting now," Claude said. "You are courageous. I know that you risk your own life in offering me sanctuary."

"If only I could help endangered children," the monk said regretfully.

"That is why I am here," Claude assured him. "To pluck our children from danger."

Claude, wearing a monk's brown robe, and Madeleine, dressed in the seamstress's plain black dress, her thick, dark hair covered with the white lace caplet of a lay sister, met in a small garden café. Seated on the rough wooden bench, they stared at each other, their eyes bright with affection and gratitude.

"Is it Purim?" she asked. "Is that why we are in costume?"

She smiled teasingly. He laughed. Gaiety was restored to them. Briefly and blessedly, they were at a remove from danger. Briefly and blessedly, they were together. Now and again they reached across the table. Their hands touched. Palm upon palm. Finger brushing finger.

In hushed tones, they planned for the days and weeks to

come. Now, at last, they would reunite with Anna Hofberg and the other children in her group. Their trek across the Pyrenees to Spain was imminent. Time was of the essence. It would be dangerous to wait any longer. Spanish couriers reported the increased presence of German patrols along escape routes. Winter was approaching. Ice and snow would render the mountain passes treacherous. Even now, the nights were cold, and lacy white coverlets of frost glittered on the ground at the break of dawn.

"We must move very soon," Claude said.

"We must move now," Madeleine corrected him.

He nodded.

They met again the next day and walked down a mountain path, following a ribbon of pale autumn sunlight, to the hamlet of Lézignan-Corbières. On a narrow road obscured by a grove of conifers, a small order of nuns maintained the orphanage where Anna and her friends, guided by Jeanne Levy, had found refuge. Their arrival at the convent was greeted with dismay by the elderly Mother Superior.

"You have placed yourself and all of us in great danger," she said. "The Germans are already suspicious. A Gestapo unit was here only last week, searching for Jewish children. Luckily, Anna's blond hair, her fair complexion, and her ability to recite the catechism deceived them. We prevented them from searching the dormitory by telling them that some of the children were ill with mumps. Ah, how those mighty storm troopers fear the disease that might threaten their manhood. But they will be back. They are persistent, those trained haters. What if they were to see you? What if they were to discover the children?"

Her voice trembled. Her arthritic fingers toyed nervously with the beads of her rosary.

"We will not be here," Madeleine assured her. "Nor will the little ones. We hope to guide the children across the border to Spain very soon."

"You must be very careful," the nun cautioned, concern replacing her anger. "Our informants in Pau tell us that the Germans have increased their presence. Because of the destruction of the bridges in Toulouse and the murders in Paris, the Germans are ever more vigilant, ever more vicious."

"What murders in Paris?" Claude asked. "Forgive our ignorance, *ma mere*. We have neither read a newspaper nor heard a radio report for several days. Not since the sabotage in Toulouse."

"Of course. You, of course, know about the bridges in Toulouse?" she asked, and they understood that it was a question that required no answer.

"But we do not know what happened in Paris," Madeleine said. "Can you enlighten us?"

The elderly nun sighed.

"It is very sad. Dr. Julius Ritter, the Nazi official who initiated that terrible program of Service de Travail Obligatoire, was assassinated. My own nephew was among the many young Frenchmen sent to Germany as a slave laborer by that cruel man. The Gestapo searched for his assassin, but when they were unsuccessful, they took revenge on the Résistance and arrested fifty Parisians. They held them hostage, hoping for informants, but when no one came forward, they shot them all in a public square. They left them there in pools of their own blood, forbidding their loved ones to bury them. I say novenas for those fifty poor souls, murdered to avenge the death of one evil Nazi. A travesty. I do not condone murder, but I hope that God will forgive me because I do not regret the assassination of Julius Ritter. I am, in fact, glad that he is gone from this earth. My only sorrow is for those he harmed in life as well as in death."

She reached for the cross that dangled from a heavy chain at her chest and held it to her lips.

"Of course God will forgive you," Madeleine said. "Our one God, yours and mine, blesses those who abhor evil and do good. You are surely blessed for all the good you have done for our children."

Still fingering her crucifix, the nun lowered her head and smiled gratefully, her anger forgotten.

"Come. I will take you to your Anna," she said.

They followed her down a narrow corridor to a small room where Anna crouched near a window, reading in the pale light that seeped through the narrow pane. She turned, tossed her book to the floor, and sprinted across the room into Madeleine's outstretched arms.

"Madeleine, Madeleine. I knew you would come. I waited and waited. I hoped and I hoped. And now you are here. Are we going to Spain? When will we go? Can we go today? Tomorrow?"

She laughed, flushed with excitement, her blue eyes sparkling as she turned to Claude.

"Claude. Oh, Claude, how wonderful that you are here, that you will go with us to Spain. And then to Palestine. I will see my brothers. Will we go to Palestine together? Oh, we must do that."

Her words tumbled forth in a wild delirium of hope and joy. She squealed with delight when they held out the small, very small, gifts they had brought her, a small bunch of dried blue flowers that Claude had gathered on his alpine trek and Madeleine had sewn into a sachet and a crescent-shaped shell with violet veins Madeleine had found on the banks of the Garonne.

Madeleine held Anna close as the child prattled on.

"Oh, how happy I am that you are here. How soon am I to join my brothers in distant Palestine? Is the journey to Palestine very long?"

She was so weary of running, of being shunted from one hiding place to another, she said again and again. She hugged Madeleine.

"Soon, so very soon, I will know happiness. Oh, it is wonderful that you are here. My friends will be so excited. All of us are ready. When do we leave? Today? Tomorrow?" she asked again.

Madeleine glanced at Claude, who turned away. She took Anna's hands in her own and spoke softly, injecting reassurance into words that she knew would disappoint.

"We cannot go to Spain just yet, Anna. Not today. Not tomorrow. We must plan and prepare. But we will leave very soon. That is my promise to you. For now, you and your friends are safe with the kind sisters."

"No! No!" Tears of disappointment streaked Anna's cheek. Her hands, clenched into fists, pummeled Madeleine with a sorrowful beat.

"I want to go now. Now. When will I see my brothers again? When will you come back?"

Madeleine cradled the girl in her arms. Anna's sorrow became her own, although the child's words were lost to her. Unable to hear, she was also unable to speak. Grief choked her voice into silence.

"Why?" Anna asked. "Why is this happening to us? Why do the Germans hate us?"

It was Claude who answered. He spoke calmly, clearly, and in the quiet of that room, Madeleine heard his every word. She had forgotten how resonant his voice could be.

"No one can understand such hatred," he said. "No one can explain it. Not I. Not Madeleine. Not the wisest of our rabbis nor the most thoughtful of our leaders. Not our courageous Mother Superior. But we know that love, in the end, triumphs over hatred, that better days will come. Be patient, Anna. Know that you are loved. And protected. It is no small thing to be loved and protected by Madeleine Levy. She catches her dreams and turns them into reality. Trust her. Trust me. We will leave for Spain and you will see your brothers again. Smile now and the three of us will go to the café in Lézignan-Corbières. We will eat fresh-baked croissants and imagine that we are on the Champs-Élysées."

And Anna did smile, a sad and wistful smile. Disappointment, after all, was not new to her. Reconciled to that which she was powerless to change, she took solace from Claude's gentle words.

"Yes. Let us go to that café and eat croissants. Perhaps they will have apricot jam. Madeleine and I love apricot jam."

She smiled and Madeleine understood that Anna was offering her the comfort of pleasant memories, of days long past when hunger had been unknown and the jam that they favored had been sweet upon their tongues.

"They will definitely have apricot jam," Madeleine promised. "This summer was a splendid season for apricots."

She remembered the summer days when she had cycled down rural roads to visit her hidden children and paused to pluck the golden orbs dangling from low-hanging branches. The hungry, frightened children had looked with wonder at the fruit she placed in their small hands. The golden skin of the juice-filled orbs was a memento of the sunlight they rarely saw, sequestered as they were in basements and haylofts, in tunnels blanketed in branches. The hidden children had eaten hesitantly, tentatively, each bite a small miracle.

She and Claude murmured their thanks to the Mother Superior and, with Anna, they walked hand in hand down the sun-dappled road into the village.

The elderly nun, still fingering her crucifix, stood in the doorway of the convent and stared after them. She had thought to remind them to be careful, very careful. Even in the small village, collaborators lurked, but she knew they had no need for her words. They were children of Abraham in Nazi-occupied France. They were conditioned to courage, conditioned to caution. She watched as they disappeared beyond a bend in the road, her lips moving in soundless prayer.

THIRTY-SIX

B ACK IN CARCASSONE, A RÉSISTANCE COURIER BROUGHT A communique from Serge. He wrote that German military successes in Greece had emboldened Hitler's generals. The Gestapo in Athens had ordered all Athenian Jews to register but had encountered the organized resistance of the local population. Princess Andrew, the great-granddaughter of Queen Victoria, hid Jews in her own home.

"Why does Serge write of this? How does all that affect the Jews of France?" Madeleine wondered. "How does it affect us, Claude?"

"Serge explains that it will soon have an impact on us," Claude replied grimly. "The Nazis are so frustrated by the Greek Resistance that Goebbels has ordered the occupying forces in France to move farther southward and crush the French Résistance. If the Jews of Greece cannot be decimated, then the Jews of France will be punished. It is maniacal logic, but our enemies are maniacs. We are at risk because our intelligence reveals that Carcassone is an obvious target. That is why Serge risked sending a courier to warn us to leave this area."

Madeleine's heart sank.

"We must have more information," she said. "What does the BBC say?"

"We will soon find out," he replied.

In the basement of the monastery, Claude watched the abbot remove his radio from its hiding place deep in the coal bin. The monk smiled sadly as he brushed the granules of black dust from the receiver.

"It is now the only radio in the village," he explained. "We keep it hidden because our beloved schoolmaster, Maître André, was arrested and sent to Brens when his radio was discovered. We fear that he was executed. Imagine the lunacy of this war. A good man is killed for the crime of listening to a radio."

Claude nodded.

"There have been similar occurrences in Toulouse," he said, and he wondered if the radio hidden in Simone's kitchen was still functioning. He would know soon enough.

He read the communique yet again. Serge wrote that the search for the saboteurs of the bridges had ended in a spurt of false arrests. That search now seemed to be abandoned, which meant that given the Gestapo drive toward Carcassone, it would be safer for both Claude and Madeleine to return to Toulouse.

Safer, Claude thought bitterly. Would they ever be safe? He shredded Serge's message as he watched the abbot coax the radio to life.

The reception was weak. They waited patiently through bouts of static and indistinct humming and smiled in relief when they heard the new BBC code for Radio Londres—Verlain's "Chanson d'Automne." The faint, ghostly melody wafted through the room.

"A suitable choice of music," the abbot said. "Autumn is indeed upon us. The season of sadness and death."

"October," Claude agreed. "Never my favorite month."

He and Madeleine had felt the new crispness in the air, the chilly brush of mountain winds drifting down from the Pyrenees. Fallen leaves of scarlet and gold crunched beneath their feet as they walked through the village to meet with the Spanish couriers who would serve as their guides. Money was exchanged. Maps were studied. The weather was discussed.

The abbot gave Claude a woolen cape. The seamstress rummaged through a trunk and found a winter coat that smelled of camphor which Madeleine gratefully accepted.

"It will soon be very cold," the couriers warned Madeleine and Claude. "The shepherds predict an early snowfall in the Pyrenees."

How soon would the snow begin to fall? Claude wondered as he leaned forward and listened to the newscaster's welcoming words. "*Ici Londres. Les Français parlent aux Français.*" Then the Morse code of dot-dot-dot-dash. V for victory. The H for honor had been eliminated. Perhaps, Claude thought, because so many French collaborators had forfeited their honor. The omission did not matter. What mattered was that they were not alone, that the Free French in Britain remained a vibrant force and Radio Londres continued to broadcast.

The newscaster's tone was somber, but then it was always somber because he never had anything positive to report. Claude could not remember a time when the news had been good. Certainly it was not good on this bleak October afternoon. He listened closely to the droning voice.

Nazi attacks on Greek Jews had accelerated. The Chief Rabbi of Athens, Elias Barzilai, had fled to Thessaly. Groups of Greek partisans, Greek Jewish scouts, and Palestinian Jews were smuggling Jewish children across the Aegean Sea to Turkish ports and then on to the coast of Haifa. It was a heroic but dubious effort, the announcer said sadly, a treacherous journey to a dangerous and uncertain destination because the British would not rescind the White Paper that limited Jewish immigration into Mandatory Palestine.

"But Palestine is your promised land," the abbot said. He was perplexed. Zionism was an alien concept to a monk isolated in Carcassone.

"It seems that promises, even God's promises, are made to be broken," Claude replied bitterly.

"Not God's promises," the abbot countered as he lit a Gauloise and passed the packet to Claude, who accepted a cigarette gratefully and inhaled deeply.

Blowing a smoke ring into the basement dimness, he marveled at the fortitude and tenacity of the Greek and Palestinian scouts. The Aegean would be frigid even on these early autumn days. According to the couriers and *passeurs*, the mountain passes of the Pyrenees were also dangerously cold. They had been warned by the Spanish guides that if he and Madeleine were to succeed in leading this last group of Jewish children across the border, they would have to leave soon. Very soon. And it was important, the *passeurs* had stressed, that the children be properly clothed and shod. The German were one enemy. The cold weather was an even more formidable adversary.

Claude sighed. The newscast ended. He helped the abbot conceal the radio beneath the black lumps of coal.

The next day, he and Madeleine made one last visit to the convent. Madeleine was relieved that Anna was away, having joined her class on a nature hike. It was the Mother Superior they had come to see.

"It is important for us to know whether the children have sturdy boots, warm clothing," Madeleine said, aware that the nun knew exactly why she was asking such a question.

The answer was both anticipated and disappointing.

"We have soled and resoled their footwear. Some of it is serviceable, but most is beyond repair. The cobbler despaired of Anna's boots. She now wears the shoes of one of our sisters, too large for her small feet, but we stuff newspapers at the toes and the heels. She manages, but they would not sustain her on a long trek," the Mother Superior said flatly.

"We have very little winter clothing," she continued. "Perhaps two anoraks. Three pair of heavy leggings. The Jewish children were brought to us in the spring or the summer. None of them arrived with any clothing but the flimsy garments they wore. You must know that the Germans requisitioned the inventory of winter clothing in every French store and factory and shipped all that they found to Berlin. German children will be warm even as our French children will shiver with cold. I do not know how you will find the garments and boots that the children will need."

"We will manage," Madeleine assured her. "We will return for our children, and we will bring everything that they will need. We have resources."

The nun asked no more questions. Too much knowledge was dangerous.

"We will await your return," she said. "But try not to delay. There has already been an early frost, which means there will be an early snowfall in the mountains."

"We have been told of that. We will not delay," Claude promised. "We know that neither time nor weather is on our side."

In fact, he thought wryly, nothing was on their side. Their only weapons were their own perseverance and determination.

"You must leave this area as soon as possible," the nun continued. "We have been informed that a Gestapo contingent will arrive today. There is a bus leaving within the hour, not for Toulouse but for Valence."

She glanced at the window where a fierce wind rattled the barren branches of a giant oak.

"Of course. Valence will, in fact, be a safer route for us. Toulouse swarms with Milice," Madeleine said. "And I will be able to see my grandmother who is in Valence."

Her spirits soared, however briefly, when she thought of seeing Lucie Dreyfus, of embracing her beloved grandmother and resting her hand upon the old woman's shoulder in the habit of her girlhood. Oh how tired she was, how very tired.

"I will send a message to my sisters at the convent there telling them to expect a visit from the granddaughter of Madame Duteil."

The nun flashed Madeleine a conspiratorial smile and turned to the window again, this time focusing her gaze on the roadway. A workman waved a flag, a signal that Gestapo vehicles were approaching. She crossed herself and hurried out. She had to warn the other sisters of the Gestapo's imminent arrival and rehearse the Jewish children yet again in the answers to the dangerous and invasive questions the unwelcome invaders asked.

Madeleine and Claude understood. Within minutes, they dashed from the convent to the depot, arriving just in time to board the Valence autobus.

The clumsy vehicle lumbered across rutted roads, lurching to stops at every hamlet so that schoolchildren might board or disembark. Because of the early frost, the children were swathed in layers of sweaters and heavy jackets, with colorful woolen hats jammed down to cover their ears.

"Where are we to find such clothing and boots?" Claude asked worriedly, pointing to the chattering children. "Look at them. Our little ones will need scarves. Mittens. Heavy socks. Warm undergarments. It was spring when I led the children across the Alps, but even then the mountain air turned bitter cold in the evening. We will be trekking across the Pyrenees at the onset of winter. If they are not properly clothed, our children could freeze to death. That has happened."

He fell silent. He would not frighten Madeleine by recounting the reports of small frozen bodies lying on mountain verges, mourned and hastily buried under mounds of snow.

"The storage room in my parents' apartment on the rue de la Dalbade is still crammed with all the clothing that my mother collected for needy children. Everything remained there when my parents were forced to flee Toulouse. I am certain that Madame Leonie, our concierge, has managed to protect the contents of the apartment. We will collect whatever we need, arrange for transport back to the orphanage, and return there at once. Our couriers are ready and willing to guide us to Pau, and that is only thirty miles from the Spanish border."

"You make it sound so simple," Claude said.

"No. I do not deceive myself. It will not be simple, but it is within our reach. Isn't it amazing what we can do when we have no choice?"

She laughed and he smiled. Her courage was contagious. Yes, she did indeed catch her dreams and turn them into reality.

It was late in the evening when they reached Valence. The gate of the convent that sheltered Lucie Dreyfus was swiftly opened by the elderly caretaker who was unsurprised by their arrival.

"Madame Duteil will be so pleased to see you," he said.

Madeleine nodded, fearful that her voice would break if she spoke, moved as she was by his kindness and concern in a world beset by cruelty.

Lucie Dreyfus waited for them in her small sitting room. Madeleine inhaled the fragrance of the herbs that her grandmother cultivated wherever she made her home. Skeins of colorful wool and half-finished knitted garments filled a corner of the room. Books were scattered on every surface—scholarly volumes, novels, collections of poetry, and Jewish texts. Her grandmother remained an eternal student, a voracious reader. The world of the intellect presented no danger. When she read, when she gathered knowledge, she was safe.

Lucie's thick, silver hair was twisted into a simple chignon, and her eyes were bright with unshed tears as she embraced her granddaughter. Her simple black wool dress was worn thin, but it fell in graceful folds. At seventy-four, she was still slender, her face unlined, her posture erect. Ever dignified, ever confident, she was, as always, a woman who refused to surrender to despair.

"How brave you are to have made this journey," she said.

"Madeleine's courage is recognized throughout the Résistance," Claude said proudly.

Madeleine shook her head. She did not want Claude to say anything more. She would not add to her grandmother's worries.

But Lucie asked no questions. She prepared tea, using a battered electric kettle, and removed a platter of cheese and baguettes from the windowsill.

"Nature itself is my icebox," she said as she set the tiny table in her room with the same care she had once lavished on the formal meals she had hosted in her elegant Paris apartment on the rue des Renaudes.

The food disappeared quickly. Madeleine realized that they had not eaten since early that morning. Normal meals at set times were now alien to them. They ate when and where they could, as indifferent to hunger as they were to their overwhelming fatigue. Food and sleep were peacetime luxuries. She sighed and saw that Claude reclined in his chair, his eyes half-closed. Lucie smiled and led him to the alcove that contained her own narrow bed.

"Rest, my son," she murmured.

Claude nodded, stretched out, and immediately fell asleep. Madeleine covered him gently with an afghan and pressed her lips against his cheeks. She remembered the many nights of her childhood when her father would return home after a late-night rotation at the hospital and then fall asleep fully clothed on the sofa. She and Simone had watched as their mother draped a blanket over him and lightly kissed his cheek. With that gentle nocturnal gesture, her mother had transmitted a lesson in love.

She kissed Claude's forehead, dimmed the light, and returned to her seat beside her grandmother.

"He is a brave young man, your Claude," Lucie said.

"Yes. Yes, he is. We care for each other, but this is such a difficult and dangerous time."

"But despite the difficulties, despite the dangers, you have been blessed with some happiness, is that not so?"

Lucie enclosed Madeleine's hand in her gentle grasp.

Madeleine hesitated. It had been many months since the word *happiness* had been vested with meaning for her. *Happiness.* She pondered the word. She would answer her grandmother honestly. She spoke very slowly.

"Yes. Claude and I have found moments of happiness, but we are always aware that we are surrounded by misery. So many of our friends and comrades have been arrested. So many have been deported. So many have died. So many of those dear to us have disappeared. I miss my uncle Pierre and my cousins, so far away in America. I worry that I might never see them again. I miss my parents and my brothers. I miss you. Claude and I dare not speak of the future. We know full well we might not have a future. Each time we part, I worry that he may be gone forever. So whatever happiness I feel is always shadowed by fear."

Her voice broke and she fought to contain her tears, yet her words had relieved the unarticulated sadness that had for so many months weighed so heavily upon her heart. As she had longed to do, she rested her head on her grandmother's shoulder.

Lucie nodded and spoke slowly, clearly so that Madeleine could hear her every word.

"I understand," she said. "I too am bereft. Like you, I find that happiness and sorrow are my twin companions. I have known a multitude of losses, grief that is often too heavy for me to bear. My son, Pierre, is in the United States, and it may well be that I will never see him and my beloved grandchildren again. I am separated from your family—your mother, my wonderful daughter, and your father who has been like my own child. Will I ever see your brothers again? Will I ever hold Simone's Yael in my arms?

"Loneliness and fear haunt my days. And yet I too am surprised by sudden spurts of joy. I look at the night sky and see the stars, and my heart leaps up. I hear the voices of the Sisters of Valence singing in celebration of God's creation, and I share their wonder at the beautiful world that has been given us. I see the way Claude looks at you and I see the love in your eyes, and I am filled with contentment. So I tell you, my Madeleine, while it is true that we live in fearsome times, this life is worth its grief."

"Yes. This life is worth its grief," Madeleine agreed. Her voice trembled at the beauty and wisdom of her grandmother's words.

She and Claude left Valence the next day. Standing in the entry of the convent, Lucie placed her hands upon their lowered heads and murmured the ancient Jewish prayer for travelers.

"May it be your will, dear God, that you lead these, my children, to peace and cause them to reach their desired destination for life, for joy, and for peace. Grant them favor, kindness, and compassion. Amen. *Selah*."

"Amen, *Selah*," Claude and Madeleine whispered in unison.

Grandmother and granddaughter embraced. Madeleine did not look back. Hand in hand, she and Claude walked down the sun-dappled road, the brilliant leaves of the season of death crunching beneath their feet.

They boarded the ancient autobus that would carry them to Toulouse, and Claude noted that the elderly driver wore a faded neckerchief imprinted with the Cross of Lorraine, the symbol of the Résistance. Wordlessly, he removed his own imprinted kerchief from his pocket and wiped his brow. The driver smiled and nodded. Oddly reassured, Claude led Madeleine to a seat in the rear. The bus lurched forward, and they slept throughout the journey.

THIRTY-SEVEN

THE BUS PULLED INTO THE DEPOT OF TOULOUSE AS THE bells of the Cathedral of Saint-Sernin chimed nine times. The hour was not late. Toulouse was a city whose citizens loved nocturnal strolls and evening gatherings at its many cafés and bistros. Madeleine's heart sank as she peered through the window of the bus and saw that the streets they drove through were deserted, every window darkened. At the depot, the few disembarking passengers glanced around nervously, checked their watches, and hurried away. Perplexed and uneasy, she and Claude looked at each other, fear in their eyes, tension in every fiber of their exhausted bodies.

"Something has happened," Claude murmured as they, too, left the bus.

He turned to the elderly driver who approached them, lighting his path in the darkened depot with a faintly glowing electric torch. Although there was no one to be seen, he held a finger to his lips, warning them to speak softly.

"What is going on, *mon ami*?" Claude asked. "Has there been an air-raid warning?"

"Not an air raid. But the Gestapo has ordered a curfew. They mandated that streets be cleared by 9:00 p.m. You must hurry to find shelter or you may be arrested."

"But something must have happened?" Claude asked insistently.

A curfew was a drastic punitive action. It not only affected social interaction but also caused economic distress. Restaurants were shuttered, evening deliveries halted. All transportation, public and private, was prohibited.

"You have not heard the news?" the driver asked.

Claude and Madeleine shook their heads.

They had not bought a newspaper when their bus made a local stop because only *La Dépêche* was on sale at the newsstand, and they would not support the Vichy-sponsored broadsheet. A foolish decision, he realized now.

"We have heard nothing," he said ruefully. "We know only that a curfew is a desperate measure."

"Yes. A desperate measure indeed. The Nazis and their collaborators are, we believe, at a point of desperation. They have been frustrated in their efforts to find the saboteurs of the bridges, and only yesterday the Police Commandant of Toulouse, a known collaborator, was assassinated right in front of his home. The shooter was a Jewish boy, driven to madness because his parents had been deported to Auschwitz. The Germans and their collaborators now fear every man, woman, and child in Toulouse. They are frightened and angry. And, as you say, desperate. Hence the curfew."

"Was the boy caught?" Claude asked.

"They caught him, and they shot him right in front of the cathedral, left his body there, still dressed in his scout uniform. A Jewish Scout, they say. He was so young, not yet eighteen. *Pauvre jeune éclaireur.* Poor young scout."

The driver touched his neckerchief and made the sign of the cross. Madeleine, gripped by terror, clutched Claude's arm.

"He was a Jewish Scout. The Nazis and the Milice will seek out everyone with a connection to the Jewish Scouts. Simone. Serge. Hélène."

Other names came to mind. Madeleine grew faint as she thought of her sister, her endangered friends, her brave comrades, many of whom had offered her refuge, often risking their own lives for her sake.

"Do you have a safe place to sleep tonight?" the driver asked.

"We do. At least I hope so," Claude said.

"Hope is not enough these days," he said.

He scrawled an address on a slip of paper and handed it to Claude.

"You may need this if your hope disappoints. It is the safest of safe houses. Just say that André sent you. André Montand."

"Thank you, André Montand," Claude said gravely. He did not offer his own name. Résistance rules were in play.

"No need to thank me. We are all Frenchmen, are we not?"

He touched his faded neckerchief and Claude, in turn, unfurled his own.

"*Liberté, égalité, fraternité,*" they whispered in unison and they went their separate ways, disappearing into the darkness of a city imprisoned in silence.

Claude and Madeleine raced through a labyrinth of streets and alleys, avoiding the main roads. When at last they reached Simone and Serge's apartment, they stared at each other, their eyes glazed by fear. It appeared to be abandoned. Blackout curtains covered the windows, empty storage cartons littered the courtyard, refuse bins overflowed, and a feral cat perched in the doorway. But drawing closer, they discerned shadowy movements behind the thick fabric of the black draperies. Claude kicked the cat away, and Madeleine pushed the door open. Serge leapt toward them, brandishing a pistol. Behind him, Simone stood motionless, her pale face frozen into a mask of fear.

"Simone, it's me, Madeleine."

Simone gasped and rushed to embrace her sister. Serge lowered his pistol, thrust it into his pocket, breathed a sigh of relief, and held his hand out to Claude. Excuses and explanations tumbled forth, an explosion of words, a staccato exchange of news. They spoke with an urgent rapidity, their voices colliding in a chorus as chaotic as the room itself.

A battered trunk crammed with clothing and linens yawned open. Burlap sacks overflowed with pots and pans, cutlery and tools. A haze of smoke and the scent of burning papers permeated the air. Documents were being incinerated in the kitchen, the ashes tossed into a fire pit in the rear of the small building.

"What is happening, Simone?" Madeleine asked.

"You came just in time," Simone said. "Another hour and we would have been gone. We could not think of how to warn you of the danger. The Germans have a list of every Jewish *Éclaireur*, and they are sweeping through the area making mass arrests. Every suspect is being sent to the camp for political prisoners at Compiègne—a death camp. No one has ever been known to leave Compiègne. They also have the names of every Résistance fighter. Vichy collaborators made sure of that."

"And of course they have known my name since my identity

was exposed on the pages of *Le Ferro*. I've just been lucky to escape their clutches thus far," Madeleine said ruefully.

"Yes, lucky. And smart. And resourceful," Claude corrected her. "I assume that I am on their list as well."

"Assume so. We know that we are. Serge and I have long been in their sights," Simone said.

She spoke with calm honed over long months of confrontations with danger.

"They were reluctant to arrest us. We were their bait. They were waiting for other Résistants to contact us," she continued.

"Waiting for us, I suppose," Claude said.

"Actually, it is Madeleine who is their prime target," Serge interposed. "We have learned that a Milice informant reported seeing her crossing the fields to the bridge on the night of the demolitions. They are circulating her photo, offering a reward for the saboteur of les Ponts Jumeaux. Madeleine, you are now the most famous Résistante in Toulouse, perhaps in all of France. Of course, they came here asking questions, but we told them that you are no longer welcome in our home, that we are angry with you because you have a non-Jewish lover. Simone told them that you and your lover had left Toulouse and crossed the border into Spain."

"And did they believe you?" Madeleine asked, clutching Claude's arm.

"Probably not. All belief is suspended," Simone replied. "They don't believe us, and we don't believe them. Sometimes they do not even believe each other. It is known that the Vichy police lie to the Gestapo, that the Gestapo lie to the Milice. But those *doryphores*, those despicable potato bugs in their green uniforms, continue to pursue us. They lurk outside our home. They follow us in the streets. One or two are posted on this street through the night.

"Fortunately, they have a great fondness for wine and beer, and we keep them well supplied. They drink well and then they sleep well And we made sure that they are sleeping especially well tonight. Late this afternoon, Serge very noisily carried a case of beer and another of wine into the shed. Of course, they plundered it as soon as darkness fell. They drank very well—and they have been sleeping very well for the past several hours. That is why they did not see you arrive."

"What happens tonight?" Claude asked.

He glanced around the chaotic room and realized that he already knew the answer to his question. Their flight was imminent.

Serge replied, his tone somber but firm. He was a man who ignored fear and embraced pragmatism.

"We have learned that they do plan to arrest us—perhaps tomorrow, perhaps the next day. Our usefulness has expired. They no longer believe that Madeleine will come here. The Résistance leadership has ordered us to leave Toulouse. They have arranged for a farmer, Monsieur Granot, to transport us to a safe house in Aveyron. He will be here just after midnight."

"It is a miracle that you arrived just in time to join us. Of course it is difficult to believe that miracles are possible in these dark days, and yet here you are. You must come with us," Simone said, gripping her sister's hands.

"You are suggesting that we go with you to Aveyron?" Claude asked, his voice tremulous with indecision.

"Of course. We will be together. It would mean survival. For now. It would mean safety. For now. Madeleine, please join us. I do not want us to be separated," Simone pleaded.

She turned to Claude, but he looked at Madeleine. She shook her head. He nodded in silent agreement. They could not go to Aveyron. Their own safety was unimportant. They were bound by the promise they had made to Anna Hofberg, by their commitment to the children who had trusted Madeleine with their lives. They would not betray the small dreamers of freedom who had trained so arduously, so fearlessly for the trek across the Pyrenees. Abandonment was not an option.

Madeleine embraced her sister, tears burning her eyes.

"We cannot go with you, Simone," she said. "We have a mission to complete. There are those who rely on us."

"As I do. I am your sister. I rely on you. I cannot bear the thought of losing you," Simone cried out, anger and fear distorting her beautiful face, the serenity that had sustained her for so many months shattered.

"You will not lose me. Claude and I know how to keep ourselves safe. Please, do not be frightened for us. We know what we must do."

She stroked Simone's hair and waited for her to be restored to calm.

"What will you do now?" Simone asked at last, acknowledging defeat, braced for honesty. "Where will you go? Most of our comrades have left Toulouse."

Claude fingered the scrap of paper the bus driver had given him.

"We will find shelter tonight. And tomorrow we will go to

the rue de la Dalbade. Is our friend, Madame Leonie, still the concierge there?" Madeleine asked.

"She is. She has remained an active Résistante, using our parents' apartment as a safe house for fugitives now and again. Of course, she has all of Maman's keys," Simone replied.

"Then she must have the keys to the storage room where Maman hid the winter clothing."

"Yes. Everything is still there. I went there only last week in search of warm jackets for my girls. But Madeleine, Maman collected boots and clothing for children. Nothing there will be of use to you and Claude."

"Claude and I have heavy coats, excellent boots. It is children's clothing that we need," Madeleine said quietly.

Simone stared at her with fear in her eyes. She understood that despite the encroaching cold of late autumn, the ominous approach of winter, and the dangerous and frequent Nazi border patrols, Madeleine and Claude were determined to guide their cadre of children across the Pyrenees. Hence the need for boots to trod along ice-encrusted trails and warm garments for protection against the onslaught of bitter mountain winds. She trembled for her sister, for Claude, for Anna Hofberg and the other children who so bravely and trustingly defied deportations and chose the hazardous road to freedom, to survival.

"Madeleine, I love you too much to lose you. You are brave. That I know. But you must also be careful," she said. "You will be in great danger."

It was Claude who answered her.

"Our Madeleine is both brave and careful. And I will be with her. I will protect her," he said. "That is my promise to you."

Madeleine, reading his lips, stared at him gratefully and embraced her sister. She dared not tell them that tentacles of terror clutched her heart, that she agonized over the fear that both care and courage might desert her. Oh, they who loved her best must not know how weak she was, how she fought to subdue the apprehensions that invaded her thoughts and haunted her dreams.

Simone said no more. Swiftly, they completed the packing, shutting the trunk, trussing up the laden blankets with lengths of rope, tying cords about the burlap sacks. Simone placed their precious radio in her own portmanteau, already crammed with her pens and ink, her stamps and etching tools, the lifesaving weapons of her lifesaving craft. She covered the battered radio with a ragged cloth, swaddling it with the tenderness of a mother shielding an infant.

"Our lifeline," she told Madeleine, who did not remind her that in Vichy France, possession of a radio might well be a death sentence.

Farmer Granot arrived as the bells of Saint-Sernin chimed the midnight hour. The wheels of his wagon were shrouded in lengths of burlap, as were the hooves of his horses. They would retreat from the city in funereal silence. They loaded the remnants of their Toulouse life onto the rough flatbed, concealing everything beneath layers of hay.

The sisters held each other close. Serge gripped Claude's shoulder. The reluctant tears of brave and powerful men trickled down their unshaven cheeks. Tenderly, Serge kissed Madeleine. With equal tenderness, Claude kissed Simone. Madeleine held the infant Yael and kissed Frederica, who clung to her. The farmer helped the little family onto his wagon. Madeleine and Claude stood in the doorway and watched as it vanished into the darkness.

"Will we ever see them again, Claude?" she whispered.

He did not reply. The reassuring words he thought to offer were stuck in his throat. He struggled to remember the traveler's supplication that Lucie Dreyfus had recited so reverently, but he recalled only a single fragment.

"Please God," he murmured, "grant them life and joy and peace."

"Amen. *Selah*," Madeleine intoned instinctively, swaying from side to side.

THIRTY-EIGHT

THEY WAITED UNTIL THE FARMER'S WAGON DISAPPEARED from sight and then, hand in hand, they hurried down the dark, deserted street, distancing themselves from the danger of a home too familiar to the Vichy police. Claude studied the address the bus driver had scrawled on that tattered scrap of notepaper. It was, he knew, their only option. A Gestapo van rumbled by, and they huddled in the recess of a building until it turned the corner. A siren sounded, and they darted into a fetid-smelling alleyway until its shriek grew faint. Panting with exhaustion, perspiring with fear, they made their way through the deserted leather market and at last reached a modest house, dark and uninviting.

Claude glanced nervously about, then knocked lightly. They heard shuffling footsteps from within, and the door opened only wide enough to emit a slender rib of light. He placed the scrap of paper into an outstretched hand.

"Quickly. *Vite.* Come in. No noise. Silence!"

"Yes. Of course. Thank you. *Merci. Merci bien.*"

They entered, weak with relief and startled by the sudden, unfamiliar warmth and the welcoming and surprising aroma of newly baked bread and a simmering pot-au-feu. An elderly woman, her cheeks flushed, blue eyes glinting, snow-white hair

twisted into a neat bun, smiled at them and wiped her hands
on the large white apron that covered her gingham housedress.

"I am Madame Montand. André Montand, my brother-
in-law, told me that you might seek shelter here. Bus drivers, of
course, know everything, and what they do not know, they surmise.
André is seldom wrong. I imagine that you are hungry. If so, you
are indeed fortunate. I have just finished cooking and baking. I
cook and bake late at night now so that the odors do not drift
out the windows and attract the attention of the gendarmes who
might then wonder why so much food is being prepared. I cannot
tell them that I must feed my Résistance comrades when they are
guests in my home. It is best that I cook while *les bâtards* sleep."

She laughed, delighted to have deceived the gendarmes,
delighted to extend hospitality to the young couple who stood
so uneasily in her doorway.

"We are. In fact, very hungry," Claude admitted gratefully,
and they followed her into the large kitchen where a single
candle provided the only light.

Madeleine dipped the warm bread into the rich gravy, struggling to remember when they had last eaten. She was deeply
grateful. Once again, she and Claude had been rescued by the
kindness of strangers. How was it, she wondered, that this war
evoked both the very best and the very worst in those caught
in its talons? Compassion and cruelty collided; human nature
was as divided as France itself. She abandoned the thought and
smiled shyly at Madame Montand.

"My name is Madeleine Levy," she said, marveling at how
simple it was for her to reveal her own identity after so many
months of hiding behind aliases.

"I know," Madame Montand said and held out a flimsy mimeographed flyer of the sort regularly distributed by the Vichy authorities.

Madeleine stared at her own poorly reproduced photograph with the caption that read: *The Jewess Who Dares Not Speak Her Name.* The badly printed text offered a reward of one hundred francs for anyone with information on her whereabouts.

"That much?" she asked Claude.

"Hardly enough," he replied, and they laughed. She thought it a miracle that laughter had not deserted them.

She turned to Madame Montand.

"Madame, I hesitate to ask yet another favor of you, but it is important that we reach my parents' apartment on the rue de la Dalbade tomorrow, and I know that the police and the Milice will be patrolling the streets. Do you think that you and your comrades can help us?"

"We will certainly try our best," the elderly woman said and carried their empty plates to the sink. She was a Toulouse housewife. War or no war, dirty dishes had to be washed.

Minutes later, they followed her up the stairs to a small room with a large bed on which two young men slept. Madam Montand spread blankets on the floor and shrugged apologetically.

"No more beds," she whispered.

"No matter," Claude assured her.

He and Madeleine lay down, and within minutes, they were fast asleep, huddled together in the nest of blankets. They awakened to the pale light of a wintry dawn, the usual silence of that hour shattered by the ominous shrieking of sirens. Claude leapt to his feet, parted the blackout shades, and stared down at the street.

"What's happening?" Madeleine asked.

"A column of police cars are speeding toward the square. Motorcycles. I see one unmarked Citroën Traction Avant approaching, and now another and yet another," he said, his voice rising.

"Gestapo vehicles," the Résistant youth who joined him at the window asserted. "They are never out in such force at such an hour. Something must have happened. Something drastic enough to warrant a reprisal. What do you think, Armand?"

His friend shrugged.

"A Maquis action. Maybe Résistance. But I hope that whatever it was was worth it. That traffic, those sirens mean the Nazi bastards are going to be making mass arrests. We must get out of Toulouse," he said.

The two young men moved swiftly, trussing up their rucksacks, thrusting knives into their high boots, and grimly checking the magazines of small pistols similar to the one Claude himself carried. The pistols, Madeleine knew, had been seized from a Gestapo supply depot during a Résistance operation and distributed to movement leaders. She had been offered one, but she had refused to accept it.

"I don't want to carry death in my pocket," she had told her combat commander. It was a decision she did not regret. Claude would protect her, she told herself as she hastily gathered up their own scattered belongings.

Claude went into the hallway, and through the open door, she discerned only the sound of voices—Claude's questioning tone and Madame Montand's terse reply—but she could not hear the words. She cursed her deafness and waited.

Claude returned to the room, grim faced and pale. He faced her and spoke very slowly, his voice raised loud enough for her to hear.

"There were bombings in the night. Two bombings, each at a different location, one Milice headquarters, the other at the Gestapo station on the rue Maignac. The damn Fascist commandant who ran the torture cells there was killed, and of course the Gestapo and their collaborators are out in force. Madame Montand says that they are arresting people at random, even rounding up schoolchildren and threatening them with deportation if they refuse to inform on their parents. No one in the city is safe. All exits are barricaded. Public transportation is suspended, and every car is being stopped," he said.

His every word was weighted with sadness.

"I don't know what we'll do," he added despairingly.

"We can help you. We know a way out of Toulouse through the sewers," Armand, the young Résistant who had shared their room, said. "Come with us."

"You must get out of the city," his friend agreed. "We know who you are, Mademoiselle Levy. Your picture has been taped to every shop window, every streetlight and phone pole. Everyone knows who you are. Someone will turn informant. And you know what that will mean."

They spoke loudly, urgently. She barely heard them, but she understood the impact of their warning.

"Of course, I know," she said, surprised at her own calm, relieved that her hands had stopped trembling. Mysteriously, the weakness she so feared had evaporated. "But we cannot leave. There is something we must accomplish before we can leave Toulouse."

They shrugged but asked no questions. They, too, had been trained to recognize the safety of silence.

"Be careful. Be very careful," Armand muttered as he shouldered his rucksack. "We wish you bonne chance. Good luck."

"Bonne chance," Madeleine and Claude echoed as the two young men who had slept beside them left, closing the door very quietly. She wondered if she would recognize them, should they ever meet again. She thought not.

"What must we do, Claude?" she asked, possibilities and impossibilities roiling through her mind.

She pondered all that had to be arranged and all that could not be arranged, the dangers known and unknown, the questions that could not be answered. How could they reach the rue de la Dalbade without being apprehended on the heavily patrolled streets? And even if they did manage to reach her parents' apartment and retrieve the winter clothing and boots for the children, how would they manage the journey southward to the orphanage with such bulky burdens? Somehow they might secure transport, but the exits from the city would be barricaded. The multitude of obstacles dizzied her. Despair soured her mouth.

She dared not think of how difficult it would be to contact the *passeurs* they counted on to lead them on the trek through the mountain passes. Later. They would deal with that later. If indeed there was a "later." She sighed and Claude pulled her close. Speaking directly into her ear, he answered her as-yet-unasked questions.

"I told Madame Montand about what we needed at your parents' apartment and why we needed it. She contacted a comrade in the Jewish Union for Resistance in Toulouse. Miraculous at such a time, on such a day, but she did it. They promised to have transport of a kind waiting for us at the rue de la Dalbade. Hopefully, the driver will take us and everything we need southward to the orphanage," he said.

"Hopefully." She repeated the word. "That is all that is left to us. Hope."

"It is enough," he replied. "We rely on hope. As always."

She nodded. She did not tell him that it was Claude himself she relied on. He had for so long been her loving companion, his tenacity and courage never wavering. Hope was his gift to her. Faith would be her gift to him. Their dreams collided. She smiled wanly and rested her head on his shoulder.

Madame Montand knocked lightly and entered the room. She smiled benignly, as calm as she had been the previous evening. A black lace caplet covered her white hair and a black shawl was draped over her white dress, the classic French country costume of a mourner. An embroidered bag dangled from her wrist.

She held out a tray that contained two large saucers of café au lait and two croissants.

"Eat and drink quickly," she said with a teasing smile. "We have a funeral to attend."

"A funeral?" Claude asked as he bit into the croissant, unsurprised that it was still warm from the oven. Had she run a *boulangerie* before the war? he wondered. Would she resume her baking when it ended? He sighed. Would any of them ever resume their lives? Would the years and months that the war had stolen from them ever be redeemed?

"Yes. A funeral," she repeated. "And the two of you are the principal mourners. Bereaved children of an aged and beloved father."

They stared at each other in confusion even as she opened the bag on her wrist and removed a black lace mantilla to which a thick black veil was attached. She handed it to Madeleine, who fingered it tentatively.

"I don't understand, madame," she said.

Madame Montand laughed.

"Of course you don't. But we have a plan. The only safe passage through the streets of Toulouse today, and perhaps for some time to come, is in a funeral cortege. Even the Gestapo dare not interfere with a burial. The Milice and their Vichy partners, devout church-goers all, oddly enough, respect the rituals for the dead. And so we three will be passengers in a limousine from a *maison funéraire*, a funeral home owned by a Résistance comrade who proudly helps us. That limousine will follow a hearse. A priest will accompany us. Our small cortege will make its way to the rue de la Dalbade, which is fortunately not far from a cemetery. *Compris?*"

She smiled, flushed with pride at the dramatic intricacy of her scheme.

"*Compris,*" Claude said, looking at Madeleine questioningly. He wanted to be certain that she had heard every word.

"*Compris,*" she echoed. "Merci, madame."

Madame Montand nodded and draped the mantilla over Madeleine, allowing it to fall to her shoulders but pinning it carefully so that the long, black folds concealed her thick hair.

"You must lower the veil to cover your face before we reach the street. Your photograph has been widely circulated, and you may be recognized. Neighbors whom I have known all my life may well betray us. That must not happen, and I pray it will not, but there are collaborators everywhere. We have learned to trust no one," she said sadly.

She sighed and left the room.

Claude and Madeleine sat side by side on the bare mattress, drinking the last of the café au lait. Claude placed the last bit of his croissant in Madeleine's *bol* because he knew how she relished sweetness.

"Will such a plan work?" Madeleine asked, stroking the long folds of the black mantilla, surprised at the softness of the fabric. Pure silk, she thought and wondered to whom it had belonged. A fashionable woman doing what she could for the Résistance, she supposed.

"I hope so," he said. "It is our only choice. We must have clothing and boots for the children. It is now only the first week of November, and snow has already fallen in the Pyrenees. Within a week, two weeks, there may well be blizzards. We must leave as soon as possible. We dare not wait. And we dare not allow the little ones to risk dying of the cold."

"I know."

She pulled the veil over her face as Madame Montand called them to join her.

Once in the street, with Claude walking behind them in somber step, Madame Montand held her arm protectively and made the sign of the cross as two neighbor women stared at her.

"My niece and nephew," she murmured. "My poor brother's children, come to Toulouse to bury their father."

The women bowed their heads reverently as a priest opened the door of the waiting limousine. Madeleine and Claude, followed by Madame Montand, climbed in and sat beside him. He smiled and they recognized Madame Montand's brother-in-law, André, the bus driver.

"I wear many uniforms," he said and laughed.

Their limousine followed the hearse in slow progression through the commercial districts of the city. In *le marché aux fleurs*, the flower market, the vendors offered only the conifer wreaths of early winter. An elderly woman shivered despite her cocoon of shawls and stared up at the darkening sky.

"*Hiver, damnable hiver*," she muttered. "Winter, damnable winter."

Madeleine thought of Anna, who always felt the cold of winter keenly. She remembered that there was a soft blue scarf and matching mittens, the color of Anna's eyes, in her mother's storage closet. They would be a welcome surprise, she thought, recalling the delight with which Anna received the smallest indulgences, how she had smiled at the faded clutch of gentians Claude had plucked in the Alps, at the delicate shell Madeleine had found on the banks of the Garonne.

She closed her eyes and retreated into sweet memories of precious hours spent with Anna, blocking out the danger of the moment. She adjusted her mantilla and tried to remember whose funeral they were supposed to be attending. Oh yes, their father, Madame Montand had said.

The shriek of a police siren catapulted her out of her brief reverie. Their driver slammed on his brakes as the squad car, its lights flashing, blocked their way.

A coarse-featured officer stomped out of his vehicle, the peaked military cap of the Milice perched on his oddly flat head and a truncheon clutched in his meaty hand.

"Out. Get out all of you," he shouted in the harsh accent peculiar to the Languedoc peasantry.

Madame Montand opened her window and stared at him reprovingly.

"Have you no shame?" she asked, her voice quivering with indignation. "Have you no respect for the dead and for those who mourn them? Do you not see that a holy priest travels with us?"

André leaned forward and made the sign of the cross. Madame Montand pointed to Madeleine and then to Claude. She held a white lace handkerchief to her eyes. Her lips trembled.

"These poor young people, my own niece and nephew, have lost their father and I have lost my beloved brother. Why do you add to our misery?"

"Papers. We must see your papers," the officer insisted. "It is a special order of the Gestapo."

"Shall we produce papers for a corpse?" she asked angrily. "Do you think we thought to carry papers with us to a graveyard? Step away and let us be on our way to bury our dead, or God will surely curse you. Is that not true, Father?"

André nodded, mumbled an incomprehensible benison, and flashed his crucifix.

The officer was flushed with indecision. His fat fingers

nervously strummed the window. Madeleine shivered. She was certain that he would arrest them. Would she and Claude be separated? Where would they be taken? Claude gripped her hand as tears trickled down her cheeks and her breath came with difficulty, but she dared not lift her veil.

The officer, his forehead now pearled with beads of sweat, whipped out a notebook and copied down the number of the limousine's license plate.

"Your name!" he barked at Madame Montand.

"Emma Bovary," she said. "Bovary. *B-O-V-A-R-Y*. Make sure you spell it correctly."

Without skipping a breath and before he could ask, she furnished an invented street address.

He shrugged, spoke briefly to their driver and to the driver of the hearse, and waved them on.

Their driver lit a Gauloise, exhaled a perfect smoke circle, and laughed harshly.

"*Quel poltron.* What a coward, a goddamn coward."

Madame Montand shrugged.

"How fortunate we are that he was indeed a coward. He may fear his Gestapo masters, but he fears his God even more," she said. "We are the beneficiaries of his cowardice and of his belief."

Weak with relief, Madeleine sat back and rested her head on Claude's shoulder as they drove on, passing pedestrians who doffed their hats and crossed themselves and a Milice unit who stood at attention in deference and respect for the mourners. Continuing on through the city center, they followed the eastern bank of the Garonne until they reached the rue de la Dalbade.

The narrow street was deserted and shrouded in silence.

The residents of Toulouse had been driven indoors by the threat of random arrests. A miasma of fear and uncertainty hung over the city. Their car came to a halt in front of the building where the Levy family had lived, and the hearse accelerated and disappeared around a corner, its subterfuge accomplished, the driver speeding toward safety.

"We leave you here," Madame Montand said. "Your comrades in the Jewish Résistance will arrive as planned. They know where to park their vehicle. Our hearts are with you."

"And our prayers," André added, even as he removed the priestly vestments and stood before them in the shabby uniform of the bus company, careful to tuck his faded scarf with the Résistance symbol of the Cross of Lorraine beneath his collar.

"We will never forget all you have done for us," Claude said, grasping his hand.

Madeleine embraced Madame Montand and kissed her on both cheeks, and then she and Claude hurried across the cobblestoned street and into the courtyard of the building she had once called home.

She glanced at the stooped apple tree whose bruised fruit she had gathered during hunger-haunted days, remembering how her mother had cooked them into a sauce that emitted a bittersweet fragrance. She looked up at the grime-encrusted windows of their fourth-floor apartment and was assaulted by memories. In her mind's eye, she saw Simone and Serge, joyous bride and groom, her brothers mock-wrestling, Claude sitting beside her on their battered sofa, her father and mother talking softly, her grandmother Lucie crocheting in a circlet of lamplight. Scenes of domestic tranquility cruelly shattered by the winds of war. She shivered and thrust all memories aside. She and Claude hurried to the concierge's doorway and prayed that Madame Leonie would be there.

Madeleine knocked and waited. One minute passed, then another. She knocked again, waited again. Terror gathered. She gagged on her fear. Was it possible that Madame Leonie, a long-time Résistance member, had been arrested? Had she fled Toulouse?

"Simone saw her only days ago," Claude whispered.

"That means nothing," Madeleine said despairingly.

She knew that a single hour, a single day in occupied France was an eternity. Anything might have happened since Simone's visit.

"What should we do?" she asked Claude, but even as she spoke, the courtyard gate opened and Madame Leonie, shrouded in an oversize black, hooded cape and carrying a string bag of groceries, stared at them. She paused, momentarily overtaken by surprise, then moved swiftly. Without uttering a sound, she unlocked her door and motioned them to enter. Hurriedly, they followed her inside. Only when she had fastened the bolt and lowered the window shades did she turn to them.

"Can it really be Madeleine Levy?" she gasped, her voice tremulous.

She shrugged out of her cape and held Madeleine close in her painfully thin arms. Her lips grazed Madeleine's cheeks, and Madeleine, in turn, kissed her on the forehead. She inhaled the remembered scent of the rouge the widowed concierge always used to mask the pallor of her skin and felt the metallic pressure of the heavy key ring at the concierge's waist.

"*Cher* Madame Leonie," she murmured.

The concierge's reply tumbled out in a meld of gladness and fear, welcome and warning.

"I never thought to see you again. Every collaborator in Toulouse, the Milice, the Vichy police, the Gestapo, they are all looking for you. They have been here, each of them, all of them. They searched your parents' apartment and went from floor to floor throughout the building. They ransacked my rooms and the basement. And they will be back. Oh, how glad I am to see you, Madeleine Levy, but it is not safe for you to be here."

"We will not be here long, madame," Claude said.

"Ah, Monsieur Lehmann. I remember your visits to the Levy family. I remember that you were a very special friend to our Madeleine."

She smiled at him and held her hand out.

"And now, I see, you are her protector," she added.

And so he was, Madeleine thought. He was her protector, her protective lover. Her mind closed over the word, claiming it, welcoming it. *Lover. Amant.*

She wondered who might have been Madame Leonie's protector through the long years of her widowhood. Had she had a lover after her husband's death? Surely her mother would know. Jeanne Levy had a talent for ferreting out secrets and delighted in sharing scraps of romantic gossip with her daughters. The random, irrelevant thought, fluttering through her mind at such an unlikely time, amused and soothed Madeleine. An odd normalcy was restored. With a new calm, she turned to the elderly concierge.

"We are here because it is important that we enter my

parents' apartment. We must have access to the storage closet. We are in urgent need of the items my mother collected. Can you help us?" Madeleine asked.

Madame Leonie nodded. She had often accepted the donations of clothing and footwear and trudged up the stairwell to deliver them to Jeanne Levy, often helping to thrust them into the closet. No questions had been asked because the answers were known. She had not hesitated then. She did not hesitate now.

"Of course I can help you. I have the keys to the apartment, the key to the padlock on the closet."

Her arthritic fingers fumbled with her key ring, and at last she released the large brass key to the apartment door and then a smaller one for the padlock. She handed both to Claude.

"There is something more I must ask you to do for us," Madeleine began, but before she could continue, Madame Leonie shook her head and spoke in a whisper.

"Quiet. Do not speak. There is someone in the courtyard. They come at all hours. Spies everywhere," she hissed bitterly.

They crouched behind the sofa as Madame Leonie knelt beside the window and peered through the slit of light beneath the black shade.

"No. It is all right. It was only the bin collector, and he is gone. I am sorry to have frightened you, but since the bombings and the assassinations, the Gestapo and the Vichy police are everywhere. The Milice are the worst. They were in the market this morning, demanding to see papers, confiscating *cartes d'identité* and making random arrests. I know they will come here again. Toulouse is very dangerous today and especially dangerous for you. I do not know what you plan, but would it not be safer if you wait until things are calmer?" she said. "Perhaps a few days, a week. I can arrange for a hiding place."

"It will be a very long time before things are calmer," Madeleine replied. "We cannot wait. Tomorrow will be as dangerous as today, only colder and darker. So it is today that we must have your help, dear Madame Leonie."

"Of course you will have my help. I understand."

She lowered her head, reluctant but accepting. She understood that the warm clothing and boots that Jeanne Levy had gathered would outfit Jewish children in their desperate odyssey across icebound mountain trails. The little ones, *les petits*, would need the protection of thick wool and soft fleece, of sturdy boots and thickly soled walking shoes. Oh, they would need so much more than that. They would need the protection of God Himself. Her heart broke for the children, for Madeleine Levy and Claude Lehmann, who would, against all odds, try to rescue them, and for the broken world of her old age. She thought to pray but could not find the words.

"What do you want me to do?" she asked instead.

"We want you to stand in the stairwell, perhaps pretend to be mopping the steps. We will rely on you to signal us if the *gendarmerie* or the Gestapo arrive. Do not shout if they should enter. Just sing *'Alouette, gentille alouette.'* There is an exit in the storage closet that accesses the fire escape. If we hear your song, I will have time enough to dash down that ladder and out through the rear door of the building," Madeleine replied.

She sighed. It was a flimsy plan, but at least it was a plan. She could move more quickly than the pursuers, who would have to climb the four floors.

"I understand. But how will you carry all that you need out of the building?"

"That will not be a problem," Madeleine assured her. "I alone will collect what is essential and bundle everything into sheets, which I will toss from the window. Claude will remain below to retrieve them, and then I will race down and join him. The Jewish Résistance will have a car waiting for us, and we will be gone. All will be done quickly. It will not be difficult. Not unduly dangerous."

The words came easily, but she was undeceived by her own facile assurances.

Madame Leonie smiled wryly and shook her head.

"It will be difficult, *ma cherie*. It will be dangerous. But then everything is difficult. Everything is dangerous. It is dangerous to breathe. It is dangerous to buy a baguette. It is dangerous to listen to the radio. So difficulties must be overcome, dangers must be ignored, and we must do what we must do. I have helped other Résistants escape from this apartment. You must do what I advise."

She turned to Claude.

"Thick vines grow on the outside wall, just beneath the windows of the Levy apartment. You will stand behind them and remain hidden by the leaves. Your view of the street will be clear enough to see the car sent by the Jewish Résistance when it approaches. Dash out only to snatch up what Madeleine tosses down to you and throw it into the car. Then you will leap into it, Madeleine will follow, and with God's help, you will be on your way," she said breathlessly.

They nodded and moved silently, swiftly. Claude passed the

keys to Madeleine. Clutching them, she raced through the dark and narrow entry of the building and climbed the four flights of stairs to the apartment she remembered so well. Madame Leonie stationed herself at the bottom of the stairwell with her mop and pail. Claude dashed outside and concealed himself in the thicket of overgrown vine leaves.

Madeleine inserted the heavy key in the lock and pushed the door open. The room was dark, the flimsy furniture shrouded in layers of dust. A necrotic odor emanated from the kitchen and a sickening stench from the water closet. She gagged against her rising nausea and hurried into the larger bedroom where her parents had slept. She saw at once that the padlock on the storage closet was rusted. A difficulty, she knew.

She inserted the key. It did not turn. Trembling, fighting a wave of panic, she tried to pull it out, but it remained in place. Fearful that it would snap, she manipulated it slowly, and at last it was released. She inserted the key again, trying a different angle. The lock clicked and she flung the door open, perceiving at once that all was just as her very organized mother had left it. Outer garments were in one pile, sweaters in another. Scarves and mittens were in large hatboxes embossed with the monogram of Lucie Dreyfus's Paris milliner, *Chapeaux de Madame Désirée*. Madeleine smiled wistfully. Yes, there had been a time when her elegant grandmother had spent happy hours trying on fashionable hats in front of a gilt-framed mirror.

But this was not the time for nostalgic reverie. She rummaged through the hatbox, selecting the thickest knits, happy to find the blue scarf and mittens that she was certain would match Anna's eyes. A fortunate omen, she thought. She tossed them onto the sheet she had pulled off the bed, adding jackets, sweaters, woolen hats, and boots, blessed thick-soled boots. She filled one sheet and then another, tied each to form a clumsy sack, and pulled them both over to the window.

Peering out, she was relieved to see Claude crouched in the labyrinth of vines directly below her. As she opened the window, a battered automobile turned the corner and parked in front of the building. She recognized the driver, David Sorel, a gaunt and dedicated leader of the Jewish Résistance, known for his courage and daring. She breathed a sigh of relief. Everything was proceeding according to their plan; everything would be all right.

Summoning all her strength, she forced the window open, lifted one unwieldy sack, and tossed it down. Claude sprinted forth, seized it, and ran to the car, thrusting it into the boot. She shoved the second bundle over the sill, and he retrieved that one as well, sprinting to the car.

Exhausted and exhilarated, Madeleine knelt for a moment beside the open window, filling her lungs with the fresh air. There, it was done. Their mission was accomplished. Against all odds, they had succeeded. She now had only to dash down the stairwell and jump into the waiting vehicle and into Claude's loving embrace. Before that day ended, they would reach the children who waited for them at Lézignan-Corbières. She imagined Anna's happiness and the excitement of the other children. Their dreams of rescue and freedom now becoming a reality.

Both exhilarated and weak with relief, she turned away from the window. She gasped. Within seconds, exhilaration morphed into shock, shock into dismay, relief into terror. Two burly Milice officers stood in the doorway. They stared at her, sneers distorting their faces, the one brandishing a pistol, the other a truncheon. Slowly, menacingly, they moved toward her.

"Madeleine Dreyfus-Levy, Jewess, we arrest you with the full authority of the National Revolution. Acting as a terrorist agent of the Résistance Intérieure Française, you have broken the laws of the Vichy government," the officer holding the pistol bellowed.

He seized her wrist and pulled her toward him. She smelled the sour wine and garlic on his breath, the stink of his sweat. Gasping for air, she broke free and rushed to the open window. The street was deserted, the car gone. David Sorel had driven away. Claude had escaped.

Good, she thought. *C'est assez.* It is enough.

Claude was safe. He would take the clothing to the children and guide them across the Pyrenees to freedom. That was enough. That would have to be enough.

Once again, her wrist was in the officer's grip, her arm then twisted painfully behind her back. Unflinching, she stared defiantly at him.

"*Vive la France. Vive liberté, égalité, fraternité. Vive de Gaulle. Vive les* Éclaireurs Israélites," she shouted defiantly, her voice vibrant, her gaze steady, her saliva spraying his face.

He raised his truncheon and brought it down with great force against her cheek. She staggered and he pushed her toward the stairwell, his knee pressed against her back, his thick fingers gripping her breast.

"Whore. Jewish whore." He spat the words out, and she felt his fetid breath upon her neck.

Madame Leonie, tears streaking her cheeks, stood in the doorway.

"I sang, Madeleine. I sang to warn you, but I had forgotten that you have difficulty hearing. I did not sing loud enough, and my warning was lost to you. How could I have forgotten? Oh, how sorry I am. So sorry."

"You will be sorrier still, you Résistance bitch!" the officer shouted as he struck her across the shoulders with the butt of his pistol.

"Leave her alone. She is an old woman. Do you not have a mother?" Madeleine shouted at him and was surprised to see his face flush with shame.

She turned to Madame Leonie.

"Do not distress yourself. You are not to blame. It does not matter. Nothing matters," she said as she was shoved out of the darkened entryway into the brightness of sunlight.

She closed her eyes against the sudden brilliance, and opening them, she gasped and bit her lip hard to make certain that she was not dreaming. She tasted her own blood and knew that she was awake and that her eyes had not deceived her. Claude stood beneath the dwarfed apple tree, his arms pinioned by two green-uniformed Vichy officers.

"Did you think I could leave you, my Madeleine?" he called as they dragged him into a prison van.

"No more than I could ever leave you," she shouted back as she, too, was shoved into the vehicle.

Its barred windows were grime streaked; its siren screamed

as the driver sped wildly away from the rue de la Dalbade, skidding against curbstones and shouting obscenities at the frightened pedestrians who scrambled out of his path.

Madeleine and Claude crawled toward each other, indifferent to the oily filth on the floor of the van and the stink of sweat and fear that hovered in the stagnant air. They huddled together in silence, aware that they were heading to the Gestapo headquarters on the rue Maignac. But where, she wondered, would they be sent from there?

Claude's hand rested on her head. He lifted strands of her thick hair, stroked her back, her shoulders, willing her to calm. She leaned into his embrace and prayed silently, reverently, that no matter where they were sent, they would not be separated. Not again. Not ever.

"Claude," she whispered.

His reply was the soft press of his lips upon her own.

THIRTY-NINE

D RANCY. THEY WERE BOTH TO BE SENT TO DRANCY, ALONG with all other imprisoned Résistants. *Drancy.* The word was whispered, passed from cell to cell of the Gestapo headquarters on rue Maignac. A prisoner in the interrogation chamber had overheard the guards talking. Another inmate had found a crumpled newspaper in a refuse bin. Rumor was confirmed and became fact.

Klaus Barbie, the infamous Butcher of Lyon, had decreed that all Résistance members imprisoned in Toulouse were to be sent to Drancy, the transit camp from which they would be transported to Auschwitz.

Claude waited. Madeleine waited. Separated and bereft, they each feared for the other. On a cold, stormy morning, their cell doors were opened, their names were called, and they were herded outside, commanded to stand in formation, drenched by the pouring rain. Shivering and fearful, they sought each other out. Their eyes met. Slowly, furtively, they glided toward each other until at last they stood side by side. He draped his ragged anorak over her quivering shoulders. His hand found hers. They dared to smile. He was alive. She was alive. They were overcome with gratitude.

They had not seen each other since their arrest days earlier.

She did not know how many days. Three, perhaps. Or four. There were no windows in the cells of the grim Gestapo fortress. Night and day had merged. There were no clocks. No hours. Only questions and beatings and more questions.

"They say we are being sent to Drancy," he murmured, gently touching the bruise on her forehead.

"Drancy. Yes. I heard that. I was once in Drancy, you know."

She spoke with difficulty. Her throat was dry, but she had grown used to thirst. Her neck was bruised because her interrogators had lashed it with a short whip during sessions that had lasted hour after hour. Yes, she had screamed. Yes, she had writhed in pain. But she had not begged for mercy, nor had she revealed a single name, a single contact. She blessed her deafness. It was a relief to be unable to hear their questions. Their failure to obtain answers, their reluctant recognition of her disability, had ignited their cruelty, but in the end, they had only wished her away because they despaired of receiving any information from her. They surrendered her to Drancy and wished her well on her way eastward to Auschwitz, the kingdom of death.

"When were you in Drancy?" Claude asked.

She did not answer. The bus doors yawned open.

"*Schnell, schnell.* Inside," the guards shouted, beating at the frightened prisoners with their spiked batons.

She gripped Claude's hand and they stumbled inside, finding a seat on a narrow, backless bench. She leaned against him and answered his question, speaking softly, dreamily.

"When Simone and I were little, my grandfather hired a car one afternoon, and he took us to Drancy on a surprise holiday. It was a new suburb, he said, just north and east of Paris."

"A surprise holiday," Claude repeated.

Yes, once there had been a world in which a grandfather could spirit his pretty granddaughters away for a pleasant afternoon, a surprise holiday. Claude tried to imagine Madeleine as a small girl, her luxuriant dark hair braided into fat pigtails, her sweet face bright with pleasure.

"My grandfather was so proud that Paris was expanding. He was proud of everything French," Madeleine continued.

Claude frowned. Alfred Dreyfus would not have been proud to learn that the new suburb of Drancy had become an internment camp. He would not have been proud of the so-called revolutionary government of Vichy nor of his own comrade in arms, Márechal Pétain, the hero of Verdun, now Hitler's puppet.

He thought to say as much to Madeleine, but she was still lost in memory of that long-ago surprise holiday.

"Drancy was to be a modern community," she continued. "We saw high-rise apartment buildings being built. A school. A library. It was going to offer working French families a wonderful way of life. It even had a lovely name. *Drancy: Un Cité de la Silence*. Drancy, a City of Silence."

"Today it is known as *un Cité de la Souffrance*, a City of Suffering," Claude said bitterly.

He did not share with her the reports he had read of Drancy. It had been taken over by the Germans immediately after the invasion. The residents had been arbitrarily dispersed and the buildings converted into police barracks that then became "detention centers," concentration camps for "undesirables"—Jews, homosexuals, gypsies, Communists.

Barbed wire encircled its perimeters, and it was now used by the Gestapo Office of Jewish Affairs as a holding area for Jewish prisoners until they could be herded into cattle cars and sent east to Auschwitz. Yes, Drancy was truly a city of suffering, the metropolis of torture ruled from Berlin by Lieutenant Colonel Adolf Eichmann, administered on-site by Alois Brunner, an SS officer rumored to be crueler than even Klaus Barbie. Terror awaited them there, Claude knew, and he shuddered to think of how it would affect Madeleine. He understood how vulnerable she was, despite her daring. He knew how she struggled to contain her fears, to retain her courage, to chase her dreams.

Seated beside her, he was relieved that she had fallen asleep, her head resting on his shoulder. A smile played on her lips. He had forgotten that she often smiled as she slept. He kissed her brow, still wet from the rain, and stared through the grime-encrusted window.

A mother and two small children stumbled to the empty seat beside him. The frightened wails of the small brother and sister competed with the pounding rain.

"Papa. Papa," they called.

Their weary mother sighed.

"André. André." Her voice was so laced with sorrow that Claude thought his heart might break.

Instead he turned to them, forced an apologetic smile, and held a finger to his lips.

"Please," he said softly, "do not awaken *ma bienne amie*."

They nodded, oddly reassured by his tender words. All love had not vanished from the world. The weary mother sang softly, her children nestled against her. Claude held Madeleine close, willing the warmth of his body to banish the chill of her fear.

Drancy was the nightmare he had feared. Chaos and cold haunted the stark camp. Families struggled to stay together. Nursing mothers huddled in corners and wept because milk had ceased to leak from breasts withered by thirst and starvation. They cradled their emaciated, weeping infants, knowing that they were destined for death. They longed for their own hearts to stop, their breath to cease.

Men, half-mad with frustration, paced back and forth, their fists clenched, muttering at their helplessness. Others gathered in prayer minyans, swaying from side to side, sharing phylacteries and prayer shawls.

"*El maaleh rachamim*—God full of mercy," they intoned, but there was no mercy, only cold clouds of their sour breath as their murmured petitions floated through the cavernous room.

Parents called shrilly to their children. Names were shouted in anger. Names were murmured with love.

Now and again, small contingents of nuns, Quakers, and Red Cross workers appeared, wheeling in urns of water or soup, pyramids of stale bread, piles of thin, coarse blankets. They wore white masks for protection against the stench of urine, feces, and vomit, but their eyes were bright with tears.

Madeleine and Claude struggled to create a semblance of order out of the turmoil that surrounded them.

"We are trained scouts, *éclaireurs*," Claude said. "We know how to organize."

She nodded and bravely copied his confidence, false as she knew it to be.

He managed to arrange for basic sanitation, demanded orderly queues for the toilets, harangued guards for water, for medical supplies, enlisted a cadre of younger men and women to assist the elderly.

Madeleine summoned all her skills and concentrated on helping the children. She organized them into orderly play groups with leaders chosen from among the restless wandering adolescents. Games were invented. Stories were told. Teachers began to hold small classes. Amid the desperation and despair, there were small eruptions of laughter, sudden spontaneous bursts of joy.

It was Claude who fashioned a pile of rags into a ball and created teams of small scurrying players briefly restored to a childhood interrupted by a war they did not understand, by hatred beyond any human understanding. In a courtyard surrounded by barbed wire, the small players raced about playing catch and tag, tossing their ball of rags into a hoop crafted of branches fallen from dying trees.

The days at Drancy passed slowly, but they saw each morning as a reprieve, each night as a triumph. They had survived, resisting still, their efforts undeterred, their love enduring.

Claude and Madeleine were outside in the barren courtyard, gathering the children together for an impromptu relay race, intent on distracting them from the sad knowledge that two toddlers had died in the night, when an elderly nun approached them.

"Mademoiselle Levy, Monsieur Claude?" she asked hesitantly.

They nodded, no longer restrained by suspicion. The worst had already happened. They were released from fear. They could answer to their own names.

Wordlessly, the nun handed Claude an envelope and hurried away, adjusting her mask, not daring to look back.

They retreated to a secluded corner and Claude opened the envelope, worn thin from being handled by too many couriers, his name barely legible beneath smeared fingerprints.

"A letter from Serge," he said, and Madeleine stared at him, willing herself to be courageous. It would be bad news, she thought. A revelation of death. But whose death? *Her parents? Her grandmother? Her brothers? Simone? Oh, not Simone. Never Simone. And not Anna.* Names fluttered through her mind. *Who? When? How? Where?* Questions collided. She gasped for air. She wondered that Claude did not hear the too rapid, too loud beat of her heart. But he did not look up from the letter. His lips were moving. He was reading aloud, but his words were lost to her.

"I can't hear you," she cried, digging her nails into his arm, leaving tears of blood on skin worn to a thinness through which his bones shimmered. "Louder! Louder!"

He turned to her, held her close, read it again, speaking directly into her ear, enunciating every word, and she listened, leaning in to him, her breath coming easier and easier as his voice gathered strength. Wondrously, a smile formed upon her lips. She had not thought to know happiness ever again, but joy filled her heart.

Serge had written that her family, her parents, her brothers, Simone and the children, her grandmother were all alive, all in places of safety. There had been word from Robert Gamzon.

The small group of children from Lizignan-Corbiere, *her* children whom she had so carefully trained, all had successfully made the trek across the Pyrenees and were in his Algiers encampment, soon to sail to Palestine.

Anna Hofberg, your precious Anna, is safe, Serge had written.

"Anna is safe," Madeleine repeated.

A stone was lifted from her heart. Her grandmother's words, so true, so powerful, came to mind, weighted with truth, with power.

This life is worth its grief, Lucie Dreyfus had said.

"This life is worth its grief," Madeleine Levy repeated.

It was a cold day, but the sun burned with an odd radiance. She heard the improbable laughter of the assembled children, watched two very thin, small girls grasp hands and whirl about in a playful dance. A miracle that children laughed, that children played.

"Come," she called to them. "I will teach you a new game. A new song."

They rushed toward her.

"*Entends-tu le coucou, Malirette?* Do you hear the cuckoo, Marilette?" she sang, holding her hand to her ear, her grandfather's gesture remembered.

"*Entends-tu le coucou, Malirette?*" they sang back in sweet chorus, their small hands fluttering to their own ears.

"*Coucou*," she sang as she pirouetted, bent, and swayed.

"*Coucou*," they repeated and imitated her dance.

She clapped her hands and turned to Claude.

"You see," she said. "My grandmother Lucie was right. This life is worth its grief."

"Yes," he replied, looking at the dancing children. "This life is surely worth its grief."

Hand in hand then, as the melancholy pastel rays of a wintry sunset streaked the darkening sky, they followed the singing children back into the grim prison fortress. They did not speak. Their certainty had no need for words. They knew that no matter what was yet to come, their lives, their love, had been worth its grief.

EPILOGUE

O N November 20, 1943, two days after Madeleine Levy's twenty-fifth birthday, she and Claude Lehmann joined Convoy Number 62, the fifteenth to leave Drancy. They were among the 1,200 Jewish prisoners who were herded into freight cars at the Bobigny station. The train arrived at Auschwitz at 2:00 a.m. on November 23 after a journey of unimaginable hardship. In January 1944, Madeleine Levy, weighing less than seventy pounds, died of typhus at Auschwitz-Birkenau.

Claude Lehmann survived the war, as did Madeleine's parents, her siblings, and her grandmother Lucie Dreyfus. Simone and Serge Perl were the parents of six children whom they raised in Paris. Ironically, Pierre Dreyfus was killed in a plane accident in Ireland in 1946. Madeleine Levy's remains were never found. Her name, age, and the inscription "deported by the Germans to Auschwitz" were etched onto the gravestone of her Dreyfus grandparents in the Montparnasse Cemetery.

In 1950, the French Fourth Republic awarded the granddaughter of Alfred and Lucie Dreyfus, the daughter of Jeanne and Pierre Paul Levy, the Military Medal, the Croix de Guerre with palm, and the Medal of the Résistance.

Zichronah l'vracha. May her memory be blessed. Her life was surely worth its grief.

READING GROUP GUIDE

1. Madeleine, with her grandfather Alfred Dreyfus as a role model, commits herself to the dangerous role of rescuing Jewish children as a Resistance fighter. What other historic or personal figures might serve as a role model to young people confronting choices that call for daring and dangerous action? Take, for example, Martin Luther King Jr., a heroic health worker, or a relative or friend whose ideals and actions you admire.

2. Given her dual roles, one as a covert Resistance fighter and the other as an agent for the Vichy government, Madeleine must often hide her true feelings. How does she accomplish this, and how might you act in similar circumstances?

3. Madeleine must balance her love for Claude against the importance of the life-saving work that engages them both. How might you confront a similar struggle in your own life? Should the needs of a larger community be prioritized rather than the yearning of an individual?

4. When Madeleine's credentials are questioned, she flirts

with her interrogator. This is counter to her usual modesty, but it is a ploy that she uses to protect the children she is intent on saving. Do you think that end justifies the means? Can you think of other situations that parallel her dilemma?

5. The dean of the Institute of Social Work speaks of lighting small candles against the darkness of tyranny. Describe the small candles that glow in various chapters of *The Paris Children*. Take, for example, the cooperation of the masons, the efforts of the nuns who shelter Lucie Dreyfus, and the bus driver. What small candles have you yourself ignited against darkness?

6. Madeleine's physician father insists that he must treat anyone who needs his help, ally or enemy. Would you agree with his attitude?

7. Although Madeleine's primary goal is to rescue endangered Jewish children, she also becomes a demolition expert. How does she confront each role? Do they require similar skills, similar courage?

8. The Resistance demands secrecy for the protection of its members. Do you think more openness would have been helpful to their operations?

9. Madeleine commits herself to helping the downed pilot before she knows whether he is English or Axis. She avers

that she must help no matter who he is because he is a human being in trouble. Do you think a Nazi combatant deserves the kind of care and concern she offers?

10. Resistance victories met with severe reprisals from the Nazi occupiers. How did the reprisals affect the surviving freedom fighters? Do you think that the greater good outweighs the suffering of the few?

11. Madeleine's grandmother assures her that "this life is worth its grief," an assurance that Madeleine accepts and embraces. How do you respond to that concept?

A CONVERSATION
WITH THE AUTHOR

What kind of research did you undertake to bring Madeleine and her France to life?

My undergraduate and graduate studies in history at Brandeis University and the Hebrew University of Jerusalem prepared me to delve into many different texts. I explored the necessary background of the Dreyfus family and the tragic years of World War II with the requisite emphasis on the German occupation of France and, more specifically, with the systematic war against the Jewish community, a genocide with a demonic focus on Jewish children. I visited both Paris and Toulouse and developed a feel for the locales. During my student days in Jerusalem, I met French Jews who had lived through that period, and their stories influenced my writing.

The Jewish Scout program figures prominently in your story. Have you yourself participated in scouting programs?

I was a very reluctant Girl Scout for a very brief period, but my two daughters and my son, during their adolescence, were avid members of Young Judea in the United States, which partners with the Tsofim, the Israeli Scout movement. Through their affiliation, I came to know many Israeli scouts and their leaders, who were often guests in our home. I also attended their meetings during my trips to Israel and listened to stories of the role that Jewish Scouts played in their heroic efforts to rescue endangered Jewish children.

Do you, like the Dreyfuses, place great emphasis on family?

My husband and I have always prioritized our children, and we are proud that, as adults, they, in turn, are caring and involved parents to our eight widely scattered grandchildren, transmitting the values that we have always held dear. Compassion, honesty, and courage are important in our family. Humor and laughter are our lodestones.

Did you have family members who, like Madeleine's grandfather, inspired you?

The short answer is that my family served as my inspiration. My parents were both born in Poland, and the stories they told of the families they left behind, many of whom became victims of the Holocaust, greatly impacted my life. My mother and father were involved in efforts to save their surviving relatives, and they emphasized the importance of helping those in need, Jewish and non-Jewish alike. There is no word for 'charity' in Hebrew. We speak of *tzedakah*, which means "justice," and it was justice and compassion that motivated Madeleine, words that were as important to my parents and grandparents as they were to the heroine of *The Paris Children*.

What inspired the words "this life is worth its grief"?

Given the sadness and injustice that often surrounds us, it is important to remember the joy and goodness that is possible.

Literature, fiction and nonfiction alike, gives us the opportunity to recognize that balance and to understand that beyond grief, there is value in the lives we live and how we live them.

What does your reading list look like these days?

Poetry (I seek out Emily Dickinson, Wallace Stevens, A. E. Housman, and Yehuda Amichai.), novels (I read and reread George Eliot, Anthony Trollope, and Cynthia Ozick.), and for true comfort, I travel to Venice with Donna Leon and her marvelous detective, Brunetti. I also try his recipes. Yes, I love cookbooks.

If you had one piece of advice for writing historic fiction, what would it be?

Read, research, read some more—dream!

What do you want your readers to take away from *The Paris Children*?

Never turn away from injustice. Do not allow history to repeat itself. Emulate Madeleine Levy, Claude Lehmann, and Simone and Serge Perl, and sustain those who fight for all that is good and moral in our complex and wonderful world because this life is worth its grief.

ACKNOWLEDGMENTS

Many thanks to my son, Harry Horowitz, whose computer skills rescued this narrative many times over. My husband, Sheldon Horowitz, an attorney who has lectured on the Dreyfus trial in numerous venues, inspired me to write about Madeleine Levy and offered insightful criticism as the book progressed. My historian son-in-law, Dr. Brian Amkraut, was always available to answer queries and offer suggestions. My editors at Sourcebooks, Anna Michels and Margaret Johnston, were wonderful midwives who ably assisted *The Paris Children* into literary life. My gratitude to all.

The Bridal Chair

Chapter One

She is gripped by a terror she cannot name, but she is certain that she is in danger, grave danger. Her breath comes in labored gasps. She is running, racing. The taps on the heels of her patent leather shoes clatter against the cobblestones, and her heart beats wildly as though struggling to match her frantic pace. Her parents grip her hands—her mother's sharp nails dig into her right palm, and her father's grasp on her left is painfully tight.

"Faster, Idotchka. Faster." They speak in unison. She trembles at the fear in their voices.

Their pursuers draw closer, booted feet beating in tympanic hate, horses' hooves pounding ominously.

She cannot go any faster. She feels her energy draining, her legs faltering. Tears streak her cheeks. How angry they will be with her if she should fall. She does not want them to be angry, her *mamochka*, her *papochka*.

And then, suddenly, their race is over, and they are lifted to the heavens. They are soaring, the three of them, hands linked, hearts lightened, flying skyward. Her parents' arms have become wings that scissor their way through a sky no longer draped in velvet darkness but wondrously studded with rainbow-colored flowers. A vagrant wind plays with her auburn curls, and she laughs as the thick tendrils tickle her cheeks. Her pinafore billows out into a great puff of whiteness that will surely keep her afloat.

She glances at her mother, who glides so easily through the air, a blackbird of a woman, her hair a cap of polished ebony, the velvet dress that hugs her slender body the color of night. She turns her head to the left and she sees that her father's beret has fallen and his fine silken hair frames his elfin face; stray strands briefly veil his bright blue eyes. He smiles; his daughter's hand is so light and trusting in his own. He is at home in this flower-strewn heaven. He will paint these skies, she knows, when they are safe and out of harm's way. But for now, their flight continues.

They float, the three of them, like zephyrs borne on soft breezes, cushioned by gentle clouds, high above the burning villages and the dark columns of soldiers tramping the country they had once called their own. Mother Russia has cast them out. They are orphaned refugees, rootless and rejected, but they are winging their way to a safe haven. They do not speak, because language is lost to them. The quiet settles over them in a soothing coverlet embroidered with hope and promise. Wordless, soundless.

Still half asleep, safe in her bed, she stretched languidly and opened her eyes to the golden light of early morning streaming through the wide window of her bedroom. A bird sang with plaintive sweetness and she hurried to the window. The solitary warbler teetered on a fragile branch of the lemon tree and then soared off into the cloudless summer sky.

"*Au revoir,*" she called softly and looked down at the garden where her parents sat opposite each other in their wicker chairs, talking softly as they sipped their morning coffee. Their voices drifted through the open window as their spoons clinked musically against their china cups.

She watched them for a moment and then turned, stripped off her white nightgown, and stood naked before her full-length mirror. She studied the curves of her body, the fine-boned contour of her face. She lifted her mass of bright hair and allowed it to fall again to her shoulders.

Her reflection reassured her. She passed her hands across the tender fullness of her breasts and felt the power of her nascent womanhood. She was no longer the frightened small girl of her nightmare. The dream was banished. The painful past was behind her. She had no need of a celestial haven. She willed herself to triumph over the sadness that too often lingered in the aftermath of her haunted sleep.

She turned her head, glanced at herself in profile, practiced a smile, practiced a frown.

Am I pretty? she wondered. *Am I beautiful? Will Michel find me much changed?*

There was an impatient knock at her bedroom door; her name was called once and then again. "Mademoiselle Ida! Mademoiselle Ida!"

The harsh voice of Katya, the Polish maid, irritable and accusatory, pierced her reverie.

"It is very late. Your parents are waiting for you."

"Tell them I'll be down in just a few minutes."

A grunt and then heavy footfalls retreated in reproach.

Ida shrugged. She knew that Katya did not like her, did not like being a maid in a Jewish home. But that was of no importance. Katya, as her mother frequently pointed out, was lucky to be working for the Chagalls. They were kind employers, Katya's wages were paid on time, she ate the same food as the family, and transport to church on Sundays and festivals was provided.

She dismissed Katya from her thoughts, splashed her face with cold water, and dressed quickly, choosing a pale blue, pearl-buttoned dress of a gossamer fabric that slipped off easily and would let her swiftly disrobe. Her father had told her that he wanted her to pose for him before she left for the alpine encampment so that he might complete the series of nude studies he had begun months earlier, alternating at whim between watercolor and gouache, charcoal and oil.

Her father had used his brush over the years to create a visual journal of her life, chronicling the days of her playful childhood, her moody adolescence, and now her emergent young womanhood. The title of each effort was scrawled in his looping script across the back of the work, a claim of ownership and provenance. There was *Ida on the Swing*, a portrait in motion, painted swiftly as she thrust herself skyward, her chubby legs vigorously pumping, the wind burnishing her cheeks. He had taken more time in painting *Ida at the Window*, capturing her as she stared dreamily through the shimmering glass while the sun sank over their Montchauvet home, setting the waters of the Seine on fire.

"What are you thinking about, Idotchka?" her father had asked that day as his brush flew across the canvas, his eyes narrowed in concentration.

She had thought then to share her recurring dream of frantic flight with him so that he might paint that nocturnal fantasy into a tactile reality, but she had remained silent. The dream was her own, not to be co-opted by his brush and palette. She took a perverse pleasure in keeping it secret. She had, after all, so few secrets from her parents. They had laid claim to every aspect of her life, keeping her close from the day of her birth. Sometimes she thought that they monitored the very breaths she took and seized upon her moods, saddened by her sadness, joyful in her joy. She choked on their vigilance; she resented their obsessive insistence that they possess every aspect of her being and then felt a disloyalty that shamed her. She was fortunate to be their daughter, the beloved legatee of their fame and fortune and unconditional love. And she loved them deeply in return.

She understood that their concern for her was born of the uncertainty and the suffering they had endured. Of course they were frightened. She accepted their fear, submitted to it. She allowed them to believe that they were the conservators of her life. But her dreams, her beautiful and terrifying nocturnal odysseys, those were her own, as was the secret she had held so close within her heart throughout the year. It thrilled her that she had managed to refrain from telling her parents about Michel. He belonged only to her.

ABOUT THE AUTHOR

Gloria Goldreich is the author of several critically acclaimed novels, including *The Bridal Chair* and National Jewish Book Award winner *Leah's Children*, among others. Her stories and essays have appeared in *Commentary*, *The Colorado Quarterly*, *McCalls*, *Redbook*, *Chatelaine*, *Hadassah Magazine*, and many other publications. She is the mother of two daughters and a son and the grandmother of eight widely scattered grandchildren. She has lectured throughout the United States and in Canada. She and her husband reside in Tuckahoe, New York.